A former police reporter for the *Los Angeles Times*, Michael Connelly is the internationally bestselling author of the Harry Bosch series, and several other bestsellers including the highly acclaimed legal thriller, *The Lincoln Lawyer*. The TV series – *Bosch* – is one of the most watched original series on Amazon Prime and is now in its fourth season. Connelly has been President of the Mystery Writers of America, and his books have been translated into thirty-nine languages. His writing has won awards all over the world, including the Edgar and Anthony Awards, and, most recently, the CWA Diamond Dagger, the highest honour in British crime writing. He spends his time in California and Florida.

To find out more, visit Michael's website or follow him on Twitter or Facebook.

www.michaelconnelly.com

@Connellybooks

/MichaelConnellyBooks

MICHAEL CONNELLY

A DARKNESS MORE THAN NIGHT

ORION

An Orion paperback

First published in Great Britain in 2000
by Orion Books
This paperback edition published in 2001
by Orion Books
an imprint of The Orion Publishing Group Ltd,
Carmelite House, 50 Victoria Embankment,
London EC4Y 0DZ

An Hachette UK company

23

Reissued 2014

A CIP catalogue record for this book is available from the British Library.

ISBN 978 1 4091 5606 2

Printed and bound in Great Britain by
Clays Ltd, Elcograf S.p.A.

The Orion Publishing Group's policy is to use papers that are natural, renewable and recyclable products and made from wood grown in sustainable forests. The logging and manufacturing processes are expected to conform to the environmental regulations of the country of origin.

www.orionbooks.co.uk

This is for Mary and Jack Lavelle,
who proved there are second acts

MICHAEL CONNELLY

A DARKNESS MORE THAN NIGHT

Prologue

Bosch looked through the small square of glass and saw that the man was alone in the tank. He took his gun out of its holster and handed it to the watch sergeant. Standard procedure. The steel door was unlocked and slid open. Immediately the smell of sweat and vomit stung Bosch's nostrils.

'How long's he been in here?'

'About three hours,' said the sergeant. 'He blew a one-eight, so I don't know what you're going to get.'

Bosch stepped into the holding tank and kept his eyes on the prone form on the floor.

'All right, you can close it.'

'Let me know.'

The door slid closed with a jarring bang and jolt. The man on the floor groaned and moved only slightly. Bosch walked over and sat down on the bench nearest to him. He took the tape recorder out of his jacket pocket and put it down on the bench. Glancing up at the glass window he saw the sergeant's face move away. He used the toe of his shoe to probe the man's side. The man groaned again.

'Wake up, you piece of shit.'

The man on the floor of the tank slowly rolled his head and then lifted it. Paint flecked his hair and vomit had caked on the front of his shirt and neck. He opened his eyes and immediately closed them against the harsh overhead lighting of the holding tank. His voice came out in a hoarse whisper.

'You again.'

Bosch nodded.
'Yeah. Me.'
'Our little dance.'
A smile cut across the three-day-old whiskers on the drunk's face. Bosch saw that he was missing a tooth he hadn't been missing last time. He reached down and put his hand on the recorder but did not turn it on yet.
'Get up. It's time to talk.'
'Forget it, man. I don't want—'
'You're running out of time. Talk to me.'
'Leave me the fuck alone.'
Bosch looked up at the window. It was clear. He looked back down at the man on the floor.
'Your salvation is in the truth. Now more than ever. I can't help you without the truth.'
'What're you, a priest now? You here to take my confession?'
'You here to give it?'
The man on the floor said nothing. After a while Bosch thought he might have fallen back asleep. He pushed the toe of his shoe into the man's side again, into the kidney. The man erupted in movement, flailing his arms and legs.
'Fuck you!' he yelled. 'I don't want you. I want a lawyer.'
Bosch was silent a moment. He picked up the recorder and slid it back into his pocket. He then leaned forward, elbows on his knees, and clasped his hands together. He looked at the drunk and slowly shook his head.
'Then I guess I can't help you,' he said.
He stood up and knocked on the window for the watch sergeant. He left the man lying on the floor.

I

'Someone's coming.'

Terry McCaleb looked at his wife and then followed her eyes down to the winding road below. He could see the golf cart making its way up the steep and winding road to the house. The driver was obscured by the roof of the cart.

They were sitting on the back deck of the house he and Graciela had rented up on La Mesa Avenue. The vicw ranged from the narrow winding road below the house to the whole of Avalon and its harbor, and then out across the Santa Monica Bay to the haze of smog that marked overtown. The view was the reason they had chosen this house to make their new home on the island. But at the moment his wife spoke, his gaze had been on the baby in his arms, not the view. He could look no farther than his daughter's wide blue and trusting eyes.

McCaleb saw the rental number on the side of the golf cart passing below. It wasn't a local coming. It was somebody who had probably come from overtown on the *Catalina Express.* Still, he wondered how Graciela knew that the visitor was coming to their house and not any of the others on La Mesa.

He didn't ask about this – she'd had premonitions before. He just waited and soon after the golf cart disappeared from sight, there was a knock at the front door. Graciela went to answer it and soon came back to the deck with a woman McCaleb had not seen in three years.

Sheriff's detective Jaye Winston smiled when she saw

the child in his arms. It was genuine, but at the same time it was the distracted smile of someone who wasn't there to admire a new baby. McCaleb knew the thick green binder she carried in one hand and the videocassette in the other meant Winston was there on business. Death business.

'Terry, howya been?' she asked.

'Couldn't be better. You remember Graciela?'

'Of course. And who is this?'

'This is CiCi.'

McCaleb never used the baby's formal name around others. He only liked to call her Cielo when he was alone with her.

'CiCi,' Winston said, and hesitated as if waiting for an explanation of the name. When none came, she said, 'How old?'

'Almost four months. She's big.'

'Wow, yeah, I can see . . . And the boy . . . where's he?'

'Raymond,' Graciela said. 'He's with some friends today. Terry had a charter and so he went with friends to the park to play softball.'

The conversation was halting and strange. Winston either wasn't really interested or was unused to such banal talk.

'Would you like something to drink?' McCaleb offered as he passed the baby to Graciela.

'No, I'm fine. I had a Coke on the boat.'

As if on cue, or perhaps indignant about being passed from one set of hands to another, the baby started to fuss and Graciela said she would take her inside. She left them standing on the porch. McCaleb pointed to the round table and chairs where they ate most nights while the baby slept.

'Let's sit down.'

He pointed Winston to the chair that would give her the best view of the harbor. She put the green binder, which McCaleb recognized as a murder book, on the table and the video on top of it.

'Beautiful,' she said.

'Yeah, she's amazing. I could watch her all—'

He stopped and smiled when he realized she was talking about the view, not his child. Winston smiled, too.

'She's beautiful, Terry. She really is. You look good, too, so tan and all.'

'I've been going out on the boat.'

'And your health is good?'

'Can't complain about anything other than all the meds they make me take. But I'm three years in now and no problems. I think I'm in the clear, Jaye. I just have to keep taking the damn pills and it should stay that way.'

He smiled and he did appear to be the picture of health. As the sun had turned his skin dark, it had worked to the opposite effect on his hair. Close cropped and neat, it was almost blond now. Working on the boat had also defined the muscles of his arms and shoulders. The only giveaway was hidden under his shirt, the ten-inch scar left by transplantation surgery.

'That's great,' Winston said. 'It looks like you have a wonderful setup here. New family, new home . . . away from everything.'

She was silent a moment, turning her head as if to take in all of the view and the island and McCaleb's life at once. McCaleb had always thought Jaye Winston was attractive in a tomboyish way. She had loose sandy-blond hair that she kept shoulder length. She had never worn makeup back when he worked with her. But she had sharp, knowing eyes and an easy and somewhat sad smile, as if she saw the humor and tragedy in everything at once. She wore black jeans and a white T-shirt beneath a black blazer. She looked cool and tough and McCaleb knew from experience that she was. She had a habit of hooking her hair behind her ear frequently as she spoke. He found that endearing for some unknown reason. He had always thought that if he had not connected with Graciela he might have tried to know Jaye Winston better. He also sensed that Winston intuitively knew that.

'Makes me feel guilty about why I came,' she said. 'Sort of.'

McCaleb nodded at the binder and the tape.

'You came on business. You could have just called, Jaye. Saved some time, probably.'

'No, you didn't send out any change-of-address or phone cards. Like maybe you didn't want people to know where you ended up.'

She hooked her hair behind her left ear and smiled again.

'Not really,' he said. 'I just didn't think people would want to know where I was. So how did you find me?'

'Asked around over at the marina on the mainland.'

'Overtown. They call it overtown here.'

'Overtown, then. They told me in the harbor master's office that you still kept a slip there but you moved the boat over here. I came over and took a water taxi around the harbor until I found it. Your friend was there. He told me how to get up here.'

'Buddy.'

McCaleb looked down into the harbor and picked out *The Following Sea*. It was about a half mile or so away. He could see Buddy Lockridge bent over in the stern. After a few moments he could tell that Buddy was washing off the reels with the hose from the freshwater tank.

'So what's this about, Jaye?' McCaleb said without looking at Winston. 'Must be important for you to go through all of that on your day off. I assume you're off on Sundays.'

'Most of them.'

She pushed the tape aside and opened the binder. Now McCaleb looked over. Although it was upside down to him, he could tell the top page was a standard homicide occurrence report, usually the first page in every murder book he had ever read. It was the starting point. His eyes went to the address box. Even upside down he could make out that it was a West Hollywood case.

'I've got a case here I was hoping you'd take a look at. In your spare time, I mean. I think it might be your sort of thing. I was hoping you'd give me a read, maybe point me someplace I haven't been yet.'

He had known as soon as he saw the binder in her hands that this was what she was going to ask him. But now that it had been asked he felt a confusing rush of sensations. He felt a thrill at the possibility of having a part of his old life again. He also felt guilt over the idea of bringing death into a home so full of new life and happiness. He glanced toward the open slider to see if Graciela was looking out at them. She wasn't.

'My sort of thing?' he said. 'If it's a serial, you shouldn't waste time. Go to the bureau, call Maggie Griffin. She'll—'

'I did all of that, Terry. I still need you.'

'How old is this thing?'

'Two weeks.'

Her eyes looked up from the binder to his.

'New Year's Day?'

She nodded.

'First murder of the year,' she said. 'For L.A. County, at least. Some people think the true millennium didn't start until this year.'

'You think this is a millennium nut?'

'Whoever did this was a nut of some order. I think. That's why I'm here.'

'What did the bureau say? Did you take this to Maggie?'

'You haven't kept up, Terry. Maggie was sent back to Quantico. Things slowed down in the last few years out here and Behavioral Sciences pulled her back. No outpost in L.A. anymore. So, yes, I talked to her. But over the phone at Quantico. She ran it through VICAP and got zilched.'

McCaleb knew she meant the Violent Criminal Apprehension Program computer.

'What about a profile?' he asked.

'I'm on a waiting list. Do you know that across the country there were thirty-four millennium-inspired murders on New Year's Eve and New Year's Day? So they have their hands full at the moment and the bigger departments like us, we're at the end of the line because the bureau figures the smaller departments with less experience and expertise and manpower need their help more.'

She waited a moment while letting McCaleb consider all of this. He understood the bureau's philosophy. It was a form of triage.

'I don't mind waiting a month or so until Maggie or somebody else over there can work something up for me, but my gut on this one tells me time is a consideration, Terry. If it is a serial, a month may be too long to wait. That's why I thought of coming to you. I am banging my head on the wall on this one and you might be our last best hope of coming up with something to move on now. I still remember the Cemetery Man and the Code Killer. I know what you can do with a murder book and some crime scene tape.'

The last few lines were gratuitous and her only false move so far, McCaleb thought. Otherwise he believed she was sincere in the expression of her belief that the killer she was looking for might strike again.

'It's been a long time for me, Jaye,' McCaleb began. 'Other than that thing with Graciela's sister, I haven't been involved in—'

'Come on, Terry, don't bullshit me, okay? You can sit here with a baby in your lap every day of the week and it still won't erase what you were and what you did. I know you. We haven't seen each other or talked in a long time but I know you. And I know that not a day goes by that you don't think about cases. Not a day.'

She paused and stared at him.

'When they took out your heart, they didn't take out what makes you tick, know what I mean?'

McCaleb looked away from her and back down at his boat. Buddy was now sitting in the main fighting chair, his feet up on the transom. McCaleb assumed he had a beer in his hand but it was too far to see that.

'If you're so good at reading people, what do you need me for?'

'I may be good but you're the best I ever knew. Hell, even if they weren't backed up till Easter in Quantico, I'd take you over any of those profilers. I mean that. You were—'

'Okay, Jaye, we don't need a sales pitch, okay? My ego is doing okay without all the—'

'Then what do you need?'

He looked back at her.

'Just some time. I need to think about this.'

'I'm here because my gut says I don't have much time.'

McCaleb got up and walked to the railing. His gaze was out to the sea. A *Catalina Express* ferry was coming in. He knew it would be almost empty. The winter months brought few visitors.

'The boat's coming in,' he said. 'It's the winter schedule, Jaye. You better catch it going back or you'll be here all night.'

'I'll have dispatch send a chopper for me if I have to. Terry, all I need from you is one day at the most. One night, even. Tonight. You sit down, read the book, look at the tape and then call me in the morning, tell me what you see. Maybe it's nothing or at least nothing that's new. But maybe you'll see something we've missed or you'll get an idea we haven't come up with yet. That's all I'm asking. I don't think it's a lot.'

McCaleb looked away from the incoming boat and turned so his back leaned against the rail.

'It doesn't seem like a lot to you because you're in the

life. I'm not. I'm out of it, Jaye. Even going back into it for a day is going to change things. I moved out here to start over and to forget all the stuff I was good at. To get good at being something else. At being a father and a husband, for starters.'

Winston got up and walked to the railing. She stood next to him but looked out at the view while he remained facing his home. She spoke in a low voice. If Graciela was listening from somewhere inside, she could not hear this.

'Remember with Graciela's sister what you told me? You told me you got a second shot at life and that there had to be a reason for it. Now you've built this life with her sister and her son and now even your own child. That's wonderful, Terry, I really think so. But that can't be the reason you were looking for. You might think it is but it's not. Deep down you know it. You were good at catching these people. Next to that, what is catching fish?'

McCaleb nodded slightly and was uncomfortable with himself for doing it so readily.

'Leave the stuff,' he said. 'I'll call you when I can.'

On the way to the door Winston looked about for Graciela but didn't see her.

'She's probably in with the baby,' McCaleb said.

'Well, tell her I said good-bye.'

'I will.'

There was an awkward silence the rest of the way to the door. Finally, as McCaleb opened it, Winston spoke.

'So what's it like, Terry? Being a father.'

'It's the best of times, it's the worst of times.'

His stock answer. He then thought a moment and added something he had thought about but never said, not even to Graciela.

'It's like having a gun to your head all the time.'

Winston looked confused and maybe even a little concerned.

'How so?'

'Because I know if anything ever happens to her, anything, then my life is over.'

She nodded.

'I think I can understand that.'

She went through the door. She looked rather silly as she left. A seasoned homicide detective riding away in a golf cart.

2

Sunday dinner with Graciela and Raymond was a quiet affair. They ate white sea bass McCaleb had caught with the charter that morning on the back side of the island near the isthmus. His charters always wanted to keep the fish they caught but then often changed their minds when they got back to the harbor. It was something about the killing instinct in men, McCaleb believed. It wasn't enough just to catch their quarry. They must kill it as well. It meant fish was often served at dinner at the house on La Mesa.

McCaleb had grilled the fish along with corn still in the husks on the porch barbecue. Graciela had made a salad and biscuits. They both had a glass of white wine in front of them. Raymond had milk. The meal was good but the silence wasn't. McCaleb looked over at Raymond and realized the boy had picked up on the vibe passed between the adults and was going along with the tide. McCaleb remembered how he had done the same thing when he was a boy and his parents were throwing silence at each other. Raymond was the son of Graciela's sister, Gloria. His father had never been part of the picture. When Glory died – was murdered – three years before, Raymond had come to live with Graciela. McCaleb met them both when he investigated the case.

'How was softball today?' McCaleb finally asked.

'It was okay, I guess.'

'Get any hits?'

'No.'

'You will. Don't worry. Just keep trying. Keep swinging.'

McCaleb nodded. The boy had wanted to go out on the charter that morning but had not been allowed. The charter was for six men from overtown. With McCaleb and Buddy, that made eight on *The Following Sea* and that was the limit the boat could carry under the rules of safety. McCaleb never broke those rules.

'Well, listen, our next charter isn't until Saturday. Right now it's only four people. In winter season I doubt we'll pick up anybody else. If it stays that way, you can come.'

The boy's dark features seemed to lighten and he nodded vigorously as he worked his fork into the pure white meat of the fish on his plate. The fork looked big in his hand and McCaleb felt a momentary sadness for the boy. He was exceedingly small for a boy of ten. This bothered Raymond a great deal and he often asked McCaleb when he would grow. McCaleb always told him that it would happen soon, though privately he thought the boy would always be small. He knew that his mother had been of average size but Graciela had told McCaleb that Raymond's father had been a very small man – in size and integrity. He had disappeared before Raymond was born.

Always picked last for the team, too small to be competitive with other boys his age, Raymond had gravitated toward pastimes other than team sports. Fishing was his passion and on off days McCaleb usually took him out into the bay to fish for halibut. When he had a charter, the boy always begged to go and when there was room he was allowed to come along as second mate. It was always McCaleb's great pleasure to put a five-dollar bill into an envelope, seal it and hand it to the boy at the end of the day.

'We'll need you in the tower,' McCaleb said. 'This party wants to go down south for marlin. It'll be a long day.'

'Cool!'

McCaleb smiled. Raymond loved being the lookout in the tower, watching for black marlin sleeping or rolling on the surface. And with a pair of binoculars, he was becoming adept at it. McCaleb looked over at Graciela to share the moment but she was looking down at her plate. There was no smile on her face.

In a few more minutes Raymond had finished eating and asked to be excused so he could play on the computer in his room. Graciela told him to keep the sound down so as not to wake the baby. The boy took his plate into the kitchen and then Graciela and McCaleb were alone.

He understood why she was silent. She knew she could not voice her objection to his getting involved in an investigation because her own request that he investigate her sister's death was what had brought them together three years before. Her emotions were caught in this irony.

'Graciela,' McCaleb began. 'I know you don't want me to do this but—'

'I didn't say that.'

'You didn't have to. I know you and I can tell by the look that's been on your face ever since Jaye was here that—'

'I just don't want everything to change, that's all.'

'I understand that. I don't want anything to change either. And it won't. All I'm going to do is look at the file and the tape and tell her what I think.'

'It won't be just that. *I* know *you*. I've seen you do this. You'll get hooked. It's what you are good at.'

'I won't get hooked. I'll just do what she asked and that's it. I'm not even going to do it here. I'm going to take what she gave me and go over to the boat. So it won't even be in the house. Okay? I don't want it in the house.'

He knew he was going to do it with or without her approval but he wanted it from her just the same. Their relationship was still so new that he seemed to always be seeking her approval. He had thought about this and wondered if it was something to do with his second chance. He had fought through a lot of guilt in the past three years but it still came up like a roadblock every few miles. Somehow he felt as though if he could just win this one woman's approval for his existence, then it would all be okay. His cardiologist had called it survivor's guilt. He had lived because someone else had died and must now attain some sense of redemption for it. But McCaleb thought the explanation was not as simple as that.

Graciela frowned but it did not detract from his view of her as beautiful. She had copper skin and dark brown hair that framed a face with eyes so darkly brown that there was almost no demarcation between iris and pupil. Her beauty was another reason he sought her approval of all things. There was something purifying about the light of her smile when it was cast on him.

'Terry, I listened to you two on the porch. After the baby got quiet. I heard what she said about what makes you tick and how a day doesn't go by that you don't think about it, what you used to do. Just tell me this, was she right?'

McCaleb was silent a moment. He looked down at his empty plate and then off across the harbor to the lights in the houses going up the opposite hillside to the inn at the top of Mount Ada. He slowly nodded and then looked back at her.

'Yes, she was right.'

'Then all of this, what we are doing here, the baby, it's all a lie?'

'No. Of course not. This is everything to me and I would protect it with everything I've got. But the answer is yes, I think about what I was and what I did. When I was with the bureau I saved lives, Graciela, plain and simple. And I took evil out of this world. Made it a little less dark out there.'

He raised his hand and gestured toward the harbor.

'Now I have a wonderful life with you and Cielo and Raymond. And I . . . I catch fish for rich people with nothing better to do with their money.'

'So you want both.'

'I don't know what I want. But I know that when she was here I was saying things to her because I knew you were listening. I was saying what I knew you wanted to hear but I knew in my heart it wasn't what I wanted. What I wanted to do was open that book right then and go to work. She was right about me, Gracie. She hadn't seen me in three years but she had me pegged.'

Graciela stood up and came around the table to him. She sat on his lap.

'I'm just scared for you, that's all,' she said.

She pulled him close.

McCaleb took two tall glasses from the cabinet and put them on the counter. He filled the first with bottled water and the second with orange juice. He then began ingesting the twenty-seven pills he had lined up on the counter, intermittently taking swallows of water and orange juice to help them go down. Eating the pills – twice a day – was his ritual and he hated it. Not because of the taste – he was long past that after three years. But because the ritual was a reminder of how dependent he was on exterior concerns for his life. The pills were a leash. He could not live long without them. Much of his world now was built around ensuring that he would always have them. He planned around them. He hoarded them. Sometimes he even dreamed about taking pills.

When he was done, McCaleb went into the living room, where Graciela was reading a magazine. She didn't look up at him when he stepped into the room, another sign that she was unhappy with what was suddenly happening in her home. He stood there waiting for a moment and when things didn't change he went down the hallway into the baby's room.

Cielo was still asleep in her crib. The overhead light was on a dimmer switch and he raised the illumination just enough so that he could see her clearly. McCaleb went to the crib and leaned down so he could listen to her breathe and see her and smell her baby scent. Cielo had her mother's coloring – dark skin and hair – except for her eyes, which were ocean blue. Her tiny hands were balled in fists as if she were showing her readiness to fight for life. McCaleb fell most in love with her when he watched her sleep. He thought about all the preparation they had gone through, the books and classes and advice from Graciela's friends at the hospital who were pediatric nurses. All of it so that they would be ready to care for a fragile life so dependent on them. Nothing had been said or read to prepare him for the opposite: the knowledge that came the first moment he held her, that his own life was now dependent on her.

He reached down to her, the spread of his hand covering her back. She didn't stir. He could feel her tiny heart beating. It seemed quick and desperate, like a whispered prayer. Sometimes he pulled the rocking chair over next to the crib and watched over her until late into the night. This night was different. He had to go. He had work to do. Blood work. He wasn't sure if he was there to simply say good-bye for the night or to somehow gain inspiration or approval from her as well. In his mind it didn't quite make sense. He just knew that he had to watch her and touch her before he went to his work.

McCaleb walked out on the pier and then down the steps to the skiff dock. He found his Zodiac among the other small boats and climbed aboard, careful to put the videotape and the murder book in the shelter of the inflatable's bow so they wouldn't get wet. He pulled the engine cord twice before it started and then headed off down the middle lane of the harbor. There were no docks in Avalon Harbor. The boats were tied to mooring buoys set in lines that followed the concave shape of the natural harbor. Because it was winter there were few boats in the harbor, but McCaleb didn't cut between the buoys. He followed the fairways, as if driving a car on the streets of a neighborhood. You didn't cut across lawns, you stayed on the roadway.

It was cold on the water and McCaleb zipped up his windbreaker. As he approached *The Following Sea* he could see the glow of the television behind the curtains of the salon. This meant Buddy Lockridge had not finished up in time to catch the last ferry and was staying over.

McCaleb and Lockridge worked the charter business together. While the boat's ownership was in Graciela's name, the marine charter license and all other documentation relating to the business were in Lockridge's name. The two had met more than three years earlier when McCaleb had docked *The Following Sea* at Cabrillo Marina in the Los Angeles Harbor and was living aboard it while restoring it. Buddy was a neighbor, living on a sailboat nearby. They had struck up a friendship that ultimately became a partnership.

During the busy spring and summer season Lockridge stayed most nights on *The Following Sea.* But during the slow times he usually caught a ferry back overtown to his own boat at Cabrillo. He seemed to have greater success finding female companions in the overtown bars than in the handful of places on the island. McCaleb assumed he would be heading back in the morning since they did not have a charter for another five days.

McCaleb bumped the Zodiac into the fantail of *The Following Sea.* He cut the engine and got out with the tape and the binder. He tied the Zodiac off on a stern cleat and headed for the salon door. Buddy was there waiting, having heard the Zodiac or felt its bump on the fantail. He slid the door open, holding a paperback novel down at his side. McCaleb glanced at the television but couldn't tell what it was he had on.

'What's up, Terror?' Lockridge asked.

'Nothing. I just need to do a little work. I'm going to be using the forward bunk, okay?'

He stepped into the salon. It was warm. Lockridge had the space heater fired up.

'Sure, fine. Anything I can do to help?'

'Nah, this isn't about the business.'

'It about that lady who came by? The sheriff's lady?'

McCaleb had forgotten that Winston had come to the boat first and gotten directions from Buddy.

'Yeah.'

'You working a case for her?'

'No,' McCaleb said quickly, hoping to limit Lockridge's interest and involvement. 'I just need to look at some stuff and give her a call back.'

'Very cool, dude.'

'Not really. It's just a favor. What are you watching?'

'Oh, nothing. Just a show about this task force that goes after computer hackers. Why, you seen it?'

'No, but I was wondering if I could borrow the TV for a little while.'

McCaleb held up the videotape. Lockridge's eyes lit up.

'Be my guest. Pop that baby in there.'

'Um, not up here, Buddy. This is – Detective Winston asked me to do this in confidence. I'll bring the TV back up as soon as I'm done.'

Lockridge's face registered his disappointment but McCaleb wasn't worried about it. He went over to the counter that separated the galley from the salon and put down the binder and tape. He unplugged the television and removed it from the locking frame that held it in place so it wouldn't fall when the boat encountered high seas. The television had a built-in videocassette player and was heavy. McCaleb lugged it down the narrow stairway and took it to the forward stateroom, which had been partially converted into an office. Two sides of the room had been lined with twin bunk beds. The bottom berth on the left had been changed into a desk and the two top bunks were used by McCaleb to store his old bureau case files – Graciela didn't want them in the house where Raymond might stumble upon them. The only problem was that McCaleb was sure that on occasion Buddy had gone through the boxes and looked at the files. And it bothered him. It was an invasion of some kind. McCaleb had thought about keeping the forward stateroom locked but knew that could be a deadly mistake. The only ceiling hatch on the lower deck was in the forward room and access to it ought not be blocked in case there was ever a need for an emergency evacuation through the bow.

He put the television down on the desk and plugged it in. He turned to go back up to the salon to retrieve the binder and tape when he saw Buddy coming down the stairs, holding the tape and leafing through the binder.

'Hey, Buddy—'

'Looks like a weird one, man.'

McCaleb reached out and closed the binder, then took it and the tape from his fishing partner's hands.

'Just taking a peek.'

'I told you, it's confidential.'

'Yeah, but we work good together. Just like before.'

It was true that by happenstance Lockridge had been a great help when McCaleb had investigated the death of Graciela's sister. But that had been an active street investigation. This was just going to be a review. He didn't need anybody looking over his shoulder.

'This is different, Buddy. This is a one-night stand. I'm just going to take a look at this stuff and then that will be it. Now let me get to work so I'm not here all night.'

Lockridge didn't say anything and McCaleb didn't wait. He closed the door to the forward bunk and then turned to the desk. As he looked down at the murder book in his hands he felt a sharp thrill as well as the familiar rising of dread and guilt.

McCaleb knew it was time to go back to the darkness.

To explore it and know it. To find his way through it. He nodded, though he was alone now. It was in acknowledgment that he had waited a long time for this moment.

3

The video was clear and steady, the lighting was good. The technical aspects of crime scene videotaping had vastly improved since McCaleb's days with the bureau. The content had not changed. The tape McCaleb watched showed the starkly lit tableau of murder. McCaleb finally froze the image and studied it. The cabin was silent, the gentle lapping sound of the sea against the boat's hull the only intrusion from outside.

At center focus was the nude body of what appeared to be a man who had been trussed with baling wire, his arms and legs held tightly behind his torso to such an extreme that the body appeared to be in a reverse fetal position. The body was face down on an old and dirty rug. The focus was too tight on the body to determine in what sort of location it had been found. McCaleb judged that the victim was a man solely on the basis of body mass and musculature. For the head of the victim was not visible. A gray plastic mop bucket had been placed entirely over the victim's head. McCaleb could see that a length of the baling wire was stretched taut from the victim's ankles, up his back and between his arms, and beneath the lip of the bucket where it wrapped around his neck. It appeared on first measure to be a ligature strangulation in which the leverage of the legs and feet pulled the wire tight around the victim's neck, causing asphyxia. In effect, the victim had been bound in such a way that he ultimately killed himself when he could no longer hold his legs folded backward in such an extreme position.

McCaleb continued studying the scene. A small amount of blood had poured onto the carpet from the bucket, indicating that some kind of head wound would be found when the vessel was removed.

McCaleb leaned back in his old desk chair and thought about his initial impressions. He had not yet opened the binder, choosing instead to watch the crime scene videotape first and to study the scene as close as possible to the way the investigators had originally seen it. Already he was fascinated by what he was looking at. He felt the implication of ritual in the scene on the television screen. He also felt the trilling of adrenaline in his blood again. He pressed the button on the remote and the video continued.

The focus pulled back as Jaye Winston entered the frame of the video. McCaleb could see more of the room now and noted that it appeared to be in a small, sparsely furnished house or apartment.

Coincidentally, Winston was wearing the same outfit she had worn when she had come to the house with the murder book and videotape. She had on rubber gloves that she had pulled up over the cuffs of her blazer. Her detective's shield hung on a black shoelace which had been tied around her neck. She took a position on the left side of the dead man while her partner, a detective McCaleb did not recognize, moved to the right side. For the first time there was talking on the video.

'The victim has already been examined by a deputy coroner and released for crime scene investigation,' Winston said. 'The victim has been photographed in situ. We're now going to remove the bucket to make further examination.'

McCaleb knew that she was carefully choosing her words and demeanor with the future in mind, a future that would include a trial for an accused killer in which the crime scene tape would be viewed by a jury. She had to appear professional and objective, completely emotionally removed from what she was encountering. Anything deviating from this could be cause for a defense attorney to seek removal of the tape from evidence.

Winston reached up and hooked her hair behind her ears and then placed both hands on the victim's shoulders. With her partner's help she turned the body on its side, the dead man's back to the camera.

The camera then came in over the victim's shoulder and closed in as Winston gently pulled the bucket handle from under the man's chin and proceeded to carefully lift it off the head.

'Okay,' she said.

She showed the interior of the bucket to the camera – blood had coagulated inside it – and then placed it in an open cardboard box used for evidence storage. She then turned back and gazed down at the victim.

Gray duct tape had been wrapped around the dead man's head to form a tight gag across the mouth. The eyes were open and distended – bugged. The cornea of each eye was rouged with hemorrhage. So was the skin around the eyes.

'CP,' the partner said, pointing to the eyes.

'Kurt,' Winston said. 'We're on sound.'

'Sorry.'

She was telling her partner to keep all observations to himself. Again, she was safeguarding the future. McCaleb knew that what her partner was pointing out was the hemorrhaging, or conjunctive petechiae, which always came with ligature strangulation. However, the observation was one that should be made to a jury by a medical examiner, not a homicide detective.

Blood matted the dead man's medium-length hair and had pooled inside the bucket against the left side of his face. Winston began manipulating the head and combing her fingers through the hair in search of the origin of the blood. She finally found the wound on the crown of the head. She pulled the hair back as much as possible to view it.

'Barney, come in close on this if you can,' she said.

The camera moved in. McCaleb saw a small, round puncture wound that did not appear to penetrate the skull. He knew that the amount of blood evidenced was not always in concert with the gravity of the wound. Even inconsequential wounds to the scalp could produce a lot of blood. He would get a formal and complete description of the wound in the autopsy report.

'Barn, get this,' Winston said, her voice up a notch from the previous monotone. 'We've got writing or something on the tape, on the gag.'

She had noticed it while manipulating the head. The camera moved in. McCaleb could make out lightly marked letters on the tape where it crossed the dead man's mouth. The letters appeared to be written in ink but the message was obliterated by blood. He could make out what appeared to be one word of the message.

'Cave,' he read out loud. 'Cave?'

He then thought maybe it was only a partial word but he couldn't think of any larger word – other than *cavern* – that contained those letters in that order.

McCaleb froze the picture and just looked. He was enthralled. What he was seeing was pulling him backward in time to his days as a profiler, when almost every case he was assigned left him with the same question: *What dark, tortured mind did this come from?*

Words from a killer were always significant and put a case on a higher plane. It most often meant that the killing was a statement, a message transmitted from killer to victim and then from the investigators to the world as well.

McCaleb stood up and reached to the upper bunk. He pulled down one of the old file boxes and let it drop heavily to the floor. Quickly lifting the lid, he began combing through the files for a notebook with some unused pages in it. It had been his ritual with the bureau to start each case he was assigned with a fresh spiral notebook. He finally came across a file with only a BAR form and a notebook in it. With so little paperwork in the file he knew it was a short case and that the notebook should have plenty of blank pages.

McCaleb leafed through the notebook and found it largely unused. He then took out the Bureau Assistance Request form and quickly read the top sheet to see what case it was. He immediately remembered it because he had handled it with one phone call. The request had come from a detective in the small town of White Elk, Minnesota, almost ten years before, when McCaleb still worked out of Quantico. The detective's report said two men had gotten into a drunken brawl in the house they shared, challenged each other to a duel and proceeded to kill each other with simultaneous shots from ten yards apart in the back yard. The detective needed no help with the double homicide case because it was cut and dried. But he was puzzled by something else. In the course of searching the victims' house, investigators had come across something strange in the basement freezer. Pushed into a corner of the freezer cabinet were plastic bags containing dozens and dozens of used tampons. They were of various makes and brands, and preliminary tests on a sampling of the tampons had identified the menstrual blood on them as having come from several different women.

The case detective didn't know what he had but feared the worst. What he wanted from the FBI's Behavioral Sciences Unit was an idea about what these bloody tampons could mean and how to proceed. More specifically, he wanted to know if the tampons could possibly be souvenirs kept by a serial killer or killers who had gone undiscovered until they happened to kill each other.

McCaleb smiled as he remembered the case. He had come across tampons in a freezer before. He called the detective and asked him three questions. What did the two men do for a living? In addition to the firearms used during the duel, were there any long weapons or a hunting license found in the apartment? And, lastly, when did bear hunting season begin in the woods of northern Minnesota?

The detective's answers quickly solved the tampon mystery. Both men worked at the airport in Minneapolis for a subcontractor that provided clean-out crews who prepared commercial airliners for flights. Several hunting rifles were found in the house but no hunting license. And, lastly, bear season was three weeks away.

McCaleb told the detective that it appeared that the men were not serial killers but had probably been collecting the contents from the tampon disposal receptacles in lavatories of the planes they cleaned. They were taking the tampons home and freezing them. When hunting season began they would most likely thaw the tampons and use them to bait bear, which can pick up the scent of blood at a great distance. Most hunters use garbage as bait but nothing is better than blood.

McCaleb remembered that the detective had actually seemed disappointed that he had no serial killer or killers at hand. He had either been embarrassed that an FBI agent sitting at a desk in Quantico had so quickly solved his mystery or he was simply annoyed that there would be no national media ride from his case. He abruptly hung up and McCaleb never heard from him again.

McCaleb tore the few pages of notes from the case out of the notebook, put them in the file with the BAR form and returned the file to its spot. He then put the lid on the box and hoisted it back up onto the shelf that had been the top bunk. He shoved the box back into place and it banged hard on the bulkhead.

Sitting back down, McCaleb glanced at the frozen image on the television screen and then considered the blank page in the notebook. Finally, he took the pen out of his shirt pocket and was about to begin writing when the door to the room suddenly opened and Buddy Lockridge stood there.

'You okay?'

'What?'

'I heard all this banging. The whole boat moved.'

'I'm fine, Buddy, I just—'

'Oh, shit, what the hell is that?'

He was staring at the TV screen. McCaleb immediately raised the remote and killed the picture.

'Buddy, look, I told you this is confidential and I can't—'

'Okay, okay, I know. I was just checking to make sure you didn't keel over or something.'

'Okay, thanks, but I'm fine.'

'I'll be up for a little while if you need something.'

'I won't, but thanks.'

'You know, you're using a lot of juice. You're going to have to run the generator tomorrow after I split.'

'No problem. I'll do it. I'll see you later, Buddy.'

Buddy pointed at the now empty television screen.

'That's a weird one.'

'Good-bye, Buddy,' McCaleb said impatiently.

He got up and closed the door while Lockridge was still standing there. This time he locked it. He returned to the seat and the notebook. He started writing and in a few moments he had constructed a list.

SCENE
1. Ligature
2. Nude
3. Head Wound
4. Tape/Gag – 'Cave'?
5. Bucket?

He studied the list for a few moments, waiting for an idea, but nothing came through. It was too early. Instinctively, he knew the wording on the tape was a key that he wouldn't be able to turn until he had the complete message. He fought the urge to open the murder book and get to it. Instead, he turned the television back on and began running the tape from the spot he had left off. The camera was in and tight on the dead man's mouth and the tape stretched tightly across it.

'We'll leave this for the coroner,' Winston said. 'You got what you can of this, Barn?'

'I got it,' said the unseen videographer.

'Okay, let's pull back and look at these bindings.'

The camera traced the baling wire from the neck to the feet. The wire looped around the neck and passed through a slip knot. It then went down the spine to where it had been wrapped several times around the ankles, which had been pulled so far back that the victim's heels now rested on his buttocks.

The wrists were bound with a separate length of wire that had been wrapped six times around and then pulled into a knot. The bindings had caused deep furrow marks in the skin of the wrists and ankles, indicating that the victim had struggled for a period before finally succumbing.

When the videography of the body was completed, Winston told the unseen man with the camera to make a video inventory of every room in the apartment.

The camera panned away from the body and took in the rest of the living-room/dining-room space. The home seemed to have been furnished out of a secondhand store. There was no uniformity, none of the pieces of furniture matched. The few framed pictures on the walls looked as though they could have come out of a room at a Howard Johnson's ten years before – all orange and aqua pastels. At the far end of the room was a tall china cabinet with no china in it. There were some books on a few of the shelves but most were barren. On top of the cabinet was something McCaleb found curious. It was a two-foot-high owl that looked hand painted. McCaleb had seen many of these before, especially in Avalon Harbor and Cabrillo Marina. Most often the owls were made of hollow plastic and placed at the tops of masts or on the bridges of power boats in a usually unsuccessful attempt to scare gulls and other birds away from the boats. The theory was that the owl would be seen by the other birds as a predator and they would stay clear, thereby leaving the boats unfouled by their droppings.

McCaleb had also seen the owls used on the exteriors of public buildings where pigeons were a nuisance. But what interested him about the plastic owl here was that he had never seen or heard of one being used inside a private home as ornamentation or otherwise. He knew that people collected all manner of things, including owls, but he had so far seen none in the apartment other than the one positioned at center on the cabinet. He quickly opened the binder and found the victim identification report. It listed the victim's occupation as house painter. McCaleb closed the binder and considered for a moment that perhaps the victim had taken the owl from a job or removed it from a structure while prepping it to be painted.

He backed the tape up and watched again as the videographer panned from the body to the cabinet atop which the owl was perched. It appeared to McCaleb that the videographer had made a 180-degree turn, meaning the owl would have been directly facing the victim, looking down upon the scene of the murder.

While there were other possibilities, McCaleb's instinct told him the plastic owl was somehow part of the crime scene. He took up the notebook and made the owl the sixth entry on his list.

The rest of the crime scene videotape fostered little interest in McCaleb. It documented the remaining rooms of the victim's apartment – the bedroom, bathroom and kitchen. He saw no more owls and took no more notes. When he got to the end of the tape he rewound it and watched it all the way through once more. Nothing new caught his attention. He ejected the tape and slid it back into its cardboard slipcase. He then carried the television back up to the salon, where he locked it into its frame on the counter.

Buddy was sprawled on the couch reading his paperback. He didn't say anything and McCaleb could tell he was hurt that McCaleb had closed and locked the door to the office on him. He thought about apologizing but decided to let it go. Buddy was too nosy about McCaleb, past and present. Maybe this rejection would let him know that.

'What are you reading?' he asked instead.

'A book,' Lockridge answered without looking up.

McCaleb smiled to himself. Now he was sure that he had gotten to Buddy.

'Well, there's the TV if you want to watch the news or something.'

'The news is over.'

McCaleb looked at his watch. It was midnight. He had not realized how much time had gone by. This had often been the case with him – while at the bureau it was routine for him to work through lunch or late into the night without realizing it when he became fully engaged in a case.

He left Buddy to sulk and went back down to the office. He closed the door again, loudly, and locked it.

4

After turning to a fresh page in his notebook, McCaleb opened the murder book. He snapped open the rings and pulled the documents out and stacked them neatly on the desk. It was a little quirk but he never liked reviewing cases by turning pages in a book. He liked to hold the individual reports in his hands. He liked squaring off the corners of the whole stack. He put the binder aside and began carefully reading through the investigative summaries in chronological order. Soon he was fully immersed in the investigation.

The homicide report had come in anonymously to the front desk of the West Hollywood substation of the Los Angeles County Sheriff's Department at noon on Monday, January 1. The male caller said there was a man dead in apartment 2B in the Grand Royale Apartments on Sweetzer near Melrose. The caller hung up without giving his name or any other message. Because the call came in on one of the non-emergency lines at the front desk it was not recorded, and there was no caller ID function on the phone.

A pair of patrol deputies were dispatched to the apartment and found the front door slightly ajar. After receiving no answer to their knocks and calls, the deputies entered the apartment and quickly determined that the anonymous caller had given correct information. A man was dead inside. The deputies backed out of the apartment and the homicide squad was called. The case was assigned to partners Jaye Winston and Kurt Mintz, with Winston as lead detective.

The victim was identified in the reports as Edward Gunn, a forty-four-year-old itinerant house painter. He had lived alone in the Sweetzer Avenue apartment for nine years.

A computer search for criminal records or known criminal activity determined that Gunn had a history of convictions for small-time crimes ranging from soliciting for prostitution and loitering to repeated arrests for public intoxication and drunk driving. He had been arrested twice for drunk driving in the three months prior to his death, including the night of December 30. He posted bail on the 31st and was released. Less than twenty-four hours later he was dead. The records also showed an arrest for a serious crime without subsequent conviction. Six years earlier Gunn had been taken into custody by the Los Angeles Police Department and questioned in a homicide. He was later released and no charges were ever filed.

According to the investigative reports Winston and her partner had put into the murder book, there was no apparent robbery of Gunn or his apartment, leaving the motive for his slaying unknown. Other residents in the eight-unit apartment building said that they had heard no disturbances in Gunn's apartment on New Year's Eve. Any sounds that might have emanated from the apartment during the murder were likely camouflaged by the sounds of a party being held by a tenant in the apartment directly below Gunn's. The party had lasted well into the morning of January 1. Gunn, according to several partygoers who were interviewed, had not attended the party or been invited.

A canvass of the neighborhood, which was primarily lined with small apartment buildings similar to the Grand Royale, found no witnesses who remembered seeing Gunn in the days leading up to his death.

All indications were that the murderer had come to

Gunn. The lack of damage to doors and windows of the apartment indicated that there had been no break-in and that Gunn might very well have known his killer. To that end, Winston and Mintz interviewed all known coworkers and associates, as well as every tenant and every person who had attended the party at the complex, in an effort to draw out a suspect. They got nothing for their effort.

They also checked all of the victim's financial records for a clue to a possible monetary motivation and found nothing. Gunn had no steady employment. He mostly loitered around a paint and design store on Beverly Boulevard and offered his services to customers on a day-work basis. He lived a hand-to-mouth existence, making just enough to pay for and maintain his apartment and a small pickup truck in which he carried his painting equipment.

Gunn had one living relative, a sister who lived in Long Beach. At the time of his death, he had not seen her in more than a year, though he happened to call her the night before his death from the holding tank of the LAPD's Hollywood Division station. He was being held there following his DUI arrest. The sister reported that she'd told her brother she could no longer keep helping him and bailing him out. She'd hung up. And she could not offer the investigators any useful information in regard to his murder.

The incident in which Gunn had been arrested six years before was fully reviewed. Gunn had killed a prostitute in a Sunset Boulevard motel room. He had stabbed her with her own knife when she attempted to stab and rob him, according to his statement in the report forwarded by the LAPD's Hollywood Division. There were minor inconsistencies between Gunn's original statement to responding patrol officers and the physical evidence but not enough for the district attorney's office to seek charges against him. Ultimately, the case was reluctantly written off as self-defense and dropped.

McCaleb noticed that the lead investigator on the case had been Detective Harry Bosch. Years earlier McCaleb had worked with Bosch on a case, an investigation he still often thought about. Bosch had been abrasive and secretive at times, but still a good cop with excellent investigative skills, intuition and instincts. They had actually bonded in some way over the emotional turmoil the case had caused them both. McCaleb wrote Bosch's name down in the notebook as a reminder to call the detective to see if he had any thoughts on the Gunn case.

He went back to reading the summaries. With Gunn's record of prior engagement with a prostitute in mind, Winston's and Mintz's next step was to comb through the murder victim's phone records as well as check and credit card purchases for indications that he might have continued to use prostitutes. There was nothing. They cruised Sunset Boulevard with an LAPD vice crew for three nights, stopping and interviewing street prostitutes. But none admitted knowing the man in the photos the detectives had borrowed from Gunn's sister.

The detectives scanned the sex want ads in the local alternative papers for an advertisement Gunn might have placed. One more time their efforts hit a wall.

Finally, the detectives took the long shot of tracking the family and associates of the dead prostitute of six years before. Although Gunn had never been charged with the killing, there was still a chance someone believed he had not acted in self-defense – someone who might have sought retribution.

But this, too, was a dead end. The woman's family was from Philadelphia. They had lost contact years before. No family member had even come out to claim the body before it was cremated at county taxpayers' expense. There was no reason for them to seek vengeance for a killing six years old when they had not cared much about the killing in the first place.

The case had hit one investigative dead end after

another. A case not solved in the first forty-eight hours had a less than 50 percent chance of being cleared. A case unsolved after two weeks was like an unclaimed body in the morgue – it was going to sit there in the cold and the dark for a long, long time.

And that was why Winston had finally come to McCaleb. He was the last resort on a hopeless case.

Finished with the summaries, McCaleb decided to take a break. He checked his watch and saw it was now almost two. He opened the cabin door and went up to the salon. The lights were off. Buddy had apparently gone to bed in the master cabin without making any noise. McCaleb opened the cold box and looked in. There was a six-pack of beer left over from the charter but he didn't want that. There was a carton of orange juice and some bottled water. He took the water and went out through the salon door to the cockpit. It was always cool on the water but this night seemed crisper than usual. He folded his arms across his chest and looked across the harbor and up the hill to the house where he knew his family slept. A single light shone from the back deck.

A momentary pang of guilt passed through him. He knew that despite his deep love for the woman and two children behind that light, he would rather be on the boat with the murder book than up there in the sleeping house. He tried to push away these thoughts and the questions they raised but could not completely blind himself to the essential conclusion that there was something wrong with him, something missing. It was something that prevented him from fully embracing that which most men seemed to long for.

He went back inside the boat. He knew that immersing himself in the case reports would shut out the guilt.

The autopsy report contained no surprises. The cause of death was as McCaleb had guessed from the video: cerebral hypoxia due to compression of the carotid arteries by ligature strangulation. The time of death was estimated to have been between midnight and 3 A.M. on January 1.

The deputy medical examiner who conducted the autopsy noted that interior damage to the neck was minimal. Neither the hyoid bone nor the thyroid cartilage was broken. This aspect, coupled with multiple ligature furrows on the skin, led the examiner to conclude that Gunn suffocated slowly while desperately struggling to keep his feet behind his torso so that the wire noose was not pulled tight around his neck. The autopsy summation suggested that the victim could have struggled in this position for as long as two hours.

McCaleb thought about this and wondered if the killer had been there in the apartment the whole time, watching the dying man struggle. Or had he set the ligature and left before his victim was dead, possibly to set some kind of alibi scheme into motion – perhaps appearing at a New Year's Eve party so that there would be multiple witnesses able to account for him at the time of the victim's death.

He then remembered the bucket and decided that the killer had stayed. The covering of the victim's face was a frequent occurrence in sexually motivated and rage killings, the attacker covering his victim's face as a means of dehumanizing the victim and avoiding eye contact. McCaleb had worked dozens of cases where he had noted this phenomenon, women who had been raped and murdered with nightgowns or pillowcases covering their faces, children with their heads wrapped in towels. He could write a list of examples that would fill the entire notebook. Instead he wrote one line on the page under Bosch's name.

UNSUB was there the whole time. He watched.

The unknown subject, McCaleb thought. So we meet again.

*

Before moving on, McCaleb looked through the autopsy report for two other pieces of information. First was the head wound. He found a description of the wound in the examiner's comments. The perimortem laceration was circular and superficial. Its damage was minimal and it was possibly a defensive wound.

McCaleb dismissed the possibility of it being a defensive wound. The only blood on the rug at the crime scene was that spilled from the bucket after it was placed over the victim's head. Plus, the flow of blood from the wound at the point of the crown was forward and over the victim's face. This indicated the head was bowed forward. McCaleb took all of this to mean that Gunn was already bound and on the floor when the blow had been struck to his head and then the bucket placed over it. His instinct told him this might have been a blow delivered with the intention of hurrying the victim's demise; an impact to the head that would weaken the victim and shorten his struggle against the ligature.

He wrote these thoughts down in the notebook and then went back into the autopsy report. He located the findings on the examination of the anus and penis. Swabs indicated no sexual activity had occurred in the time prior to death. McCaleb wrote down *No Sex* in the notebook. Beneath this he wrote the word *Rage* and circled it.

McCaleb realized that many, if not all, of the suspicions and conclusions he was coming up with had probably already been reached by Jaye Winston. But this had always been his routine in analyzing murder scenes. He made his own judgments first, then looked to see how they stacked up next to the primary investigator's conclusions afterward.

After the autopsy he went to the evidence analysis reports. He first looked at the recovered evidence list and noticed that the plastic owl he had seen on the videotape had not been bagged and tagged. He felt sure that it should have been and made a note of it. Also missing from the list was any mention of a weapon recovery. It appeared that whatever had been used to open up the wound on Gunn's scalp had been taken away from the scene by the killer. McCaleb made a note of this as well because it was another piece of information supportive of a profile of the killer as organized, thorough and cautious.

The report on the analysis of the tape used to gag the victim was folded into a separate envelope that McCaleb found in one of the binder's pockets. In addition to a computer printout and an addendum there were several photographs that showed the full length of the tape after it had been cut and peeled away from the victim's face and head. The first set of photos documented the tape front and back as it was found, with a significant amount of coagulated blood obscuring the message written on it. The next set of photos showed the tape front and back after the blood had been removed with a solution of soapy water. McCaleb stared at the message for a long moment even though he knew he would never be able to decipher it on his own.

Cave Cave Dus Videt

He finally put the photos aside and picked up the accompanying reports. The tape was found to be clear of fingerprints but several hairs and microscopic fibers were collected from the underside adhesive. The hair was determined to have belonged to the victim. The fibers were held pending further orders for analysis. McCaleb knew this meant there was a time and cost constraint. The fibers would not be analyzed until the investigation reached a point where there were fibers from a suspect's possessions that also could be analyzed and compared. Otherwise, the costly and time-consuming analysis of the collected fibers would be for nothing. McCaleb had seen this sort of investigative prioritizing before. It was a routine in local law enforcement not to take expensive steps until necessary. But he was a bit surprised that it had not been deemed necessary in this case. He concluded that Gunn's background as a one-time murder suspect might have dropped him into a lower class of victim, one for which the extra step is not taken. Maybe, McCaleb thought, this was why Jaye Winston had come to him. She hadn't said anything about paying him for his time – not that he could accept a monetary payment anyway.

He moved on to an addendum report that had been filed by Winston. She had taken a photograph of the tape and the message to a linguistics professor at UCLA who had identified the words as Latin. She was then referred to a retired Catholic priest who lived in the rectory at St. Catherine's in Hollywood and had taught Latin at the church's school for two decades until it was dropped from the curriculum in the early seventies. He easily translated the message for Winston.

As McCaleb read the translation he felt the feathery run of adrenaline rise up his spine to his neck. His skin tightened and he felt a sensation that came close to lightheadedness.

Cave Cave Dus Videt
Cave Cave D(omin)us Videt
Beware Beware God Sees

'Holy shit,' McCaleb said quietly to himself.

It was not said as an exclamation. Rather, it was the phrase he and fellow bureau profilers had used to informally classify cases in which religious overtures were part of the evidence. When God was discovered to be part of the probable motivation for a crime, it became a 'holy shit' case when spoken of in casual conversation. It also changed things significantly, for God's work was never done. When a killer was out there using His name as part of the imprint of a crime, it often meant there would be more crimes. It was said in the bureau profiling offices that God's killers never stopped of their own volition. They had to be stopped. McCaleb now understood Jaye

Winston's apprehension about letting this case gather dust. If Edward Gunn was the first known victim, then somebody else was likely in the sights of the killer right now.

McCaleb scribbled down a translation of the killer's message and some other thoughts. He wrote *Victim Acquisition* and underlined it twice.

He looked back at Winston's report and noticed that at the bottom of the page containing the translation there was a paragraph marked with an asterisk.

> *Father Ryan stated that the word 'Dus' as seen on the duct tape was a short form of 'Deus' or 'Dominus' primarily found in medieval Bibles as well as church carvings and other artwork.

McCaleb leaned back in his chair and drank from the water bottle. He found this final paragraph the most interesting of the whole package. The information it contained could be a means by which the killer might be isolated in a small group and then found. Initially the pool of potential suspects was huge – it would essentially include anyone who had had access to Edward Gunn on New Year's Eve. But the information from Father Ryan narrowed it significantly to those who had knowledge of medieval Latin, or someone who had gotten the word *Dus* and possibly the whole message from something he had seen.

Perhaps something in a church.

5

McCaleb was too jazzed by what he had read and seen to think about sleep. It was four-thirty and he knew he would complete this night awake and in the office. It was probably too early in Quantico, Virginia, for anyone to be in the Behavioral Sciences Unit but he decided to make the call anyway. He went up to the salon, got the cell phone out of the charger and punched in the number from memory. When the general operator answered he asked to be transferred to Special Agent Brasilia Doran's desk. There were a lot of people he could have asked for but he had decided on Doran because they had worked well together – and often from long distances – when he had been in the bureau. Doran also specialized in icon identification and symbology.

The call was picked up by a machine and while listening to Doran's outgoing message McCaleb quickly tried to decide whether to leave a message or just call back. Initially, he thought it would be better to hang up and try to catch Doran live later because a personal call is much more difficult to deflect than a taped message. But then he decided to put faith in their former camaraderie, even if he had been out of the bureau for nearly five years.

'Brass, it's Terry McCaleb. Long time no see. Uh, listen, I'm calling because I need a favor. Could you call me back as soon as you get a moment? I'd really appreciate it.'

He gave the number for his cell phone, thanked her and hung up. He could take the phone with him back to the house and wait for the call there but that would mean that Graciela might overhear the conversation with Doran and he didn't want that. He went back down to the forward bunk and started through the murder book documents again. He checked every page again for something that stood out in its inclusion or exclusion. He took a few more notes and made a list of things he still needed to do and know before drawing up a profile. But primarily he was just waiting for Doran. She finally returned his call at five-thirty.

'Long time is right,' she said by way of greeting.

'Too long. How y'doin', Brass?'

'Can't complain because nobody listens.'

'I heard you guys are looking for the Drano over there.'

'You're right about that. We are clogged and flogged. You know last year we sent half the staff to Kosovo to help in the war crimes investigations. On six-week rotations. That just killed us. We are still so far behind it's getting critical.'

McCaleb wondered if she was giving him the woe-is-me pitch so he might not ask the favor he had mentioned on the message. He decided to go ahead with it anyway.

'Well, then you aren't going to like hearing from me,' he said.

'Oh boy, I'm shaking in my boots. What do you need, Terry?'

'I'm doing a favor for a friend out here. Sheriff's homicide squad. Taking a look at a homicide and—'

'Did he already run it through here?'

'It's a she. And, yeah, she ran it on the VICAP box and got blanked. That's all. She got the word on how backed up you guys are on profiling and came to me instead. I sort of owe her one so I said I'd take a look.'

'And now you want to cut in line, right?'

McCaleb smiled and hoped she was smiling as well on the other end of the line.

'Sort of. But I think it's a quickie. It's just one thing I want.'

'Then out with it. What?'

'I need an iconography baseline. I'm following a hunch on something.'

'Okay. Doesn't sound too involving. What's the symbol?'

'An owl.'

'An owl? Just an owl?'

'More specifically, a plastic owl. But an owl just the same. I want to know if it's turned up before and what it means.'

'Well, I remember the owl on the bag of potato chips. What's that brand?'

'Wise. I remember. It's an East Coast brand.'

'Well, there you go. The owl is smart. He is wise.'

'Brass, I was hoping for something a little more—'

'I know, I know. Tell you what, I'll see what I can find. The thing to remember is, symbols change. What means one thing at one time might mean something completely different at another time. You just looking for contemporary uses and examples?'

McCaleb thought for a moment about the message on the duct tape.

'Can you throw in the medieval time period?'

'Sounds like you got a weird one – but ain't they all. Let me guess, a holy shit case?'

'Could be. How'd you know that?'

'Oh, all that medieval Inquisition and church stuff. Seen it before. I've got your number. I'll try to get back today.'

McCaleb thought about asking her to run an analysis of the message from the duct tape but decided not to pile it on. Besides, the message must have been included on the computer run Jaye Winston completed. He thanked her and was about to disconnect when she asked about his health and he told her he was fine.

'You still living on that boat I heard about?'

'Nope. I'm living on an island now. But I still have the boat. I've got a wife and new baby daughter, too.'

'Wow! Is this the Terry "TV Dinner" McCaleb I used to know?'

'Same one, I guess.'

'Well, it sounds like you got your stuff together.'

'I think I finally do.'

'Then be careful with it. What are you doing chasing a case again?'

McCaleb hesitated in his reply.

'I'm not sure.'

'Don't bullshit me. We both know why you're doing it. Tell you what, let me see what I can find out and I'll call you back.'

'Thanks, Brass. I'll be waiting.'

McCaleb went into the master cabin and shook Buddy Lockridge awake. His friend startled and began swinging his arms wildly.

'It's me, it's me!'

Before he calmed down, Buddy clapped McCaleb on the side of the head with a book he had fallen asleep holding.

'What are you doing?' Buddy exclaimed.

'I'm trying to wake you, man.'

'What for? What time is it?'

'It's almost six. I want to take the boat across.'

'Now?'

'Yeah, now. So get up and help me. I'll get the lines.'

'Man, now? We're going to hit the layer. Why don't you wait until it burns off?'

'Because I don't have the time.'

Buddy reached up and turned on the reading lamp that was attached to the cabin wall just above the headboard. McCaleb noticed the book he was reading was called *The Wire in the Blood.*

'Something sure put a wire in your blood, man,' he said as he rubbed his ear where the book had hit him.

'Sorry about that. Why you in such a hurry to cross, anyway? It's that case, isn't it?'

'I'll be on top. Let's get it going.'

McCaleb headed out of the cabin. Buddy called after him as he expected he would.

'You going to need a driver?'

'No, Buddy. You know I've been driving a couple years now.'

'Yeah, but you might need help with the case, man.'

'I'll be all right. Hurry up, Bud, I want to get over there.'

McCaleb took the key off the hook next to the salon door and went out and climbed up into the bridge. The air was still chilled and tendrils of dawn light were working their way through the morning mist. He flicked on the Raytheon radar and started the engines. They turned over immediately – Buddy had taken the boat over to Marina del Rey the week before to have them overhauled.

McCaleb left them idling while he climbed back down and went to the fantail. He untied the stern line and then the Zodiac and led it around to the bow. He tied the Zodiac to the line from the mooring buoy after releasing it from the forward cleat. The boat was free now. He turned in the bow pulpit and looked up at the bridge just as Buddy, his hair a wiry nest from sleep, slid into the pilot seat. McCaleb signaled that the boat was loose. Buddy pushed the throttles forward and *The Following Sea* began to move. McCaleb picked the eight-foot gaff pole up off the deck and used it to keep the buoy off the bow as the boat made the turn into the fairway and slowly headed toward the mouth of the harbor.

McCaleb stayed in the pulpit, leaning back against the railing and watching the island slip away behind the boat. He looked up once again toward his house and saw only the one light still on. It was too early for his family to be awake. He thought about the mistake he had knowingly just made. He should have gone up to the house and told

Graciela what he was doing, tried to explain it. But he knew it would lose him a lot of time and that he would never be able to explain it to her satisfaction. He decided to just go. He would call his wife after the crossing and he would deal with the consequences of his decision later.

The cool air of the shark-gray dawn had tightened the skin on his arms and neck. He turned in the bow pulpit and looked forward and across the bay to where he knew overtown lay hidden beneath the marine layer. Not being able to see what he knew to be there gave him an ominous feeling and he looked down. The water the bow cut through was flat and as blue-black as a marlin's skin. McCaleb knew he needed to get up into the bridge to help Buddy. One of them would drive while the other kept an eye on the radar screen to chart a safe course to Los Angeles Harbor. Too bad, he thought, that there would be no radar for him to use once he was on land again and trying to chart his way through the case that now gripped him. A mist of a different kind awaited him there. And these thoughts of trying to see his way through turned his mind to the thing about the case that had hooked him so deeply.

Beware Beware God Sees

The words turned in his head like a newfound mantra. There was someone in the cloaking mist ahead who had written those words. Someone who had acted on them in an extreme capacity at least once and who would likely act on them again. McCaleb was going to find that person. And in doing so, he wondered, whose words would he be acting on? Was there a true God sending him on this journey?

He felt a touch on his shoulder and startled and turned, nearly dropping the gaff pole overboard. It was Buddy.

'Jesus, man, don't do that!'

'You all right?'

‘I was till you scared the hell out of me. What are you doing? You should be driving.’

McCaleb glanced over his shoulder to make sure they were clear of the harbor markers and into the open bay.

‘I don’t know,’ Buddy said. ‘You looked like Ahab standing out here with that gaff. I thought something was wrong. What are you doing?’

‘I was thinking. Do you mind? Don’t sneak up on me like that, man.’

‘Well, I guess that makes us even then.’

‘Just go drive the boat, Buddy. I’ll be up in a minute. And check the generator – might as well juice the batteries.’

As Buddy moved away McCaleb felt his heart even out again. He stepped off the pulpit and snapped the gaff back into its clamps on the deck. As he was bent over he felt the boat rise and fall as it went over a three- or four-foot roller. He straightened up and looked around for the origin of the wake. But he saw nothing. It had been a phantom moving across the flat surface of the bay.

6

Harry Bosch raised his briefcase like a shield and used it to push his way through the crowd of reporters and cameras gathered outside the doors of the courtroom.

'Let me through, please, let me through.'

Most of them didn't move until he used the briefcase to lever them out of the way. They were desperately crowding in and reaching tape recorders and cameras toward the center of the human knot where the defense lawyer was holding court.

Bosch finally made it to the door, where a sheriff's deputy was pressed against the handle. He recognized Bosch and stepped sideways so he could open the door.

'You know,' Bosch said to the deputy, 'this is going to happen every day. This guy has more to say outside court than inside. You might want to think about setting up some rules so people can get in and out.'

As Bosch went through the door, he heard the deputy tell him to talk to the judge about it.

Bosch walked down the center aisle and then through the gate to the prosecution table. He was the first to arrive. He pulled the third chair out and sat down. He opened his briefcase on the table, took out the heavy blue binder and put it to the side. He then closed and snapped the briefcase locks and put it down on the floor next to his chair.

Bosch was ready. He leaned forward and folded his arms on top of the binder. The courtroom was still, almost empty except for the judge's clerk and a court reporter who were getting ready for the day. Bosch liked these times. The quiet before the storm. And he knew without a doubt that a storm was surely coming. He nodded to himself. He was ready, ready to dance with the devil once more. He realized that his mission in life was all about moments like these. Moments that should be savored and remembered but that always caused a tight fisting of his guts.

There was a loud metallic clacking sound and the door to the side holding cell opened. Two deputies led a man through the door. He was young and still tanned somehow despite almost three months in lockup. He wore a suit that would easily take the weekly paychecks of the men on either side of him. His hands were cuffed at his sides to a waist chain which looked incongruous with the perfect blue suit. In one hand he clasped an artist's sketch pad. The other held a black felt-tip pen, the only kind of writing instrument allowed in lockdown.

The man was led to the defense table and positioned in front of the middle seat. He smiled and looked forward as the cuffs and the chain were removed. A deputy put a hand on the man's shoulder and pushed him down into the seat. The deputies then moved back and took positions in chairs to the man's rear.

The man immediately leaned forward and opened the sketch pad and went to work with his pen. Bosch watched. He could hear the point of the pen scratching furiously on the paper.

'They don't allow me a charcoal, Bosch. Do you believe that? What threat could a piece of charcoal possibly be?'

He hadn't looked at Bosch as he said it. Bosch didn't reply.

'It's the little things like that that bother me the most,' the man said.

'Better get used to it,' Bosch said.

The man laughed but still did not look at Bosch.

'You know, somehow I knew that was exactly what you were going to say.'

Bosch was quiet.

'You see, you are so predictable Bosch. All of you are.'

The rear courtroom door opened and Bosch turned his eyes away from the defendant. The attorneys were coming in now. They were about to start.

7

By the time McCaleb got to the Farmers' Market he was thirty minutes late for the meeting with Jaye Winston. He and Buddy had made the crossing in an hour and a half and McCaleb had called the sheriff's detective after they tied up at Cabrillo Marina. They arranged to meet but then he found the battery in the Cherokee dead because the car hadn't been used in two weeks. He had to get Buddy to give him a jump from his old Taurus and that had taken up the time.

He walked into Dupar's, the corner restaurant in the market, but didn't see Winston at any of the tables or the counter. He hoped she hadn't come and gone. He chose an unoccupied booth that afforded the most privacy and sat down. He didn't need to look at a menu. They had chosen the Farmer's Market to meet because it was near Edward Gunn's apartment and because McCaleb wanted to eat breakfast at Dupar's. He had told Winston that more than anything else about Los Angeles, he missed the pancakes at Dupar's. Often when he and Graciela and the children made their once-a-month trip overtown to buy clothing and supplies not available on Catalina, they ate a meal at Dupar's. It didn't matter whether it was breakfast, lunch or dinner, McCaleb always ordered pancakes. Raymond did, too. But he was boysenberry while McCaleb was traditional maple.

McCaleb told the waitress he was waiting for another party but ordered a large orange juice and a glass of water. After she brought the two glasses he opened his leather bag and took out the plastic pill box. He kept a week's supply of his pills on the boat and another couple days' worth in the glove box of the Cherokee. He'd prepared the box after docking. Alternating gulps of orange juice and water, he downed the twenty-seven pills that made up his morning dosage. He knew their names by their shapes and colors and tastes; Prilosec, Imuran, digoxin. As he methodically went through the lineup he noticed a woman in a nearby booth watching, her eyebrows arched in wonder.

He would never get rid of the pills. They were as certain for him as the proverbial death and taxes. Over the years some would be changed, some subtracted and new ones added, but he knew he would be swallowing pills and washing away their awful tastes with orange juice for the rest of his life.

'I see you ordered without me.'

He looked up from the last three cyclosporine pills he was about to take as Jaye Winston slid into the opposite side of the booth.

'Sorry, I'm so late. Traffic on the ten was a complete bitch.'

'It's all right. I was late, too. Dead battery.'

'How many of those you take now?'

'Fifty-four a day.'

'Unbelievable.'

'I had to turn a hallway closet into a medicine cabinet. The whole thing.'

'Well, at least you're still here.'

She smiled and McCaleb nodded. The waitress came to the table with a menu for Winston but she said they had better order.

'I'll have what he's having.'

McCaleb ordered a large stack with melted butter. He told the waitress they would share one order of well-done bacon.

'Coffee?' asked the waitress. She looked as though this

might have been the one-millionth pancake order she had taken.

'Yes, please,' said Winston. 'Black.'

McCaleb said he was fine with the orange juice.

When they were alone McCaleb looked across the table at Winston.

'So, you get ahold of the manager?'

'He's going to meet us at ten-thirty. The place is still vacant but it has been cleaned. After we released it, the vic's sister came up and went through his things, took what she wanted.'

'Yeah, I was afraid of something like that.'

'The manager didn't think it was very much – the guy didn't have much.'

'What about the owl?'

'He didn't remember the owl. Frankly, I didn't either until you mentioned it this morning.'

'It's just a hunch. I'd like to take a look at it.'

'Well, we'll see if it's there. What else do you want to do? I hope you didn't come all the way across just to look at the guy's apartment.'

'I was thinking about checking out the sister. And maybe Harry Bosch, too.'

Winston was silent but he could tell by her demeanor she was waiting for an explanation.

'In order to profile an unknown subject, it's important to know the victim. His routines, personality, everything. You know the drill. The sister and, to a lesser extent, Bosch can help with that.'

'I only asked you to look at the book and the tape, Terry. You're going to make me start feeling guilty here.'

McCaleb paused while the waitress brought Winston's coffee and put down two small glass pitchers containing boysenberry and maple syrup. After she went away he spoke.

'You knew I'd get hooked, Jayne. "Beware, beware, God sees?" I mean, come on. You're going to tell me you thought I'd look it all over and phone in the report? Besides, I'm not complaining. I'm here because I want to be. If you feel guilty, you can buy the pancakes.'

'What did your wife say about it?'

'Nothing. She knows it's something I have to do. I called her from the dock after I crossed. It was too late for her to really say anything by then anyway. She just told me to pick up a bag of green corn tamales at El Cholo before I headed back. They sell 'em frozen.'

The pancakes came. They stopped talking and McCaleb politely waited for Winston to choose a syrup first but she was using a fork to move her pancakes around on her plate and he finally couldn't wait. He doused his stack with maple syrup and started eating. The waitress came back by and put a check down. Winston quickly grabbed it.

'The sheriff will pay for this.'

'Tell him thanks.'

'You know, I don't know what you expect from Harry Bosch. He told me he'd only had a handful of contacts with Gunn in the six years since the prostitute case.'

'When were those, when he got popped?'

Winston nodded as she poured boysenberry syrup on her pancakes.

'That means he would have seen him the night before he was killed. I didn't see anything about it in the book.'

'I haven't written it up. There's not much to it. The watch sergeant called him and told him Gunn was in the drunk tank on a DUI.'

McCaleb nodded.

'And?'

'And he came in to look at the guy. That was it. He said they didn't even talk because Gunn was too blitzed.'

'Well . . . I still want to talk to Harry. I worked a case with him once. He's a good cop. Intuitive and observant. He might know something I could use.'

'That is, if you can get to talk to him.'

'What do you mean?'

'You don't know? He's riding the prosecution table on the David Storey murder case. Up in Van Nuys. Don't you watch the news?'

'Ah, damn, I forgot about that. I remember reading his name in the newspapers after they took Storey down. That was, what, in October? They're already in trial?'

'They sure are. No delays and they didn't need a prelim because they went through the grand jury. They started jury selection right after the first. Last I heard, they had the panel so openers will probably be this week, maybe even today.'

'Shit.'

'Yeah, good luck getting to Bosch. I'm sure this is just what he'll want to hear about.'

'Are you saying you don't want me to talk to him?'

Winston shrugged her shoulders.

'No, I'm not saying that at all. Do whatever you want to do. I just didn't think you'd be doing so much legwork on this. I can talk to my captain about maybe getting a consulting fee for you but—'

'Don't worry about it. The sheriff's buying breakfast. That's enough.'

'Doesn't seem like it.'

He didn't tell her that he'd work the case for free, just to be back in the life for a few days. And he didn't tell her that he couldn't take any money from her anyway. If he made any 'official' income he would lose his eligibility for the state medical assistance that paid for the fifty-four pills he swallowed every day. The pills were so expensive that if he had to pay for them himself he'd be bankrupt inside six months, unless he happened to be drawing a six-figure salary. It was the ugly secret behind the medical miracle that had saved him. He got a second chance at life, just as long as he didn't use it to try to earn a living. It was the reason the charter business was in Buddy Lockridge's name. Officially, McCaleb was an unpaid deckhand.

Buddy simply rented the boat for charter from Graciela, the rent being 60 percent of all charter fees after expenses.

'How are your pancakes?' he asked Winston.

'The best.'

'Damn right.'

8

The Grand Royale was a two-story eyesore, a deteriorating stucco box whose attempt at style began and ended with the modish design of the letters of its name tacked over the entranceway. The streets of West Hollywood and elsewhere in the flats were lined with such banal designs, the high-density apartments that crowded out smaller bungalow courts in the fifties and sixties. They replaced true style with phony ornamental flourishes and names that reflected exactly what they were not.

McCaleb and Winston entered the second-floor apartment that had belonged to Edward Gunn with the building manager, a man named Rohrshak – 'Like the test, only spelled different.'

If he hadn't known where to look, McCaleb would have missed what was left of the bloodstain on the carpet where Gunn had died. The carpet had not been replaced. Instead it had been shampooed, leaving only a small, light brown trace stain that would probably be mistaken by the next renter as the remnant of a soda or coffee spill.

The place had been cleaned and readied for renting. But the furnishings were the same. McCaleb recognized them from the crime scene video.

He looked across the room at the china cabinet but it was empty. There was no plastic owl perched atop it. He looked at Winston.

'It's gone.'

Winston turned to the manager.

'Mr. Rohrshak. The owl that was on top of that cabinet.

We think it was important. Are you sure you don't know what happened to it?'

Rohrshak spread his arms wide and then dropped them to his side.

'No, I don't know. You asked before and I thought, "I don't remember any owl." But if you say so . . .'

He shrugged his shoulders and jutted his chin, then nodded as if reluctantly agreeing that there had been an owl on the china cabinet.

McCaleb read his body language and words as the classic mannerisms of a liar. Deny the existence of the object you have stolen and you eliminate the theft. He assumed Winston had picked up on it as well.

'Jaye, you have a phone? Can you call the sister to double-check?'

'I've been holding out until the county buys me one.'

McCaleb had wanted to keep his phone free in case Brass Doran called back but put his leather bag down on an overstuffed couch and dug out his phone and handed it to her.

She had to get the sister's number out of a notebook in her briefcase. While she made the call McCaleb walked slowly around the apartment, taking it all in and trying to get a vibe from the place. In the dining area he stopped in front of the round wooden table with four straight-back chairs placed around it. The crime scene analysis report said that three of the chairs had numerous smears, partials and complete latent fingerprints on them – all of them belonging to the victim, Edward Gunn. The fourth chair, the one found on the north side of the table, was completely devoid of fingerprint evidence in any condition. The chair had been wiped down. Most likely, the killer had done this after handling the chair for some reason.

McCaleb checked his directions and went to the chair on the north side of the table. Careful not to touch the back of it, he hooked his hand under the seat and pulled it away from the table and over to the china cabinet. He positioned it at center and then stepped up onto the seat. He raised his arms as if placing something on top of the cabinet. The chair wobbled on its uneven legs and McCaleb instinctively reached one hand to the top edge of the china cabinet to steady himself. Before he grabbed on he realized something and stopped himself. He braced his forearm across the frame of one of the cabinet's glass doors instead.

'Steady there, Terry.'

He looked down. Winston was standing next to him. His phone was folded closed in her hand.

'I am. So does she have the bird?'

'No, she didn't know what I was talking about.'

McCaleb raised himself on his toes and looked over the top edge of the cabinet.

'She tell you what she did take?'

'Just some clothes and some old photos of them when they were kids. She didn't want anything else.'

McCaleb nodded. He was still looking up and down the top of the cabinet. There was a thick layer of dust on top.

'You say anything about me coming down to talk to her?'

'I forgot. I can call her back.'

'You have a flashlight, Jaye?'

She dug through her purse and then handed up a small penlight. McCaleb flicked it on and held it at a low angle to the top of the cabinet. The light made the surface dust more distinct and now he could clearly see an octagonal-shaped impression that had been left by something that had been put on top of the cabinet and the dust. The base of the owl.

He next moved the light along the edges of the top board, then turned it off and got down off the chair. He handed Jaye the penlight.

'Thanks. You might want to think about getting a print team back out here.'

'How come? The owl's not up there, is it?'

McCaleb glanced at Rohrshak for a moment.

'Nope, it's gone. But whoever put it up there used that chair. When it wobbled they grabbed a hold.'

He took a pen out of his pocket and reached up and tapped the front edge of the cabinet in the area where he had seen finger impressions in the dust.

'It's pretty dusty but there might be prints.'

'What if it was whoever took the owl?'

McCaleb looked pointedly at Rohrshak when he answered.

'Same thing. There might be prints.'

Rohrshak looked away.

'Can I use this again?'

Winston held up his phone.

'Go ahead.'

As Winston called for a print team, McCaleb dragged the chair into the middle of the living room, positioning it a few feet from the bloodstain. He then sat down on it and took in the room. In this position the owl would have looked down on the killer as well as the victim. Some instinct told McCaleb that this was the configuration the killer had wanted. He looked down at the bloodstain and imagined he was looking down at Edward Gunn struggling for his life and slowly losing the battle. The bucket, he thought. Everything fit but the bucket. The killer had set the stage but then couldn't watch the play. He needed the bucket so that he wouldn't see his victim's face. It bothered McCaleb that it didn't fit.

Winston came over and handed him the phone.

'There's a crew just finishing a break-in on Kings. They'll be here in fifteen minutes.'

'That's lucky.'

'Very. What are you doing?'

'Just thinking. I think he sat here and watched but then couldn't take it. He struck the victim on the head, to maybe hurry it up. Then he got the bucket and put it on so he wouldn't have to watch.'

Winston nodded.

'Where'd the bucket come from? There was nothing in the—'

'We think it came from under the sink in the kitchen. There's a ring, a water ring on the shelf that fits the base of the bucket. It's on a supplemental Kurt typed up. He must've forgotten to put it in the book.'

McCaleb nodded and stood up.

'You're going to wait for the print crew, right?'

'Yes, it shouldn't be long.'

'I'm going to take a walk.'

He headed for the open door.

'I will go with you,' Rohrshak said.

McCaleb turned.

'No, Mr. Rohrshak, you need to stay here with Detective Winston. We need an independent witness to monitor what we do in the apartment.'

He glanced over Rohrshak's shoulder at Winston. She winked, telling him she understood the phony story and what he was doing.

'Yes, Mr. Rohrshak. Please stay here, if you don't mind.'

Rohrshak shrugged his shoulders again and raised his hands.

McCaleb went down the stairs to the enclosed courtyard in the center of the apartment building. He turned in a complete circle and his eyes traveled up to the line of the flat roof. He didn't see the owl anywhere and turned and walked out through the entrance hall to the street.

Across Sweetzer was the Braxton Arms, a three-story, L-shaped apartment building with exterior walkways and stairwells. McCaleb crossed and found a six-foot security gate and fence at the entrance. It was more for show than as a deterrent. He took off his windbreaker, folded it and pushed it between two of the gate's bars. He then brought his foot up onto the gate's handle, tested it with his weight, then hoisted himself up to the top of the gate. He dropped down on the other side and looked around to see if anyone was watching him. He was clear. He grabbed his windbreaker and headed for the stairwell.

He walked up to the third level and followed the walkway to the front of the building. His breathing was loud and labored from climbing the gate and then the stairs. When he got to the front he put his hands on the safety railing and leaned forward until he had caught his breath. He then looked across Sweetzer to the flat roof of the apartment building where Edward Gunn had lived. Again, the plastic owl wasn't there.

McCaleb leaned his forearms down on the railing and continued to labor for breath. He listened to the cadence of his heart as it finally settled. He could feel sweat popping on his scalp. He knew it wasn't his heart that was weak. It was his body, weakened by all the drugs he took to keep his heart strong. It frustrated him. He knew that he would never be strong, that he would spend the rest of his life listening to his heart the way a night burglar listens to creaks in the floor.

He looked down when he heard a vehicle and saw a white van with the sheriff's seal on the driver's door pull to a stop in front of the apartment building across the street. The print crew had arrived.

McCaleb glanced at the roof across the street once more and then turned to head back down, defeated. He suddenly stopped. There was the owl. It was perched atop a compressor for a central air-conditioning system on the roof of the L-extension of the building he was in.

He quickly went to the stairs and climbed up to the roof landing. He had to work his way around some furniture that was stacked and stored on the landing but found the door unlocked and hurried across the flat, gravel-strewn roof to the air conditioner.

McCaleb first studied the owl before touching it. It matched his memory of the owl on the crime scene tape.

Its base was an octagonal stump. He knew it was the missing owl. He removed the wire that had been wrapped around the base and attached to the intake grill of the air conditioner. He noticed that the grill and metal covering of the unit were covered with old bird droppings. He surmised that the droppings were a maintenance problem and Rohrshak, who apparently managed this building as well as the one across the street, had taken the owl from Gunn's apartment to use to keep the birds away.

McCaleb took the wire and looped it around the owl's neck so that he could carry it without touching it, though he doubted there would be any usable fingerprint or fiber evidence remaining on it. He lifted it off the air conditioner and headed back to the stairs.

When McCaleb stepped back into Edward Gunn's apartment he saw two crime scene techs getting equipment out of a toolbox. A stepladder was standing in front of the china cabinet.

'You might want to start with this,' he said.

He watched Rohrshak's eyes widen as he entered the room and placed the plastic owl on the table.

'You manage the place across the street, don't you, Mr. Rohrshak?'

'Uh . . .'

'It's okay. It's easy enough to find out.'

'Yes, he does,' Winston said, bending down to look at the owl. 'He was over there when we needed him on the day of the murder. He lives there.'

'Any idea how this ended up on the roof?' McCaleb asked.

Rohrshak still didn't answer.

'Guess it just flew over, right?'

Rohrshak couldn't take his eyes off the owl.

'Tell you what, you can go now, Mr. Rohrshak. But stay around your place. If we get a print off the bird or the cabinet, we're going to need to take a set of yours for comparison.'

Now Rohrshak looked at McCaleb and his eyes grew even wider.

'Go on, Mr. Rohrshak.'

The building manager turned and slowly headed out of the apartment.

'And shut the door, please,' McCaleb called after him.

After he was gone and the door was shut Winston almost burst into laughter.

'Terry, you're being so hard on him. He didn't really do anything wrong, you know. We cleared the place, he let the sister take what she wanted and then what was he supposed to do, try to rent the place with this stupid owl up there?'

McCaleb shook his head.

'He lied to us. That was wrong. I almost blew a gasket climbing that building across the street. He could have just told us it was up there.'

'Well, he's properly scared now. I think he learned his lesson.'

'Whatever.'

He stepped back so one of the techs could go to work on the owl while the other climbed the ladder to work on the top of the cabinet.

McCaleb studied the bird as the tech brushed on black fingerprint powder. It appeared that the owl was hand painted. It was dark brown and black on its wings, head and back. Its chest was a lighter brown with some yellow highlighting. Its eyes were a shiny black.

'Has this been outside?' the tech asked.

'Unfortunately,' McCaleb answered, remembering the rains that had swept off the mainland and out to Catalina the week before.

'Well, I'm not getting anything.'

'Figures.'

McCaleb looked at Winston, his eyes portraying renewed anger with Rohrshak.

'Nothing up here, either,' the other tech said. 'Too much dust.'

9

The trial of David Storey was being held in the Van Nuys courthouse. The crime the case centered on was not remotely connected to Van Nuys or even the San Fernando Valley, but the courthouse had been chosen by schedulers in the district attorney's office because Department N was available and it was the single largest courtroom in the county – constructed out of two courtrooms several years earlier to comfortably hold the two juries as well as the attendant media crush of the Menendez brothers murder case. The Menendezes' slaying of their parents had been one of several Los Angeles court cases in the previous decade to capture the media's and, therefore, the public's attention. When it was over, the DA's office did not bother deconstructing the huge courtroom. Somebody there had the foresight to realize that in L.A. there would always be a case that could fill Department N.

And at the moment it was the David Storey case.

The thirty-eight-year-old film director, known for films that pushed the limits of violence and sexuality within an R rating, was charged with the murder of a young actress he had taken home from the premiere of his most recent film. The twenty-three-year-old woman's body was found the next morning in the small Nichols Canyon bungalow she shared with another would-be actress. The victim had been strangled, her nude body arranged in her bed in a pose investigators believed to be part of a careful plan by her killer to avoid discovery.

The case's elements – power, celebrity, sex and money – and the added Hollywood connection served to bring the case maximum media attention. David Storey worked on the wrong side of the camera to be a fully realized celebrity himself, but his name was known and he wielded the awesome power of a man who had delivered seven box office hits in as many years. The media were drawn to the Storey trial in the way young people are drawn by the dream of Hollywood. The advance coverage clearly delineated the case as a parable on unchecked Hollywood avarice and excess.

The case also had a degree of secrecy not usually seen in criminal trials. The prosecutors assigned to the case took their evidence to a grand jury in order to seek charges against Storey. The move allowed them to bypass a preliminary hearing, where most of the evidence accumulated against a defendant is usually made public. Without that fount of case information, the media were left to mine their sources in both the prosecution and defense camps. Still, little about the case was leaked to the media other than generalities. The evidence the prosecution would use to tie Storey to the murder remained cloaked, and all the more cause for the media frenzy around the trial.

It was just that frenzy that had convinced the district attorney to move the trial to the large Department N courtroom in Van Nuys. The second jury box would be used to accommodate more media members in the courtroom, while the unused deliberation room would be converted into a media room where the video feed could be watched by the second- and third-tier journalists. The move, which would give all media – from the *National Enquirer* to the *New York Times* – full access to the trial and its players, guaranteed the proceedings would become the first full-blooded media circus of the new century.

In the center ring of this circus, sitting at the prosecution table, was Detective Harry Bosch, the lead investigator of the case. All the pretrial media analysis came down to one conclusion: the charges against David Storey would rise and fall with Bosch. All evidence in support of the murder charge was said to be circumstantial; the foundation of the case would come from Bosch. The one solid piece of evidence that had been leaked to the media was that Bosch would testify that in a private moment, with no other witnesses or devices at hand to record the statement, Storey had smugly admitted to him that he had committed the crime and boasted that he would surely get away with it.

McCaleb knew all of this as he walked into the Van Nuys courthouse shortly before noon. He stood in line to go through the metal detector and felt a reminder of all that had changed in his life. When he had been a bureau agent all he needed to do was hold his badge up and walk around the line. Now he was just a citizen. He had to wait.

The fourth-floor hallway was crowded with people milling about. McCaleb noticed that many clutched stacks of eight-by-ten black-and-white glossies of the movie stars they hoped would be attending the trial – either as witnesses or as spectators in support of the defendant. He walked to the double-door entrance to Department N but one of the two sheriff's deputies posted there told him the courtroom was at full capacity. The deputy pointed to a long line of people standing behind a rope. He said it was the line for people waiting to go in. Every time one person left the courtroom another could go in. McCaleb nodded and stepped away from the doors.

He saw that further down the hallway was an open door with people milling about it. He recognized one man as a reporter on a local television news program. He guessed it was the media room and headed that way.

When he got to the open door he could look in and see two large televisions mounted high up in either corner above the room where there were several people crowded around a large jury table. Reporters. They were typing on laptop computers, taking notes on pads, eating sandwiches from to-go bags. The center of the table was crowded with plastic coffee and soda cups.

He looked up at one of the televisions and saw that court was still in session though it was now past noon. The camera focused on a wide angle and he recognized Harry Bosch sitting with a man and a woman at the prosecution table. It did not look as though he was paying attention to the proceedings. A man McCaleb recognized stood at the lectern between the prosecution and defense tables. He was J. Reason Fowkkes, the lead defense attorney. At the table to his left sat the defendant, David Storey.

McCaleb could not hear the audio feed but he knew that Fowkkes was not delivering his opening statement. He was looking up at the judge, not in the direction of the jury box. Most likely last-minute motions were being argued by the attorneys before openers began. The twin television screens switched to a new camera, this angle directly on the judge, who began speaking, apparently delivering his rulings. McCaleb noted the name plate in front of the judge's bench. It said Superior Court Judge John A. Houghton.

'Agent McCaleb?'

McCaleb turned from the television to see a man he recognized but couldn't immediately place standing next to him.

'Just McCaleb. Terry McCaleb.'

The man perceived his difficulty and held out his hand.

'Jack McEvoy. I interviewed you once. It was pretty brief. It was about the Poet investigation.'

'Oh, right, I remember now. That was a while back.'

McCaleb shook his hand. He did remember McEvoy. He had become entwined in the Poet case and then wrote a book about it. McCaleb had had a very peripheral part in the case – when the investigation had shifted to Los Angeles. He never read McEvoy's book but was sure he had not added anything to it and likely wasn't mentioned in it.

'I thought you were from Colorado,' he said, recalling that McEvoy had worked for one of the papers in Denver. 'They sent you out to cover this?'

McEvoy nodded.

'Good memory. I was from there but I live out here now. I work freelance.'

McCaleb nodded, wondering what else there was to say.

'Who are you covering this for?'

'I've been writing a weekly dispatch on it for the *New Times*. Do you read it?'

McCaleb nodded. He was familiar with the *New Times*. It was a weekly tabloid with an anti-authority, muckraking stance. It appeared to subsist mostly on entertainment ads, ranging from movies to the escort services that filled its back pages. It was free and Buddy always seemed to leave issues lying around the boat. McCaleb looked at it from time to time but hadn't noticed McEvoy's name before.

'I'm also doing a general wrap for *Vanity Fair*,' McEvoy said. 'You know, a more discursive, dark-side-of-Hollywood piece. I'm thinking about another book, too. What brings you here? Are you . . . involved with this in some . . .'

'Me, no. I was in the area and I have a friend involved. I was hoping I might be able to get a chance to say hello to him.'

As he told the lie McCaleb looked away from the writer and back through the door to the televisions. The full courtroom camera angle was now being shown. It looked like Bosch was gathering things into a briefcase.

'Harry Bosch?'

McCaleb looked back at him.

'Yeah, Harry. We worked a case together before and . . . uh, what's going on in there now, anyway?'

'Final motions before they start. They started with a closed session and they're just doing some housekeeping. Not worth being in there. Everybody thinks the judge will probably finish before lunch and then give the lawyers the rest of the day to work on openers. They start tomorrow at ten. You think things are crowded here now? Wait till tomorrow.'

McCaleb nodded.

'Oh, well, okay then. Uh, nice seeing you again, Jack. Good luck with the story. And the book, if it comes to that.'

'You know, I would have liked to write your story. You know, with the heart and everything.'

McCaleb nodded.

'Well, I owed Keisha Russell one and she did a good job with it.'

McCaleb noticed people start to push their way out of the media room. Behind them he could see on the television screens that the judge had left the bench. Court was out of session.

'I better go down the hall and see if I can catch Harry. Good to see you again, Jack.'

McCaleb offered his hand and McEvoy shook it. He then followed the other reporters down to the courtroom doors.

The main doors to Department N were opened by the two deputies and out flowed the crowd of lucky citizens who had gotten seats during the session, which had most likely been mind-numbingly boring. Those who had not made it inside pushed up close for a glimpse of a celebrity but they were disappointed. The celebrities wouldn't start showing until the next day. Opening statements were like the opening credits of a film. That's where they would want to be seen.

At the tail end of the crowd came the lawyers and staff. Storey had been returned to lockup but his attorney strode right to the semicircle of reporters and began giving his view of what had transpired inside. A tall man with jet-black hair, a deep tan and ever-shifting green eyes took a position directly behind the lawyer to cover his back. He was striking and McCaleb thought he recognized him but he couldn't think from where. He looked like one of the actors Storey normally put in his films.

The prosecutors came out and soon had their own knot of reporters to deal with. Their answers were shorter than the defense lawyer's. They often declined to comment when asked questions about the evidence they would present.

McCaleb watched for Bosch and finally saw him slip out last. Bosch skirted the crowd by staying close to the wall and headed toward the elevators. One reporter moved in on him but he held up his hand and waved her away. She stopped and moved back like a loose molecule to the pack standing around J. Reason Fowkkes.

McCaleb followed Bosch down the hall and caught him when he stopped to wait for an elevator.

'Hey, Harry Bosch.'

Bosch turned, already putting on his no-comment face, when he saw it was McCaleb.

'Hey . . . McCaleb.'

He smiled. The men shook hands.

'Looks like the world's worst eight-by-ten case,' McCaleb said.

'You're telling me. What are you doing here? Don't tell me you're writing a book on this thing.'

'What?'

'All these ex-bureau guys writing books nowadays.'

'Nah, that's not me. Actually, though, I was hoping I could maybe buy you lunch. There's something I wanted to talk to you about.'

Bosch looked at his watch and was deciding something.

'Edward Gunn.'

Bosch looked up at him.

'Jaye Winston?'

McCaleb nodded.

'She asked me to take a look.'

The elevator came and they stepped onto it with a crowd of people who had been in the courtroom. They all seemed to be looking at Bosch while trying not to show it. McCaleb decided not to continue until they were off.

On the first floor they headed toward the exit.

'I told her I'd profile it. A quick one. To do it I need to get a handle on Gunn. I thought maybe you could tell me about that old case and about what kind of guy he was.'

'He was a scumbag. Look, I have about forty-five minutes max. I need to get on the road. I'm running down wits today, making sure everybody's ready to go after openers.'

'I'll take the forty-five if you can spare it. Any place to eat around here?'

'Forget the cafeteria here – it's awful. There's a Cupid's up on Victory.'

'You cops always eat at the best.'

'It's why we do what we do.'

10

They ate their hot dogs at an outdoor table without an umbrella. Though it was a mildly warm winter day, McCaleb found himself sweating. On any given day the Valley could be counted on to be fifteen to twenty degrees warmer than Catalina and he wasn't used to the change. His internal heating and cooling systems had never been normal since the transplant and he was prone to quick chills and sweats.

He began with some small talk about Bosch's current case.

'You ready to become Hollywood Harry with this case?'

'Yeah, no thanks,' Bosch said between bites of what was billed as a Chicago dog. 'I think I'd rather be on midnight shift in the Seventy-seventh.'

'Well, you think you got it together? You got him?'

'Never know. The DA's office hasn't won a big one since disco. I don't know how it will go. The lawyers all say it depends on the jury. I always thought it was the quality of the evidence but I'm just a dumb detective. John Reason brought in O. J.'s jury consultant and they're acting pretty happy with the twelve in the box. Shit, John Reason. See, I'm even calling the guy by the name the reporters use. It shows how good he is at controlling things, sculpting things.'

He shook his head and took another bite of his lunch.

'Who is the big guy I saw him with?' McCaleb asked. 'The guy standing behind him like Lurch.'

'Rudy Valentino, his investigator.'

'That's his name?'

'No, it's Rudy Tafero. He's former LAPD. He worked Hollywood detectives until a few years back. People in the bureau called him Valentino 'cause of his looks. He got off on it. Anyway, he went private. Has a bail bonds license. Don't ask me how but he started getting security contracts with a lot of Hollywood people. He showed up on this one right after we popped Storey. In fact, Rudy brought Storey to Fowkkes. Probably got a nice finder's fee for that.'

'And how about the judge? How's he going to be?'

Bosch nodded as if he had found something good in the conversation.

'Shootin' Houghton. He's no Second Chance Lance. He's no bullshit. He'll slap Fowkkes down if he needs to. At least we have that going for us.'

'Shootin' Houghton?'

'Under that black robe he's usually strapped – or at least most people think so. About five years ago he had a Mexican Mafia case, and when the jury came in guilty a bunch of the defendants' buddies and family in the audience got mad and nearly started a riot in the courtroom. Houghton pulled his Glock and put a round into the ceiling. It quieted things down pretty quick. Ever since he's been reelected by the highest percentage of any incumbent judge in the county. Go in his courtroom and check the ceiling. The bullet hole's still there. He won't let anybody fix it.'

Bosch took another bite and looked at his watch. He changed the subject, talking with his mouth full.

'Nothing personal but I take it they've hit the wall on Gunn if they're going to outside help already.'

McCaleb nodded.

'Something like that.'

He looked down at the chili dog in front of him and wished he had a knife and fork.

'What's wrong? We didn't have to come here.'

'Nothing. I was just thinking. Between pancakes at

Dupar's this morning and this, I might need another heart by dinner.'

'You want to stop your heart, next time you go to Dupar's top it off with a stop at Bob's Donuts. Right there in the Farmers' Market. Raised glaze. A couple of those and you'll feel your arteries harden and snap like icicles hanging off a house. They never came up with suspect one, right?'

'Right. Nothing.'

'So what makes you so interested?'

'Same as Jaye. Something about this one. We think whoever it was might be just starting.'

Bosch just nodded. His mouth was full.

McCaleb appraised him. His hair was shorter than McCaleb had remembered it. More gray but that was to be expected. He still had the mustache and the eyes. They reminded him of Graciela's, so dark there was almost no delineation between iris and pupil. But Bosch's eyes were weary and slightly hooded by wrinkles at the corners. Still, they were always moving, observing. He sat leaning slightly forward, as if ready to move. McCaleb remembered that there had always been a spring-loaded feel to Bosch. He felt as though at any moment or for any reason Bosch could put the needle into the red zone.

Bosch reached inside his suit coat and took out a pair of sunglasses and put them on. McCaleb wondered if that had been in response to realizing that McCaleb had been studying him. He bent down, raised up his chili dog and finally took a bite. It tasted delicious and deadly at the same time. He put the dripping mess back on the paper plate and wiped his hand on a napkin.

'So tell me about Gunn. You said he was a scumbag. What else?'

'What else? That's about it. He was a predator. Used women, bought women. He murdered that girl in that motel room, no doubt in my mind.'

'But the DA kicked the case.'

'Yeah. Gunn claimed self-defense. He said some things that didn't add up but not enough to add up to charges. He claimed self-defense and there wasn't going to be enough to go against that in a trial. So they no-billed it, end of story, on to the next case.'

'Did he ever know you didn't believe him?'

'Oh, sure. He knew.'

'Did you try to sweat him at all?'

Bosch gave him a look that McCaleb could read through the sunglasses. The last question went to Bosch's credibility as an investigator.

'I mean,' McCaleb said quickly, 'what happened when you tried to sweat him?'

'Actually, the truth is we never really got the chance. There was a problem. See, we did set it up. We brought him in and put him in one of the rooms. My partner and I were planning to leave him there a while, let him percolate a little and think about things. We were going to do all the paper, put it in the book and then take a run at him, try to break his story. We never got the chance. I mean, to do it right.'

'What happened?'

'Me and Edgar – that's my partner, Jerry Edgar – we went down the hall to get a cup of coffee and talk about how we were going to play it. While we were down there the squad lieutenant sees Gunn sitting in the interview room and doesn't know what the fuck he's doing there. He takes it upon himself to go in and make sure the guy's been properly advised of his rights.'

McCaleb could see the anger working its way into Bosch's face, even six years after the fact.

'You see, Gunn had come in as a witness and ostensibly as the victim of a crime. He said she came at him with the knife and he turned it on her. So we didn't need to advise him. The plan was to go in there, shake his story down and get him to make a mistake. Once we had that, then we were going to advise him. But this dipshit lieutenant didn't know any of this and he just went in and advised the guy. After that, we were dead. He knew we were coming after him. He asked for a lawyer as soon as we walked into the room.'

Bosch shook his head and looked out onto the street. McCaleb followed his eyes. Across Victory Boulevard was a used-car lot with red, white and blue pennants flapping in the wind. To McCaleb, Van Nuys was always synonymous with car lots. They were all over, new and used.

'So what did you say to the lieutenant?' he asked.

'Say? I didn't say anything. I just shoved him through the window of his office. I got a suspension out of it – involuntary stress leave. Jerry Edgar eventually took the case in to the DA and they sat on it a while and then finally kicked it.'

Bosch nodded. His eyes rested on his empty paper plate.

'I sort of blew it,' he said. 'Yeah, I blew it.'

McCaleb waited a moment before speaking. A gust of wind blew Bosch's plate off the table and the detective watched it skitter across the picnic area. He made no move to chase it down.

'You still working for that lieutenant?'

'Nope. He's no longer with us. Not too long after that he went out one night and didn't come home. They found him in his car up in the tunnel in Griffith Park near the Observatory.'

'What, he killed himself?'

'No. Somebody did it for him. It's still open. Technically.'

Bosch looked back at him. McCaleb dropped his eyes and noticed that Bosch's tie tack was a tiny pair of silver handcuffs.

'What else can I tell you?' Bosch said. 'None of this had anything to do with Gunn. He was just a fly in the ointment – the ointment being the bullshit they call the justice system.'

'Doesn't sound like you had time to do much background on him.'

'None, actually. All that I told you took place in the span of eight or nine hours. Afterward, with what happened, I was off the case and the guy walked out the door.'

'But you didn't give up. Jaye told me you visited him in the drunk tank the night before he got himself killed.'

'Yeah, he got popped on a duice while cruising whores on Sunset. He was in the tank and I got a call. I went in to take a look, maybe jerk his chain a little, see if he was ready to talk. But the guy was piss drunk, just lying there on the floor in the puke. So that was it. You could say that we didn't communicate.'

Bosch looked at McCaleb's unfinished chili dog and then his watch.

'Sorry, but that's all I got. You going to eat that or can we go?'

'Couple more bites, couple more questions. Don't you want to have a smoke?'

'I quit a couple years ago. I only smoke on special occasions.'

'Don't tell me, it was the Marlboro-man-gone-impotent sign on Sunset.'

'No, my wife wanted us both to quit. We did.'

'Your wife? Harry, you're full of surprises.'

'Don't get excited. She's come and gone. But at least I don't smoke anymore. I don't know about her.'

McCaleb just nodded, feeling he had stepped too far into the other man's personal world. He got back to the case.

'So any theories on who killed him?'

McCaleb took another bite while Bosch answered.

'My guess is he probably met up with somebody just like himself. Somebody who crossed a line somewhere. Don't get me wrong, I hope you and Jaye get the guy. But so far, whoever he or she is hasn't done anything I'm too upset about. Know what I mean?'

'It's funny you mentioned a "she." You think it could have been a woman?'

'I don't know enough about it. But like I said, he preyed on women. Maybe one of them put a stop to it.'

McCaleb just nodded. He couldn't think of anything else to ask. Bosch had been a long shot anyway. Maybe he'd known it would come to this and he just wanted to reconnect with Bosch for other reasons. He spoke with his eyes down on his paper plate.

'You still think about the girl on the hill, Harry?'

He didn't want to say out loud the name Bosch had given her.

Bosch nodded.

'From time to time I do. It sticks with me. They all do, I guess.'

McCaleb nodded.

'Yeah. So nothing . . . nobody ever made a claim on her?'

'Nope. And I tried with Seguin one last time, went up to see him at Q last year, about a week before he got the juice. Tried one more time to find out from him but he just smiled at me. It was like he knew it was the last thing he could hold over me or something. He enjoyed it, I could tell. So I got up to leave and I told him to enjoy himself in hell and know what he said to me? He said, "I hear it's a dry heat."'

Bosch shook his head.

'Fucker. I drove up and back on my day off. Twelve hours in the car and the air conditioner didn't work.'

He looked directly at McCaleb and even through the shades McCaleb again felt the bond he had known so long ago with this man.

Before he could say anything he heard his phone begin to chirp from the pocket of his windbreaker, which was folded on the bench next to him. He struggled with the jacket to find the pocket and got to the phone before the caller hung up. It was Brass Doran.

'I have some stuff for you. Not a lot, but maybe a start.'

'You someplace I can call you back in a few minutes?'

'Actually, I'm in the central conference room. We're about to brainstorm a case and I'm the leader. It could be a couple hours before I'm free. You could call me at home tonight if you—'

'No, hold on.'

He held the phone down and looked at Bosch.

'I better take this. I'll talk to you later if anything comes up, okay?'

'Sure.'

Bosch started getting up. He was going to carry his Coke with him.

'Thanks,' McCaleb said, extending his hand. 'Good luck with the trial.'

Bosch shook his hand.

'Thanks. We'll probably need it.'

McCaleb watched him walk out of the picnic area and to the sidewalk leading back to the courthouse. He brought the phone back up then.

'Brass?'

'Here. Okay, you were talking about owls in general, right? You don't know the specific kind or breed, right?'

'Right. It's just a generic owl, I think.'

'What color is it?'

'Uh, it's brown mostly. Like on the back and the wings.'

As he spoke he took a couple of folded pages of notebook paper and a pen out of his pockets. He shoved his half-eaten chili dog out of the way and got ready to take notes.

'Okay, modern iconography is what you'd expect. The owl is the symbol of wisdom and truth, denotes knowledge, the view of the greater picture as opposed to the small detail. The owl sees in the night. In other words, seeing through the darkness is seeing the truth. It is learning the truth, therefore, knowledge. And from knowledge comes wisdom. Okay?'

McCaleb didn't need to take notes. What Doran had said was obvious. But just to keep his head in it he wrote down a line.

Seeing in the dark = Wisdom

He then underlined the last word.

'Okay, fine. What else?'

'That's basically what I have as far as contemporary application. But when I go backward it gets pretty interesting. Our friend the owl has totally rejuvenated his reputation. He used to be a bad guy.'

'Tell me, Brass.'

'Get your pencil out. The owl is seen repeatedly in art and religious iconography from early medieval through late Renaissance periods. It is found often depicted in religious allegorical displays – paintings, church panels and stations of the cross. The owl was—'

'Okay, Brass, but what did it mean?'

'I'm getting to that. Its meaning could be different from depiction to depiction and according to species depicted. But essentially its depiction was the symbol of evil.'

McCaleb wrote the word down.

'Evil. Okay.'

'I thought you'd be more excited.'

'You can't see me. I'm standing on my hands here. What else you have?'

'Let me run down the list of hits. These are taken from the extracts, the critical literature of the art of the period. References to depictions of owls come up as the symbol of – and I quote – doom, the enemy of innocence, the Devil himself, heresy, folly, death and misfortune, the bird of darkness, and finally, the torment of the human soul in its inevitable journey to eternal damnation. Nice, huh? I like that last one. I guess they didn't sell too many bags of potato chips with owls on them back in the fourteen hundreds.'

McCaleb didn't answer. He was busy scribbling down the descriptions she had read to him.

'Read that last one again.'

She did and he wrote it down verbatim.

'Now, there is more,' Doran said. 'There is also some interpretation of the owl as being the symbol of wrath as well as the punishment of evil. So it obviously was something that meant different things at different times *and* to different people.'

'The punishment of evil,' McCaleb said as he wrote it down.

He looked at the list he had written.

'Anything else?'

'Isn't that enough?'

'Probably. Was there anything about books showing some of this stuff or the names of artists or writers who used the so-called "bird of darkness" in their work?'

McCaleb heard some pages turning over the phone and Doran was silent for a few moments.

'I don't have a lot here. No books but I can give you the name of some of the artists mentioned and you could probably get something over the Internet or maybe the library at UCLA.'

'All right.'

'I have to do this quickly. We're about to go here.'

'Give it to me.'

'All right, I have an artist named Bruegel who painted a huge face as the gateway to hell. A brown owl was nesting in the nostril of the face.'

She started laughing.

'Don't ask me,' she said. 'I'm just giving you what I found.'

'Fine,' McCaleb said, writing the description down. 'Go on.'

'Okay, two others noted for using the owl as the symbol

of evil were Van Oostanen and Dürer. I don't have specific paintings.'

He heard more pages turning. He asked for spellings of the artists' names and wrote them down.

'Okay, here it is. This last guy's work is supposedly replete with owls all over the place. I can't pronounce his first name. It's spelled H-I-E-R-O-N-Y-M-U-S. He was Netherlandish, part of the Northern Renaissance. I guess owls were big up there.'

McCaleb looked at the paper in front of him. The name she had just spelled seemed familiar to him.

'You forgot his last name. What's his last name?'

'Oh, sorry. It's Bosch. Like the spark plugs.'

McCaleb sat frozen. He didn't move, he didn't breathe. He stared at the name on the page, unable to write the last part that Doran had just given him. Finally, he turned his head and looked out of the picnic area to the spot on the sidewalk where he had last seen Harry Bosch walking away.

'Terry, you there?'

He came out of it.

'Yeah.'

'That's really all I have. And I have to go. We're starting here.'

'Anything else on Bosch?'

'Not really. And I'm out of time.'

'Okay, Brass. Listen, thanks a lot. I owe you one for this.'

'And I'll collect one day. Let me know how it all comes out, okay?'

'You got it.'

'And send me a photo of that little girl.'

'I will.'

She hung up and McCaleb slowly closed his phone. He wrote a note at the bottom of the page reminding him to send Brass a photo of his daughter. It was just an exercise in avoiding the name of the painter he had written down.

'Shit,' he whispered.

He sat with his thoughts for a long time. The coincidence of receiving the eerie information just minutes after eating with Harry Bosch was unsettling. He studied his notes for a few more moments but knew they did not contain the immediate information he needed. He finally reopened the phone and called 213 information. A minute later he called the personnel office of the Los Angeles Police Department. A woman answered after nine rings.

'Yes, I'm calling on behalf of the L.A. County Sheriff's Department and I need to contact a particular LAPD officer. Only I don't know where he works. I only have his name.'

He hoped the woman wouldn't ask what he meant by *on behalf of*. There was what seemed to be a long silence and then he heard the sound of typing on a keyboard.

'Last name?'

'Uh, it's Bosch.'

He spelled it and then looked down at his notes, ready to spell the first name.

'And the first na – never mind, there's only one. Higher – ronny – mus. Is that it? I can't pronounce it, I don't think.'

'Hieronymus. Yes, that's it.'

He spelled the name and asked if it was a match. It was.

'Well, he's a detective third grade and he works in Hollywood Division. Do you need that number?'

McCaleb didn't answer.

'Sir, do you need—'

'No, I have it. Thank you very much.'

He closed the phone, looked at his watch, and then reopened the phone. He called Jaye Winston's direct number and she picked up right away. He asked if she had gotten anything back from the lab on the examination of the plastic owl.

'Not yet. It's only been a couple hours and one of them

was lunch. I'm going to give it until tomorrow before I start knocking on their door.'

'Do you have time to make a few calls and do me a favor?'

'What calls?'

He told her about the icon search Brass Doran had conducted but left out any mention of Hieronymus Bosch. He said that he wanted to talk with an expert on Northern Renaissance painting but thought the arrangements could be made more quickly and cooperation would be more forthcoming if the request came from an official homicide detective.

'I'll do it,' Winston said. 'Where should I start?'

'I'd try the Getty. I'm in Van Nuys now. If somebody will see me I could be there in a half hour.'

'I'll see what I can do. You talk to Harry Bosch?'

'Yeah.'

'Anything new?'

'Not really.'

'I didn't think so. Hang tight. I'll call you back.'

McCaleb dumped what was left of his lunch into one of the trash barrels and headed back toward the courthouse, where he had left the Cherokee parked on a side street by the state parole offices. As he walked he thought about how he had lied by omission to Winston. He knew he should have told her about the Bosch connection or coincidence, whichever it was. He tried to understand what it was that made him hold it back. He found no answer.

His phone chirped just as he got to the Cherokee. It was Winston.

'You have an appointment at the Getty at two. Ask for Leigh Alasdair Scott. He's an associate curator of paintings.'

McCaleb got out his notes and wrote the name down, using the front hood of the Cherokee, after asking Winston to spell it.

'That was quick, Jaye. Thanks.'

'We aim to please. I spoke directly to Scott and he said if he couldn't help you he would find someone who could.'

'You mention the owl?'

'No, it's your interview.'

'Right.'

McCaleb knew he had another chance to tell her about Hieronymus Bosch. But again he let it pass.

'I'll call you later, okay?'

'See ya.'

He closed the phone and unlocked the car. He looked over the roof at the parole offices and saw a large white banner with blue lettering hanging across the facade above the building's entrance.

WELCOME BACK THELMA!

He got into the car wondering whether the Thelma being welcomed back was a convict or an employee. He drove off in the direction of Victory Boulevard. He'd take it to the 405 and then head south.

11

As the freeway rose to cross the Santa Monica Mountains in the Sepulveda Pass, McCaleb saw the Getty rise in front of him on the hilltop. The structure of the museum itself was as impressive as any of the great artworks housed within. It looked like a castle sitting atop a medieval hill. He saw one of the double trams slowly working its way up the side of the hill, delivering another group to the altar of history and art.

By the time he parked at the bottom of the hill and caught his own tram ride up, McCaleb was fifteen minutes late for his appointment with Leigh Alasdair Scott. After getting directions from a museum guard, McCaleb hurried across the travertine stone plaza to a security entrance. Having checked in at the counter he waited on a bench until Scott came for him.

Scott was in his early fifties and spoke with an accent McCaleb placed as originating in either Australia or New Zealand. He was friendly and happy to oblige the L.A. County sheriff's office.

'We have had occasion to offer our help and expertise to detectives in the past. Usually in regard to authenticating artwork or offering historical background to specific pieces,' he said as they walked down a long hallway to his office. 'Detective Winston indicated this would be different. You need some general information on the Northern Renaissance?'

He opened a door and ushered McCaleb into a suite of offices. They stepped into the first office past the security counter. It was a small office with a view through a large window across the Sepulveda Pass to the hillside homes of Bel-Air. The office felt crowded because of the bookshelves lining two walls and the cluttered worktable. There was just room for two chairs. Scott pointed McCaleb to one while he took the other.

'Actually, things have changed a bit since Detective Winston spoke to you,' McCaleb said. 'I can be more specific about what I need now. I've been able to narrow down my questions to a specific painter of that period. If you can tell me about him and maybe show me some of his work, that would be a big help.'

'And what is his name?'

'I'll show it to you.'

McCaleb took out his folded notes and showed him. Scott read the name aloud with obvious familiarity. He pronounced the first name Her-ron-i-mus.

'I thought that was how you said it.'

'Rhymes with anonymous. His work is actually quite well known. You are not familiar with it?'

'No. I never did much studying of art. Does the museum have any of his paintings?'

'None of his works are in the Getty collection but there is a descendant piece in the conservation studio. It is undergoing heavy restoration. Most of his verified works are in Europe, the most significant representations in the Prado. Others scattered about. I am not the one you should be talking to, however.'

McCaleb raised his eyebrows in way of a question.

'Since you have narrowed your query to Bosch specifically, there is someone here you would be better advised to talk to. She is a curatorial assistant. She also happens to be working on a catalogue raisonné on Bosch – a rather long-term project for her. A labor of love, perhaps.'

'Is she here? Can I speak to her?'

Scott reached for his phone and pushed the speaker button. He then consulted an extensions list taped to the table next to it and punched in three digits. A woman answered after three rings.

'Lola Walter, can I help you?'

'Lola, it's Mr. Scott. Is Penelope available?'

'She's working on *Hell* this morning.'

'Oh, I see. We'll go to her there.'

Scott hit the speaker button, disconnecting the call, and headed toward the door.

'You're in luck,' he said.

'Hell?' McCaleb asked.

'It's the descendant painting. If you'll come with me please.'

Scott led the way to an elevator and they went down one floor. Along the way Scott explained that the museum had one of the finest conservation studios in the world. Consequently, works of art from other museums and private collections were often shipped to the Getty for repair and restoration. At the moment a painting believed to have come from a student of Bosch's or a painter from his studio was being restored for a private collector. The painting was called *Hell.*

The conservation studio was a huge room partitioned into two main sections. One section was a workshop where frames were restored. The other section was dedicated to the restoration of paintings and was broken into a series of work bays that ran along a glass wall with the same views Scott had in his office.

McCaleb was led to the second bay, where there was a woman standing behind a man seated before a painting attached to a large easel. The man wore an apron over a dress shirt and tie and a pair of what looked like jeweler's magnifying glasses. He was leaning toward the painting and using a paintbrush with a tiny brush head to apply what looked like silver paint to the surface.

Neither the man nor the woman looked at McCaleb and Scott. Scott held his hands up in a *Hold here* gesture while the seated man completed his paint stroke. McCaleb looked at the painting. It was about four feet high and six feet wide. It was a dark landscape depicting a village being burned to the ground in the night while its inhabitants were being tortured and executed by a variety of otherworldly creatures. The upper panels of the painting, primarily depicting the swirling night sky, were spotted with small patches of damage and missing paint. McCaleb's eyes caught on one segment of the painting below this which depicted a nude and blindfolded man being forced up a ladder to a gallows by a group of birdlike creatures with spears.

The man with the brush completed his work and placed the brush on the glass top of the worktable to his left. He then leaned back toward the painting to study his work. Scott cleared his throat. Only the woman turned around.

'Penelope Fitzgerald, this is Detective McCaleb. He is involved in an investigation and needs to ask about Hieronymus Bosch.'

He gestured toward the painting.

'I told him you would be the most appropriate member of staff to speak with.'

McCaleb watched her eyes register surprise and concern, a normal response to a sudden introduction to the police. The seated man did not even turn around. This was not a normal response. Instead he picked up his brush and went back to work on the painting. McCaleb held his hand out to the woman.

'Actually, I'm not officially a detective. I've been asked by the sheriff's department to help out with an investigation.'

They shook hands.

'I don't understand,' she said. 'Has a Bosch painting been stolen?'

'No, nothing like that. This is a Bosch?'

He gestured toward the painting.

'Not quite. It may be a copy of one of his pieces. If so, then the original is lost and this is all we have. The style and design are his. But it's generally agreed to be the work of a student from his workshop. It was probably painted after Bosch was dead.'

As she spoke her eyes never left the painting. They were sharp and friendly eyes that easily betrayed her passion for Bosch. He guessed that she was about sixty and had probably dedicated her life to the study and love of art. She had surprised him. Scott's brief description of her as an assistant working on a catalog of Bosch's work had made McCaleb think she would be a young art student. He silently chastised himself for making the assumption.

The seated man put his brush down again and picked up a clean white cloth off the worktable to wipe his hands. He swiveled in his chair and looked up when he noticed McCaleb and Scott. It was then that McCaleb knew he had made a second error of assumption. The man had not been ignoring them. He just hadn't heard them.

The man flipped the magnifiers up to the top of his head while reaching beneath the apron to his chest and adjusted a hearing aid control.

'I am sorry,' he said. 'I didn't know we had visitors.'

He spoke with a hard German accent.

'Dr. Derek Vosskuhler, this is Mr. McCaleb,' Scott said. 'He's an investigator and he needs to steal Mrs. Fitzgerald away from you for a short while.'

'I understand. This is fine.'

'Dr. Vosskuhler is one of our restoration experts,' Scott volunteered.

Vosskuhler nodded and looked up at McCaleb and studied him in the way he might study a painting. He made no move to extend his hand.

'An investigation? In regard to Hieronymus Bosch, is it?'

'In a peripheral way. I just want to learn what I can about him. I'm told Mrs. Fitzgerald is the expert.'

McCaleb smiled.

'No one is an expert on Bosch,' Vosskuhler said without

a smile. 'Tortured soul, tormented genius . . . how will we ever know what is truly in a man's heart?'

McCaleb just nodded. Vosskuhler turned and appraised the painting.

'What do you see, Mr. McCaleb?'

McCaleb looked at the painting and didn't answer for a long moment.

'A lot of pain.'

Vosskuhler nodded approvingly. Then he stood and looked closely at the painting, flipping the glasses down and leaning close to the upper quarter panel, his lenses just inches from the night sky above the burning village.

'Bosch knew all of the demons,' he said without turning from the painting. 'The darkness . . .'

A long moment went by.

'A darkness more than night.'

There was another long moment of silence until Scott abruptly punctuated it by saying he needed to get back to his office. He left then. And after another moment Vosskuhler finally turned from the painting. He didn't bother flipping up the glasses when he looked at McCaleb. He slowly reached into his apron and switched off sound to his ears.

'I, too, must go back to work. Good luck with your investigation, Mr. McCaleb.'

McCaleb nodded as Vosskuhler sat back in his swivel chair and picked up his tiny brush again.

'We can go to my office,' Fitzgerald said. 'I have all the plate books from our library there. I can show you Bosch's work.'

'That would be fine. Thank you.'

She headed toward the door. McCaleb delayed a moment and took one last look at the painting. His eyes were drawn to the upper panels, toward the swirling darkness above the flames.

Penelope Fitzgerald's office was a six-by-six pod in a room

shared by several curatorial assistants. She pulled a chair into the tight space from a nearby pod where no one was working and told McCaleb to sit down. Her desk was L-shaped, with a laptop computer set up on the left side and a cluttered work space on the right. There were several books stacked on the desk. McCaleb noticed that behind one stack was a color print of a painting very much in the same style as the painting Vosskuhler was working on. He pushed the books a half foot to the side and bent down to look at the print. It was in three panels, the largest being the centerpiece. Again it was a ramble. Dozens and dozens of figures spread across the panels. Scenes of debauchery and torture.

'Do you recognize it?' Fitzgerald said.

'I don't think so. But it's Bosch, right?'

'His signature piece. The triptych called *The Garden of Earthly Delights.* It's in the Prado in Madrid. I once stood in front of it for four hours. It wasn't enough time to take it all in. Would you like some coffee or some water or anything, Mr. McCaleb?'

'No, I'm fine. Thank you. You can call me Terry if you want.'

'And you can call me Nep.'

McCaleb put a quizzical look on his face.

'Childhood nickname.'

He nodded.

'Now,' she said. 'In these books I can show you every piece of Bosch's identified work. Is it an important investigation?'

McCaleb nodded.

'I think so. It's a homicide.'

'And you are some kind of consultant?'

'I used to work for the FBI here in L.A. The sheriff's detective assigned to the case asked me to look at it and see what I think. It led me here. To Bosch. I am sorry but I can't get into the details of the case and I know that will probably be frustrating to you. I want to ask questions but I can't really answer any from you.'

'Darn.' She smiled. 'It sounds really interesting.'

'Tell you what, if there is ever a point I can tell you about it, I will.'

'Fair enough.'

McCaleb nodded.

'From what Dr. Vosskuhler said, I take it that there isn't a lot known about the man behind the paintings.'

Fitzgerald nodded.

'Hieronymus Bosch is certainly considered an enigma and he probably always will be.'

McCaleb unfolded his notepaper on the table in front of him and started taking notes as she spoke.

'He had one of the most unconventional imaginations of his time. Or any time for that matter. His work is quite extraordinary and still subject these five centuries later to restudy and reinterpretation. However, I think you will find that the majority of the critical analysis to date holds that he was a doomsayer. His work is informed with the portents of doom and hellfire, of warnings of the wages of sin. To put it more succinctly, his paintings primarily carried variations on the same theme: that the folly of humankind leads us all to hell as our ultimate destiny.'

McCaleb was writing quickly, trying to keep up. He wished he had brought a tape recorder.

'Nice guy, huh?' Fitzgerald said.

'Sounds like it.' He nodded to the print of the triptych. 'Must've been fun on a Saturday night.'

She smiled.

'Exactly what I thought when I was in the Prado.'

'Any redeeming qualities? He took in orphans, was nice to dogs, changed flat tires for old ladies, anything?'

'You have to remember his time and place to fully understand what he was doing with his art. While his work is punctuated with violent scenes and depictions of torture and anguish, this was a time when those sorts of things were not unusual. He lived in a violent time; his work clearly reflects that. The paintings also reflect the medieval belief in the existence of demons everywhere. Evil lurks in all of the paintings.'

'The owl?'

She stared blankly at him for a moment.

'Yes, the owl is one symbol he used. I thought you said you were unfamiliar with his work.'

'I *am* unfamiliar with it. It was an owl that brought me here. But I shouldn't go into that and I shouldn't have interrupted you. Please go on.'

'I was just going to add that it is telling when you consider that Bosch was a contemporary of Leonardo, Michelangelo and Raphael. Yet if you were to look at their works side by side you would have to believe Bosch – with all the medieval symbols and doom – was a century behind.'

'But he wasn't.'

She shook her head as though she felt sorry for Bosch.

'He and Leonardo da Vinci were born within a year or two of each other. By the end of the fifteenth century, da Vinci was creating pieces that were full of hope and celebration of human values and spirituality while Bosch was all gloom and doom.'

'That makes you feel sad, doesn't it?'

She put her hands on the top book in the stack but didn't open it. It was simply labeled BOSCH on the spine and there was no illustration on the black leather binding.

'I can't help but think about what could have been if Bosch had worked side by side with da Vinci or Michelangelo, what could have happened if he had used his skill and imagination in celebration rather than damnation of the world.'

She looked down at the book and then back up at him.

'But that is the beauty of art and why we study and celebrate it. Each painting is a window to the artist's soul and imagination. No matter how dark and disturbing, his vision is what sets him apart and makes his paintings unique. What happens to me with Bosch is that the paintings serve to carry me into the artist's soul and I sense the torment.'

He nodded and she looked down and opened the book.

The world of Hieronymus Bosch was as striking to McCaleb as it was disturbing. The landscapes of misery that unfolded in the pages Penelope Fitzgerald turned were not unlike some of the most horrible crime scenes he had witnessed, but in these painted scenes the players were still alive and in pain. The gnashing of teeth and the ripping of flesh were active and real. His canvases were crowded with the damned, humans being tormented for their sins by visible demons and creatures given image by the hand of a horrible imagination.

At first he studied the color reproductions of the paintings in silence, taking it all in the way he would first observe a crime scene photograph. But then a page was turned and he looked at a painting that depicted three people gathered around a sitting man. One of those standing used what looked like a primitive scalpel to probe a wound on the crown of the sitting man's head. The image was depicted in a circle. There were words painted above and below the circle.

'What is this one?' he asked.

'It's called *The Stone Operation*,' Fitzgerald said. 'It was a common belief at the time that stupidity and deceit could be cured by the removal of a stone from the head of the one suffering the malady.'

McCaleb leaned over her shoulder and looked closely at the painting, specifically at the location of the surgery wound. It was in a location comparable to the wound on Edward Gunn's head.

'Okay, you can go on.'

Owls were everywhere. Fitzgerald did not have to point them out most of the time, their positions were that obvious. She did explain some of the attendant imagery. Most often in the paintings when the owl was depicted in a tree, the branch upon which the symbol of evil perched was leafless and gray – dead.

She turned the page to a three-panel painting.

'This is called *The Last Judgment*, with the left panel subtitled *The Fall of Mankind* and the right panel simply and obviously called *Hell*.'

'He liked painting hell.'

But Nep Fitzgerald didn't smile. Her eyes studied the book.

The left panel of the painting was a Garden of Eden scene with Adam and Eve at center taking the fruit from the serpent in the apple tree. On a dead branch of a nearby tree an owl watched the transaction. On the opposite panel Hell was depicted as a dark place where birdlike creatures disemboweled the damned, cut their bodies up and placed them in frying pans to be slid into fiery ovens.

'All of this came from this guy's head,' McCaleb said. 'I don't . . .'

He didn't finish because he was unsure what he was trying to say.

'A tormented soul,' Fitzgerald said and turned the page.

The next painting was another circular image with seven separate scenes depicted along the outer rim and a portrait of God at center. In a circle of gold surrounding the portrait of God and separating him from the other scenes were four Latin words McCaleb immediately recognized.

'Beware, beware, God sees.'

Fitzgerald looked up at him.

'You obviously have seen this before. Or you just happen to know fifteenth-century Latin. This must be one strange case you are working on.'

'It's getting that way. But I only know the words, not the painting. What is it?'

'It's actually a tabletop, probably created for a church

rectory or a holy person's house. It's the eye of God. He is at center and what he sees as he looks down are these images, the seven deadly sins.'

McCaleb nodded. By looking at the distinct scenes he could pick out some of the more obvious of the sins; gluttony, lust and pride.

'And now his masterpiece,' his tour guide said as she turned the page.

She came to the same triptych she had pinned to the wall of the pod. *The Garden of Earthly Delights*. McCaleb studied it closely now. The left panel was a bucolic scene of Adam and Eve being placed in the garden by the creator. An apple tree stood nearby. The center panel, the largest, showed dozens of nudes coupling and dancing in uninhibited lust, riding horses and beautiful birds and wholly imagined creatures from the lake in the foreground. And then the last panel, the dark one, was the payoff. Hell, a place of torment and anguish administered by monster birds and other ugly creatures. The painting was so detailed and enthralling that McCaleb understood how someone might stand before it – the original – for four hours and still not see everything.

'I am sure you are grasping the ideas of Bosch's often repeated themes by now,' Fitzgerald said. 'But this is considered the most coherent of his works as well as the most beautifully imagined and realized.'

McCaleb nodded and pointed to the three panels as he spoke.

'You have Adam and Eve here, the good life until they eat that apple. Then in the center you have what happens after the fall from grace: life without rules. Freedom of choice leads to lust and sin. And where does all of this go? Hell.'

'Very good. And if I could just point out a few specifics that might interest you.'

'Please.'

She started with the first panel.

'The earthly paradise. You are correct in that it depicts Adam and Eve before the Fall. This pool and fountain at center represent the promise of eternal life. You already noted the fruit tree at left center.'

Her finger moved across the plate to the fountain structure, a tower of what looked like flower petals that somehow delivered water in four distinct trickles to the pool below. Then he saw it. Her finger stopped below a small dark entrance at the center of the fountain structure. The face of an owl peered from the darkness.

'You mentioned the owl before. Its image is here. You see all is not right in this paradise. Evil lurks and, as we know, will ultimately win the day. According to Bosch. Then, going to the next panel we see the imagery again and again.'

She pointed out two distinct representations of owls and two other depictions of owl-like creatures. McCaleb's eyes held on one of the images. It showed a large brown owl with shiny black eyes being embraced by a nude man. The owl's coloring and eyes matched that of the plastic bird found in Edward Gunn's apartment.

'Do you see something, Terry?'

He pointed to the owl.

'This one. I can't really go into it with you but this one, it matches up with the reason I am here.'

'A lot of symbols are at work in this panel. That is one of the obvious ones. After the Fall, man's freedom of choice leads him to debauchery, gluttony, folly and avarice, the worst sin of all in Bosch's world being lust. Man wraps his arms around the owl; he embraces evil.'

McCaleb nodded.

'And then he pays for it.'

'Then he pays for it. As you notice in the last panel, this is a depiction of hell without fire. Rather, it is a place of myriad torments and endless pain. Of darkness.'

McCaleb stared silently for a long time, his eyes moving

across the landscape of the painting. He remembered what Dr. Vosskuhler had said.

A darkness more than night.

12

Bosch cupped his hands and held them against the window next to the front door of the apartment. He was looking into the kitchen. The counters were spotless. No mess, no coffee maker, not even a toaster. He started to get a bad feeling. He stepped over to the door and knocked once more. He then paced back and forth waiting. Looking down he saw an outline on the pavement of where a welcome mat had once been.

'Damn,' he said.

He reached into his pocket and took out a small leather pouch. He unzipped it and removed two small steel picks he had made from hacksaw blades. Glancing around he saw no one. He was in a shielded alcove of a large apartment complex in Westwood. Most residents were probably still at work. He stepped up to the door and went to work with the picks on the deadbolt. Ninety seconds later he had the door open and he went inside.

He knew the apartment was vacant as soon as he stepped in but he covered every room anyway. All of them were empty. Hoping for an empty prescription bottle he even checked the bathroom medicine cabinet. There was a used razor made of pink plastic on a shelf, nothing else.

He walked back into the living room and took out his cell phone. He had just put Janis Langwiser's cell phone on the speed dial the day before. She was co-prosecutor on the case and they had worked on Bosch's testimony throughout the weekend. His call found her still in the trial team's temporary office in the Van Nuys courthouse.

'Listen, I don't want to rain on the parade but Annabelle Crowe is gone.'

'What do you mean, gone?'

'I mean gone, baby, gone. I'm standing in what was her apartment. It's empty.'

'Shit! We really need her, Harry. When did she move out?'

'I don't know. I just discovered she was gone.'

'Did you talk to the apartment manager?'

'Not yet. But he's not going to know much more than how long ago she split. If she's running from the trial she wouldn't be leaving any forwarding addresses with the management.'

'Well, when did you talk to her last?'

'Thursday. I called her here. But that line is disconnected today. No forwarding number.'

'Shit!'

'I know. You said that.'

'She got the subpoena, right?'

'Yeah, she got it Thursday. That's why I called. To make sure.'

'Okay, then maybe she'll be here tomorrow.'

Bosch looked around the empty apartment.

'I wouldn't count on it.'

He looked at his watch. It was after five. Because he had been so sure about Annabelle Crowe, she had been the last witness he was going to check on. There had been no hint that she was going to split. Now he knew he would be spending the night trying to run her down.

'What can you do?' Langwiser asked.

'I've got some information on her I can run down. She's got to be in town. She's an actress, where else is she going to go?'

'New York?'

'That's where real actors go. She's a face. She'll stay here.'

'Find her, Harry. We'll need her by next week.'

'I'll try.'

There was a moment of silence while they both considered things.

'You think Storey got to her?' Langwiser finally asked.

'I'm wondering. He could've gotten to her with what she needs – a job, a part, a paycheck. When I find her I'll be asking that.'

'Okay, Harry. Good luck. If you get her tonight, let me know. Otherwise, I'll see you in the morning.'

'Right.'

Bosch closed the phone and put it down on the kitchen counter. From his jacket pocket he took out a thin stack of three-by-five cards. Each card had the name of one of the witnesses he was responsible for vetting and preparing for trial. Home and work addresses as well as phone numbers and pager numbers were noted on the cards. He checked the card assigned to Annabelle Crowe and then punched her pager number into his phone. A recorded message said the pager was no longer in service.

He clapped the phone closed and looked at the card again. The name and number of Annabelle Crowe's agent were listed at the bottom. He decided that the agent might be the one tie she wouldn't sever.

He put the phone and cards back into his pockets. This was one inquiry he was going to make in person.

13

McCaleb made the crossing by himself, *The Following Sea* arriving at Avalon Harbor just as darkness did. Buddy Lockridge had stayed behind at Cabrillo Marina because no new charters had come up and he wouldn't be needed until Saturday. As he arrived at the island McCaleb radioed the harbor master's boat on channel 16 and got help mooring the boat.

The added weight of the two heavy books he had found in the used-books section at Dutton's bookstore in Brentwood plus the smaller cooler filled with frozen tamales made the walk up the hill to his house exhausting. He had to stop twice on the side of the road to rest. Each time he sat down on the cooler and took one of the books out of his leather bag so that he could once more study the dark work of Hieronymus Bosch – even in the shadows of evening.

Since his visit to the Getty, the images in the Bosch paintings were never far from his thoughts. Nep Fitzgerald had said something at the end of the meeting in her office. Just before closing the book on the plates reproducing *The Garden of Earthly Delights* she looked at him with a small smile, as if she had something to say but was hesitant.

'What?' he said.

'Nothing really, just an observation.'

'Go ahead and make it. I'd like to hear it.'

'I was just going to mention that a lot of the critics and

scholars who view Bosch's work see corollaries to contemporary times. That's the mark of a great artist – if his work stands the test of time. If it has the power to connect to people and . . . and maybe influence them.'

McCaleb nodded. He knew she wanted him to tell her what he was working on.

'I understand what you are saying. I'm sorry but at the moment I can't tell you about this. Maybe someday I will, or someday you will just know what it was. But thank you. You have helped a lot, I think. I don't know for sure yet.'

Sitting on the cooler now, McCaleb remembered the conversation. Corollaries to contemporary times, he thought. And crimes. He opened the larger of the two books he had bought and opened it to a color illustration of Bosch's masterpiece. He studied the owl with black eyes and all of his instincts told him he was on to something significant. Something very dark and dangerous.

When he got home Graciela took the cooler from him and opened it on the kitchen counter. She took three of the green corn tamales out and put them on a plate for defrosting in the microwave.

'I'm making chili relenos, too,' she said. 'It's a good thing you called from the boat or we would've gone ahead and eaten without you.'

McCaleb let her vent. He knew she was angry about what he was doing. He walked over to the table where Cielo was propped in a bouncing chair. She was staring up at the ceiling fan and moving her hands in front of her, getting used to them. McCaleb bent down and kissed both of them and then her forehead.

'Where's Raymond?'

'In his room. On the computer. Why did you only get ten?'

He looked over at her as he slid into a chair next to Cielo. She was putting the other tamales into a plastic Tupperware container for freezing.

'I took the cooler in and told them to fill it. That's how many fit, I guess.'

She shook her head, annoyed with him.

'We'll have one extra.'

'Then throw it out or invite one of Raymond's friends over for dinner next time. Who cares, Graciela? It's a tamale.'

Graciela turned and looked at him with dark, upset eyes that immediately softened.

'You're sweaty.'

'I just walked up the hill. The shuttle was closed for the night.'

She opened an overhead cabinet and took out a plastic box holding a thermometer. There was a thermometer in every room in the house. She took this one out and shook it and came over to him.

'Open.'

'Let's use the electronic.'

'No, I don't trust them.'

She put the end of the thermometer under his tongue and then used her hand to gently bring his jaw up and close his mouth. Very professional. She had been an emergency room nurse when he met her and was now the school nurse and an office clerk at Catalina Elementary. She had just gone back to work after the Christmas holiday. McCaleb sensed that she wanted to be a full-time mother, but they couldn't afford it so he never brought it up directly. He hoped that in a couple of years the charter service would be more established and they would have the choice then. Sometimes he wished they had kept a share of the money for the book-and-movie deal but he also knew that their decision to honor Graciela's sister by not making money from what happened had been the only choice. They had given half the money to the Make a Wish Foundation and put the other half in a trust fund for Raymond. It would pay for college if he wanted that.

Graciela held his wrist and checked his pulse while he sat silently watching her.

'You're high,' she said, dropping his wrist. 'Open.'

He opened his mouth and she took out the thermometer and read it. She went to the sink and washed it, then returned it to its case and the cabinet. She didn't say anything and McCaleb knew that meant his temperature was normal.

'You wish I had a fever, don't you?'

'Are you crazy?'

'Yes, you do. That way you could tell me to stop this.'

'What do you mean, tell you to stop it? Last night you said it was just going to be last night. Then this morning you said it was just going to be today. What are you telling me now, Terry?'

He looked over at Cielo and held out a finger for her to grasp.

'It's not over.' He now looked back at Graciela. 'Some things came up today.'

'Some *things?* Whatever they are, give them to Detective Winston. It's her job. It's not your job to be doing this.'

'I can't. Not yet. Not until I am sure.'

Graciela turned and walked back to the counter. She put the plate with the tamales on it into the microwave and set it for defrost.

'Will you take her in and change her? It's been a while. And she'll need a bottle while I make dinner.'

McCaleb carefully raised his daughter out of the bouncing seat and put her on his shoulder. She made some fussing noises and he gently patted her back to calm her. He walked over to Graciela's back, put his arm around the front of her and pulled her backward into him. He kissed the top of her head and held his face in her hair.

'It will all be over soon and we'll be back to normal.'

'I hope so.'

She touched his arm, which crossed her body beneath

her breasts. The touch of her fingertips was the approval he sought. It told him this was a rough spot but they were okay. He held her tighter, kissed the back of her neck and then let her go.

Cielo watched the slowly moving mobile that hung over the changing table as he put a new diaper on her tiny body. Cardboard stars and half moons hung from threads. Raymond had made it with Graciela as a Christmas present. An air current from somewhere in the house gently turned it and Cielo's dark blue eyes focused on it. McCaleb bent down and kissed her forehead.

After wrapping her in two baby blankets he took her out to the porch and gave her the bottle while gently moving in the rocking chair. Looking down at the harbor he noticed he had left on the instrument lights on *The Following Sea*'s bridge. He knew he could call the harbor master on the pier and whoever was working nights could just motor over and turn them off. But he knew he'd be going back to the boat after dinner. He would get the lights then.

He looked down at Cielo. Her eyes were closed but he knew she was awake. She was working the bottle forcefully. Graciela had stopped full-time breastfeeding when she had gone back to work. Bottle feedings were new and he found them to be perhaps the single most pleasurable moments of being a new father. He often whispered to his daughter during these times. Promises mostly. Promises that he would always love her and be with her. He told her never to be afraid or feel alone. Sometimes when she would suddenly open her eyes and look at him, he sensed that she was communicating the same things back to him. And he felt a kind of love he had never known before.

'Terry.'

He looked up at Graciela's whisper.

'Dinner's ready.'

He checked the bottle and saw it was almost empty.

'I'll be there in a minute,' he whispered.

After Graciela left them he looked down at his daughter. The whispering had made her open her eyes. She stared up at him. He kissed her on the forehead and then just held her gaze.

'I have to do this, baby,' he whispered.

The boat was cold inside. McCaleb turned on the salon lights and then positioned the space heater in the center of the room and turned it on low. He wanted to warm up but not too much, for then he might get sleepy. He was still tired from the exertions of the day.

He was down in the front cabin going through his old files when he heard the cell phone start to chirp from his leather bag up in the salon. He closed the file he was studying and took it with him as he bounded up the stairs to the salon and grabbed the phone out of his bag. It was Jaye Winston.

'So how'd it go at the Getty? I thought you were going to call me back.'

'Oh, well it ran late and I wanted to get back to the boat and get across before dark. I forgot to call.'

'You're back on the island?'

She sounded disappointed.

'Yeah, I told Graciela this morning I'd be back. But don't worry, I'm still working on a few things.'

'What happened at the Getty?'

'Nothing much,' he lied. 'I talked to a couple people and looked at some paintings.'

'You see any owls that match ours?'

She laughed as she asked the question.

'A couple close ones. I got some books I want to look through tonight. I was going to call you, see if maybe we could get together tomorrow.'

'When? I've got a meeting in the morning at ten and another at eleven.'

'I was thinking the afternoon anyway. There's something I have to do in the morning myself.'

He didn't want to tell her that he wanted to watch the opening statements in the Storey trial. He knew they'd be carried live on *Court TV*, which he got up at the house with the satellite dish.

'Well, I could probably get a chopper to take me out there but I'll have to check with aero first.'

'No, I'll be coming back over.'

'You will? Great! You want to come here?'

'No, I was thinking about something more quiet and private.'

'How come?'

'I'll tell you tomorrow.'

'Getting mysterious on me. This isn't a scam to get the sheriff's to pay for pancakes again, is it?'

They both laughed.

'No scam. Any chance you could come out to Cabrillo and meet me at my boat?'

'I'll be there. What time?'

He made the appointment for three o'clock thinking that would give him plenty of time to prepare a profile and figure out how he would tell her what he had to say. It would also give him enough time to be ready for what he hoped she would allow him to do that night.

'Anything on the owl?' he asked once they had the meeting arranged.

'Very little, none of it good. Inside there are manufacturing markings. The plastic mold was made in China. The company ships them to two distributors over here, one in Ohio and one in Tennessee. From there they probably go all over. It's a long shot and a lot of work.'

'So you're going to drop it.'

'No, I didn't say that. It's just not a priority. It's on my partner's plate. He's got calls out. We'll see what he gets from the distributors, evaluate and decide where to go from there.'

McCaleb nodded. Prioritizing investigative leads and even investigations themselves was a necessary evil. But it still bothered him. He was sure the owl was a key and knowing everything about it would be useful.

'Okay, so we're all set?' she asked.

'About tomorrow? Yeah, we're set.'

'We'll see you at three.'

'We?'

'Kurt and I. My partner. You haven't met him yet.'

'Uh, look, tomorrow could it just be me and you? Nothing against your partner but I'd just like to talk to you tomorrow, Jaye.'

There was a moment of silence before she responded.

'Terry, what's going on with you?'

'I just want to talk to you about this. You brought me in, I want to give what I have to you. If you want to bring your partner in on it after, that's fine.'

There was another pause.

'I'm getting a bad vibe from all of this, Terry.'

'I'm sorry, but that's the way I want it. I guess you have to take it or leave it.'

His ultimatum made her go silent even longer this time. He waited for her.

'All right, man,' she finally said. 'It's your show. I'll take it.'

'Thanks, Jaye. I'll see you then.'

They hung up. He looked at the old case file he had pulled and still held in his hand. He put the phone down on the coffee table and leaned back on the couch and opened the file.

14

At first they called it the Little Girl Lost case because the victim had no name. The victim was thought to be about fourteen or fifteen years old; a Latina – probably Mexican – whose body was found in the bushes and among the debris below one of the overlooks off Mulholland Drive. The case belonged to Bosch and his partner at the time, Frankie Sheehan. This was before Bosch worked homicide out of Hollywood Division. He and Sheehan were a Robbery–Homicide team and it had been Bosch who contacted McCaleb at the bureau. McCaleb was newly returned to Los Angeles from Quantico. He was setting up an outpost for the Behavioral Sciences Unit and Violent Criminal Apprehension Program. The Little Girl Lost case was one of the first submitted to him.

Bosch came to him, bringing the file and the crime scene photos to his tiny office on the thirteenth floor of the federal building in Westwood. He came without Sheehan because the partners had disagreed on whether to bring the bureau in on the case. Cross-agency jealousies at work. But Bosch didn't care about all of that. He cared about the case. He had haunted eyes. The case was clearly working on him as much as he worked on it.

The body had been found nude and violated in many ways. The girl had been manually strangled by her killer's gloved hands. No clothes or purse were found on the hillside. Fingerprints matched no computerized records. The girl matched no description on an active missing persons case anywhere in Los Angeles County or on national crime computer systems. An artist's rendering of the victim's face put on the TV news and in the papers brought no calls from a loved one. Sketches faxed to five hundred police agencies across the Southwest and to the State Judicial Police in Mexico drew no response. The victim remained unclaimed and unidentified, her body reposing in the refrigerator at the coroner's office while Bosch and his partner worked the case.

There was no physical evidence found with the body. Aside from being left without her clothes or any identifying property, the victim had apparently been washed with an industrial-strength cleaner before being dumped late at night off Mulholland.

There was only one clue with the body. An impression in the skin of the left hip. Postmortem lividity indicated the blood in the body had settled on the left half, meaning the body had been lying on its left side in the time between thestilling of the heart and the dropping of the body down the hillside where it came to rest face down on a pile of empty beer cans and tequila bottles. The evidence indicated that during the time that the blood settled, the body had been lying on top of the object that left the impression on the hip.

The impression consisted of the number 1, the letter J and part of a third letter that could have been the upper left stem of an H, a K or an L. It was a partial reading of a license plate.

Bosch formed the theory that whoever had killed the girl with no name had hidden the body in the trunk of a car until it was time to dump it. After carefully cleaning the body the killer had put it into the trunk of his car, mistakenly putting it down on part of a license plate that had been taken off the car and also placed in the trunk. Bosch's theory was that the license plate had been removed and possibly replaced with a stolen plate as one more safety measure that would help the killer avoid detection if his car happened to be spotted by a suspicious passerby at the Mulholland overlook.

Though the skin impression gave no indication of what state issued the license plate, Bosch went with the percentages. From the state Department of Motor Vehicles he obtained a list of every car registered in Los Angeles County that carried a plate beginning 1JH, 1JK and 1JL. The list contained over three thousand names of car owners. He and his partner cut 40 percent of it by discounting the female owners. The remaining names were slowly fed into the National Crime Index computer and the detectives came up with a list of forty-six men with criminal records ranging from minor to the extreme.

It was at this point that Bosch came to McCaleb. He wanted a profile of the killer. He wanted to know if he and Sheehan were on the right track in suspecting that the killer had a criminal history, and he wanted to know how to approach and evaluate the forty-six men on the list.

McCaleb considered the case for nearly a week. He looked at each of the crime scene photos twice a day – first thing in the morning and last thing before going to sleep – and studied the reports often. He finally told Bosch that he believed they were on the right course. Using data accumulated from hundreds of similar crimes and analyzed in the bureau's VICAP program, he was able to provide a profile of a man in his late twenties with a history of having committed crimes of an escalating nature and likely including offenses of a sexual nature. The crime scene suggested the work of an exhibitionist – a killer who wanted his crime to be public and to instill horror and fear in the general population. Therefore, the location of the body dump site would have been chosen for these reasons as opposed to reasons of convenience.

In comparing the profile to the list of forty-six names, Bosch narrowed the possibilities to two suspects: a Woodland Hills office building custodian who had a record of arson and public indecency and a stage builder who worked for a studio in Burbank and had been arrested for the attempted rape of a neighbor when he was a teenager. Both men were in their late twenties.

Bosch and Sheehan leaned toward the custodian because of his access to industrial cleaners, like the one that had been used to wash the victim's body. However, McCaleb liked the stage builder as a suspect because the attempted rape of the neighbor in his youth indicated an impulsive action that was more in tune with the profile of the current crime's perpetrator.

Bosch and Sheehan decided to informally interview both men and invited McCaleb along. The FBI agent stressed that the men should be interviewed in their own homes so that he would have the opportunity to study them in their own environment as well as look for clues in their belongings.

The stage builder was first. His name was Victor Seguin. He seemed shell-shocked by seeing the three men at his door and the explanation Bosch gave for their visit. Nevertheless he invited them in. As Bosch and Sheehan calmly asked questions McCaleb sat on a couch and studied the clean and neat furnishings of the apartment. Within five minutes he knew they had the right man and nodded to Bosch – their prearranged signal.

Victor Seguin was informed of his rights and arrested. He was placed in the detectives' car and his small home under the landing zone of Burbank Airport was sealed until a search warrant could be obtained. Two hours later, when they reentered with the search warrant, they found a sixteen-year-old girl bound and gagged but alive in a soundproof coffin-like crawl space constructed by the stage builder beneath a trap door hidden under his bed.

Only after the excitement and adrenaline high of having broken a case and saved a life began to subside did Bosch finally ask McCaleb how he knew they had their man. McCaleb walked the detective over to the living-room bookcase, where he pointed out a well-worn copy of a book called *The Collector*, a novel about a man who abducts several women.

Seguin was charged with the unidentified girl's murder and the kidnapping and rape of the young woman the investigators rescued. He denied any guilt in the murder and pressed for a deal by which he would plead guilty to the kidnapping and rape of the survivor only. The DA's office declined any deal and proceeded to trial with what they had – the survivor's gut-wrenching testimony and the license plate impression on the dead girl's hip.

The jury convicted on all counts after less than four hours' deliberation. The DA's office then floated a possible deal to Seguin: a promise not to go for the death penalty during the second phase of the trial if the killer agreed to tell investigators who his first victim was and from where he had abducted her. To take the deal Seguin would have to drop his pose of innocence. He passed. The DA went for the death penalty and got it. Bosch never learned who the dead girl was and McCaleb knew it haunted him that no one apparently cared enough to come forward.

It haunted McCaleb, too. On the day he came to the penalty phase of the trial to testify, he had lunch with Bosch and noticed that a name had been written on the tabs of his files on the case.

'What's that?' McCaleb asked excitedly. 'You ID'd her?'

Bosch looked down and saw the name on the tabs and turned the files over.

'No, no ID yet.'

'Well, what's that?'

'Just a name. I sort of gave her a name, I guess.'

Bosch looked embarrassed. McCaleb reached over and turned the files back over to read the name.

'Cielo Azul?'

'Yeah, she was Spanish, I gave her a Spanish name.'

'It means blue sky, right?'

'Yeah, blue sky. I, uh . . .'

McCaleb waited. Nothing.

'What?'

'Well . . . I'm not that religious, you know what I mean?'

'Yes.'

'But I sort of figured if nobody down here wanted to claim her, then hopefully . . . maybe there's somebody up there that will.'

Bosch shrugged his shoulders and looked away. McCaleb could see his face turning red in the upper cheeks.

'It's hard to find God's hand in what we do. What we see.'

Bosch just nodded and they didn't speak about the name again.

McCaleb lifted the last page of the file marked Cielo Azul and looked at the inside rear flap of the manila folder. It had become his habit over time at the bureau to jot notes on the back flap, where they would not readily be seen because of the attached file pages. These were notes he made about the investigators who submitted the cases for profiling. McCaleb had come to realize that insights about the investigator were sometimes as important as the information in the case file. For it was through the investigator's eyes that McCaleb first viewed many aspects of the crime.

His case with Bosch had come up more than ten years earlier, before he began his more extensive profiling of the investigators as well as the cases. On this file he had written Bosch's name and just four words beneath it.

Thorough – Smart – M. M. – A. A.

He looked at the last two notations now. It had been part of his routine to use abbreviations and shorthand when making notes that needed to be kept confidential. The last two notations were his reading on what motivated

Bosch. He had come to believe that homicide detectives, a breed of cop unto themselves, called upon deep inner emotions and motivations to accept and carry out the always difficult task of their job. They were usually of two kinds, those who saw their jobs as a skill or a craft, and those who saw it as a mission in life. Ten years ago he had put Bosch into the latter class. He was a man on a mission.

This motivation in detectives could then be broken down even further as to what gave them this sense of purpose or mission. To some the job was seen as almost a game; they had some inner deficit that caused them to need to prove they were better, smarter and more cunning than their quarry. Their lives were a constant cycle of validating themselves by, in effect, invalidating the killers they sought by putting them behind bars. Others, while carrying a degree of that same inner deficit, also saw themselves with the additional dimension of being speakers for the dead. There was a sacred bond cast between victim and cop that formed at the crime scene and could not be severed. It was what ultimately pushed them into the chase and enabled them to overcome all obstacles in their path. McCaleb classified these cops as avenging angels. It had been his experience that these cop/angels were the best investigators he ever worked with. He also came to believe that they traveled closest to that unseen edge beneath which lies the abyss.

Ten years before, he had classified Harry Bosch as an avenging angel. He now had to consider whether the detective had stepped too close to that edge. He had to consider that Bosch might have gone over.

He closed the file and pulled the two art books out of his bag. Both were simply titled *Bosch*. The larger one, with full-color reproductions of the paintings, was by R. H. Marijnissen and P. Ruyffelaere. The second book, which appeared to carry more analysis of the paintings than the other, was written by Erik Larsen.

McCaleb started with the smaller book and began

scanning through the pages of analysis. He quickly learned that, as Penelope Fitzgerald had said, there were many different and even competing views of Hieronymus Bosch. The Larsen book cited scholars who called Bosch a humanist and even one who believed him to be part of a heretical group that believed the earth was a literal hell ruled over by Satan. There were disputes among the scholars about the intended meanings of some of the paintings, about whether some paintings could actually be attributed to Bosch, about whether the painter had ever traveled to Italy and viewed the work of his Renaissance contemporaries.

Finally, McCaleb closed the book when he realized that, at least for his purposes, the words about Hieronymus Bosch might not be important. If the painter's work was subject to multiple interpretations, then the only interpretation that mattered would be that of the person who killed Edward Gunn. What mattered was what that person saw and took from the paintings of Hieronymus Bosch.

He opened the larger book and began to slowly study the reproductions. His viewing of reproduction plates of the paintings at the Getty had been hurried and encumbered by his not being alone.

He put his notebook on the arm of the couch with the plan to keep a tabulation of the number of owls he saw in the paintings as well as descriptions of each bird. He quickly realized that the paintings were so minutely detailed in the smaller-scale reproductions that he might be missing things of significance. He went down to the forward cabin to find the magnifying glass he had always kept in his desk at the bureau for use while examining crime scene photos.

As he was bent over a box full of office supplies he had cleared out of his desk five years before, McCaleb felt a slight bump against the boat and straightened up. He had tied the Zodiac up on the fantail, so it could not have been his own skiff. He was considering this when he felt the unmistakable up-and-down movement of the boat indicating that someone had just stepped aboard. His mind focused on the salon door. He was sure he had left it unlocked.

He looked down into the box he had just been sorting through and grabbed the letter opener.

As he came up the steps into the galley McCaleb surveyed the salon and saw no one and nothing amiss. It was difficult seeing past the interior reflection on the sliding door but outside in the cockpit, silhouetted by the streetlights on Crescent Street, there was a man. He stood with his back to the salon as if admiring the lights of the town going up the hill.

McCaleb moved quickly to the slider and pulled it open. He held the letter opener at his side but with the point of the blade up. The man standing in the cockpit turned around.

McCaleb lowered his weapon as the man stared at it with wide eyes.

'Mr. McCaleb, I—'

'It's all right, Charlie, I just didn't know who it was.'

Charlie was the night man in the harbor office. McCaleb didn't know his last name. But he knew that he often visited Buddy Lockridge on nights Buddy stayed over. McCaleb guessed that Buddy was a soft touch for a quick beer every now and then on the long nights. That was probably why Charlie had rowed his skiff over from the pier.

'I saw the lights and thought maybe Buddy was here,' he said. 'I was just paying a visit.'

'No, Buddy's overtown tonight. He probably won't be back till Friday.'

'Okay, then. I'll just be going. Everything all right with you? The missus isn't making you sleep on the boat, is she?'

'No, Charlie, everything's fine. Just doing a little work.'

He held up the letter opener as if that explained what he was doing.

'All right then, I'll be heading back.'

'Good night, Charlie. Thanks for checking on me.'

He went back inside and down to the office. He found the magnifying glass, with a light attachment, at the bottom of the box of office supplies.

For the next two hours he went through the paintings. The eerie landscapes of phantasmic demons surrounding human prey enthralled him once again. As he studied each work he marked particular findings such as the owls with yellow Post-its so that he could easily return to them.

McCaleb amassed a list of sixteen direct depictions of owls in the paintings and another dozen portrayals of owl-like creatures or structures. The owls were darkly painted and lurking in all the paintings like sentinels of judgment and doom. He looked at them and couldn't help but think of the analogy of the owl as detective. Both creatures of the night, both watchers and hunters – firsthand observers of the evil and pain humans and animals inflict upon each other.

The single most significant finding McCaleb made during his study of the paintings was not an owl. Rather, it was the human form. He made the discovery as he used the lighted glass to examine the center panel of a painting called *The Last Judgment.* Outside the depiction of hell's oven, where sinners were thrown, there were several bound victims waiting to be dismembered and burned. Among this grouping McCaleb found the image of a nude man bound with his arms and legs behind him. The sinner's extremities had been stretched into a painful reverse fetal position. The image closely reflected what he had seen at center focus in the crime scene videotape and photos of Edward Gunn.

McCaleb marked the finding with a Post-it and closed the book. When the cell phone on the couch next to him chirped just then, he bolted upright with a start. He checked his watch before answering and saw it was exactly midnight.

The caller was Graciela.

'I thought you were coming back tonight.'

'I am. I just finished and I'm on my way.'

'You took the cart down, right?'

'Yeah. So I'll be fine.'

'Okay, see you soon.'

'Yes, you will.'

McCaleb decided to leave everything on the boat, thinking that he needed to clear his mind before the next day. Carrying the files and the heavy books would only remind him of the heavy thoughts he carried within. He locked the boat and took the Zodiac to the skiff dock. At the end of the pier he climbed into the golf cart. He rode through the deserted business district and up the hill toward home. Despite his efforts to deflect them, his thoughts were of the abyss. A place where creatures with sharp beaks and claws and knives tormented the fallen in perpetuity. He knew one thing for sure at this point. The painter Bosch would have made a good profiler. He knew his stuff. He had a handle on the nightmares that rattle around inside most people's minds. As well as those that sometimes get out.

15

Opening statements in the trial of David Storcy were delayed while the attorneys argued over final motions behind closed doors with the judge. Bosch sat at the prosecution table and waited. He tried to clear his mind of all extraneous diversions, including his fruitless search for Annabelle Crowe the night before.

Finally, at ten forty-five, the attorneys came into the courtroom and moved to their respective tables. Then the defendant – today wearing a suit that looked like it would cover three deputies' paychecks – was led into court from the holding cell and, at last, Judge Houghton took the bench.

It was time to begin and Bosch felt the tension in the courtroom ratchet up a considerable notch. Los Angeles had raised – or perhaps lowered – the criminal trial to the level of worldwide entertainment, but it was never seen that way by the players in the courtroom. They were playing for keeps and in this trial perhaps more than most there was a palpable sense of the enmity between the two opposing camps.

The judge instructed the deputy sheriff who acted as his bailiff to bring in the jury. Bosch stood with the others and turned and watched the jurors file in silently and take their seats. He thought he could see excitement in some of their faces. They had been waiting through two weeks of jury selection and motions for things to start. Bosch's eyes rose above them to the two cameras mounted on the wall over the jury box. They gave a full view of the courtroom, except for the jury box.

After everyone was seated Houghton cleared his throat and leaned forward to the bench microphone while looking at the jurors.

'Ladies and gentlemen, how are you this morning?'

There was a murmured response and Houghton nodded.

'I apologize for the delay. Please remember that the justice system is in essence run by lawyers. As such it runs slowwwwwwly.'

There was polite laughter in the courtroom. Bosch noticed that the attorneys – prosecution and defense – dutifully joined in, a couple of them overdoing it. It had been his experience that while in open court a judge could not possibly tell a joke that the lawyers did not laugh at.

Bosch glanced to his left, past the defense table, and saw the other jury box was packed with members of the media. He recognized many of the reporters from television newscasts and press conferences in the past.

He scanned the rest of the courtroom and saw the public observation benches were densely packed with citizens, except for the row directly behind the defense table. There sat several people with ample room on either side who looked as if they'd spent the morning in a makeup trailer. Bosch assumed they were celebrities of some sort, but it wasn't a realm he was familiar with and he could not identify any of them. He thought about leaning over to Janis Langwiser and asking but then thought better of it.

'We needed to clean up some last-minute details in my chambers,' the judge continued to the jury. 'But now we're ready to start. We'll begin with opening statements and I need to caution you that these are not statements of fact but rather statements about what each side *thinks* the facts are and what they will endeavor to prove during the course of the trial. These statements are not to be considered by you to contain evidence. All of that comes later on. So listen closely but keep an open mind because a lot is still coming down the pipe. Now we're going to start off with the prosecution and, as always, give the defendant the last word. Mr. Kretzler, you may begin.'

The lead prosecutor stood and moved to the lectern positioned between the two lawyers' tables. He nodded to the jury and identified himself as Roger Kretzler, deputy district attorney assigned to the special crimes section. He was a tall and gaunt prosecutor with a reddish beard beneath short dark hair and rimless glasses. He was at least forty-five years old. Bosch thought of him as not particularly likable but nevertheless very capable at his job. And the fact that he was still in the trenches prosecuting cases when others his age had left for the higher-paying corporate or criminal defense worlds made him all the more admirable. Bosch suspected he had no home life. On nights before the trial when a question about the investigation had come up and Bosch would be paged, the call-back number was always Kretzler's office line – no matter how late it was.

Kretzler identified his co-prosecutor as Janis Langwiser, also of the special crimes unit, and the lead investigator as LAPD detective third grade Harry Bosch.

'I am going to make this short and sweet so all the sooner we will be able to get to the facts, as Judge Houghton has correctly pointed out. Ladies and gentlemen, the case you will hear in this courtroom certainly has the trappings of celebrity. It has event status written all over it. Yes, the defendant, David N. Storey, is a man of power and position in this community, in this celebrity-driven age we live in. But if you strip away the trappings of power and glitter from the facts – as I promise we will do over the next few days – what you have here is something as basic as it is all too common in our society. A simple case of murder.'

Kretzler paused for effect. Bosch checked the jury. All eyes were fastened on the prosecutor.

'The man you see seated at the defense table, David N. Storey, went out with a twenty-three-year-old woman named Jody Krementz on the evening of last October twelfth. And after an evening that included the premiere of his latest film and a reception, he took her to his home in the Hollywood Hills where they engaged in consensual sexual intercourse. I don't believe you will find argument from the defense table about any of this. We are not here about that. But what happened during or after the sex is what brings us here today. On the morning of October thirteenth the body of Jody Krementz was found strangled and in her own bed in the small home she shared with another actress.'

Kretzler flipped up a page of the legal pad on the lectern in front of him even though it seemed clear to Bosch and probably everyone else that his statement was memorized and rehearsed.

'In the course of this trial the State of California will prove beyond a reasonable doubt that it was David Storey who took Jody Krementz's life in a moment of brutal sexual rage. He then moved or caused to be moved the body from his home to the victim's home. He arranged the body in such a way that the death might appear accidental. And following this, he used his power and position in an effort to thwart the investigation of the crime by the Los Angeles Police Department. Mr. Storey, who you will learn has a history of abusive behavior toward women, was so sure that he would walk away untouched from his crime that in a moment of—'

Kretzler chose this moment to turn from the lectern and look down upon the seated defendant with a disdainful look. Storey stared straight ahead unflinchingly and the prosecutor finally turned back to the jury.

'—shall we say candor, he actually boasted to the lead

investigator on the case, Detective Bosch, that he would do just that, walk away from his crime.'

Kretzler cleared his throat, a sign he was ready to bring it all home.

'We are here, ladies and gentlemen of the jury, to find justice for Jody Krementz. To make it our business that her murderer not walk away from his crime. The State of California asks, and I personally ask, that you listen carefully during the trial and weigh the evidence fairly. If you do that, we can be sure that justice will be served. For Jody Krementz. For all of us.'

He picked up the pad from the lectern and turned to move back to his seat. But then he stopped, as if a second thought had just occurred to him. Bosch saw it as a well-practiced move. He thought the jury would see it that way as well.

'I was just thinking that we all know it has been part of our recent history here in Los Angeles to see our police department put on trial in these high-profile cases. If you don't like the message, then by all means shoot the messenger. It is a favorite from the defense bar's bag of tricks. I want you all to promise yourselves that you will remain vigilant and keep your eyes on the prize, that prize being truth and justice. Don't be fooled. Don't be misdirected. Trust yourself on the truth and you'll find the way.'

He stepped over to his seat and sat down. Bosch noticed Langwiser reaching over and gripping Kretzler's forearm in a congratulatory gesture. It, too, was part of the well-practiced play.

The judge told the jurors that in light of the brevity of the prosecution's address the trial would proceed to the defense statement without a break. But the break came soon enough anyway when Fowkkes stood and moved to the lectern and proceeded to spend even less time than Kretzler addressing the jury.

'You know, ladies and gentlemen, all this talk about

shoot the messenger, don't shoot the messenger, well let me tell you something about that. Those fine words you got from Mr. Kretzler there at the end, well let me tell you every prosecutor in this building says those at the start of every trial in this place. I mean they must have 'em printed up on cards they carry in their wallets, it seems to me.'

Kretzler stood and objected to what he called such 'wild exaggeration' and Houghton admonished Fowkkes but then advised the prosecutor that he might make better use of his objections. Fowkkes moved on quickly.

'If I was outta line, I'm sorry. I know it's a touchy thing with prosecutors and police. But all I'm saying, folks, is that where there's smoke there's usually fire. And in the course of this trial we are going to try to find our way through the smoke. We may or may not come upon a fire but one thing I do know for sure we will come upon is the conclusion that this man—'

He turned and pointed strongly at his client.

'—this man, David N. Storey, is without a shadow of a doubt not guilty of the crime he is charged with. Yes, he is a man of power and position but, remember, it is not a crime to be so. Yes, he knows a few celebrities but, last time I checked *People* magazine, this too was not yet a crime. Now I think you may find elements of Mr. Storey's personal life and appetites to be offensive to you. I know I do. But remember that these do not constitute crimes that he is charged with in these proceedings. The crime here is *murder*. Nothing less and nothing more. It is a crime of which David Storey is *NOT* guilty. And no matter what Mr. Kretzler and Ms. Langwiser and Detective Bosch and their witnesses tell you, there is absolutely no evidence of guilt in this case.'

After Fowkkes bowed to the jury and sat down, Judge Houghton announced the trial would break for an early lunch before testimony began in the afternoon.

Bosch watched the jury file out through the door next to

the box. A few of them looked back over their shoulders at the courtroom. The juror who was last in line, a black woman of about fifty, looked directly back at Bosch. He lowered his eyes and then immediately wished he hadn't. When he looked back up she was gone.

16

McCaleb turned off the television when the trial broke for lunch. He didn't want to hear all the analysis of the talking heads. He thought the best point had been scored by the defense. Fowkkes had made a smooth move telling the jury that he, too, found his client's personal life and habits offensive. He was telling them that if he could stand it, so could they. He was reminding them that the case was about taking a life, not about how one lived a life.

He went back to preparing for his afternoon meeting with Jaye Winston. He'd gone back to the boat after breakfast and gathered up his files and books. Now, with a pair of scissors and some tape, he was putting together a presentation he hoped would not only impress Winston but convince her of something McCaleb was having a difficult time believing himself. In a way, putting together the presentation was a dress rehearsal for putting on a case. In that respect, McCaleb found the time he labored over what he would show and say to Winston very useful. It allowed him to see logic holes and prepare answers for the questions he knew Winston would ask.

While he considered exactly what he would say to Winston, she called on his cell phone.

'We might have a break on the owl. Maybe, maybe not.'

'What is it?'

'The distributor in Middleton, Ohio, thinks he knows where it came from. A place right here in Carson called Bird Barrier.'

'Why does he think that?'

'Because Kurt faxed photos of our bird, and the man he was dealing with in Ohio noticed that the bottom of the mold was open.'

'Okay. What's it mean?'

'Well, apparently these are shipped with the base enclosed so it can be filled with sand to make the bird stand up in wind and rain and whatever.'

'I understand.'

'Well, they have one subdistributor who orders the owls with the bottom of the base punched out. Bird Barrier. They take them with the open base because they fit the owls on top of some kind of gizmo that shrieks.'

'What do you mean, shrieks?'

'You know, like a real owl. I guess it helps really scare birds away. You know what Bird Barrier's slogan is? "Number one when it comes to birds going number two." Cute, huh? That's how they answer the phone there.'

McCaleb's mind was churning too quickly to register humor. He didn't laugh.

'This place is in Carson?'

'Right, not far from your marina. I've got to go to a meeting now but I was going to drop by before coming to see you. You want to meet there instead? Can you make it over in time?'

'That would be good. I'll be there.'

She gave him the address, which was about fifteen minutes from Cabrillo Marina, and they agreed to meet there at two. She said that the company's president, a man named Cameron Riddell, had agreed to see them.

'Are you bringing the owl with you?' McCaleb asked.

'Guess what, Terry? I've been a detective going on twelve years now. *And* I've had a brain even longer.'

'Sorry.'

'See you at two.'

After clicking off the phone, McCaleb took a leftover tamale out of the freezer, cooked it in the microwave and then wrapped it in foil and put it in his leather bag for eating while crossing the bay. He checked on his daughter, who was in the family room sleeping in the arms of their part-time nanny, Mrs. Perez. He touched the baby's cheek and left.

Bird Barrier was located in a commercial and upscale warehouse district that hugged the eastern side of the 405 Freeway just below the airfield where the Goodyear blimp was tethered. The blimp was in its place and McCaleb could see the leashes that held it straining against the afternoon wind coming in from the sea. When he pulled into the Bird Barrier lot he noticed an LTD with commercial hubs that he knew had to be Jaye Winston's car. He was right. She was sitting in a small waiting room when he came in through a glass door. On the floor next to her chair were a briefcase and a cardboard box sealed at the top with red tape marked EVIDENCE. She immediately got up and went to a reception window through which McCaleb could see a seated young man wearing a telephone headset.

'Can you tell Mr. Riddell we're both here?'

The young man, who was apparently on a call, nodded to her.

A few minutes later they were ushered into Cameron Riddell's office. McCaleb carried the box. Winston made the introductions, calling McCaleb her colleague. It was the truth but it also concealed his badgeless status.

Riddell was a pleasant-looking man in his mid-thirties who seemed anxious to help in the investigation. Winston put on a pair of latex gloves from her briefcase, then ran a key along the red tape on the box and opened it. She removed the owl and placed it on Riddell's desk.

'What can you tell us about this, Mr. Riddell?'

Riddell remained standing behind his desk and leaned across to look at the owl.

'I can't touch it?'

'Tell you what, why don't you put these on.'

Winston opened her briefcase and handed another pair of gloves from the cardboard dispenser to Riddell. McCaleb just watched, having decided that he would not jump in unless Winston asked him to or she made an obvious omission during the interview. Riddell struggled with the gloves, slowly pulling them on.

'Sorry,' Winston said. 'They're medium. You look like a large.'

Once he had the gloves on, Riddell picked the owl up with both hands and studied the underside of the base. He looked up into the hollow plastic mold and then held the bird directly in front of him, seemingly studying the painted eyes. He then placed it on the corner of the desk and went back around to his seat. He sat down and pressed a button on an intercom.

'Monique, it's Cameron. Can you go to the back and get one of the screeching owls off the line and bring it in to me? I need it now, too.'

'On my way.'

Riddell took off the gloves and flexed his fingers. He then looked at Winston, having sensed that she was the important one. He gestured to the owl.

'Yes, it's one of ours but it's been . . . I don't know what the word you would use would be. It's been changed, modified. We don't sell them like this.'

'How so?'

'Well, Monique's getting us one so you can see, but essentially this one has been repainted a little bit and the screeching mechanism has been removed. Also, we have a proprietary label we attach here at the base and that's gone.'

He pointed to the rear of the base.

'Let's start with the painting,' Winston said. 'What was done?'

Before Riddell answered, there was a single knock on the door and a woman came in carrying another owl which was wrapped in plastic. Riddell told her to put it down on the desk and remove the plastic. McCaleb noticed that she made a face when she saw the painted black eyes of the owl Winston had brought. Riddell thanked her and she left the office.

McCaleb studied the side-by-side owls. The evidence owl had been painted darker. The Bird Barrier owl had five colors on its feathers, including white and light blue, as well as plastic eyes with pupils rimmed in a reflective amber color. Also, the new owl was sitting atop a black plastic base.

'As you can see, the owl you brought has been repainted,' Riddell said. 'Especially the eyes. When you paint over them like that, you lose a lot of the effect. These are called foil-reflect eyes. The layer of foil in the plastic catches light and gives the eyes the appearance of movement.'

'So the birds think it is real.'

'Exactly. You lose that when you paint them like this.'

'We don't think the person that painted this was worried about birds. What else is different?'

Riddell shook his head.

'Just that the plumage has been darkened quite a bit. You can see that.'

'Yes. Now you said the mechanism has been removed. What mechanism?'

'We get these from Ohio and then we paint them and attach one of two mechanisms. What you see here is our standard model.'

Riddell picked the owl up and showed them the underside. The black plastic base swiveled as he turned it. It made a loud screeching sound.

'Hear the screech?'

'Yes, that's enough, Mr. Riddell.'

'Sorry. But you see, the owl sits on this base and reacts to the wind. As it turns, it emits the screech and sounds like a predator. Works well, as long as the wind is blowing. We also have a deluxe model with an electronic insert in the base. It contains a speaker that emits recorded sounds of predator birds like the hawk. No reliance on wind.'

'Can you get one without either one of the inserts?'

'Yes, you can purchase a replacement that fits over one of our proprietary bases. In case the owl is damaged or lost. With exposure, particularly in marine settings, the paint lasts two to three years and after that the owl might lose some of its effectiveness. You have to repaint or simply get a new owl. The reality is, the mold is the least expensive part of the ensemble.'

Winston looked over at McCaleb. He had nothing to add or ask in the line of questioning she was pursuing. He simply nodded at her and she turned back to Riddell.

'Okay, then, I think we want to see if there is a method of tracing this owl from this point to its eventual owner.'

Riddell looked at the owl for a long moment as if it might be able to answer the question itself.

'Well, that could be difficult. It's a commodity item. We sell several thousand a year. We ship to retail outlets as well as sell through mail-order catalogs and an internet website.'

He snapped his fingers.

'There is one thing that will cut it down some, though.'

'What's that?'

'They changed the mold last year. In China. They did some research and decided the horned owl was considered a higher threat to other birds than the round head. They changed to the horns.'

'I'm not quite following you, Mr. Riddell.'

He held up a finger as if to tell her to wait a moment. He then opened a desk drawer and dug through some paperwork. He came out with a catalog and quickly started turning pages. McCaleb saw that Bird Barrier's primary business was not plastic owls, but large-scale bird deterrent systems that encompassed netting and wire coils and spikes. Riddell found the page showing the plastic owls and turned the catalog so that Winston and McCaleb could view it.

'This is last year's catalog,' he said. 'You see the owl has the round head. The manufacturer changed last June, about seven months ago. Now we have these guys.'

He pointed to the two owls on the table.

'The feathering turns up into the two points, or ears, on the top of the head. The sales rep said these are called horns and that these types of owls are sometimes called devil owls.'

Winston glanced at McCaleb, who raised his eyebrows momentarily.

'So you're saying this owl we have was ordered or bought since June,' she said to Riddell.

'More like since August or maybe September. They changed in June but we probably didn't start receiving the new mold until late July. We also would have sold off our existing supplies of the round head first.'

Winston then questioned Riddell about sales records and determined that information from mail-order and website purchases was kept complete and current on the company's computer files. But point-of-purchase sales from shipments to major hardware and home and marine products retailers would obviously not be recorded. He turned to the computer on his desk and typed in a few commands. He then pointed to the screen, though McCaleb and Winston were not at angles where they could see it.

'All right, I asked for sales of those part numbers since August one,' he said.

'Part numbers?'

'Yes, for the standard and deluxe models and then the replacement molds. We show we self-shipped four hundred and fourteen total. We also shipped six hundred even to retailers.'

'And what you're telling us is that we can only trace, through you at least, the four hundred fourteen.'

'Correct.'

'You have the names of buyers and the addresses the owls were shipped to there?'

'Yes, we do.'

'And are you willing to share this information with us without need of a court order?'

Riddell frowned as if the question was absurd.

'You said you're working on a murder, right?'

'Right.'

'We don't require a court order. If we can help, we want to help.'

'That's very refreshing, Mr. Riddell.'

They sat in Winston's car and reviewed the computer printouts Riddell had given them. The evidence box containing the owl was between them on the seat. There were three printouts, divided by orders for the deluxe, standard or replacement owls. McCaleb asked to see the replacement list because his instincts told him the owl in Edward Gunn's apartment had been bought for the express purpose of playing a part in the murder scene and therefore no attachment mechanisms were needed. Additionally, the replacement owl was the least expensive.

'We better find something here,' Winston said as her eyes scanned the list of purchasers of the standard owl model. 'Because chasing down buyers through the Home Depots and other retailers is going to mean court orders and lawyers and – hey, the Getty's on here. They ordered four.'

McCaleb looked over at her and thought about that. Finally, he shrugged his shoulders and went back to his list. Winston moved on as well, continuing her listing of the difficulties they would face if they had to go to the retail outlets where the horned owl was sold. McCaleb tuned her out when he got to the third-to-last name on his list. He traced his finger from a name he recognized along a line on the printout detailing the address the owl was shipped to, method of payment, origin of purchase order and the name of the person receiving it if different from purchaser. His breath must have caught, because Winston picked up on his vibe.

'What?'

'I got something here.'

He held the printout across the seat to her and pointed to the line.

'This buyer. Jerome Van Aiken. He had one shipped the day before Christmas to Gunn's address and apartment number. The order was paid for by a money order.'

She took the printout from him and started reading the information.

'Shipped to the Sweetzer address but to a Lubbert Das care of Edward Gunn. Lubbert Das. Nobody named Lubbert Das came up in the investigation. I don't remember that name on the residents list of that building, either. I'll call Rohrshak to see if Gunn ever had a roommate with that name.'

'Don't bother. Lubbert Das never lived there.'

She looked up from the pages and over at him.

'You know who Lubbert Das is?'

'Sort of.'

Her brow creased deeply.

'Sort of? *Sort of?* What about Jerome Van Aiken?'

He nodded. Winston dropped the pages on the box between them. She looked at him with an expression that imparted both curiosity and annoyance.

'Well, Terry, I think it's about time you started telling me what you know.'

McCaleb nodded again and put his hand on the door handle.

'Why don't we go over to my boat? We can talk there.'

'Why don't we talk right here, right fucking now?'

McCaleb tried a small smile on her.

'Because it's what you'd call an audiovisual demonstration.'

He opened the door and got out, then looked back in at her.

'I'll see you over there, okay?'

She shook her head.

'You better have one hell of a profile worked out for me.'

Then he shook his head.

'I don't have a profile ready for you yet, Jaye.'

'Then what *do* you have?'

'A suspect.'

He closed the door then and he could hear her muffled curses as he walked to his car. As he crossed the parking lot a shadow fell over him and everything else. He looked up to see the Goodyear blimp cross overhead, totally eclipsing the sun.

17

They reconvened fifteen minutes later on *The Following Sea*. McCaleb got out some Cokes and told Winston to sit on the stuffed chair at the end of the coffee table in the salon. In the parking lot he had told her to bring the plastic owl with her to the boat. He now used two paper towels to remove it from its box and place it on the table in front of her. Winston watched him, her lips tight with annoyance. McCaleb told her he understood her anger at being manipulated on her own case but added that she would be back in control of things as soon as he presented his findings.

'All I can say, Terry, is that this better be fucking good.'

He remembered that he had once noted on the inside file flap on the first case he ever worked with her that she was prone to using profanity when under stress. He had also noted that she was smart and intuitive. He hoped now that those characteristics had not changed.

He stepped over to the counter where he had his presentation file waiting. He opened it and took the top sheet over to the coffee table. He pushed the Bird Barrier printout aside and put the sheet down at the base of the plastic owl.

'What do you think? This our bird?'

Winston leaned forward to study the color image he had put down. It was an enlarged detail from the Bosch painting *The Garden of Earthly Delights* showing the nude man embracing the dark owl with shining black eyes. He had cut it and other details from the Marijnissen book. He watched as Winston's eyes moved back and forth between the plastic owl and the detail from the painting.

'I'd say it's a match,' she finally said. 'Where'd you get this, the Getty? You should have told me about this yesterday, Terry. What the fuck is going on?'

McCaleb raised his hands in a calming gesture.

'I'll explain everything. Just let me show you this stuff the way I want to. Then I'll answer any question you ask.'

She waved a hand, indicating he could go on. He went over to the counter and got the second sheet and brought it over. He put it down in front of her.

'Same painter, different painting.'

She looked. It was a detail from *The Last Judgment* depicting the sinner bound in the reverse fetal position, waiting to be delivered to hell.

'Don't do this to me. Who painted these?'

'I'll tell you in a minute.'

He went back to the counter and the file.

'Is this guy still alive?' she called after him.

He walked the third sheet over and put it down on the table next to the other two.

'He's been dead about five hundred years.'

'Jesus.'

She picked up the third sheet and looked closely at it. It was the full copy of the *Seven Deadly Sins* tabletop.

'That's supposed to be God's eye seeing all the sins of the world,' McCaleb explained. 'You recognize the words in the center, running around the iris?'

'Beware, beware . . .' she whispered the translation. 'Oh, God, we've got a real nut here. Who is this?'

'One more. This one really falls into place now.'

He went back to the file for the fourth time and came back with another reproduction of a painting from the Bosch book. He handed it to her.

'It's called *The Stone Operation.* In medieval times it was believed by some that an operation to remove a stone from the brain was a cure for stupidity and deceit. Note the location of the incision.'

'I noted, I noted. Just like our guy. What's all of this around here?'

She traced the exterior of the circular painting with a finger. In the outer black margin were words that were once ornately painted in gold but which had deteriorated over time and were almost indecipherable.

'The translation is "Master, cut out the stone. My name is Lubbert Das." The critical literature on the painter who created this piece notes that in his time the name Lubbert was a derisive name applied to those who were perverted or stupid.'

Winston put the sheet down on top of the others and raised her hands, palms out.

'All right, Terry, enough. Who was the painter and who is this suspect you say you've come up with?'

McCaleb nodded. It was time.

'The painter's name was Jerome Van Aiken. He was Netherlandish, considered to be one of the greats of the Northern Renaissance. But his paintings were dark, full of monsters and phantasmic demons. Owls, too. Lots of owls. The literature suggests the owls found in his paintings symbolized everything from evil to doom to the fall of mankind.'

He sorted through the sheets on the coffee table and held up the detail of the man embracing the owl.

'This kind of says it all about him. Man's embracing of evil – the devil owl, to use Mr. Riddell's description – leads to the inevitable destiny of hell. Here's the whole painting.'

He went back to the file and brought to her the full copy of *The Garden of Earthly Delights.* He watched her eyes as she studied the images. He saw repulsion as well as fascination. He pointed out the four owls he had found in the painting, including the detail he had already shown her.

She suddenly pulled the sheet aside and looked at him.

'Wait a minute. I know I've seen this before. In a book or maybe an art class I took at CSUN. But I never heard of this Van Aiken, I don't think. He painted this?'

McCaleb nodded.

'*The Garden of Earthly Delights.* Van Aiken painted it but you've never heard of him because he wasn't known by his real name. He used the Latin version of Jerome and took the name of his hometown for a last name. He was known as Hieronymus Bosch.'

She just looked at him for a long moment as it all clicked together, the images he had shown her, the names on the printout, her knowledge of the Edward Gunn case.

'Bosch,' she said, almost as an expulsion of breath. 'Is Hieronymus . . .?'

She didn't finish. McCaleb nodded.

'Yeah, that's Harry's real name.'

They were both pacing in the salon now, heads down but careful not to collide. Talking in sprints, a bad but fast-moving jazz in their blood.

'This is too far out there, McCaleb. Do you know what you are saying?'

'I know exactly what I'm saying. And don't think that I didn't think long and hard about it before I said it. I consider him to be a friend, Jaye. There was . . . I don't know, at one time I thought we were a lot alike. But look at this stuff, look at the connections, the parallels. It fits. It all fits.'

He stopped and looked at her. She kept pacing.

'He's a cop! A homicide cop, for God's sake.'

'What, are you going to tell me it's beyond the realm because he's a cop? This is Los Angeles – the modern Garden of Earthly Delights. With all the same temptations and demons. You don't even have to go beyond the city limits for examples of cops crossing the line – dealing drugs, robbing banks, even murder.'

'I know, I know. It's just that . . .'

She didn't finish.

'At minimum it fits well enough that you know we have to take a good hard look.'

She stopped and looked back at him.

'We? Forget it, Terry. I asked you to take a look at the book, not run down the leads. You're out after this.'

'Look, if I didn't run some of this down you'd have nothing. This owl would still be sitting on top of that guy Rohrshak's other building.'

'I'll give you that. And thank you very much. But you're a civilian. You're out.'

'I'm not walking away, Jaye. If I'm the one who puts Bosch under the glass, then I'm not walking away from it.'

Winston sat down heavily in the chair.

'All right, can we talk about that when and if we come to it? I'm still not sold on this.'

'Good. I'm not either.'

'Well, you sure made a nice show of giving me the pictures and building your case.'

'All I am saying is that Harry Bosch is connected to this. And that cuts two ways. One, he did it. Two, he's been set up. He's been a cop a long time.'

'Twenty-five, thirty years. The list of people he's put in the penitentiary has got to be a yard long. And the ones who have been in and out is probably half the list. It'll take a fucking year to run all of them down.'

McCaleb nodded.

'And don't think he didn't know that.'

She looked up sharply at him. He started pacing again, his head down. After too long a silence he glanced up and saw her staring at him.

'What?'

'You really like Bosch for this, don't you? You know something else.'

'No, I don't. I am trying to stay open. All avenues of possibility need to be pursued.'

'Bullshit, you're driving down one avenue.'

McCaleb didn't answer. He felt enough guilt about it without Winston having to apply more.

'Okay,' she said. 'Then why don't you spell it out for me? And don't worry, I'm not going to hold it against you when you end up wrong.'

He stopped and looked at her.

'Come on, spell it out for me.'

McCaleb shook his head.

'I'm not all the way there yet. All I know is that what we have here is way, *way* beyond the realm of coincidence. So there has to be an explanation.'

'So tell me the explanation involving Bosch. I know you. You've been thinking about it.'

'All right, but remember, it's all theory at this point.'

'I'll remember. Go.'

'First of all, you start with *Detective* Hieronymus Bosch believing – no, make that *knowing* – that this guy, Edward Gunn, walked on a homicide. Okay, then you have Gunn turn up strangled and looking like a figure out of a picture by the *painter* Hieronymus Bosch. You throw in one plastic owl and at least a half dozen other connection points between the two Boschs, let alone the name, and there it is.'

'What's there? Those connections don't mean it was Bosch who did it. You said it yourself, someone could have set this up for us to find and put on Bosch.'

'I don't know what it is. Gut instinct, I guess. There's something about Bosch – something off the page.'

He remembered how Vosskuhler had described the paintings.

'A darkness more than night.'

'What's that supposed to mean?'

McCaleb waved off the question. He reached over and picked up the detail of the owl embraced by the man. He held it up in front of her face.

'Look at the darkness there. In the eyes. There's something about Harry that is the same.'

'Now you're getting downright spooky, Terry. What are you saying, in a previous life Harry Bosch was a painting? I mean, listen to what you are saying here.'

He put the sheet back down and stepped away from her, shaking his head.

'I don't know *how* to say it,' he said. 'There's just something there. A connection of some kind between them that is more than the name.'

He made a motion of waving away the thought.

'All right, then let's move on,' Winston said. 'Why now, Terry? If it is Bosch, why now? And why Gunn? He walked away from him six years ago.'

'It's interesting that you say walked away from *him* and not justice.'

'I didn't mean anything by it. You just like to take—'

'Why now? Who knows? But there was that re-encounter the night before in the drunk tank and before that there was the time in October and it goes further back. Whenever this guy ended up in the can Bosch was there.'

'But on that last night Gunn was too drunk to talk.'

'Says who?'

She nodded. They only had Bosch's account of the drunk-tank encounter.

'All right, fine. But why Gunn? I mean, I don't want to put a qualitative judgment on a murderer or his victims but, come on, the guy stabbed a prostitute in a Hollywood hot sheet hotel. We all know that some count more than others and this one couldn't have counted for much. If you read the book, you saw – her own family didn't even care about her.'

'Then there's something missing, something else that we don't know. Because Harry cared. I don't think he's the kind who ever counts one case, one person more important than another, anyway. But there's something about

Gunn we don't know yet. There has to be – six years ago it was enough for Harry to shove his lieutenant through a window and take a suspension for it. It was enough for him to visit Gunn every time he got hooked up and put in a cell.'

McCaleb nodded to himself.

'We need to find the trigger. The stressor. The thing that forced the action now as opposed to a year ago, two years ago, whenever.'

Winston abruptly stood up.

'Would you stop saying "we"? And, you know, there is something you are conveniently missing here. Why would this man, this veteran cop and homicide detective, kill this guy and leave all of these clues leading back to himself? It makes no sense – not with Harry Bosch. He'd be too smart for that.'

'Only from this side of it. These things may only seem obvious now that we have discovered them. And you are forgetting the act of murder itself is evidence of aberrant thinking, of a dissembling personality. If Harry Bosch has veered off the path and crashed into the ditch – into the abyss – then we can't assume anything about his thinking or planning of a murder. His leaving of these markers could be symptomatic.'

She waved off his explanation.

'That's the Quantico dance there. Too much mumbo jumbo.'

Winston picked the copy of *The Garden of Earthly Delights* off the table and studied it.

'I talked to Harry about this case two weeks ago,' she said. 'You talked to him yesterday. He wasn't exactly climbing the walls and foaming at the mouth. And look at this trial he's riding now. He's cool, calm and has his shit together. Know what some of the guys in the office call him, the ones who know him? The Marlboro Man.'

'Yeah, well, he stopped smoking. And maybe this Storey

case was the stressor. A lot of pressure. It's gotta come out someplace.'

McCaleb could tell she wasn't listening. Her eyes had caught on something in the painting. She dropped the sheet and picked up the detail of the dark owl embraced by the nude man.

'Let me ask you something,' she said. 'If our guy sent the owl directly from that warehouse to our victim, then how the fuck did it get this nice custom paint job?'

McCaleb nodded.

'Good question. He must've painted it right there in the apartment. Maybe while watching Gunn try to stay alive.'

'There was no paint like this found in the apartment. And we checked the building's dumpster, too. I saw no paint.'

'He took it with him, got rid of it somewhere else.'

'Or maybe plans to use it again on the next one.'

She paused and thought for a long moment. McCaleb waited.

'So what do we do?' she finally asked.

'So it's "we" now?'

'For now. I changed my mind. I can't take this inside. Too dangerous. If it's wrong I could kiss everything goodbye.'

McCaleb nodded.

'Do you and your partner have other cases?'

'We've got three open files, including this one.'

'Well, put him on one of the others while you work this one – with me. We work on Bosch until we have something solid – one way or the other – that you can take in and make official.'

'And what do I do, call up Harry Bosch and tell him I need to talk to him because he's a suspect in a murder?'

'I'll take Bosch first. It will be less obvious if I make the first run. Let me get a feel for him and, who knows, maybe my current instincts will be wrong. Or maybe I'll find the trigger.'

'That's easier said than done. We move too close and he'll know. I don't want this blowing up in our faces – my face, in particular.'

'That's where I can be an advantage.'

'Yeah? How so?'

'I'm not a cop. I'll be able to get closer to him. I need to get inside his house, see how he lives. Meantime, you—'

'Wait a minute. You're not talking about breaking into his house. I can't be a party to that.'

'No, nothing illegal.'

'Then how are you going to get in?'

'Knock on the door.'

'Good luck. What were you going to say? Meantime, I do what?'

'You work the outside line, the obvious stuff. Trace down the money order for the owl. Find out more about Gunn and the murder six years ago. Find out about the incident between Harry and his old lieutenant – and find out about the lieutenant. Harry said the guy went out one night and ended up dead in a tunnel.'

'Damn, I remember that. That was related to Gunn?'

'I don't know. But Bosch made some kind of elliptical reference to it yesterday.'

'I can pull stuff on it and I can ask questions about the other stuff. But any one of these moves could get back to Bosch.'

McCaleb nodded. He thought it was a risk that had to be taken.

'You know anybody who knows him?' he said.

She shook her head in annoyance.

'Look, don't you remember? Cops are paranoid people. The minute I ask one question about Harry Bosch, people are going to know what we are doing.'

'Not necessarily. Use the Storey case. It's high profile. Maybe you've been watching the guy on TV and he doesn't look so good. "Is he all right? What's going on with him?" Like that. Make it like you're gossiping.'

She didn't look mollified. She stepped over to the sliding door and looked out across the marina. She leaned her forehead against the glass.

'I know his former partner,' she said. 'There's an informal group of women who get together once a month. We all work homicide from all the local departments. About a dozen of us. Harry's old partner Kiz Rider just got moved from Hollywood to Robbery–Homicide. The big time. But I think they were close. He was kind of a mentor. I might be able to hit on her. If I use a little finesse.'

McCaleb nodded and thought of something.

'Harry told me he was divorced. I don't know how long ago but you could ask Rider about him like, you know, you're interested and what's he like, that sort of thing. You ask like that and she might give you the real lowdown.'

Winston looked away from the slider and back at McCaleb.

'Yeah, that will make us good friends when she finds out it was all bullshit and I was setting up on her ex-partner – her mentor.'

'If she's a good cop she'll understand. You had to clear him or bag him and either way you wanted to do it as quietly as possible.'

Winston looked back out the door.

'I'm going to need deniability on this.'

'Meaning?'

'Meaning if we do this and you go in there and it all blows up, I need to be able to walk away.'

McCaleb nodded. He wished she hadn't said it but he could see her need to protect herself.

'I'm just telling you up front, Terry. If it all goes to hell it's going to look like you overstepped, that I asked you to take a look at the book and you went off on your own. I'm sorry but I have to protect myself here.'

'I understand, Jaye. I can live with it. I'll take my chances.'

18

Winston was silent for a long time while she stared out the salon's door. McCaleb sensed that she was building up to something and just waited.

'I'll tell you a story about Harry Bosch,' she finally said. 'The first time I ever met him was about four years ago. It was a joint case. Two kidnap–murders. The one in Hollywood was his, the one in West Hollywood was mine. Young women, girls really. Physical evidence tied the cases together. We were basically working them separately but would meet for lunch every Wednesday to compare notes.'

'Did you profile it?'

'Yeah. This was when Maggie Griffin was still out here at the bureau. She worked something up for us. The usual. Anyway, things heated up when a third one disappeared. A seventeen-year-old this time. The evidence from the first two indicated the doer was keeping them alive four or five days before he got tired of them and killed them. So we had a big clock on us. We got reinforcements and we were running down common denominators.'

McCaleb nodded. It sounded as though they were going by the book on tracking a serial.

'A long shot came up,' she said. 'All three of the victims used the same dry cleaner on Santa Monica near La Cienega. The latest – the girl – had a summer job at Universal and took her uniforms in for dry cleaning. Anyway, before we even went in there to the management we went into the employee parking lot and took down tags to run, just in case we got something before we had to go in and announce ourselves. And we got a hit. The manager himself. He'd gotten popped about ten years before on a public indecency. We pulled the jacket and it was a garden-variety flasher case. He pulled up in a car next to a bus stop and opened the door so the woman on the bench could get a look at his johnson. Turned out she was an undercover – they knew a wagger was working the neighborhood and put out decoys. Anyway, he got probation and counseling. He lied about it on his application at the job and over the years worked his way up to manager of the shop.'

'Higher job, higher stress, higher level of offense.'

'That's what we thought. But we didn't have any evidence. So Bosch had an idea. He said all of us – me, him and our partners – would go see this guy, his name was Hagen, at his home. He said an FBI agent once told him to always brace a suspect at home if you get the chance because sometimes you get more from the surroundings than you get from their mouths.'

McCaleb suppressed a smile. It had been a lesson Bosch learned on the Cielo Azul case.

'So we followed Hagen home. He lived over in Los Feliz in a big old rundown house off Franklin. This was the fourth day of the third woman's disappearance, so we knew we were running out of time. We knocked on his door and the plan was to act like we didn't know about his record and that we were just there to enlist his help in checking out employees in the shop. You know, to see how he reacted or if he made a slip.'

'Right.'

'Well, we were in there in this guy's living room and I was doing most of the talking because Bosch wanted to see how the guy took it. You know, a woman in control. And we weren't there but five minutes when Bosch suddenly stood up and said, "It's him. She's here somewhere." And when he said that, Hagen up and bolted for the door. He didn't get far.'

'Was it a bluff or part of the plan?'

'Neither. Bosch just knew. On this little table next to the couch was one of those baby monitor things, you know? Bosch saw that and he just knew. It was the wrong end. It was the transmitter part. It meant the receiver was somewhere else. If you have a kid it's the other way around. You listen in the living room for noise from the baby room. But this was backwards. The profile from Griffin said this guy was a controller, that he likely used verbal coercion on his victim. Bosch saw that transmitter and something just clicked; this guy had her somewhere and got off on talking to her.'

'He was right?'

'Dead on. We found her in the garage in an unplugged freezer with three air holes drilled in it. It was like a coffin. The receiver part of the monitor was in there with her. She later told us that Hagen talked to her incessantly whenever he was in the house. He sang to her, too. Top forties. He'd change the words and sing about raping and killing her.'

McCaleb nodded. He wished he had been there on the case, for he knew what Bosch had felt, that sudden moment of coalescing, when the atoms smash together. When you just knew. A moment as thrilling as it was dreadful. The moment every homicide detective privately lives for.

'The reason I tell this story is because of what Bosch did and said after. Once we had Hagen in the back seat of one of the cars and started searching the house, Bosch stayed in the living room with that baby monitor. He turned it on and he spoke to her. He never stopped until we found her. He said, "Jennifer, we're here. It's all right, Jennifer, we're coming. You're safe and we're coming for you. Nobody's going to hurt you." He never stopped talking to her, soothing her like that.'

She stopped for a long moment and McCaleb saw her eyes were on the memory.

'After we found her we all felt so good. It was the best high I've ever had on this job. I went to Bosch and said, "You must have kids. You spoke to her like she was one of your own." And he just shook his head and said no. He said, "I just know what it's like to be alone and in the dark." Then he sort of walked away.'

She looked from the door back at McCaleb.

'Your talking about darkness reminded me of that.'

He nodded.

'What do we do if we come to a point that we know flat out that it was him?' she asked, her face turned back to the glass.

McCaleb answered quickly so that he wouldn't have to think about the question.

'I don't know,' he said.

After Winston had put the plastic owl back in the evidence box, gathered all of the pages he had shown her and left, McCaleb stood at the sliding door and watched her make her way up the ramp to the gate. He checked his watch and saw there was a lot of time before he needed to get ready for the night. He decided he would watch some of the trial on *Court TV*.

He looked back out the door and saw Winston putting the evidence box into the trunk of her car. Behind him somebody cleared his throat. McCaleb abruptly turned and there was Buddy Lockridge in the stairwell looking up at him from the lower deck. He had a pile of clothes clasped in his arms.

'Buddy, what the hell are you doing?'

'Man, that's one weird case you're working on.'

'I said *what* the hell are you doing?'

'I was going to do laundry and I came over here 'cause half my stuff was down in the cabin. Then you two showed up and when you started talking I knew I couldn't come up.'

He held the pile of clothes in his arms up as proof of his story.

'So I just sat down there on the bed and waited.'

'And listened to everything we said.'

'It's a crazy case, man. What are you going to do? I've seen that Bosch guy on *Court TV*. He kind of looks like he's wound a little too tight.'

'I know what I'm not going to do. I'm not going to talk about this with you.'

He pointed to the glass door.

'Leave, Buddy, and don't tell a word of this to anybody. You understand me?'

'Sure, I understand. I was just—'

'Leaving.'

'Sorry, man.'

'So am I.'

McCaleb opened the slider and Lockridge walked out like a dog with his tail between his legs. McCaleb had to hold himself back from kicking him in the rear. Instead he angrily slid the door closed and it banged loudly in its frame. He stood there looking out through the glass until he saw Lockridge make it all the way up the ramp and over to the facilities building where there was a coin laundry.

His eavesdropping had compromised the investigation. McCaleb knew he should page Winston immediately and tell her, see how she wanted to handle it. But he let it go. The truth was, he didn't want to make any move that might take him out of the investigation.

19

After putting his hand on the Bible and promising the whole truth, Harry Bosch took a seat in the witness chair and glanced up at the camera mounted on the wall above the jury box. The eye of the world was upon him, he knew. The trial was being broadcast live on *Court TV* and locally on Channel 9. He tried to give no appearance of nervousness. But the fact was that more than the jurors would be studying him and judging his performance and personality. It was the first time in many years of testifying in criminal trials that he did not feel totally at ease. Being on the side of the truth was not a comfort when he knew the truth had to run a treacherous obstacle course set before it by a wealthy, connected defendant and his wealthy, connected attorney.

He put the blue binder – the murder book – down on the front ledge of the witness box and pulled the microphone toward him, creating a high-pitched squeal that hurt every set of ears in the courtroom.

'Detective Bosch, please don't touch the microphone,' Judge Houghton intoned.

'Sorry, Your Honor.'

A deputy sheriff who acted as the judge's bailiff came over to the witness box, turned the microphone off and adjusted its location. When Bosch nodded at its new position, the bailiff turned it back on. The judge's clerk then asked Bosch to state his full, formal name and spell it for the record.

'Very well,' the judge said after Bosch finished. 'Ms. Langwiser?'

Deputy District Attorney Janis Langwiser got up from the prosecution table and went to the attorney's lectern. She carried a yellow legal tablet with her questions on it. She was second seat at the prosecution table but had worked with the investigators since the start of the case. It had been decided that she would handle Bosch's testimony.

Langwiser was a young up-and-coming lawyer in the DA's office. In the span of a few short years she had risen from a position of filing cases for more experienced lawyers in the office to handle to taking them all the way to court herself. Bosch had worked with her before on a politically sensitive and treacherous case known as the Angels Flight murders. The experience resulted in his recommendation of her as second chair to Kretzler. Since working with her again, Bosch had found his earlier impressions were well founded. She had complete command and recall of the facts of the case. While most other lawyers would have to sift through evidence reports to locate a piece of information, she would have the information and its location in the reports memorized. But her skill was not confined to the minutiae of the case. She never took her eye off the big picture – the fact that all their efforts were focused on putting David Storey away for good.

'Good afternoon, Detective Bosch,' she began. 'Could you please tell the jury a bit about your career as a police officer.'

Bosch cleared his throat.

'Yes. I've been with the Los Angeles Police Department twenty-eight years. I have spent more than half of that time investigating homicides. I am a detective three assigned to the homicide squad of the Hollywood Division.'

'What does "detective three" mean?'

'It means detective third grade. It is the highest detective rank, equivalent to sergeant, but there are no detective sergeants in the LAPD. From detective three the next rank up would be detective lieutenant.'

'How many homicides would you say you have investigated in your career?'

'I don't keep track. I would say at least a few hundred in fifteen years.'

'A few *hundred*.'

Langwiser looked over at the jury when she stressed the last word.

'Give or take a few.'

'And as a detective three you are currently a supervisor on the homicide squad?'

'I have some supervisory duties. I am also the lead officer on a three-person team that handles homicide investigations.'

'As such you were in charge of the team that was called to the scene of a homicide on October thirteenth of last year, correct?'

'That is correct.'

Bosch glanced over at the defense table. David Storey had his head down and was using his felt-tip pen to draw on the sketch pad. He'd been doing it since jury selection began. Bosch's eyes traveled to the defendant's attorney and locked on those of J. Reason Fowkkes. Bosch held the stare until Langwiser asked her next question.

'This was the murder of Donatella Speers?'

Bosch looked back over at Langwiser.

'Correct. That was the name she used.'

'It was not her real name?'

'It was her stage name, I guess you would call it. She was an actress. She changed her name. Her real name was Jody Krementz.'

The judge interrupted and asked Bosch to spell the names for the court reporter, then Langwiser continued.

'Tell us the circumstances of the call out. Walk us

through it, Detective Bosch. Where were you, what were you doing, how did this become your case?'

Bosch cleared his throat and had reached to the microphone to pull it closer when he remembered what happened the last time. He left the microphone where it was and leaned forward to it.

'My two partners and I were eating lunch at a restaurant called Musso and Frank's on Hollywood Boulevard. It was Friday and we usually eat there if we have the time. At eleven forty-eight my pager went off. I recognized the number as belonging to my supervisor, Lieutenant Grace Billets. While I was calling her, the pagers of my partners, Jerry Edgar and Kizmin Rider, also went off. At that point we knew we had probably drawn a case. I got ahold of Lieutenant Billets and she directed my team to one-thousand-one Nichols Canyon Road, where patrol officers had earlier responded along with paramedics to an emergency call at that location. They reported a young woman was found dead in her bed under suspicious circumstances.'

'You then went to the address?'

'No. I had driven all three of us to Musso's. So I drove back to the Hollywood station, which is a few blocks away, and dropped off my partners so they could get their own vehicles. Then all three of us proceeded separately to the address. You never know where you might have to go from a crime scene. It's good procedure for each detective to have his or her own car.'

'At this time did you know who the victim was or what the suspicious circumstances of her death were?'

'No, I did not.'

'What did you find when you got there?'

'It was a small two-bedroom house overlooking the canyon. Two patrol cars were on the scene. The paramedics had already left once it was determined the victim was dead. Inside the house were two patrol officers and a patrol sergeant. In the living room there was a woman seated on the couch. She was crying. She was introduced to me as Jane Gilley. She shared the house with Ms. Krementz.'

Bosch stopped there and waited for a question. Langwiser was bent over the prosecution table whispering to her co-prosecutor, Roger Kretzler.

'Ms. Langwiser, does that conclude your questioning of Detective Bosch?' Judge Houghton asked.

Langwiser jerked upright, not having noticed that Bosch had stopped.

'No, Your Honor.'

She moved back to the lectern.

'Go on, Detective Bosch, tell us what happened after you entered the house.'

'I spoke to Sergeant Kim and he informed me that there was a young woman who was deceased in her bed in the bedroom to the right rear of the house. He introduced the woman on the couch and he said that his people had backed out of the bedroom without disturbing anything once the paramedics determined that the victim was dead. I then went down the short hallway to the bedroom and entered.'

'What did you find in there?'

'I saw the victim in the bed. She was a white female of slim build and blond hair. Her identification would later be confirmed as Jody Krementz, age twenty-three.'

Langwiser asked permission to show a set of photographs to Bosch. Houghton allowed it and Bosch identified the police evidence photos as being that of the victim in situ – as the body had been seen at first by police. The body was face up. The bedclothes were pulled to the side to reveal the body to be nude with the legs spread about two feet apart at the knees. The large breasts held their full shape despite the body being in a horizontal position, an indication of breast implants. The left arm was extended over the stomach. The palm of the left hand covered the pubic region. Two fingers of the left hand penetrated the vagina.

The victim's eyes were closed and her head rested on a pillow but at a sharp angle to her neck. Wrapped tightly around her neck was a yellow scarf with one end looped up and over the top crossbar of the bed's headboard. The end of the scarf came off the crossbar and extended to the victim's right hand on the pillow above her head. The end of the silk scarf was wrapped several times around the hand.

The photographs were in color. A purplish-red bruise could be seen on the victim's neck where the scarf had tightened against the skin. There was a rouge-like discoloration in and around the eye sockets. There was also a bluish discoloration running down the complete left side of the body, including the left arm and leg.

After Bosch identified the photographs as being of Jody Krementz in situ, Langwiser asked that they be shown to the jury. J. Reason Fowkkes objected, stating that the photos would be highly inflammatory and prejudicial for jurors to see. The judge overruled the objection but told Langwiser to choose just one photo which would be representative of the lot. Langwiser chose the photo taken closest to the victim and it was handed to a man who sat in the first seat of the jury. While the photo was slowly passed from juror to juror and then to the alternates, Bosch watched their faces tighten with shock and horror. He pushed back on his seat and drank from a paper cup of water. After he drained it he caught the eye of the sheriff's deputy and signaled for a refill. He then pulled himself back close to the microphone.

After the photo made its way through the jury, it was delivered to the clerk. It would be returned to the jurors, along with all other exhibits presented during the trial, during deliberation of a verdict.

Bosch watched Langwiser return to the lectern to continue the questioning. He knew she was nervous.

They'd had lunch together in the basement cafeteria of the other court building and she had voiced her concerns. Though she was second seat to Kretzler, it was a big trial with potential career enhancing or destroying aspects for both of them.

She checked her legal pad before going on.

'Detective Bosch, did there come a time after you had inspected the body that you declared the death to be subject to a homicide investigation?'

'Right away – before my partners even got there.'

'Why is that? Did it not appear to be an accidental death?'

'No, it—'

'Ms. Langwiser,' Judge Houghton interrupted. 'One question at a time, please.'

'Sorry, Your Honor. Detective, did it not appear to you that the woman may have accidentally killed herself?'

'No, it did not. It appeared to me that someone attempted to make it look that way.'

Langwiser looked down at her pad for a long moment before going on. Bosch was pretty sure the pause was planned, now that the photograph and his testimony had secured the full attention of the jury.

'Detective, are you familiar with the term autoerotic asphyxia?'

'Yes, I am.'

'Could you please explain it to the jury?'

Fowkkes stood up and objected.

'Y'Honor, Detective Bosch may be a lot of things but there has been no proffer made to the court that he is an expert in human sexuality.'

There was a murmur of quiet laughter in the courtroom. Bosch saw a couple of the jurors suppress smiles. Houghton hit his gavel once and looked at Langwiser.

'What about that, Ms. Langwiser?'

'Your Honor, I can make a proffer.'

'Proceed.'

'Detective Bosch, you said you have worked hundreds of homicides. Have you investigated deaths that turned out not to be caused by homicide?'

'Yes, probably hundreds of those as well. Accidental deaths, suicides, even deaths by natural causes. It is routine for a homicide detective to be called out to a death scene by patrol officers to help in making a determination as to whether a death should be investigated as a homicide. This is what happened in this case. The patrol officers and their sergeant weren't sure what they had. They called it in as suspicious and my team got the call out.'

'Have you ever been called out or investigated a death that was ruled, either by you or the medical examiner's office, an accidental death by autoerotic asphyxia?'

'Yes.'

Fowkkes stood up again.

'Same objection, Y'Honor. This is leading to an area where Detective Bosch is not an expert.'

'Your Honor,' Langwiser said. 'It has clearly been established that Detective Bosch is an expert in the investigation of death – that would include all kinds. He has seen this before. He can testify to it.'

There was a note of exasperation in her voice. Bosch thought it was intended for the jury, not Houghton. It was a subliminal way of communicating to the twelve that she wanted to get at the truth, while others wanted to block the way.

'I tend to agree, Mr. Fowkkes,' Houghton said after a slight pause. 'Objections to this line of questioning are overruled. Proceed, Ms. Langwiser.'

'Thank you, Your Honor. So then, Detective Bosch, you are familiar with cases of autoerotic asphyxia?'

'Yes, I have worked on three or four. I have also studied the literature on the subject. It is referenced in books on homicide investigation techniques. I have also read summaries of in-depth studies conducted by the FBI and others.'

'Was this before this case occurred?'

'Yes, before.'

'What is autoerotic asphyxia? How does it occur?'

'Ms. Langwiser,' the judge began.

'Sorry, Your Honor. Restating. What is autoerotic asphyxia, Detective Bosch?'

Bosch took a drink of water, using the time to draw his thoughts together. They had gone over these questions during lunch.

'It is an accidental death. It occurs when the victim attempts to increase sexual sensations during masturbation by cutting off or disrupting the flow of arterial blood to the brain. This is usually done with a form of ligature around the neck. The tightening of the ligature results inhypoxia – the diminishing of oxygenation of the brain. It is believed by people who . . . uh, practice this that hypoxia – the light-headedness that ensues – heightens masturbatory sensations. However, it can lead to accidental death if the victim goes too far, to the point where he damages the carotid arteries and/or passes out with the ligature still tightly in place and asphyxiates.'

'You said "he," Detective. But in this case the victim is a woman.'

'This case does not involve autoerotic asphyxia. The cases I have seen and investigated involving this form of death all involved male victims.'

'Are you saying that in this case the death was made to look like autoerotic asphyxia?'

'Yes, that was my immediate conclusion. It remains so today.'

Langwiser nodded and paused. Bosch sipped some water. As he brought the cup up to his mouth he glanced at the jury. Everyone in the box seemed to be paying close attention.

'Walk us through it, Detective. What led you to that conclusion?'

'Can I refer to my reports?'

'Please.'

Bosch opened the binder in front of him. The first four pages were the OIR – the original incident report. He turned to the fourth page, which included the lead officer's summary. The report had actually been typed out by Kiz Rider, though Bosch was the LO on the case. He quickly scanned the summary to refresh his mind, then looked up at the jury.

'Several things contradicted the death being an accident caused by autoerotic asphyxia. First off, I was immediately concerned because statistically it is rare that this occurs with female victims. It is not one hundred percent males but it is close. This knowledge made me pay very close attention to the body and the crime scene.'

'Would it be fair to say you were immediately skeptical of the crime scene?'

'Yes, that would be fair.'

'Okay, go on. What else concerned you?'

'The ligature. In almost all cases involving this that I have been aware of firsthand or through the literature on the subject, the victim uses some sort of padding around the neck to prevent bruising or breaking of the skin. Most often a piece of heavy clothing like a sweater or a towel is wrapped around the neck. The ligature is then wrapped around this padding. It prevents the ligature from making a contusion line running around the neck. In this case there was no padding.'

'And what did that mean to you?'

'Well, it didn't make sense if you looked at it from the victim's viewpoint. I mean, if you were to assume that she had engaged in this activity, then the scene didn't make sense. It would mean that she didn't use any kind of padding because she didn't mind having the bruises on her neck. This to me was a contradiction between what we had there at the scene and common sense. Add in that she was an actress – which I knew right away because she had a stack of head shots on the bureau – and the contradiction was even greater. She relied on her physical presence and attributes while seeking acting work. That she would knowingly engage in an activity, sexual or otherwise, that would leave visible bruises on her neck – I just didn't buy it. That and other things led me to conclude the scene was a setup.'

Bosch looked over at the defense table. Storey still had his head down and was working on the sketch pad as though he were sitting on a bench in a park somewhere. Bosch noticed Fowkkes was writing on a legal tablet. Harry wondered if he had said something in his last answer that could somehow be turned against him. He knew Fowkkes was an expert in taking phrases of testimony and giving them new meaning when taken out of context.

'What other things added to this conclusion?' Langwiser asked him.

Bosch looked at the OIR summary page again.

'The biggest single thing was the indication from postmortem lividity that the body had been moved.'

'In layman's terms, Detective, what does postmortem lividity mean?'

'When the heart ceases to pump blood through the body, the blood then settles in the lower half of the body, depending on the position of the body. Over time it creates a bruising effect on the skin. If the body is moved, the bruising remains in the original position because the blood has coagulated. Over time the bruising becomes more apparent.'

'What happened in this case?'

'In this case there was clear indication that the blood had settled in the left side of the body, meaning the victim's body had been lying on the left side at or shortly after the time of death.'

'However, that was not the way the body was found, correct?'

'That is correct. The body was found in the supine position – lying on the back.'

'What did you conclude from this?'

'That the body had been moved after death. That the woman had been positioned on her back as part of the setup to make her death look like an autoerotic asphyxiation.'

'What did you think was the cause of death?'

'At that point I wasn't sure. I just didn't think it was as presented. The bruising on the neck beneath the ligature led me to believe we were looking at a strangulation – just not at her own hands.'

'At what point did your partners arrive on the scene?'

'While I was making the initial observations of the body and crime scene.'

'Did they come to the same conclusions as you?'

Fowkkes objected, saying the question called for an answer that would be hearsay. The judge sustained the objection. Bosch knew it was a minor point. If Langwiser wanted the conclusions of Edgar and Rider on the record, she could just call them to testify.

'Did you attend the autopsy of Jody Krementz's body?'

'Yes, I did.' He flipped through the binder until he found the autopsy protocol. 'On October seventeenth. It was conducted by Dr. Teresa Corazón, chief of the medical examiner's office.'

'Was a cause of death determined by Dr. Corazón during autopsy?'

'Yes, the cause of death was asphyxiation. She was strangled.'

'By ligature?'

'Yes.'

'Now doesn't this contradict your theory that the death was not caused by autoerotic asphyxiation?'

'No, it confirmed it. The pose of autoerotic asphyxiation was used to cover the strangulation murder of the victim. The interior damage to both carotid arteries, to the muscular tissue of the neck and the hyoid bone, which was crushed, led Dr. Corazón to confirm that death was at the hand of another. The damage was too great to be knowingly self-inflicted.'

Bosch realized he was holding a hand to his neck as he described the injuries. He dropped it back down to his lap.

'Did the medical examiner find any independent evidence of homicide?'

He nodded.

'Yes, examination of the victim's mouth determined that there was a deep laceration caused by biting on the tongue. Such injury is common in cases of strangulation.'

Langwiser flipped a page over on her tablet.

'Okay, Detective Bosch, let's go back to the crime scene. Did you or your partners interview Jane Gilley?'

'Yes, I did. Along with Detective Rider.'

'From that interview were you able to ascertain where the victim had been in the twenty-four hours prior to the discovery of her death?'

'Yes, we first determined that she had met the defendant several days earlier at a coffee shop. He invited her to attend a premiere of a movie as his date on the night of October twelfth at the Chinese Theater in Hollywood. He picked her up between seven and seven-thirty that night. Ms. Gilley watched from a window in the house and identified the defendant.'

'Did Ms. Gilley know when Ms. Krementz returned that night?'

'No. Ms. Gilley left the house shortly after Ms. Krementz went on her date and spent the night elsewhere. Consequently, she did not know when her roommate returned home. It was when Ms. Gilley returned to the house at eleven A.M. on October thirteenth that she discovered Ms. Krementz's body.'

'What was the name of the movie which was premiered the night before?'

'It was called *Dead Point*.'

'And who directed it?'

'David Storey.'

Langwiser waited through a long pause before looking at her watch and then up at the judge.

'Your Honor,' she said, 'I am going to move into a new line of questioning now with Detective Bosch. If appropriate, this might be the best time to break for the day.'

Houghton pulled back the baggy black sleeve of his robe and looked at his watch. Bosch looked at his. It was a quarter to four.

'Okay, Ms. Langwiser, we'll adjourn until nine o'clock tomorrow morning.'

Houghton told Bosch he could step down from the witness stand. He then admonished the jurors not to read newspaper accounts or watch TV reports on the trial. Everyone stood as the jurors filed out. Bosch, who was now standing next to Langwiser at the prosecution table, glanced over at the defense side. David Storey was looking at him. His face betrayed no emotion at all. But Bosch thought he saw something in his pale blue eyes. He wasn't sure but he thought it was mirth.

Bosch was the first to look away.

20

After the courtroom emptied, Bosch conferred with Langwiser and Kretzler about their missing witness.

'Anything yet?' Kretzler asked. 'Depending on how long John Reason keeps you up there, we're going to need her tomorrow afternoon or the next morning.'

'Nothing yet,' Bosch said. 'But I've got something in the works. In fact, I better get going.'

'I don't like this,' Kretzler said. 'This could blow up. If she's not coming in, there's a reason. I've never been a hundred percent on her story.'

'Storey could have gotten to her,' Bosch offered.

'We need her,' Langwiser said. 'It shows pattern. You have to find her.'

'I'm on it.'

He got up from the table to leave.

'Good luck, Harry,' Langwiser said. 'And, by the way, so far I think you're doing very well up there.'

Bosch nodded.

'The calm before the storm.'

On his way down the hall to the elevators Bosch was approached by one of the reporters. He didn't know his name but he recognized him from the press seats in the courtroom.

'Detective Bosch?'

Bosch kept walking.

'Look, I've told everybody, I'm not commenting until the trial is over. I'm sorry. You'll have to get—'

'No, that's okay. I just wanted to see if you hooked up with Terry McCaleb.'

Bosch stopped and looked at the reporter.

'What do you mean?'

'Yesterday. He was looking for you here.'

'Oh, yeah, I saw him. You know Terry?'

'Yeah, I wrote a book a few years ago about the bureau. I met him then. Before he got the transplant.'

Bosch nodded and was about to move on when the reporter put out his hand.

'Jack McEvoy.'

Bosch reluctantly shook his hand. He recognized the name. Five years earlier the bureau had tracked a serial cop killer to L.A., where it was believed he was about to strike his next victim – a Hollywood homicide detective named Ed Thomas. The bureau had used information from McEvoy, a reporter for the *Rocky Mountain News* in Denver, to track the so-called Poet and Thomas's life was never threatened. He was retired from the force now and running a bookshop down in Orange County.

'Hey, I remember you,' Bosch said. 'Ed Thomas is a friend of mine.'

Both men appraised each other.

'You're covering this thing?' Bosch asked, an obvious question.

'Yeah. For the *New Times* and *Vanity Fair*. I'm thinking about a book, too. So when it's all over, maybe we can talk.'

'Yeah, maybe.'

'Unless you're doing something with Terry on it.'

'With Terry? No, that was something else yesterday. No book.'

'Okay, then keep me in mind.'

McEvoy dug into his pocket for his wallet and then removed a business card.

'I mostly work out of my home in Laurel Canyon. Feel free to give me a call if you want.'

Bosch held the card up.

'Okay. I gotta go. See you around, I guess.'

'Yeah.'

Bosch walked over and pushed the button for an elevator. He looked at the card again while he waited and thought about Ed Thomas. He then put the card into the pocket of his suit jacket.

Before the elevator came he looked down the hallway and saw McEvoy was still in the hallway, now talking to Rudy Tafero, the defense's investigator. Tafero was a big man and he was leaning forward, close to McEvoy, as if it was some sort of conspiratorial rendezvous. McEvoy was writing in a notebook.

The elevator opened and Bosch stepped on. He watched them until the doors closed.

Bosch took Laurel Canyon Boulevard over the hill and dropped down into Hollywood ahead of the evening traffic. At Sunset he took a right and pulled to the curb a few blocks into West Hollywood. He fed the meter and went into the small, drab white office building across Sunset from a strip bar. The two-story courtyard building catered to small production companies. They were small offices with small overheads. The companies lived from movie to movie. In between there was no need for opulent offices and space.

Bosch checked his watch and saw that he was right on time. It was quarter to five and the audition was set for five. He took the stairs up to the second floor and went through a door with a sign saying NUFF SAID PRODUCTIONS. It was a three-room suite, one of the biggest in the building. Bosch had been there before and knew the layout: a waiting room with a secretary's desk, the office of Bosch's friend, Albert 'Nuff' Said, and then a conference room. A woman behind the secretary's desk looked up at Bosch as he stepped in.

'I'm here to see Mr. Said. My name's Harry Bosch.'

She nodded and picked up the phone and punched a number. Bosch could hear it beep in the other room and recognized Said's voice answering.

'It's Harry Bosch,' the secretary said.

Bosch heard Said order her to send him in. He headed that way before she was off the phone.

'Go on in,' she said to his back.

Bosch stepped into an office that was furnished simply with a desk, two chairs, a black leather couch and a television/video console. The walls were crowded with framed one-sheet posters advertising Said's movies and other mementos, such as the back panels of the producers' chairs with the names of the movies printed on them. Bosch had known Said at least fifteen years, ever since the older man had hired him as a technical adviser on a movie thinly based on one of Bosch's cases. They had kept in touch sporadically over the ensuing decade, Said usually calling Bosch when he had a technical question about a police procedure he was using in a movie. Most of Said's productions were never seen on the silver screen. They were television and cable movies.

Albert Said stood up behind the desk and Bosch extended his hand.

'Hey, Nuff, howzit going?'

'Going fine, my friend.'

He pointed to the television.

'I watched your fine performance on *Court TV* today. Bravo.'

He politely clapped his hands. Bosch waved the demonstration off and looked at his watch again.

'Thanks. So are we all set here?'

'I believe so. Marjorie will have her wait for me in the conference room. You can take it from there.'

'I appreciate this, Nuff. Let me know what I can do to square it.'

'You can be in my next movie. You have a real presence,

my friend. I watched the whole thing today. I taped it if you would like to see for yourself.'

'No, I don't think so. I don't think we'll have the time anyway. What have you got going these days?'

'Oh, you know, waiting for the light to turn green. I have a project I think is about to go with overseas financing. It is about this cop who gets sent to prison and the trauma of being stripped of his badge and his respect and everything gives him amnesia. And so there he is in prison and he can't remember which guys he put there and which ones he didn't. He's in a constant fight to survive. The one convict who befriends him turns out to be a serial killer he sent there in the first place. It's a thriller, Harry. What do you think? Steven Segal is reading the script.'

Said's bushy black eyebrows were arched into sharp points on his forehead. He was clearly excited by the premise of the movie.

'I don't know, Nuff,' Bosch said. 'I think it's been done before.'

'Everything's been done before. But what do you think?'

Bosch was saved by the bell. In the silence after Said's question they both could hear the secretary talking to someone in the next room. Then the speakerphone on Said's desk beeped and the secretary said, 'Ms. Crowe is here. She will be waiting in the conference room.'

Bosch nodded at Said.

'Thanks, Nuff,' he whispered. 'I'll take it from here.'

'Are you sure?'

'I'll let you know if I need any help.'

He turned to the office door but then went back to the desk and put out his hand.

'I may have to split kind of fast. So I'll say good-bye. Good luck with that project. Sounds like another winner.'

They shook hands.

'Yes, we shall see,' Said said.

Bosch left the office and crossed a small hallway and

entered the conference room. There was a square, glass-topped table at center with a chair on each side. Annabelle Crowe sat in the chair on the side opposite the door. She was studying a black-and-white photograph of herself as Bosch entered. She looked up with a bright smile and perfect teeth. The smile held for a little longer than a second and then crashed off her face like a Malibu mudslide.

'What – what are you doing here?'

'Hello, Annabelle, how've you been?'

'This is an audition – you can't just—'

'You're right, this is an audition. I am auditioning you for the role of witness in a murder trial.'

The woman stood up. Her head shot and a résumé slipped off the table to the floor.

'You can't just – what is going on here?'

'You know what is going on. You moved and left no forwarding. Your parents wouldn't help. Your agent wouldn't help me. The only way I could get to you was to set up an audition. Now sit down and we're going to talk about where you've been and why you're ducking the trial.'

'So there is no part?'

Bosch almost laughed. She still didn't get it.

'No, no part.'

'And they're not remaking *Chinatown?*'

This time he did laugh but quickly covered.

'One of these days they'll get around to it. But you're too young for the part and I'm no Jake Gittes. Sit down, please.'

Bosch started to pull out the chair opposite hers. But she refused to sit down. She looked very put out. She was a beautiful young woman with a face that often got her what she wanted. But not this time.

'I said sit down,' Bosch said sternly. 'You have to understand something here, Miss Crowe. You broke the law when you did not respond to a court-issued subpoena to appear today. That means if I want, I can just place you under arrest and we can talk about this in lockup. Or the alternative is that we sit down here because they're letting us use the nice room and talk about this in a civilized manner. Your choice, Annabelle.'

She dropped back into her chair. Her mouth was a thin, tight line. The lipstick she had carefully painted on for a casting session was already starting to crack and wear. Bosch studied her for a long moment before beginning.

'Who got to you, Annabelle?'

She looked at him sharply.

'Look,' she said, 'I was scared, okay? I still am. David Storey is a powerful man. He has some scary people behind him.'

Bosch leaned across the table.

'Are you saying you were threatened by him? By them?'

'No, I am not saying that. They didn't need to threaten me. I know the picture.'

Bosch leaned back away from her and quietly studied her. Her eyes moved everywhere around the room but to him. The traffic noise from out on Sunset filtered through the room's one closed window. Somewhere in the building a toilet was flushed. Finally, she looked at Bosch.

'What? What do you want?'

'I want you to testify. I want you to make a stand against this guy. For what he tried to do to you. For Jody Krementz. And Alicia Lopez.'

'Who is Alicia Lopez?'

'Another one we found. She wasn't lucky like you.'

Bosch could read the turmoil on her face. She clearly viewed testifying as some sort of danger.

'If I testify I'll never work again. And maybe worse.'

'Who told you that?'

She didn't answer.

'Come on, who? Did that come from them, your agent, who?'

She hesitated and then shook her head as if she couldn't believe she was talking to him.

'I was working out at Crunch and I was on a Stairmaster and this guy got on the machine next to me. He was reading the newspaper. It was folded to the story he was reading. And I was minding my own business when suddenly he just started talking. He never looked at me. He just talked while he was looking down at the newspaper. He said the story he was reading was about the David Storey trial and how he'd hate to be a witness who went against him. He said that person would never work in this town again.'

She stopped but Bosch waited. He studied her. Her anguish in recounting the story seemed genuine. She was on the verge of tears.

'And I . . . I got so panicked with him right there next to me I just got off the machine and ran into the locker room. I stayed in there for an hour and even then I was scared that he might still be out there waiting for me. Watching me.'

She started crying. Bosch got up and left the room and looked into the bathroom in the hallway. There was a box of tissues. He took it back with him to the conference room and handed it to Annabelle Crowe. He sat back down.

'Where is Crunch?'

'Just down the street from here. Sunset and Crescent Heights.'

Bosch nodded. He knew where it was now. The same shopping and entertainment complex where Jody Krementz had met David Storey in a coffee shop. He wondered if there was a connection. Maybe Storey belonged to Crunch. Maybe he got a workout pal to threaten Annabelle Crowe.

'Did you get a look at the guy?'

'Yes, but it doesn't matter. I don't know who he was. I never saw him before or since.'

Bosch thought about Rudy Tafero.

'Do you know who the defense team's investigator is? A guy named Rudy Tafero? He's tall, black hair and a nice tan. Good-looking guy?'

'I don't know who that is but he's not the man who was there that day. This man was short and bald. He had glasses.'

The description didn't register with Bosch. He decided to let it go for the time being. He'd have to let Langwiser and Kretzler know about the threat. They might want to take it to Judge Houghton. They might want to have Bosch go to Crunch and start asking questions, see if he could confirm anything.

'So what are you going to do?' she asked. 'Are you going to make me testify?'

'It's not up to me. The prosecutors will decide after I tell them your story.'

'Do you believe it?'

Bosch hesitated and then nodded.

'You still have to show up. You're under subpoena. Be there between twelve and one tomorrow and they'll let you know what they want to do.'

Bosch knew that they would make her testify. They wouldn't care if the threat was real or not. They had the case to worry about. Annabelle Crowe would be sacrificed to get David Storey. A small fish to get a big fish, the name of the game.

Bosch made her empty her purse. He looked through her things and found an address and phone number written down. It was a temp apartment in Burbank. She admitted that she had put her belongings in storage and was living in the temp, waiting for the trial to be over.

'I'm going to give you a break, Annabelle, and not hold you in lockup overnight. But I found you this time and I can find you again. You don't show up tomorrow and I'll come looking for you. And you'll go right to lockup at Sybil Brand, you understand that?'

She nodded her head.

'You going to be there?'

She nodded again.

'I should've never come to you people.'

Bosch nodded. She was right.

'It's too late for that,' he said. 'You did the right thing. Now you have to live with it. That's the funny thing about the courts. You decide to be brave and stick your neck out and they don't let you back down from it.'

21

Art Pepper was on the stereo and Bosch was on the telephone with Janis Langwiser when there was a knock on his screen door. He stepped into the hallway from the kitchen and saw a figure looking in through the mesh. Annoyed by the intrusion of a solicitor, he walked to the door and was about to simply close it without a word when he recognized the visitor as Terry McCaleb. Still on the phone and listening to Langwiser fume about possible witness tampering, he flicked on the outside light, opened the screen door and signaled McCaleb in.

McCaleb made a signal that he would be quiet until Bosch was off the call. Bosch watched him walk through the living room and step out onto the rear deck to look down at the lights of the Cahuenga Pass. He tried to concentrate on what Langwiser was saying but he was curious as to why McCaleb would drive all the way up into the hills to see him.

'Harry, are you listening?'

'Yeah. What was that last part?'

'I said do you think Shootin' Houghton will delay the trial if we open up an investigation.'

Bosch didn't have to think long to answer that.

'No way. The show must go on.'

'Yeah, that's what I figure. I'm going to call Roger and see what he wants to do. Anyway, it's the least of our worries. As soon as you mention Alicia Lopez on the stand there's going to be a brutal fight.'

'I thought we already won that. Houghton ruled—'

'It doesn't mean Fowkkes won't try a new attack. We're not clear yet.'

There was a pause. There had not been much confidence in her voice.

'I guess I'll see you tomorrow, Harry.'

'All right, Janis, I'll see you.'

Bosch clicked the phone off and put it back in its cradle in the kitchen. When he stepped back out McCaleb was standing in the living room, looking at the shelves over the stereo, at a framed photograph of Bosch's wife in particular.

'Terry, what's up?'

'Hey, Harry, sorry to drop in unannounced like this. I didn't have your home number to call first.'

'How'd you find the place? You want a beer or something?'

Bosch pointed to his chest.

'Can you have a beer?'

'I can now. Just got clearance, in fact. I can drink again. In moderation. A beer sounds good.'

Bosch went into the kitchen. McCaleb continued talking from the living room.

'I've been here before. You don't remember?'

Bosch came out with two open bottles of Anchor Steam. He handed one to McCaleb.

'You need a glass? When were you here?'

McCaleb took the bottle.

'Cielo Azul.'

He took a long pull from the bottle, answering Bosch's question about the glass.

Cielo Azul, Bosch thought and then he remembered. They had gotten drunk on the back porch once, both of them dulling the edges of a case that was too terrible to think deeply about with a sober mind. He remembered being embarrassed about it the next day, about how he had lost control and kept rhetorically asking in an alcohol-slowed voice, 'Where is God's hand, where is God's hand?'

'Oh, yeah,' Bosch said. 'One of my finer existential moments.'

'Yeah. Except the place is different now. The old one slide down the hill in the quake?'

'Just about. Red-tagged, the whole bit. Started over from the ground up.'

'Yeah, I didn't recognize it. I drove up here looking for the old place. But then I saw the Shamu and figured there couldn't be another cop in the neighborhood.'

Bosch thought about the black-and-white parked in the carport. He hadn't bothered to take it to the station to exchange for his personal car. It would save him time in the morning by allowing him to drive straight to court. The car was a slickback – a black-and-white without the emergency lights on top. Detectives from the divisions used them as part of a program designed to make it look as if there were more cops on the street than there really were.

McCaleb reached over and clicked Bosch's bottle with his own.

'To Cielo Azul,' he said.

'Yeah,' Bosch said.

He drank from the bottle. It was ice cold and good. His first beer since the start of the trial. He decided he would keep it to one, even if McCaleb pressed on.

'This your ex?' McCaleb asked, pointing to the photo on the shelves.

'My wife. Not my ex, yet – at least as far as I know. But I guess it's heading that way.'

Bosch stared at the photo of Eleanor Wish. It was the only picture of her he had.

'That's too bad, man.'

'Yeah. So what's up, Terry? I've got some stuff I have to go over for—'

'I know, the trial. I'm sorry to intrude, man. I know

that's gotta be all-consuming. I just had a couple things on the Gunn case I wanted to clear up. But also I wanted to tell you something. I mean, show you, too.'

He pulled his wallet out of his back pocket, opened it and took out a photo. He handed it to Bosch. The photo had taken on the contour line of the wallet. It showed a dark-haired baby in the arms of a dark-haired woman.

'That's my daughter, Harry. And my wife.'

Bosch nodded and studied the photo. Both mother and child had dark hair and skin and were quite beautiful. He knew they were probably even more so to McCaleb.

'Beautiful,' he said. 'The baby looks brand new. So tiny.'

'She's about four months now. That picture's a month old, though. Anyway, I forgot to tell you yesterday at lunch. We named her Cielo Azul.'

Bosch's eyes came up from the photo to McCaleb's. They held for a moment and then he nodded.

'Nice.'

'Yeah, I told Graciela I wanted to do it and I told her why. She thought it was a good idea.'

Bosch handed the photo back.

'I hope someday the kid does, too.'

'Me, too. We call her CiCi most of the time. Anyway, remember that night up here, how you kept asking that question about the hand of God and how you couldn't find it in anything anymore? That happened to me, too. I lost it. This kind of job . . . it's hard not to. Then . . .'

He held up the photo.

'Here it is right here. I found it again. The hand of God. I see it in her eyes.'

Bosch looked at him for a long moment and then nodded.

'Good for you, Terry.'

'I mean, I'm not trying to come off like . . . I mean I'm not trying to convert you or anything. I'm just saying I found that thing that was missing. And I don't know if you're still looking for it . . . I just wanted to say, you know, that it is out there. Don't give up.'

Bosch glanced away from McCaleb and out the glass doors to the darkness.

'For some people I'm sure it is.'

He drained his bottle and went into the kitchen to break his promise to himself to have only one. He called back to McCaleb to see if he was ready for a second but his visitor passed. As he bent into the open refrigerator he paused and closed his eyes as the cool air caressed his face. He thought about what McCaleb had just told him.

'You don't think you are one of them?'

Bosch jerked up at the sound of McCaleb's voice. He was standing in the kitchen's doorway.

'What?'

'You said it was out there for some people. You don't think you are one of them?'

Bosch took a beer out of the refrigerator and slid it into the bottle opener mounted on the wall. He snapped the bottle open and drank deeply from it before answering.

'What is this, Terry, twenty questions? You thinking of becoming a priest or something?'

McCaleb smiled and shook his head.

'Sorry, Harry. A new father, you know? I guess I want to tell the world, that's all.'

'That's nice. You want to talk about Gunn now?'

'Sure.'

'Let's go out and look at the night.'

They walked out to the back deck and both looked at the view. The 101 was its usual ribbon of light, a glowing vein cutting through the mountains. The sky was clear, the smog having been washed out by rain the week before. Bosch could see the lights on the floor of the Valley seemingly extending into infinity. Closer to the house there was only darkness held in the brush on the hillside below. He could smell the eucalyptus from below; it was always strongest after the rain.

McCaleb was the first to speak.

'You've got a nice place here, Harry. A nice spot. You must hate having to ride down into the plague every morning.'

Bosch looked over at him.

'Not as long as I get a shot at the carriers every now and then. People like David Storey. I don't mind that.'

'And what about the ones who walk away? Like Gunn.'

'Nobody walks away, Terry. If I believed that they did, then I couldn't do this. Sure we might not get every one of them, but I believe in the circle. The big wheel. What goes around comes around. Eventually. I might not see the hand of God too often like you do but I believe in that.'

Bosch put his bottle down on the railing. It was empty and he wanted another but knew he had to put on the brakes. He'd need every brain cell he could muster in court the next day. He thought about a cigarette and knew there was a fresh pack in a kitchen cabinet. But he decided to hold off on that, too.

'Then I guess what happened with Gunn must be a confirmation of your faith in the big wheel theory.'

Bosch didn't say anything for a long time. He just stared out across the valley of light.

'Yeah,' he finally said. 'I guess it does.'

He broke his stare away and turned his back on the view. He leaned against the railing and looked at McCaleb again.

'So what about Gunn? I thought I told you everything there was to tell yesterday. You've got the file, right?'

McCaleb nodded.

'You probably did and I do have the file. But I was just wondering if anything else came up. You know, if maybe our conversation jump-started your thinking on it.'

Bosch sort of laughed and picked up the bottle before remembering it was empty.

'Terry, come on, man, I'm in the middle of a trial. I'm

on the stand, I've been chasing down an AWOL wit. I mean I stopped thinking about your investigation the minute I got up from the table at Cupid's. What exactly do you want from me?'

'Nothing, Harry. I don't want anything from you that you don't have. I just thought it might be worth a shot, is all. I'm working on this thing and scratching around for anything. I thought maybe . . . don't worry about it.'

'You're a weird guy, McCaleb. I'm remembering that now. The way you used to stare at crime scene photos. You want another beer?'

'Yeah, why not?'

Bosch pushed off the railing and reached over for his bottle and then McCaleb's. It was still at least a third full. He put it back down.

'Well, finish that.'

He went into the house and got two more beers out of the refrigerator. This time McCaleb was standing in the living room when he came back from the kitchen. He handed Bosch his empty bottle and Bosch wondered for a moment if he had finished it or poured the beer over the side of the deck. He took the empty into the kitchen and when he came back McCaleb was standing at the stereo studying a CD case.

'This what's playing?' he asked. 'Art Pepper meets the Rhythm Section?'

Bosch stepped over.

'Yeah. Art Pepper and Miles's side men. Red Garland on piano, Paul Chambers on bass, Philly Joe Jones on drums. Recorded here in L.A., January 19, 1957. One day. The cork in the neck of Pepper's sax was supposedly cracked but it didn't matter. He had one shot with these guys. He made the most of it. One day, one shot, one classic. That's the way to do it.'

'These guys were in Miles Davis's band?'

'At the time.'

McCaleb nodded. Bosch leaned close to look at the CD cover in McCaleb's hands.

'Yeah, Art Pepper,' he said. 'When I was growing up I never knew who my father was. My mother, she used to have a lot of this guy's records. She hung out at some of the jazz clubs where he'd play. Handsome devil, Art was. For a hype. Just look at that picture. Too cool to fool. I made up this whole story about how he was my old man and he wasn't around 'cause he was always on the road and making records. Almost got to the point I believed it. Later on – I mean years later – I read a book about him. It said he was junk sick when they took that picture. He puked as soon as it was over and went back to bed.'

McCaleb studied the photograph on the CD. A handsome man leaning against a tree, his sax cradled in his right arm.

'Well, he could play,' McCaleb said.

'Yeah, he could,' Bosch agreed. 'Genius with a needle in his arm.'

Bosch stepped over and turned the volume up slightly. The song was 'Straight Life,' Pepper's signature composition.

'Do you believe that?' McCaleb asked.

'What, that he was a genius? Yeah, he was with the sax.'

'No, I mean do you think that every genius – musician, artist, even a detective – has a fatal flaw like that? The needle in the arm.'

'I think everybody's got a fatal flaw, whether they're a genius or not.'

Bosch turned it up louder. McCaleb put his beer down on top of one of the floor speakers. Bosch picked it up and handed it back. He used his palm to wipe the wet ring off the wood surface. McCaleb turned the music down.

'Come on, Harry, give me something.'

'What are you talking about?'

'I made the journey up here. Give me something on Gunn. I know you don't care about him – the wheel turned and he didn't walk away. But I don't like the way this one looked. This guy – whoever he is – is still out there. And he's going to do this again. I can tell.'

Bosch shrugged his shoulders like he still didn't care.

'All right, here's something. It's thin but it might be worth a try. When he was in the tank the night before he got put down and I checked in on him, I also talked with the Metro guys who brought him in on the duice. They said they asked him where he'd been drinking and he said he'd come out of a place called Nat's. It's on the Boulevard about a block from Musso's and on the south side.'

'Okay, I can find it,' McCaleb said, a what-about-it tone in his voice. 'What's the connection?'

'Well, see, Nat's was the same place he'd been drinking that night six years ago that I first made his acquaintance. It's where he picked up that woman, the one he killed.'

'So he was a regular.'

'Looks it.'

'Thanks, Harry. I'll check it out. How come you didn't tell this to Jaye Winston?'

Bosch shrugged his shoulders.

'I guess I didn't think about it and she didn't ask.'

McCaleb almost put his beer down on the speaker again but instead handed it to Bosch.

'I might go check down there tonight.'

'Don't forget.'

'Forget what?'

'You hook the guy who did it, you shake his hand for me.'

McCaleb didn't respond. He looked around the place as if he had just walked in.

'Can I use the bathroom?'

'Down the hall on the left.'

McCaleb headed that way while Bosch took the bottles into the kitchen and put them in the recycle bin with the others. He opened the refrigerator and saw he was down to one soldier left in the six-pack he'd bought on the way home from tricking Annabelle Crowe. He closed the refrigerator when McCaleb stepped into the room.

'That's a crazy fucking picture you got hanging in the hallway,' he said.

'What? Oh, yeah. I like that picture.'

'What's it supposed to mean?'

'I don't know. I guess it means the big wheel keeps turning. Nobody walks away.'

McCaleb nodded.

'I suppose.'

'You heading down there to Nat's?'

'Thinking about it. You want to go?'

Bosch considered it even though he knew it would be foolish. He had to review half of the murder book in preparation for his continuing testimony the next morning.

'Nah, I better do some work here. Get ready for tomorrow.'

'Okay. How'd it go today, anyway?'

'So far so good. But we're playing softball right now – direct. Tomorrow the ball goes to John Reason and he throws it back inside and fast.'

'I'll watch the news.'

McCaleb stepped over and stuck his hand out. Bosch shook it.

'Be careful out there.'

'You, too, Harry. Thanks for the beers.'

'No problem.'

He walked McCaleb to the door and then watched him get into a black Cherokee parked on the street. It started up immediately and pulled away, leaving Bosch standing in the lighted doorway.

Bosch locked up and turned off the living-room lights. He left the stereo on. It would automatically turn off at the end of Art Pepper's classic moment in time. It was early but Bosch was tired from the pressures of the day and the alcohol moving in his blood. He decided he would sleep now and wake up early to prepare for his testimony. He went into the kitchen and got the last bottle of beer out of the refrigerator.

On the way down the hall to his bedroom he stopped and looked at the framed picture McCaleb had referred to. It was a print of the Hieronymus Bosch painting called *The Garden of Earthly Delights*. He'd had it for a long time, since he was a kid. The surface of the print was warped and scratched. It was in bad shape. It had been Eleanor who moved it from the living room to the hallway. She didn't like it being in the place where they sat every night. Bosch never understood whether that was because of what was in the painting or because the print was old and deteriorated.

As he looked at the landscape of human debauchery and torment depicted in the painting, Bosch thought about maybe moving it back to its spot in the living room.

In Bosch's dream he was moving through dark water, unable to see his hands in front of his own face. There was a ringing sound and he pushed upward through the darkness.

He came awake. The light was on but all was silent. The stereo was off. He started to look at his watch when the phone rang again and he quickly grabbed it off the bedside table.

'Yeah.'

'Hey, Harry, it's Kiz.'

His old partner.

'Kiz, what's up?'

'You okay? You sound . . . out of it.'

'I'm fine. I was just . . . I was asleep.'

He looked at his watch. It was just after ten.

'Sorry, Harry, I thought you'd be burning the oil, getting ready for tomorrow.'

'I'm going to get up early and do it.'

'Well, you did good today. We had the box on in the squad. Everybody was pulling for you.'

'I'll bet. How is it going down there?'

'It's going. In a way I'm starting over. I've got to prove myself to them.'

'Don't worry about it. You'll be passing those guys like they're standing still. Just like you did with me.'

'Harry . . . you're the best. I learned more from you than you'll ever know.'

Bosch hesitated. He was genuinely touched by what she had said.

'That's nice of you to say, Kiz. You should call me more often.'

She laughed.

'Well, that's not why I'm calling. I told a friend I'd do this. It reminds me of high school but here goes. There's somebody that is interested in you. I said I'd check to see if you were back out in the field, if you know what I mean?'

Bosch didn't even have to think before answering.

'Nah, Kiz, I'm not. I . . . I'm not giving up on Eleanor yet. I'm still hoping she'll call or show up and maybe we can work it out. You know how it is.'

'I do. And that's cool, Harry. I just said I'd ask. But if you change your mind, she's a neat lady.'

'I know her?'

'Yeah, you know her. Jaye Winston, over at the sheriff's. We're in a women's group together. Dicks without Dicks. We got to talking about you tonight.'

Bosch didn't say anything. A strange constricting feeling filled his gut. He didn't believe in coincidences.

'Harry, you there?'

'Yeah, I'm here. I was just thinking about something.'

'Well, I'll let you go. And listen, Jaye asked me not to give you her name. You know, she just wanted to ask about you and put an anonymous feeler out. So next time you both run across each other on the job it wouldn't be embarrassing. So you didn't get it from me, right?'

'Right. She asked you questions about me?'

'A few. Nothing big. I hope you don't mind. I told her she made a good choice. I said if I wasn't, you know, the way I was, I'd be interested too.'

'Thanks, Kiz,' Bosch said but his mind was flying.

'Well, look, I'm gonna go. I'll see you. Knock 'em dead tomorrow, okay?'

'I'll try.'

She hung up and Bosch slowly put the phone back in its cradle. The tightening in his gut got more intense. He started thinking about McCaleb's visit and what he had asked and what Harry had said. Now Winston was asking questions about him.

He did not believe it was a coincidence. It was clear to Bosch that they had a bead on him. They were looking at him for the Edward Gunn killing. And he knew he had probably given McCaleb the right amount of psychological insight to believe he was on the right course.

Bosch drained the bottle of beer that was on the nightstand. The last swallow was room temperature and sour. He knew there were no more bottles in the refrigerator. He got up to get a cigarette instead.

22

Nat's was a railroad car-sized bar that was like a lot of Hollywood haunts – favored during daylight hours by hard-core drinkers, during early evening hours by casual hookers and their clientele, and late at night by the black leather and tattoo crowd. It was the kind of place where a person would stand out as a target if he tried to pay for drinks with a gold credit card.

McCaleb had stopped at Musso's for dinner – his body clock demanding nourishment before a complete shut-down occurred – and didn't get to Nat's until after ten. While eating his chicken pot pie he had wondered whether going to the bar to ask questions about Gunn was even worth the time. The tip had come from the suspect. Would the suspect knowingly point the investigator in the right direction? It seemed not, but McCaleb factored in Bosch's drinking and his being unaware of McCaleb's true mission during the visit to the house on the hill. The tip might very well be valid and he decided no part of the investigation should be overlooked.

As he walked in it took him a few seconds to adjust to the dim, reddish lighting. When the room became clear he saw it was half empty. It was the time between the early evening crowd and the late night group. Two women – one black, one white – sitting at one end of the bar that ran along the left side of the room sized him up and McCaleb could see *cop* register in their eyes at the same moment *hookers* registered in his. It secretly pleased him that he still had the look. He walked by them and further into the lounge. The booths lining the right side of the room were mostly full. No one in these bothered to give him a glance.

He stepped up to the bar between two empty stools and signaled one of the bartenders.

An old Bob Seger song, 'Night Moves,' was blaring from a jukebox in the back. The bartender leaned over the bar so she could get McCaleb's order. She was wearing a buttoned black vest with no shirt underneath. She had long straight black hair and a thin gold hoop pierced her left eyebrow.

'What can I get you?'

'Some information.'

McCaleb slid a driver's-license picture of Edward Gunn across the counter. It was a three-by-five blowup that had been in the files Winston gave him. The bartender looked at it for a moment and then back up at McCaleb.

'What about him? He's dead.'

'How do you know that?'

She shrugged her shoulders.

'I don't know. Word just got around, I guess. You a cop?'

McCaleb nodded, lowered his voice so the music would cover it and said, 'Something like that.'

The bartender leaned further over the bartop so she could hear him. This position opened the top of her vest, exposing most of her small but round breasts. There was a tattoo of a heart wrapped in barbed wire on the left side. It looked like a bruise on a pear, not very appetizing. McCaleb looked away.

'Edward Gunn,' he said. 'He was a regular, right?'

'He came in a lot.'

McCaleb nodded. Her acknowledgment confirmed Bosch's tip.

'You work New Year's Eve?'

She nodded.

'You know if he came in that night?'

She shook her head.

'I can't remember. A lot of people were in here New Year's Eve. We had a party. I don't know if he was here or not. It wouldn't surprise me, though. People came and went.'

McCaleb nodded toward the other bartender. A Latino who also wore a black vest with no shirt beneath.

'What about him? Think he'd remember?'

'No, 'cause he only started last week. I'm breaking him in.'

A thin smile played on her face. McCaleb ignored it. 'Twisting the Night Away' began playing. The Rod Stewart version.

'How well did you know Gunn?'

She let out a short burst of laughter.

'Honey, this is the kind of place where people don't exactly like to let on who they are or what they are. How well did I know him? I knew him, okay? Like I said, he came in. But I didn't even know his name until he was dead and people started talking about him. Somebody said Eddie Gunn got himself killed and I said, "Who the fuck is Eddie Gunn?" They had to describe him. The whiskey rocks who always had the paint in his hair. Then I knew who Eddie Gunn was.'

McCaleb nodded. He reached inside his coat pocket and brought out a folded piece of newspaper. He slid it across the bartop. She leaned down to look, showing another view of her breasts. McCaleb thought it was intentional.

'This is that cop, the one from the trial, right?'

McCaleb didn't answer the question. The newspaper had been folded to a photo of Harry Bosch that had run that morning in the *Los Angeles Times* as an advance on the testimony expected to begin in the Storey trial. It was a candid shot of Bosch standing outside the courtroom door. He probably didn't even know it had been taken.

'You seen him in here?'

'Yeah, he comes in. Why are you asking about him?'

McCaleb felt a charge go up the back of his neck.

'When does he come in?'

'I don't know, from time to time. I wouldn't call him a regular. But he'd come in. And he wouldn't stay long. A one-timer – one drink and out. He's . . .'

She pointed a finger up and cocked her head to the side as she rifled through her interior files. She then slashed her finger down as if making a notch.

'Got it. Bottled beer. Asks for Anchor Steam every time because he always forgets we don't carry it – too expensive, we'd never sell it. He then settles for the old thirty-three.'

McCaleb was about to ask what that was when she answered his unspoken question.

'Rolling Rock.'

He nodded.

'Was he in here New Year's Eve?'

She shook her head.

'Same answer. I don't remember. Too many people, too many drinks, too many days since then.'

McCaleb nodded and pulled the newspaper back across the bar and put it in his pocket.

'He in some kind of trouble, that cop?'

McCaleb shook his head. One of the women at the end of the bar tapped the corner of her empty glass on the bartop and called to the bartender.

'Hey, Miranda, you got payin' customers over here.'

The bartender looked around for her partner. He was gone, apparently in the back room or the bathroom.

'Gotta go to work,' she said.

McCaleb watched her go to the end of the bar and make two fresh vodka rocks for the hookers. During a lull in the music, he overheard one of them tell her to stop talking to the cop so he would leave. As Miranda headed back toward McCaleb's position one of the hookers called after her.

'And stop giving him the freebie or he'll never leave.'

McCaleb acted like he didn't hear it. Miranda exhaled like she was tired when she got to him.

'I don't know where Javier went. I can't be standing here talking to you all night.'

'Let me ask you one last thing,' he said. 'You ever remember the cop being in here with Eddie Gunn at the same time – either together or apart?'

She thought a moment and leaned forward.

'Maybe, it could've happened. But I don't remember.'

McCaleb nodded. He was pretty sure that was the best he could get out of her. He wondered if he should leave some money on the bar. He'd never been good at that sort of thing when he was an agent. He never knew when it would be appropriate and when it would be insulting.

'Can I ask you something now?' Miranda asked.

'What?'

'You like what you see?'

He felt his face immediately begin to color with embarrassment.

'I mean, you were looking enough. I just thought I'd ask.'

She glanced over at the hookers and shared a smile. They were all enjoying McCaleb's embarrassment.

'They're real nice,' he said as he stepped away from the bar, leaving a twenty-dollar bill for her. 'I'm sure they keep people coming back. Probably kept Eddie Gunn comin' in.'

He headed toward the door and she called after him, her words hitting him in the back all the way to the door.

'Then maybe you oughta come back and try 'em out some time, *Officer!*'

As he went through the door he heard the hookers whoop and slap hands in a high five.

McCaleb sat in the Cherokee in front of Nat's and tried to shake off the embarrassment. He concentrated on the information he had gotten from the bartender. Gunn was a regular and might or might not have been in there on the last night of his life. Secondly, she was familiar with Bosch as a customer. He, too, might or might not have been in there on the last night of Gunn's life. The fact that this information had indirectly come from Bosch was puzzling. Again, he wondered why Bosch – if he was Gunn's killer – had given him a valid clue to follow. Was it arrogance, a belief that he would never be considered a suspect and therefore not be brought up during the questioning at the bar? Or could there be a deeper psychological motivation? McCaleb knew that many criminals make mistakes that ensure their apprehension because subconsciously they do not want to get away with their crimes. The big wheel theory, McCaleb thought. Maybe Bosch was subconsciously making sure the wheel turned for him as well.

He opened his cell phone and checked the signal. It was good. He called Jaye Winston's home number. He checked his watch while the phone was ringing and thought that it was not too late to call. After five rings she finally picked up.

'It's me. I've got some stuff.'

'So do I. But I'm still on the phone. Can I call you when I'm done?'

'Yeah, I'll be here.'

He clicked off and sat in the car waiting and thinking about things. He watched through the windshield as the white hooker from the bar stepped through the door with a man in a baseball cap in tow. They both lit cigarettes and headed down the sidewalk toward a motel called the Skylark.

His phone chirped. It was Winston.

'It's coming together, Terry. I'm a believer.'

'What did you get?'

'You first. You said you got some stuff.'

'No, you. What I got is minor. It sounds like you hooked something big.'

'Okay, listen to this. Harry Bosch's mother was a prostitute. In Hollywood. She got murdered when he was a little kid. And whoever did it got away with it. How is that for psychological underpinnings, Mr. Profiler?'

McCaleb didn't answer. The new information was stunning and provided many of the missing pieces in the working theory. He watched the hooker and her customer at the window of the motel office. The man passed cash through and received a key. They went in through a glass door.

'Gunn kills a prostitute and walks away,' Winston said when he didn't respond. 'Just like what happened with his mother.'

'How'd you find this out?' McCaleb finally asked.

'I made that call we talked about. To my friend, Kiz. I acted like I was interested in Bosch and asked her if she knew if he was, you know, over his divorce yet. She told me what she knew about him. The stuff about his mother apparently came out a few years ago in a civil trial when Bosch got sued for a wrongful death – the Dollmaker, you remember that one?'

'Yeah, the LAPD refused to call us in on that one. That was also a guy who killed prostitutes. Bosch killed him. He was unarmed.'

'There's a psychology going on here. A goddamn pattern.'

'What happened to Bosch after his mother was killed?'

'Kiz didn't really know. She called him an institutional man. It happened when he was ten or eleven. After that he grew up in youth halls and foster homes. He went into the service and then the department. The point is, this is the thing we were missing. The thing that turned a no-count case into something Bosch wouldn't let go.'

McCaleb nodded to himself.

'And there's more,' Winston said. 'I went through all the accumulated files – extraneous things I didn't put in the murder book. I looked at the autopsy on the woman

Gunn killed six years ago. Her name was Frances Weldon, by the way. There was one thing in there that seems significant in light of what we now know about Bosch. Examination of the uterus and hips showed that at some point she'd had a child.'

McCaleb shook his head.

'Bosch wouldn't have known that. He pushed his lieutenant through a window and was on suspension by the time there was an autopsy.'

'True. But he could and probably did look at the case files after he came back. He would have known that Gunn did to some other kid what was done to him. You see, it is all fitting. Eight hours ago I thought you were grasping at straws. Now it looks to me like you're dead on.'

It didn't feel all that good to be dead on. But he understood Winston's excitement. When cases fell together the excitement could sometimes obscure the reality of the crime.

'What happened to her kid?' he asked.

'No idea. She probably gave the child up after the birth. That doesn't matter. What matters is what it meant to Bosch.'

She was right. But McCaleb didn't like the loose end.

'Going back to your call to Bosch's old partner. Is she going to call him and tell him you asked about him?'

'She already did.'

'This is tonight?'

'Yeah, this all just went down. That was that call, her getting back to me. He passed. He told her he was still holding out hope for his wife coming back.'

'Did she tell him it was you who was interested?'

'She wasn't supposed to.'

'But she probably did. This might mean he knows we're looking at him.'

'That's impossible. How?'

'I was just up there tonight. I was in his house. Then the

same night he gets this call about you. A guy like Harry Bosch, he doesn't believe in coincidences, Jaye.'

'Well, when you were up there, how did you handle it?' Winston finally asked.

'Like we said. I wanted more info on Gunn but sidetracked into talking about Bosch. That's why I was calling you. I got some interesting stuff. Nothing that compares to what you got but stuff that also fits. But if he got this call about you right after I was there . . . I don't know.'

'Tell me about your stuff.'

'All little stuff. He's got the photo of the estranged wife prominently displayed in the living room. I was there less than an hour and the guy downed three beers. So there's the alcohol syndrome. Symptomatic of interior pressures. He also spoke of something he called "the big wheel." It's part of his belief system. He doesn't see the hand of God in things. He sees the big wheel. What goes around comes around. He said guys like Gunn don't really get away. Something always catches up to them. The wheel. I used some specific phrases to see if I could draw a reaction or disagreement. I called the world outside his door the plague. He didn't disagree. He said he could deal with the plague as long as he got his shots at the carriers. It's all very subtle, Jaye, but it's all there. He's got a Bosch print on the wall in the hallway. *The Garden of Earthly Delights.* It's got our owl in it.'

'So, he's named after the guy. If my name was Picasso I'd have a Picasso print on the wall.'

'I acted like I'd never seen it before and asked him what it meant. All he said was that it was the big wheel turning. That's what it meant to him.'

'Little pieces that fit.'

'There's still work to be done.'

'Well, are you still on it? Or are you going back?'

'For the time being I'm on it. I'll be staying over

tonight. But I have a charter Saturday. I have to go back for that.'

She didn't say anything.

'You got anything else?' he finally asked.

'Yeah, I almost forgot.'

'What?'

'The owl from Bird Barrier. It was paid for with a money order from the Postal Service. I got the number from Cameron Riddell and ran a trace on it. It was bought December twenty-second at the post office on Wilcox in Hollywood. It's about four blocks from the police station where Bosch works.'

He shook his head.

'The laws of physics.'

'What do you mean?'

'For every action there is an equal and opposite reaction. When you look into the abyss the abyss looks into you. You know, all the clichés. They're clichés because they're true. You don't go into the darkness without it going into you and taking its piece. Bosch may have gone in too many times. He's lost his way.'

They were silent for a little while after that and then made plans to meet the following day. As he hung up he saw the hooker leaving the Skylark by herself and heading back up toward Nat's. She was wearing a denim jacket which she pulled tight around her against the cool night air. She adjusted her wig as she walked toward the bar where she would seek another customer.

Watching her and thinking about Bosch, McCaleb was reminded of all he had and how lucky in life he had been. He was reminded that luck could be a fleeting thing. It had to be earned and then guarded with everything you had. He knew he was not doing that now. He was leaving things unguarded while he went into the dark.

23

Trial resumed twenty-five minutes after the scheduled nine o'clock start because of the prosecution's unsuccessful bid to seek both sanctions against the defense for witness intimidation and a delay while the statements of Annabelle Crowe were fully investigated. Sitting behind his cherry-wood desk in chambers, Judge Houghton encouraged the investigation but said the trial would not be delayed to accommodate it and no sanctions or other penalties would be issued unless evidence corroborating the witness's statements could be found. He warned the prosecutors and Bosch, who had taken part in the closed-door meeting by recounting his interview with Crowe, not to leak word of the witness's accusations to the media.

Five minutes later they were convened in the courtroom and the jurors were brought to their two rows of seats. Bosch returned to the witness stand and was reminded by the judge that he was still under oath. Janis Langwiser went back to the lectern with her legal pad.

'Now, Detective Bosch, we left off yesterday with your conclusion in regard to the death of Jody Krementz being determined to be a homicide. Is that correct?'

'Yes.'

'And that conclusion was based not only on your investigation but on the investigation and autopsy conducted by the coroner's office as well, correct?'

'Correct.'

'Could you please tell the jurors how the investigation

proceeded once you had established the death as a homicide?'

Bosch turned in his seat so that he was looking directly at the jury box as he spoke. The movement was jarring. He had a pounding ache on the left side of his head that was so intense he wondered if people could actually see his temple throbbing.

'Well, my two partners – Jerry Edgar and Kizmin Rider – and I began to sit through – I mean, sift through the physical evidence we had accumulated. We also began conducting extensive interviews with those who knew the victim and were known to have been with her in the last twenty-four hours of her life.'

'You mentioned physical evidence. Please explain to the jury what physical evidence you had accumulated.'

'Actually, there was not a whole lot gathered. There were fingerprints throughout the house that we needed to run down. And there also was a quantity of fiber and hair evidence gathered from on and about the victim's body.'

J. Reason Fowkkes quickly objected before Bosch could continue his answer.

'Objection to the phrase "on or about" as being vague and misleading.'

'Your Honor,' Langwiser countered, 'I think if Mr. Fowkkes gave Detective Bosch a chance to finish the answer to the question there would be nothing vague or misleading. But interrupting a witness in mid-answer to say the answer is vague or misleading is not appropriate.'

'Overruled,' Judge Houghton said, before Fowkkes could get in a rejoinder. 'Let the witness complete his answer and then we'll see how vague it is. Go ahead, Detective Bosch.'

Bosch cleared his throat.

'I was going to say that several samples of pubic hair not—'

'What is "several," Your Honor,' Fowkkes said. 'My

ongoing objection is to the lack of precision this witness is offering the jury.'

Bosch looked at Langwiser and saw how mad she was getting.

'Judge,' she said, 'could we please have direction from the court as to when objections can be raised? Defense counsel is seeking to constantly interrupt the witness because he knows we are moving into an area that is particularly devastating to his—'

'Ms. Langwiser, this isn't the time for closing arguments,' the judge said, cutting her off. 'Mr. Fowkkes, unless you are seeing a dire miscarriage of justice, I want objections stated either before a witness speaks or after he has completed at least a sentence.'

'Your Honor, the consequences *are* dire here. The state is trying to take away my client's life, simply because his moral views are—'

'Mr. Fowkkes!' the judge boomed. 'That goes for you, too, on the closing arguments. Let's continue the testimony, shall we?'

He turned to Bosch.

'Detective, continue – and try to be a little more precise in your answers.'

Bosch looked at Langwiser and saw her close her eyes momentarily. The judge's offhand direction to Bosch had been what Fowkkes was going for. A hint to the jurors that there might be vagueness, maybe even obfuscation in the prosecution's case. Fowkkes had successfully goaded the judge into appearing to agree with his objections.

Bosch glanced over at Fowkkes and saw him sitting with arms folded and a satisfied, if not smug, look on his face. Bosch looked back down at the murder book in front of him.

'Can I refer to my notes?' he asked.

He was told he could. He opened the binder and turned to the evidence reports. Looking at the medical examiner's evidence collection report, he began again.

'Prior to autopsy an evidence-collecting brush was passed through the victim's pubic hair. The comb collected eight samples of pubic hair that subsequent laboratory testing showed to have come from someone other than the victim.'

He looked up at Langwiser.

'Were those pubic hairs from eight different people?'

'No, the lab tests identified them as coming from the same unknown person.'

'And what did this indicate to you?'

'That the victim likely had sexual relations with someone between the time of her last bathing and her death.'

Langwiser looked down at her notes.

'Was there any other hair evidence collected on the victim or at the scene of the crime, Detective?'

Bosch turned a page in the murder book.

'Yes, a single strand of hair measuring two and one half inches long was found entangled on the clasp of a gold necklace the victim wore around her neck. The clasp was located at the back of the victim's neck. This, too, was identified during lab analysis as coming from someone other than the victim.'

'Going back for a moment to the pubic hair. Were there any other indications or evidence collected from the body or the crime scene indicating the victim had engaged in sexual relations in the time between bathing and her death?'

'No, there wasn't. No semen was collected from the vagina.'

'Is there a conflict between that and the finding of the pubic hair?'

'No conflict. It was simply an indication that a condom could have been used during the sex act.'

'Okay, moving on, Detective. Fingerprints. You mentioned fingerprints were found in the house. Please tell us about that area of the investigation.'

Bosch turned to the fingerprint report in the binder.

'There were a total of sixty-eight exemplars of fingerprints gathered inside the house where the victim was found. The victim and her roommate accounted for fifty-two of these. It was determined that the remaining sixteen were left by a total of seven people.'

'And who were these people?'

Bosch read the list of names from the binder. Through questioning from Langwiser he explained who each person was and how the detectives traced down when and why they had been in the house. They were friends of the roommates as well as family members, a former boyfriend and a prior date. The prosecution team knew that the defense would attempt to go to town on the prints, using them as red herrings to bait the jury away from the facts of the case. So the testimony moved slowly as Bosch tediously explained the location and origin of each fingerprint found and identified in the house. He ended with testimony about a full set of fingerprints found on the headboard of the bed in which the victim was found. He and Langwiser knew that these were the prints that Fowkkes would get the most yardage out of, so Langwiser attempted to minimize the potential damage by having it revealed during her examination of the witness.

'How far from the victim's body were these prints located?'

Bosch looked at the report in the binder.

'Two point three feet.'

'Exactly where on the headboard?'

'On the outside facing, between the headboard and the wall.'

'Was there a lot of space there?'

'About two inches.'

'How would someone get their fingerprints there?'

Fowkkes objected, saying it was outside Bosch's realm of expertise to determine how a set of fingerprints got anywhere, but the judge allowed the question.

'Only two ways I can think of,' Bosch answered. 'They

got there when the bed was not pushed quite up to the wall. Or the person who left the prints had reached their fingers through the opening in the slats of the headboard and left them while holding onto that particular cross board.'

Langwiser introduced a photo taken by a fingerprint technician as an exhibit and it was shown to the jury.

'To accomplish the latter explanation you offered, the person would have to be lying in the bed, would they not?'

'It would seem that way.'

'Face down?'

'Yes.'

Fowkkes stood to object but the judge sustained it before the lawyer uttered a word.

'You are going too far afield with suppositions, Ms. Langwiser. Move on.'

'Yes, Your Honor.'

She referred to her pad for a moment.

'This print on the victim's bed, didn't that make you think the person who left it should be considered a prime suspect?'

'Not initially. It is impossible to tell how long a print has been at a specific location. Plus we had the additional factor that we knew the victim had not been killed in her bed, but rather taken to the bed after being killed elsewhere. It appeared to us that the location of the print was not a place that would have been touched by the killer when he put the body in the bed.'

'Who did these prints belong to?'

'A man named Allan Wiess, who had dated Ms. Krementz on three prior occasions, the most recent date being three weeks before her death.'

'Did you interview Allan Wiess?'

'Yes, I did. Along with Detective Edgar.'

'Did he acknowledge ever being in the victim's bed?'

'Yes, he did. He said he slept with her on that last occasion that he saw her, three weeks prior to her death.'

'Did he say he touched the bed board in the location you have shown us where the fingerprints were located?'

'He said he could have done it but he did not specifically remember doing it.'

'Did you investigate Allan Weiss's activities on the night of Jody Krementz's death?'

'Yes, we did. He had a solid alibi.'

'And what was that?'

'He told us he was in Hawaii at a real estate seminar. We checked airline and hotel records as well as with the seminar's producers. We confirmed he was there.'

Langwiser looked at Judge Houghton and said that it would be a good time to take the morning break. The judge said it was a little early but granted the request and ordered the jurors back in fifteen minutes.

Bosch knew she wanted the break now because she was about to move into questions about David Storey and wanted them clearly separated from all the other testimony. As he stepped off the witness stand and went back to the prosecution table, Langwiser was flipping through some files. She spoke to him without looking up.

'What's wrong, Harry?'

'What do you mean?'

'You're not crisp. Not like yesterday. Are you nervous about something?'

'No. Are you?'

'Yeah, the whole thing. We've got a lot riding on this.'

'I'll be crisper.'

'I'm serious, Harry.'

'So am I, Janis.'

He then walked away from the prosecution table and out through the courtroom.

He decided he would get a cup of coffee at the second-floor cafeteria. But first he stepped into the restroom next to the elevators and went to one of the sinks to splash cold water on his face. He bent fully over the sink, careful not to get water on his suit. He heard a toilet flush and when he straightened up and looked in the mirror he saw Rudy Tafero pass behind him and go to the sink furthest away. Bosch bent down again and brought more water up and held it. Its chill felt good against his eyes and eased his headache.

'What's it like, Rudy?' he asked without looking at the other man.

'What's what like, Harry?'

'You know, doing the devil's bidding. You get any sleep at night?'

Bosch walked over to the paper towel dispenser and tore off several sheets to dry his hands and face. Tafero came over and tore off a towel and began drying his hands.

'It's funny,' Tafero said. 'The only time in my life I had trouble sleeping was when I was a cop. I wonder why that was.'

He balled the towel in his hands and threw it into the wastebasket. He smiled at Bosch and then walked out. Bosch watched him go, still rubbing his hands on the towels.

24

Bosch could feel the coffee working in his blood. The second wind was coming. The headache was easing. He was ready. This would be how they planned it, how they had choreographed it. He leaned forward to the microphone and waited for the question.

'Detective Bosch,' Langwiser said from the lectern, 'did there come a time when the name David Storey came up in your investigation?'

'Yes, almost immediately. We received information from Jane Gilley, who was Jody Krementz's roommate, that on the last night of Jody's life she had a date with David Storey.'

'Did there come a time when you questioned Mr. Storey about that last night?'

'Yes. Briefly.'

'Why briefly, Detective Bosch? This *was* a homicide.'

'That was Mr. Storey's choosing. We attempted several times to interview him on that Friday that the body was discovered and the next day as well. He was difficult to locate. Finally, through his attorney, he agreed to be interviewed the next day, which was Sunday, on the condition that we come to him and conduct the interview in his office at Archway Studios. We reluctantly agreed to do it that way but did so in the spirit of cooperation and because we needed to talk to this man. At that point we were two days into the case and had not been able to talk to the last person known to have seen the victim alive. When we arrived at the office, Mr. Storey's personal attorney, Jason Fleer, was there. We began interviewing Mr. Storey but in less than five minutes his attorney terminated the interview.'

'Was this conversation tape-recorded?'

'Yes, it was.'

Langwiser made the motion to play the recording and it was approved by Judge Houghton over Fowkkes's objection. Fowkkes had asked the judge to simply allow jurors to read his already prepared transcripts of the short interview. But Langwiser objected to that, saying that she had not had time to check the transcripts for accuracy and that it was important for the jurors to hear David Storey's tone and demeanor. With the wisdom of Solomon the judge ruled that the tape would be heard and that the transcripts would be handed out anyway as an aid to the jurors. He encouraged Bosch and the prosecution team to read along as well so they could check the transcript for accuracy.

BOSCH: My name is Detective Hieronymus Bosch of the Los Angeles Police Department. I am accompanied by my partners, Detectives Jerry Edgar and Kizmin Rider. The date is October 15, 2000. We are interviewing David Storey in his offices at Archway Studios in regard to case number zero-zero-eight-nine-seven. Mr. Storey is accompanied by his attorney, Jason Fleer. Mr. Storey, Mr. Fleer? Any questions before we begin?

FLEER: No questions.

BOSCH: Oh, and, obviously, we are recording this statement. Mr. Storey, did you know a woman named Jody Krementz? Also known as Donatella Speers.

STOREY: You know the answer to that.

FLEER: David . . .

STOREY: Yes, I knew her. I was with her last Thursday night. It does not mean I killed her.

FLEER: David, please. Answer only the questions they ask you.

STOREY: Whatever.

BOSCH: Can I continue?

FLEER: By all means. Please.

STOREY: Yes, by all means. Please.

BOSCH: You mentioned that you were with her on Thursday evening. This was a date?

STOREY: Why ask things you already know the answer to? Yes, it was a date, if you want to call it that.

BOSCH: What do you want to call it?

STOREY: Doesn't matter.

(pause)

BOSCH: Could you give us a framework of time that you were with her?

STOREY: Picked her up at seven-thirty, dropped her off about midnight.

BOSCH: Did you enter her home when you came to pick her up?

STOREY: Matter of fact, I didn't. I was running very late and called on my cell phone to tell her to come outside because I didn't have time to come in. I think she wanted me to meet her roommate – another actress, no doubt – but I didn't have the time.

BOSCH: So when you pulled up she was waiting outside.

STOREY: That's what I said.

BOSCH: Seven-thirty until midnight. That is four and a half hours.

STOREY: You are good at math. I like that in a detective.

FLEER: David, let's try to get this done.

STOREY: I am.

BOSCH: Could you tell us what you did during the time period you were with Jody Krementz?

STOREY: We covered the three Fs. Film, food and a fuck.

BOSCH: Excuse me?

STOREY: We went to the premiere of my movie, then we went to the reception and had something to eat, then I took her to my place and we had sex. Consensual sex, Detective. Believe it or not, people do it on dates all the time. And not just Hollywood people. It happens across this great country of ours. It's what makes it great.

BOSCH: I understand. Did you take her home when you were finished?

STOREY: Always the gentleman, I did.

BOSCH: Did you enter her house at this time?

STOREY: No. I was in my fucking bathrobe. I just drove up, she got out and went inside. I then drove back home. Whatever happened after that I don't know. I am not involved in this in any way, shape or form. You people are—

FLEER: David, please.

STOREY: – completely full of shit if for one fucking moment you think—

FLEER: David, stop!

(pause)

Detective Bosch, I think we need to stop this.

BOSCH: We're in the middle of an interview here and—

FLEER: David, where are you going?

STOREY: Fuck these people. I'm going out for a smoke.

BOSCH: Mr. Storey has just left the office.

FLEER: I think at this point he is exercising his rights under the Fifth Amendment. This interview is over.

The tape went blank and Langwiser turned it off. Bosch looked at the jury. Several of them were looking at Storey. His arrogance had come through loud and clear on the tape. This was important because they would soon be asking the jury to believe that Storey had privately boasted to Bosch about the murder and how he would get away with it. Only an arrogant man would do that. The prosecution needed to prove Storey was not only a murderer, but an arrogant one at that.

'Okay, then,' Langwiser said. 'Did Mr. Storey return to continue the interview?'

'No, he did not,' Bosch answered. 'And we were asked to leave.'

'Did Mr. Storey's denial of any involvement in the murder of Jody Krementz end your interest in him?'

'No, it did not. We had an obligation to investigate the case fully and that included either ruling him in or ruling him out as a suspect.'

'Was his behavior during the short interview cause for suspicion?'

'You mean his arrogance? No, he—'

Fowkkes jumped up with an objection.

'Your Honor, one man's arrogance is another man's confidence in his innocence. There is no—'

'You are right, Mr. Fowkkes,' Houghton said.

He sustained the objection, struck Bosch's answer and turned to the jurors to tell them to ignore the remark.

'His behavior during the interview was not cause for suspicion,' Bosch began again. 'His being the last known person to be with the victim was cause for our immediate attention and focus. His lack of cooperation was suspicious but at this point we were keeping an open mind about everything. My partners and I have a combined total of more than twenty-five years' experience investigating homicides. We know that things are not always what they seem.'

'Where did the investigation go next?'

'We continued all avenues of investigation. One of those avenues was obviously Mr. Storey. Based on his statement that he and the victim had gone to his home on their date, my partners filed a search warrant application in Municipal Court and received approval to search David Storey's home.'

Langwiser brought the search warrant forward to the

judge and it was received into evidence. She took it back with her to the lectern. Bosch then testified that the search of the home on Mulholland Drive was conducted at 6 A.M. two days after the initial interview with Storey.

'The search warrant authorized you to seize any evidence of Jody Krementz's murder, any evidence of her belongings and any evidence of her presence in that location, is that correct?'

'Correct.'

'Who conducted the search?'

'Myself, my partners and a two-man forensics team. We also had a photographer, for video and stills. A total of six.'

'How long did the search last?'

'Approximately seven hours.'

'Was the defendant present during the search?'

'For most of it. He had to leave at one point for a meeting with a movie actor he said he couldn't postpone. He was gone approximately two hours. During that time his personal attorney, Mr. Fleer, remained in the house and monitored the search. We were never left alone in the house, if that is what you are asking.'

Langwiser flipped through the pages of the search warrant, coming to the end of it.

'Now, Detective, when you seize any items during a court-approved search, you are required by law to keep an inventory on the search warrant receipt, correct?'

'Yes.'

'This receipt is then filed with the court, correct?'

'Yes.'

'Can you tell us then, why is this receipt blank?'

'We did not take any items from the house during the search.'

'You found nothing that indicated that Jody Krementz had been inside Mr. Storey's house, as he had told you she had been?'

'Nothing.'

'This search took place how many days after the

evening Mr. Storey told you he had taken Ms. Krementz to his house and engaged in sexual relations with her?'

'Five days from the night of the murder, two days from our interview with Mr. Storey.'

'You found nothing in support of Mr. Storey's statement.'

'Nothing. The place was clean.'

Bosch knew she was trying to turn a negative into a positive, somehow trying to imply that the unsuccessful search was an indication of Storey's guilt.

'Would you call this an unsuccessful search?'

'No. Success doesn't enter into it. We were looking for evidence that would corroborate his statement as well as any evidence of possible foul play relating to Ms. Krementz. We found nothing in the house indicative of this. But sometimes it is not what you find, it's what you don't.'

'Can you explain that to the jury?'

'Well, it is true we didn't take any evidence from the house. But we found something missing that would later become important to us.'

'And what was that?'

'A book. A missing book.'

'How did you know it was missing if it wasn't there?'

'In the living room of the house there was a large built-in bookcase. Each shelf was full of books. On one shelf there was a space – a slot – where a book had been but was now gone. We could not find what book that might be. There were no books sitting out loose in the house. At the time it was just a small thing. Someone had obviously taken a book from the shelf and not replaced it. It was just kind of curious to us that we could not figure out where or what it was.'

Langwiser offered two still photographs of the bookcase taken during the search as exhibits. Houghton accepted them over a routine objection from Fowkkes. The photos showed the bookcase in its entirety and a close-up of the second shelf with the open space between a book called

The Fifth Horizon and a biography of the film director John Ford called *Print the Legend.*

'Now, Detective,' Langwiser said, 'you said that at the time you did not know if this missing book had any importance or bearing on the case, correct?'

'That is right.'

'Did you eventually determine what book had been taken from the shelf?'

'Yes, we did.'

Langwiser paused. Bosch knew what she was going to do. The dance had been choreographed. He thought of her as a good storyteller. She knew how to string it along, keep people hooked in, take them to the edge of the cliff and then pull them back.

'Well, let's take things in order,' she said. 'We'll come back to the book. Now did you have occasion to talk to Mr. Storey on the day of the search?'

'He mostly kept to himself and was on the phone most of the time. But we spoke when we first knocked on the door and announced the search. And then at the end of the day when I told him we were leaving and that we were not taking anything with us.'

'Did you wake him up when you came at six in the morning?'

'Yes, we did.'

'Was he alone in the house?'

'Yes.'

'Did he invite you in?'

'Not at first. He objected to the search. I told him—'

'Excuse me, Detective, we might make this easier if we show it. You said there was a videographer with you. Was he running the camera when you knocked at six in the morning?'

'Yes, he was.'

Langwiser then made the appropriate motions to introduce the search video. It was accepted under objection from the defense. A large television was rolled into the courtroom and placed at center in front of the jury box. Bosch was asked to identify the tape. The lights in the courtroom were dimmed and it was played.

The tape began with a focus on Bosch and the others outside the red front door of a house. He identified himself and the address and the case number. He spoke quietly. He then turned and knocked sharply on the door. He announced it was the police and knocked sharply again. They waited. Bosch knocked on the door every fifteen seconds until it was finally opened about two minutes after the first pounding. David Storey looked out through the opening, his hair disheveled, his eyes showing exhaustion.

'What?' he asked.

'We have a search warrant here, Mr. Storey,' Bosch said. 'It allows us to conduct a search of these premises.'

'You have to be fucking kidding.'

'No, we're not, sir. Could you step back and let us in? The sooner we're in the sooner we're out.'

'I'm calling my lawyer.'

Storey closed and locked the door. Bosch immediately stepped up and put his face close to the jamb. He called out loudly.

'Mr. Storey, you have ten minutes. If this door is not opened by six-fifteen then we're going to take it down. We have a court-ordered search warrant and we will execute it.'

He turned back to the camera and made the cut signal across his throat.

The video jumped to another focus on the door. The time readout in the bottom corner now showed it was 6:13 A.M. The door opened and Storey stepped back and signaled the search team in. His hair looked as though it had been combed with his hands. He was wearing black jeans and a black T-shirt. He was in bare feet.

'Do what you have to do and get out. My lawyer's coming and he's going to watch you people. You break one fucking thing in this house and I'm going to sue the shit out of you. This is a David Serrurier house. You so much as put a scratch on one of the walls and it'll be your jobs. All of you.'

'We'll be careful, Mr. Storey,' Bosch said as he walked in.

The cameraman was the last to enter the house. Storey looked into the lens as if seeing it for the first time.

'And get that shit off of me.'

He made a motion and the camera angle shot upward to the ceiling. It remained there while the voices of the videographer and Storey continued off camera.

'Hey! Don't touch the camera!'

'Then get it out of my face!'

'Okay. Fine. Just don't touch the camera.'

The screen went blank and the lights of the courtroom came back up. Langwiser continued the questioning.

'Detective Bosch, did you or members of the search team have further . . . conversation with Mr. Storey after that?'

'Not during the search. Once his lawyer got there Mr. Storey stayed in his office. When we searched his office he moved into the bedroom. When he was leaving for his appointment I questioned him briefly about that and he left. That was about it as far as it went during the search and while we were inside the house.'

'What about at the end of the day – seven hours later – when the search was completed, did you speak to the defendant again?'

'Yes, I spoke to him briefly at the front door. We were packed up and ready to leave. The lawyer had left. I was in my car with my partners. We were backing out when I realized I had forgotten about giving Mr. Storey a copy of the search warrant. It's required by law. So I went back to his door and knocked on it.'

'Did Mr. Storey answer the door himself?'

'Yes, he answered after about four hard knocks. I gave him the receipt and told him it was required.'

'Did he say anything to you?'

Fowkkes stood up and objected for the record but the issue had already been disposed of in pretrial motions and rulings. The judge noted the objection for the record and overruled it for the record. Langwiser asked the question again.

'Can I refer to my notes?'

'Please.'

Bosch turned to the notes he had taken in the car right after the conversation.

'First, he said, "You didn't find a goddamn thing, did you?" And I told him he was right, that we weren't taking anything with us. He then said, "Because there was nothing to take." I nodded and was turning to leave when he spoke again. He said, "Hey, Bosch." I turned back and he leaned toward me and said, "You'll never find what you are looking for." I said, "Oh really, what is it that I am looking for?" He didn't respond. He just looked at me and smiled.'

After a pause, Langwiser asked, 'Was that the end of it?'

'No. I sensed at that point that I might be able to bait him into saying more. I said to him, "You did it, didn't you?" He continued to smile and then he slowly nodded. And he said, "And I'll get away with it." He said, "I'm a —"

'Bullshit! You're a fucking liar!'

It was Storey. He had stood up and was pointing at Bosch. Fowkkes had his hand on him and was trying to pull him back into his place. A deputy sheriff, who had been positioned at a desk to the rear of the defense table was up and moving toward Storey from behind.

'The defendant will sit DOWN!' the judge boomed from the bench at the same moment he brought the gavel down.

'He's fucking lying!'

'Deputy, sit him down!'

The deputy moved in, put both hands on Storey's shoulders from behind and roughly pulled him back down into his seat. The judge pointed another deputy toward the jury.

'Remove the jury.'

While the jurors were quickly hustled into the deliberation room, Storey continued to struggle with the deputy and Fowkkes. As soon as the jurors were gone he seemed to relax his efforts and then calmed. Bosch looked over at the reporters, trying to see if any of them had noted how Storey's demonstration ended as soon as the jurors were out of sight.

'Mr. Storey!' the judge yelled from a standing position. 'That behavior and language is not acceptable in this courtroom. Mr. Fowkkes, if you can't control your client, my people will. One more outburst and I will have him gagged and chained to that chair. Am I clear on this?'

'Absolutely, Your Honor. I apolo—'

'That is a zero tolerance rule. Any outburst from here on out and he'll be shackled. I don't care who he is or who his friends are.'

'Yes, Your Honor. We understand.'

'I am taking five minutes and then we'll start again.'

The judge abruptly left the bench, his feet resounding loudly as he quickly took the three steps down. He disappeared through a door to the rear hallway that led to his chambers.

Bosch looked over at Langwiser and her eyes betrayed her delight at what had just happened. To Bosch it was a trade-off. On one hand the jurors saw the defendant acting angry and out of control – possibly exhibiting the same rage that had led to murder. But on the other hand, he was registering his objection to what was happening to him in the courtroom. And that could register an empathic response from the jurors. Storey had to reach only one of them in order to walk.

Before the trial Langwiser had predicted that they would draw Storey into an outburst. Bosch had thought she was wrong. He thought Storey was too cool and calculating. Unless, of course, the outburst was a calculated move. Storey was a man who directed dramatic scenes and characters for a living. Bosch knew he should have seen that a time might come when he would be unwittingly used as a supporting actor in one of those scenes.

25

The judge returned to the bench two minutes after leaving and Bosch wondered if he had retreated to his chambers to put a holster on under the robes. As soon as he sat down Houghton looked at the defense table. Storey was sitting with his face somberly pointed down at the sketch pad in front of him.

'Are we ready?' the judge asked.

All parties murmured they were ready. The judge called for the jury and they were brought in, most of them looking directly at Storey as they entered.

'Okay, folks, we're going to try this again,' Judge Houghton said. 'The exclamations you heard a few minutes ago from the defendant are to be ignored. They are not evidence, they are not anything. If Mr. Storey wants to personally deny the charges or anything else said about him in testimony, he'll get that chance.'

Bosch watched Langwiser's eyes dance. The judge's comments were his way of slapping back at the defense. He was setting up the expectation that Storey would testify during the defense phase. If he didn't, then it could be a letdown for the jurors.

The judge turned it back over to Langwiser, who continued her questioning of Bosch.

'Before we were interrupted, you were testifying about your conversation with the defendant at the door to his house.'

'Yes.'

'You quoted the defendant as saying, "And I'll get away with it," is that correct?'

'Correct.'

'And you took this comment to be referring to the death of Jody Krementz, correct?'

'That's what we were talking about, yes.'

'Did he say anything else after that?'

'Yes.'

Bosch paused, wondering if Storey would make another outburst. He didn't.

'He said, "I am a god in this town, Detective Bosch. You don't fuck with the gods." '

Nearly ten seconds of silence went by before Langwiser was prompted by the judge to move on.

'What did you do after the defendant made this statement to you?'

'Well, I was kind of taken aback. I was surprised that he would say this to me.'

'You were not recording the conversation, is that correct?'

'That is correct. It was just a conversation at the door after I knocked.'

'So what happened next?'

'I went to the car and immediately wrote out these notes of the conversation so I would have it verbatim from when it was freshest in my mind. I told my partners what had just transpired and we decided to call the district attorney's office for advice as to whether this admission to me would give us probable cause to arrest Mr. Storey. Um, what happened was that none of us could get a signal on our cell phones because we were up there in the hills. We left the house and drove to the fire station on Mulholland just east of Laurel Canyon Boulevard. We asked to use a phone there and I made the call to the DA.'

'And who did you speak with?'

'You. I recounted the case, what had transpired during the search and what Mr. Storey said at the door. It was decided to continue the investigation at that point and not make the arrest.'

'Did you agree with that decision?'

'Not at the time. I wanted to arrest him.'

'Did Mr. Storey's admission change the investigation?'

'It pretty much closed the focus. The man had admitted the crime to me. We began looking only at him.'

'Did you ever consider that perhaps the admission was an empty boast, that at the same time you were in essence baiting the defendant, he was baiting you?'

'Yes, I considered it. But ultimately I believed he made the statements because they were true and because he believed he was in an invincible position at that point.'

There was a sharp ripping sound as Storey tore the top page off his sketch pad. He crumpled the paper and bounced it across the table. It hit a computer screen and bounced off the table to the floor.

'Thank you, Detective,' Langwiser said. 'Now, you said the decision was to continue the investigation. Can you tell the jury what that entailed?'

Bosch described how he and his partners had interviewed dozens of witnesses who had seen the defendant and the victim at the film premiere or at the reception that followed in a circus tent erected in a nearby parking lot. They also interviewed dozens more people who knew Storey or had worked with him. Bosch acknowledged that none of these interviews had produced information important to the investigation.

'You mentioned earlier that during the search of the defendant's home you became curious about a missing book, correct?'

'Yes.'

Fowkkes objected.

'There has been no evidence whatsoever about a missing book. There was a space on the shelf. It does not mean there was ever a book in that place.'

Langwiser promised she would tie it all up promptly and the judge overruled.

'Did there come a time when you determined what book had been in that space on the shelf in the defendant's home?'

'Yes, in the course of our gathering of background information on Mr. Storey, my partner, Kizmin Rider, who was aware of his work and professional reputation, remembered that she had read a story about him in a magazine called *Architectural Digest.* She was able to do an Internet search and determine that the issue she remembered was from February of last year. She then ordered a copy of the magazine from the publisher. What she had remembered was that there were photos in the article of Mr. Storey in his house. She remembered his bookshelves because she is an avid reader and was curious about what books this movie director would have on his shelves.'

Langwiser made a motion to introduce the magazine as her next exhibit. It was received by the judge and Langwiser gave it to Bosch on the witness stand.

'Is that the magazine your partner received?'

'Yes.'

'Could you turn to the story on the defendant and describe the photograph on the opening page of the story?'

Bosch flipped to a marker in the magazine.

'It is a photograph of David Storey sitting on the couch in the living room of his house. To his left are the bookshelves.'

'Can you read the titles of the books on the spines of the books?'

'Some of them. They are not all clear.'

'When you received this magazine from the publisher, what did you do with it?'

'We saw that not all of the books were clear. We contacted the publisher again and attempted to borrow the negative of this photo. We dealt with the editor in chief, who would not allow the negatives out of the office. He cited media law and free-press restraints.'

'So what happened next?'

'The editor said he would even fight a court order. An attorney from the city attorney's office was called in and began negotiating with the magazine's lawyer. The result was that I flew to New York City and was allowed access to the negative in the photo lab in the *Architectural Digest* offices.'

'For the record, what date were you there?'

'I took a redeye on October twenty-ninth. I was at the magazine's office the following morning. It was a Monday, October thirtieth.'

'And what did you do there?'

'I had the magazine's photo lab manager make blowups of the shot containing the bookshelves.'

Langwiser introduced two large blowup photographs on hard backing as her next exhibits. After they were approved over unsustained objection she put them on easels set in front of the jury. One showed the bookcase in full while the other was a blowup of one shelf. The image was grainy but the titles on the spines of the books could be read.

'Detective, did you compare these photos with those taken during the search of the defendant's house?'

'Yes, we did.'

Langwiser asked permission to set up a third and fourth easel and to put blowup photos taken during the search of the full bookcase and the shelf with the space for a missing book. The judge approved. She then asked Bosch to step down from the witness stand and use a pointer to explain what he found during his comparison study. It was obvious to anyone looking at the photos what he found but Langwiser was painstakingly going through the motions so that no juror could be confused.

Bosch put the pointer on the photo showing the open

space in the shelved books. He then brought it over and put the tip on a book that was in the same spot.

'When we searched the house on October seventeenth there was no book here between *The Fifth Horizon* and *Print the Legend*. Here in this photo, taken ten months before, there is a book between *The Fifth Horizon* and *Print the Legend*.'

'And what is the title of that book?'

'*Victims of the Night*.'

'Okay, and did you look at photos you had from the search of the full bookcase in order to see if this book, *Victims of the Night*, had been shelved elsewhere?'

Bosch pointed to the October 17 blowup of the entire bookcase.

'We did. It's not there.'

'Did you find this book anywhere in the house?'

'No, we did not.'

'Thank you, Detective. You can return to the witness stand now.'

Langwiser introduced a copy of *Victims of the Night* as an exhibit and handed it to Bosch.

'Can you tell the jury what that is, Detective?'

'It is a copy of *Victims of the Night*.'

'Is that the book that was on the defendant's shelf when his photograph was taken for *Architectural Digest* in January of last year?'

'No, it's not. It's a copy of the same book. I bought it.'

'Where?'

'A place called Mystery Bookstore in Westwood.'

'Why did you buy it there?'

'I called around. It was the only place I could find that had it in stock.'

'Why was it so hard to find?'

'The man at Mystery Bookstore told me it was a small printing by a small publisher.'

'Did you read this book?'

'Parts of it. It is mostly photographs of unusual crime scenes and accident scenes, that sort of thing.'

'Is there anything in there that struck you as unusual or perhaps relating to the killing of Jody Krementz?'

'Yes, there is a photograph of a death scene on page seventy-three that immediately drew my attention.'

'Describe it, please.'

Bosch opened the book to a marker. He spoke as he looked at the full-page photograph on the right side of the book.

'It shows a woman in a bed. She's dead. A scarf is tied around her neck and looped over one of the bars of the headboard. She is nude from the waist down. Her left hand is between her legs and two of her fingers have penetrated the vagina.'

'Can you read the caption beneath the photo, please?'

'It says, "Autoerotic Death: This woman was found in her bed in New Orleans, a victim of autoerotic asphyxia. It is estimated that around the world more than five hundred people die from this accidental misadventure each year." '

Langwiser asked and received permission to place two more blowup photos on the easels as exhibits. She placed them right over two of the bookshelf photos. Side by side the photos were of Jody Krementz's body in her bed and of the page from *Victims of the Night.*

'Detective, did you make a comparison between the photo of the victim in this case, Jody Krementz, and the photo from the book?'

'Yes, I did. I found them to be very similar.'

'Did it appear to you that the body of Ms. Krementz could have been staged, using the photo from the book as a model or baseline?'

'Yes, it did.'

'Did you ever have occasion to ask the defendant what happened to his copy of the book *Victims of the Night*?'

'No, since the day of the search of his home, Mr. Storey

and his attorneys have refused repeated requests for an interview.'

Langwiser nodded and looked at the judge.

'Your Honor, may I take these exhibits down and offer them to the court clerk?'

'Please do,' the judge responded.

Langwiser made a show of taking the photos of the two dead women down first by folding them in toward each other like two sides of a mirror closing. It was a little thing but Bosch saw thc jurors watching.

'Okay, Detective Bosch,' Langwiser said when the easels were cleared. 'Did you make any inquiries or do any further investigation into autoerotic deaths?'

'Yes. I knew that if this case ever moved to a trial that the classification of the death as a homicide staged to look like this sort of accident might be challenged. I was also curious about what that caption in the book said. Frankly, I was surprised by the figure of five hundred deaths a year. I did some checking with the FBI and found that the figure was actually accurate, if not low.'

'And did that cause you to do any further research?'

'Yes, on a more local level.'

With Langwiser prompting, Bosch testified that he checked through records at the medical examiner's office for deaths due to autoerotic asphyxia. His search went back five years.

'And what did you find?'

'In those five years, sixteen deaths in Los Angeles County classified as accidental death by misadventure had been attributed specifically to autoerotic asphyxia.'

'And how many of these cases involved female victims?'

'Only one case involved a female.'

'Did you examine this case?'

Fowkkes was up with an objection and this time asked for a sidebar conference. The judge allowed it and the attorneys gathered at the side of the bench. Bosch could not hear the whispered conversation but knew that

Fowkkes was most likely trying to stop the direction of the testimony. Langwiser and Kretzler had anticipated he would move once more to block any mention of Alicia Lopez in front of the jurors. It would likely be the pivotal decision in the trial – for both sides.

After five minutes of whispered argument, the judge sent the lawyers back to their places and told the jurors that the issue before the court would take longer than anticipated. He adjourned for another fifteen-minute break. Bosch returned to the prosecution table.

'Something new?' Bosch asked Langwiser.

'No, the same old argument. For some reason the judge wants to hear it again. Wish us luck.'

The lawyers and the judge retreated to chambers to argue the point. Bosch was left at the table. He used his cell phone to check messages at his home and office. There was one message at work. It was from Terry McCaleb. He thanked Bosch for the tip from the night before. He said he got some good information at Nat's and that he'd be in touch. Bosch erased it and closed the phone, wondering what it was that McCaleb had picked up.

When the lawyers returned through the rear door of the courtroom, Bosch read the judge's decision in their faces. Fowkkes looked dour, with his eyes downcast. Kretzler and Langwiser came back smiling.

After the jurors were brought back and the trial resumed, Langwiser went directly in for the hit. She asked the court reporter to read back the last question before the objection.

'Did you examine this case?' the reporter read.

'Let's strike that,' Langwiser said. 'Let's not confuse the issue. Detective, the one female case of the sixteen you found in the medical examiner's records, what was the name of the deceased in that case?'

'Alicia Lopez.'

'Can you tell us a little bit about her?'

'She was twenty-four and lived in Culver City. She worked as an administrative assistant to the vice-president of production at Sony Pictures, also in Culver City. She was found dead in her bed on the twentieth of May, nineteen ninety-eight.'

'She lived alone?'

'Yes.'

'What were the circumstances of her death?'

'She was found in her bed by a coworker who became concerned when she had missed two days of work following the weekend without calling in. The coroner estimated she had been dead three to four days by the time she was found. Decomposition of the body was extensive.'

'Ms. Langwiser?' Judge Houghton interrupted. 'It was agreed that you would lay foundation connecting the cases quickly.'

'I'm right there, Your Honor. Thank you. Detective, did anything about this case alert you or draw your attention in any way?'

'Several things. I looked at photos taken at the death scene and though decomposition was extensive I was able to note that the victim in this case was in a posture closely paralleling that of the victim in the present case. I also noted that the ligature in the Lopez case was also used without a buffering, which was the same with the present case. I also knew from our backgrounding investigation of Mr. Storey that at the time of Ms. Lopez's death he wasmaking a film for a company called Cold House Films, a company which was being financed in part by Sony Pictures.'

In the moment following his answer Bosch noticed that the courtroom had become unusually still and silent. No one was whispering in the gallery or clearing their throat. It was as if everyone – jurors, lawyers, spectators and media – all decided to hold their breath at once. Bosch glanced at the jurors and saw that almost all of them were looking at the defense table. Bosch looked there as well and saw Storey, his face still aimed downward, silently seething. Langwiser finally broke the silence.

'Detective, did you make further inquiries about the Lopez case?'

'Yes, I spoke to the detective who handled it for the Culver City Police Department. I also made inquiries about Ms. Lopez's job at Sony.'

'And what did you learn about her that would have bearing on the present case?'

'I learned that at the time of her death she was acting as a liaison between the studio and the field production of the film David Storey was directing.'

'Do you recall the name of that film?'

'*The Fifth Horizon.*'

'Where was it being filmed?'

'In Los Angeles. Mostly in Venice.'

'And as a liaison would Ms. Lopez have had any direct contact with Mr. Storey?'

'Yes. She spoke with him by phone or in person every day of the shoot.'

Again the silence seemed to be roaring. Langwiser milked it for as long as she could and then started driving home the nails.

'Let me see if I have all of this straight, Detective. Your testimony is that in the past five years there has been only one death of a female in Los Angeles County attributed to autoerotic asphyxia and that the present case involving the death of Jody Krementz was staged to appear as an autoerotic asphyxia?'

'Objection,' Fowkkes interjected. 'Asked and answered.'

'Overruled,' Houghton said without argument from Langwiser. 'The witness may answer.'

'Yes,' Bosch said. 'Correct.'

'And that both of these women knew the defendant, David Storey?'

'Correct.'

'And that both of these deaths show similarities to a

photograph of an autoerotic death contained in a book known at one time to be in the defendant's collection at home?'

'Correct.'

Bosch looked over at Storey as he said it, hoping he would look up so that they could lock eyes one more time.

'What did the Culver City Police Department have to say about this, Detective Bosch?'

'Based upon my inquiries they have reopened the case. But they are hampered.'

'Why is that?'

'The case is old. Because it was originally ruled an accidental death, not all the records were kept in archives. Because decomposition was advanced at the time of the body's discovery it is hard to make definitive observations and conclusions. And the body cannot be exhumed because it was cremated.'

'It was? By whom?'

Fowkkes stood and objected but the judge said the argument had already been heard and overruled. Langwiser prompted Bosch before Fowkkes had even sat back down.

'By whom, Detective Bosch?'

'By her family. But it was paid for . . . the cremation, the service, everything was paid for by David Storey as a gift in Alicia Lopez's memory.'

Langwiser loudly flipped up a page on her legal tablet. She was on a roll and everybody knew it. It was what cops and prosecutors called being in the tube. It was a surfing reference. It meant they had ridden the case into the water tunnel where everything was going smoothly and perfectly and was surrounding them in glorious balance.

'Detective, subsequent to this part of the investigation, did there come a time when a woman named Annabelle Crowe came to see you?'

'Yes. A story had broken in the *Los Angeles Times* about

the investigation and how David Storey was the focus. She read the story and came forward.'

'And who is she?'

'She's an actress. She lives in West Hollywood.'

'And what bearing did she have on this case?'

'She told me that she had dated David Storey at one time last year and he choked her while they were having sex.'

Fowkkes made another objection, this one without the force of his other protestations. But again he was overruled, as the testimony had been cleared by the judge in earlier motions.

'Where did Ms. Crowe say this incident took place?'

'In Mr. Storey's home on Mulholland Drive. I asked her to describe the place and she was able to do so accurately. She had been there.'

'Couldn't she have seen the issue of *Architectural Digest* that showed photos of the defendant's home?'

'She was able to describe in accurate detail areas of the master bedroom and bath that were not shown in the magazine.'

'What happened to her when the defendant choked her?'

'She told me she passed out. When she awoke Mr. Storey was not in the room. He was taking a shower. She grabbed her clothing and fled from the home.'

Langwiser underlined that with a long silence. She then flipped the pages of her pad down, glanced over at the defense table and then looked up at Judge Houghton.

'Your Honor, that is all I have for Detective Bosch at this time.'

26

McCaleb got to El Cochinito at quarter to twelve. He hadn't been inside the store-front restaurant in Silver Lake in five years but he remembered the place had only a dozen or so tables and they were usually taken quickly at lunchtime. And often those tables were taken by cops. Not because the name of the restaurant was a draw – the Little Pig – but because the food was of high quality and low cost. It had been McCaleb's experience that cops were highly skilled in finding such establishments among the many restaurants in any city. When he had traveled on assignment for the bureau, he would always ask the local street cops for recommendations on food. He had rarely been disappointed.

While he waited for Winston he carefully studied the menu and planned his meal. In the past year his palate had finally returned with a vengeance. For the first eighteen months of his life after surgery, his sense of taste had deserted him. He had not cared what he ate because it all tasted the same – bland. Even a heavy dousing of habañera sauce on everything from sandwiches to pasta only registered a minor blip on his tongue. But then, slowly, his taste started coming back and it became a second rebirth for him following the transplant itself. He now loved everything Graciela made. He even loved everything *he* made – and this despite his general ineptitude with anything other than the barbecue grill. He ate everything with a gusto he'd never had before, even before the transplant. A peanut butter and jelly sandwich in the middle of the night was something he privately savored as much as a trip overtown with Graciela to dine in style at Jozu on Melrose. Consequently, he had started filling out, gaining back the twenty-five pounds he'd lost while his own heart had withered and he'd waited for a new one. He was now back to his pre-illness weight of 180 and food intake, for the first time in four years, was something he had to watch. On his last cardio checkup, his doctor had taken notice and raised a warning. She told him that he had to slow down the intake of calories and fat.

But not at this lunch. He had been waiting a long time for a chance to come to this place. Years earlier he had spent a good bit of time in Florida on a serial case and the only good that had come out of it was his love of Cuban food. When he later transferred to the Los Angeles field office it was hard to find a Cuban restaurant that compared with the places where he had eaten in Ybor City outside of Tampa. Once on an L.A. case he'd come across a patrol cop who he learned was of Cuban descent. McCaleb asked him where he went to eat when he wanted real home cooking. The cop's answer was El Cochinito. And McCaleb quickly became a regular.

McCaleb decided that studying the menu was a waste of time because he had known all along what he wanted. Lechon asada with black beans and rice, fried bananas and yucca on the side and don't bother telling the doctor. He just wished Winston would hurry up and get there so he could place his order.

He put the menu aside and thought about Harry Bosch. McCaleb had spent most of the morning on the boat, watching the trial on television. He thought Bosch's performance on the witness stand had been outstanding. The revelation that Storey had been linked to another death was shocking to McCaleb and apparently to the media horde as well. During the breaks the talking heads in the studio were beside themselves with excitement over the prospect of this new fodder. They cut at one point to the hallway outside the courtroom where J. Reason Fowkkes was being peppered with questions about these new developments. Fowkkes, for probably the only time in his life, was not commenting. The talking heads were left to speculate about this new information and to comment on the methodical yet thoroughly gripping procession of the prosecution's case.

Still, watching the trial only caused uneasiness within McCaleb. He had a difficult time coming to terms with the idea that the man he had watched so capably describing the aspects and moves of a difficult investigation was also the man he was investigating, the man his gut instincts told him had committed the same kind of crime he was now involved in prosecuting.

At noon, their agreed-upon meeting time, McCaleb looked up from his thoughts to see Jaye Winston come through the restaurant's front door. She was followed by two men. One was black and one was white and that was the best way to differentiate between them because they wore almost identical gray suits and maroon ties. Before they even got to his table McCaleb knew they were bureau men.

Winston had a look of washed-out resignation on her face.

'Terry,' she said before sitting down, 'I want you to meet a couple guys.'

She indicated the black agent first.

'This is Don Twilley and this is Marcus Friedman. They're with the bureau.'

All three of them pulled out chairs and sat down. Friedman sat next to McCaleb, Twilley directly across from him. Nobody shook hands.

'I've never had Cuban food before,' Twilley said as he pulled a menu from the napkin stand. 'Is it good here?'

McCaleb looked at him.

'No. That's why I like to eat here.'

Twilley's eyes came up from the menu and he smiled.

'I know, stupid question.' He looked down at the menu and then back up at McCaleb. 'You know I know about you, Terry. You're a fucking legend in the FO. Not 'cause of the heart, 'cause of the cases. I'm glad to finally meet you.'

McCaleb looked over at Winston with a look that said what the hell is going on?

'Terry, Marc and Don are from the civil rights section.'

'Yeah? That's great. Did you guys come all the way from the field office to meet the legend and try Cuban food, or is there something else?'

'Uh . . .' Twilley began.

'Terry, the shit's hit the fan,' Winston said. 'A reporter called my captain this morning to ask if we were investigating Harry Bosch as a suspect in the Gunn case.'

McCaleb leaned back in his seat, shocked by the news. He was about to respond when the waiter came to the table.

'Give us a couple minutes,' Twilley said gruffly to the man, waving him off with a dismissive gesture, which annoyed McCaleb.

Winston continued.

'Terry, before we go further with this, I have to know something. Did you leak this?'

McCaleb shook his head in disgust.

'Are you kidding me? You're asking *me* that?'

'Look, all I know is that it didn't come from me. And I didn't tell anyone, not Captain Hitchens and not even my own partner, let alone a reporter.'

'Well, it wasn't me. Thanks for asking.'

He glanced at Twilley and then back at Winston. He hated having this dispute with Jaye in front of them.

'What are these guys doing here?' he asked. Then looking at Twilley again, he added, 'What do you want?'

'They're taking over the case, Terry,' Winston answered. 'And you're out.'

McCaleb looked back at Winston. His mouth opened a little before he realized how he looked and closed it.

'What are you talking about? I'm out? I'm the only one in. I've been working this as—'

'I know, Terry. But things are different now. After the reporter called Hitchens I had to tell him what was happening, what we'd been doing. He threw a fit and after he was done throwing a fit he decided the best way to handle this was to go to the bureau with it.'

'The civil rights section, Terry,' Twilley said. 'Investigating cops is our bread and butter. We'll be able to—'

'Fuck you, Twilley. Don't try that bureau rap with me. I used to be in the club, remember? I know how it goes. You guys will come in, piggyback my trail and then waltz Bosch past the cameras on the way to the lockup.'

'Is that what this is about?' Friedman said. 'Getting the credit?'

'You don't have to worry about that, Terry,' Twilley said. 'We can put you in front of the cameras if that's what you want.'

'It's *not* what I want. And don't call me Terry. You don't even fuckin' know me.'

He looked down at the table, shaking his head.

'Fuck, I've been waiting to come back to this place for a long time and now I don't even feel like eating.'

'Terry . . .' Winston said, not offering anything else.

'What, you're going to tell me this is right?'

'No. It's not right or wrong. It's just the way it is. The investigation is official now. You're not official. You knew this could happen from the start.'

He reluctantly nodded. He brought his elbows up onto the table and put his face into his hands.

'Who was the reporter?'

When Winston didn't answer he dropped his hands and looked pointedly at her.

'Who?'

'A guy named Jack McEvoy. He works for the *New Times*, an alternative weekly that likes to stir up shit.'

'I know what it is.'

'You know McEvoy?' Twilley asked.

McCaleb's cell phone began to chirp. It was in the pocket of his jacket draped over his chair. It got caught in the pocket as he tried to get it out. He anxiously struggled with it because he assumed it would be Graciela. Other than Winston and Buddy Lockridge, he'd only given the number to Brass Doran in Quantico and he had finished his business with her.

He finally answered after the fifth chirp.

'Hey, Agent McCaleb, it's Jack McEvoy from the *New Times*. You got a couple minutes to talk?'

McCaleb looked across the table at Twilley, wondering if he could hear the voice on the phone.

'Actually, I don't. I'm in the middle of something here. How'd you get this number?'

'Information on Catalina. I called the number and your wife answered. She gave me your cell. That a problem?'

'No, no problem. But I can't talk now.'

'When can we talk? It's important. Something's come up that I really want to talk—'

'Just call me later. In an hour.'

McCaleb closed the phone and put it down on the table. He looked at it, half expecting McEvoy to call back right away. Reporters were like that.

'Terry, everything all right?'

He looked up at Winston.

'Yeah, fine. My charter tomorrow. He wanted to know about the weather.'

He looked at Twilley.

'What was your question again?'

'Do you know Jack McEvoy? The reporter who called Captain Hitchens.'

McCaleb paused, looking at Winston and then back at Twilley.

'Yeah, I know him. You know I know him.'

'That's right, the Poet case. You had a piece of that.'

'A small piece.'

'When was the last time you talked to McEvoy?'

'Well, that would've been, let's see . . . that would have been a couple days ago.'

Winston visibly stiffened. McCaleb looked over at her.

'Relax, would you, Jaye? I ran into McEvoy at the Storey trial. I went up there to talk to Bosch. McEvoy's covering it for *New Times* and he said hello – I hadn't talked to him in five years. And I did *not* tell him what I was doing or what I was working on. In fact, at the time I saw him Bosch wasn't even a suspect.'

'Well, did he see you with Bosch?'

'I'm sure he did. Everybody did. There's as much media up there as there was for O. J. Did he specifically mention me to your captain?'

'If he did, Hitchens didn't tell me.'

'All right, then, if it wasn't you and it wasn't me, where else did the leak come from?'

'That's what we are asking you,' Twilley said. 'Before we come into this case we want to know the lay of the land and who's talking to who.'

McCaleb didn't reply. He was getting claustrophobic. Between the conversation and Twilley being in his face, and the people standing around in the small restaurant waiting for tables, he was beginning to feel like he couldn't breathe.

'What about this bar you went to last night?' Friedman asked.

McCaleb leaned back and looked over at him.

'What about it?'

'Jaye told us what you told her. You specifically asked about Bosch *and* Gunn there, right?'

'Yeah, right. And what? You think the bartender then jumped on the phone and called the *New Times* and asked for Jack McEvoy? All because I showed her a picture of Bosch? Give me a fucking break.'

'Hey, it's a media-conscious town. People are plugged in. People sell stories, info, data all the time.'

McCaleb shook his head, refusing to buy into the possibility that the bartender in the vest had enough intelligence to put together what he was doing and to then make a call to a reporter.

Suddenly, he realized who did have the intelligence and information to do it. Buddy Lockridge. And if it had been him, it might as well have been McCaleb who leaked the story. He felt sweat start to warm his scalp as he thought about Lockridge hiding down on the lower deck while he had made his case against Bosch to Winston.

'Did you have anything to drink while you were in the bar? I hear you take a mess of pills every day. Mixing that with alcohol . . . you know, loose lips sink ships.'

Twilley had asked the question but McCaleb looked sharply at Winston. He was stung with a sense of betrayal by the whole scene and at how quickly things had shifted. But before he could say anything he saw the apology in her eyes and he knew she wished things had been handled differently. He finally looked back at Twilley.

'You think maybe I mixed a few too many drinks and pills, Twilley? That it? You think I started shooting my mouth off in the bar?'

'I don't think that. I'm just asking, okay? No reason to get defensive here. I'm just trying to figure out how this reporter knows what he thinks he knows.'

'Well, figure it out without me.'

McCaleb pushed back his chair to get up.

'Try the lechon asada,' he said. 'It's the best in the city.'

As he began to get up, Twilley reached across the table and grabbed his forearm.

'Come on, Terry, let's talk about this,' Twilley said.

'Terry, please,' Winston said.

McCaleb pulled his arm loose from Twilley's grip and stood up. He looked over at Winston.

'Good luck with these guys, Jaye. You'll probably need it.'

Then he looked down at Friedman and then Twilley.

'And fuck you guys very much.'

He made his way through the crowd of people waiting and out the front door. Nobody followed him.

He sat in the Cherokee parked on Sunset and watched the restaurant while letting the anger slowly leach out of his body. On one level McCaleb knew the moves Winston and her captain were making were the right moves. But on another he didn't like being moved out of his own case. A case was like a car. You could be driving it or riding in the front or back. Or you could be left on the side of the road as the car went by. McCaleb had just gone from having his hands on the wheel to thumbing it from the side of the road. And it hurt.

He began to think about Buddy Lockridge and how he would handle him. If he determined that it had been Buddy who had talked to McEvoy after eavesdropping on McCaleb's briefing of Winston on the boat, then he would cleanly sever all ties to him. Partner or not, he wouldn't be able to work with Buddy again.

He realized that Buddy had the number to his cell phone and could have been the one who gave it to McEvoy. He got the phone out and called his home. Graciela answered, Fridays being one of her half days at the school.

'Graciela, did you give my cell number to anybody lately?'

'Yes, a reporter who said he knew you and needed to speak with you right away. A Jack something. Why, is something wrong?'

'No, nothing's wrong. I was just checking.'

'Are you sure?'

McCaleb got a call-waiting beep. He looked at his watch. It was ten to one. McEvoy wasn't supposed to call back until after one.

'Yes, I'm sure,' he told Graciela. 'Look, I've got another call. I'll be home by dark tonight. I'll see you then.'

He switched to the other call. It was McEvoy, who explained that he was at the courthouse and had to get back into the trial at one or he'd lose his precious seat. He couldn't wait the full hour to call back.

'Can you talk now?' he asked.

'What do you want?'

'I need to talk to you.'

'You keep saying that. About what?'

'Harry Bosch. I'm working on a story about—'

'I don't know anything about the Storey case. Only what's on TV.'

'It's not that. It's about the Edward Gunn case.'

McCaleb didn't answer. He knew this was not good. Dancing with a reporter over something like this could only lead to trouble. McEvoy spoke into the silence.

'Is that what you wanted to see Harry Bosch about the other day when I saw you here? Are you working on the Gunn case?'

'Listen to me. I can honestly tell you that I am not working on the Edward Gunn case. Okay?'

Good, McCaleb thought. So far he hadn't lied.

'*Were* you working on the case? For the sheriff's department?'

'Can I ask you something? Who told you this? Who said I was working this case?'

'I can't answer that. I have to protect my sources. If you want to give me information I will protect your identity as well. But if I give up a source, I'm fucked in this business.'

'Well, I'll tell you what, Jack. I'm not talking to you unless you are talking to me, know what I mean? It's a two-way street. You want to tell me who is saying this shit about me and I'll talk to you. Otherwise, we've got nothing to say to each other.'

He waited. McEvoy said nothing.

'I thought so. Take it easy, Jack.'

He closed the phone. Whether McEvoy had mentioned his name or not to Captain Hitchens, it was clear that McEvoy was tapped in to a credible pipeline of information. And again McCaleb narrowed it down to one person besides himself and Jaye Winston.

'Goddamnit!' he said out loud in the car.

A few minutes after one he watched Jaye Winston come out of El Cochinito. McCaleb was hoping for the chance to corner her and talk to her alone, maybe tell her about Lockridge. But Twilley and Friedman followed her out and all three got into the same car. A bureau car.

McCaleb watched them pull out into traffic and drive off in the direction of downtown. He got out of the Cherokee and went back into the restaurant. He was starved. There were no tables available so he made an order to go. He'd eat in the Cherokee.

The old woman who took his order looked up at him with sad brown eyes. She said it had been a busy week and the kitchen had just run out of lechon asada.

27

John Reason surprised the spectators, the jurors and probably most of the media when he reserved his cross-examination of Bosch until the defense's case began, but it had been anticipated by the prosecution team. If the defense strategy was to shoot themessenger, that messenger was Bosch and the best place from which to take the shot was during the presentation of the defense's side. That way, Fowkkes's attack on Bosch could be part of an orchestrated attack on the entire case against David Storey.

Following a lunch break during which Bosch and the prosecutors were relentlessly pursued by the media with questions about Bosch's testimony, the prosecution began to move quickly with the momentum gained in the morning's session. Kretzler and Langwiser took turns examining a series of witnesses with short stays on the stand.

The first of these was Teresa Corazón, chief of the medical examiner's office. Under Kretzler's questioning, she testified to her findings during the autopsy and put Jody Krementz's time of death at some point between midnight and 2 A.M. on Friday, October 13. She also gave corroborating testimony on the rarity of autoerotic deaths involving female victims.

Once more Fowkkes reserved the right to question the witness during the defense phase of the trial. Corazón was dismissed after less than a half hour on the stand.

Now that his own testimony was completed – as far as

the prosecution's case went – it was not vital for Bosch to be in the courtroom for every moment of the trial. While Langwiser called the next witness – a lab tech who would identify the hair samples gathered from the victim's body as belonging to Storey – Bosch walked Corazón to her car. They had been lovers many years before in what current culture would term a casual relationship. But while there may not have been any love involved, there had been nothing casual about it to Bosch. In his view it had been two people who looked at death every day pushing it away with the ultimate life-affirming act.

Corazón had broken it off after she was named to the top slot in the coroner's office. Their relationship since that point had been strictly professional, though Corazón's new position reduced her time in the autopsy suites and Bosch did not see her often. The Jody Krementz case was different. Corazón had instinctively known it might become a case that drew the bead of the media horde and had taken the autopsy herself. It had paid off. Her testimony would be seen across the nation and probably around the globe. She was attractive, smart, skilled and thorough. That half hour on the stand would be like a half-hour commercial for lucrative jobs as an independent examiner or commentator. Bosch knew one thing about her from his time with her: Teresa Corazón always had her eye on the next step.

She was parked in the garage next to the state parole office on the back side of the justice complex. They spoke of banalities – the weather, Harry's attempts to stop smoking – until Corazón brought the case up.

'It seems to be going well.'

'So far.'

'It'd be nice if we won one of these big ones for a change.'

'It would.'

'I watched you testify this morning. In my office I had the TV on. You did very well, Harry.'

He knew her tone. She was leading to something.

'But?'

'But you look tired. And you know they're going to come after you. This kind of case, if they destroy the cop they destroy the case.'

'O. J. one-oh-one.'

'Right. So are you ready for them?'

'I think so.'

'Good. Just rest up.'

'Easier said than done.'

As they approached the garage Bosch looked over at the parole office and saw a gathering of the staff out front for some kind of presentation. The group was standing below a banner hanging from the roof line that said WELCOME BACK THELMA. A man in a suit was presenting a plaque to a heavyset black woman who was leaning on a cane.

'Oh . . . that's that parole agent,' Corazón said. 'The one who got shot last year. By that hit man from Vegas?'

'Right, right,' Bosch said, remembering the story. 'She came back.'

He noticed that there were no television cameras recording the presentation. A woman got shot in the line of duty and then fought her way back to the job. It apparently wasn't worth wasting videotape over.

'Welcome back,' he said.

Corazón's car was on the second floor. It was a two-seat, shining black Mercedes.

'I see the outside work must be going pretty well,' Bosch said.

Corazón nodded.

'In my last contract I got four weeks' professional leave. I'm making the most of it. Trials, TV, that sort of thing. I did a case on that autopsy show on HBO, too. It airs next month.'

'Teresa, you're going to be world famous before we know it.'

She smiled and stepped close to him and straightened his tie.

'I know what you think about it, Harry. That's okay.'

'Doesn't matter what I think about it. Are you happy?'

She nodded.

'Very.'

'Then I'm happy for you. I better get back in there. I'll see you, Teresa.'

She suddenly rose on her toes and kissed him on the cheek. It had been a long time since he had gotten one of those.

'I hope you make it through, Harry.'

'Yeah, me too.'

Bosch stepped out of the elevator into the hallway and headed toward the Department N courtroom. He saw a line of people cordoned off by the courtroom door: people waiting for a spectator seat to possibly open. A few reporters were milling about the open door of the pressroom but everybody else was at stations, watching the trial.

'Detective Bosch?'

Bosch turned. Standing in a pay-phone alcove was Jack McEvoy, the reporter he had met the day before. He stopped.

'I saw you walk out and I hoped I'd catch you.'

'I have to get back in there.'

'I know. I just wanted to tell you that it is very important that I talk to you about something. The sooner the better.'

'What are you talking about? What's so important?'

'Well, it's about you.'

McEvoy stepped out of the alcove so that he was closer to Bosch and did not have to speak as loud.

'What about me?'

'Do you know you are under investigation by the sheriff's department?'

Bosch looked up the hall toward the courtroom door and then back at McEvoy. The reporter was slowly bringing a pad of paper and pen up in his hands. He was ready to take notes.

'Wait a minute.' Bosch put his hand on the notebook. 'What are you talking about? What investigation?'

'Edward Gunn, you remember him? He's dead and you're their suspect.'

Bosch just stared at him, his mouth coming slightly open.

'I wondered if you wanted to comment on this. You know, defend yourself. I'll be writing a story for next week's edition and wanted you to have the chance to tell your—'

'No, no comment. I have to get back.'

Bosch turned and walked a few paces toward the courtroom door but then stopped. He walked back to McEvoy, who was writing in the notebook.

'What are you writing? I didn't say anything.'

'I know. That's what I'm writing.'

McEvoy looked up from the notebook to him.

'You said next week,' Bosch said. 'When does it come out?'

'*New Times* is published every Thursday morning.'

'So until when do I have, if I decide to talk to you?'

'About Wednesday lunch. But that will be pressing it. I won't be able to do much then but drop in some quotes. The time to talk is now.'

'Who told you this? Who's your source?'

McEvoy shook his head.

'I can't discuss sources with you. What I want to talk about is this allegation. Did you kill Edward Gunn? Are you some kind of avenging angel? That's what they think.'

Bosch studied the reporter for a long moment before finally speaking.

'Don't quote me on this, but fuck you. You know what I mean? I don't know if this is a bullshit bluff or not, but let me give you some advice. You better make damn sure you've got it right before you put anything in that paper of yours. A good investigator always knows the motivation of his sources – it's called having a bullshit meter. Yours better be working real well.'

He turned and walked quickly to the courtroom door.

Langwiser had just finished with the hair specialist when Bosch came back into the courtroom. Once again Fowkkes stood up and reserved the right to recall the witness during the defense case.

While the witness came through the gate behind the attorneys' lectern, Bosch slipped past him and went to his seat at the prosecution table. He didn't look at or say anything to Langwiser or Kretzler. He folded his arms and looked down at the notepad he had left on the table. He realized he had adopted the same position and posture he had seen David Storey take at the defense table. The posture of a guilty man. Bosch quickly dropped his arms to his lap and looked up at the seal of the State of California which hung on the wall above the judge's bench.

Langwiser got up and called the next witness, a fingerprint technician. His testimony was quick and more corroboration of Bosch's testimony. It went unchallenged by Fowkkes. The technician was followed to the stand by the patrol officer who answered the first call from Krementz's roommate and then by his sergeant, who was the next to arrive.

Bosch barely listened to the testimony. There was nothing new in it and his mind was racing in another direction. He was thinking about McEvoy and the story he was working on. He knew he should inform Langwiser and Kretzler but wanted time to think about things. He decided to hold off until after the weekend.

The victim's roommate, Jane Gilley, was the first witness to appear who was not part of the law enforcement community. She was tearful and sincere in her testimony, confirming details of the investigation already revealed by Bosch but also adding more personal bits of information. She testified about how excited Jody Krementz had been at the prospect of dating a major Hollywood player and how both of them had spent the day before her date getting manicures, pedicures and hair stylings.

'She paid for me,' Gilley testified. 'That was so sweet.'

Her testimony put a very human face on what so far had been an almost antiseptic analysis by law enforcement professionals of a murder.

When Gilley's examination by Langwiser was concluded, Fowkkes finally broke with his pattern and announced he had a few questions for the witness. He stepped to the lectern without any notes. He clasped his hands behind his back and leaned slightly forward to the microphone.

'Now, Ms. Gilley, your roommate was an attractive young woman, wasn't she?'

'Yes, she was beautiful.'

'And was she popular? In other words, did she date a lot of fellows?'

Gilley nodded hesitantly.

'She went out.'

'A lot, a little, how often?'

'It would be hard to say. I wasn't her social secretary and I have my own boyfriend.'

'I see. Then let's take, say, the ten weeks prior to her death. How many of those ten weeks would you say went by without Jody going out on a date?'

Langwiser stood up and objected.

'Your Honor, this is ridiculous. It has nothing to do with the night of October twelfth going into the morning of the thirteenth.'

'Oh, but Your Honor, I think it does,' Fowkkes responded. 'And I think Ms. Langwiser knows it does. If you allow me a little bit of string here, I will be able to quickly tie it up.'

Houghton overruled the objection and told Fowkkes to ask the question again.

'In the ten weeks prior to her death, how many weeks went by without Jody Krementz having a date with a man?'

'I don't know. Maybe one. Maybe none.'

'Maybe none,' Fowkkes repeated. 'And, Ms. Gilley, how many of those weeks would you say your roommate had at least two dates?'

Langwiser objected again but was overruled again.

'I don't know the answer,' Gilley said. 'A lot of them.'

'A lot of them,' Fowkkes repeated.

Langwiser rose and asked the judge to direct Fowkkes not to repeat the witness's answer unless it was in the form of a question. The judge complied and Fowkkes went on as if he had not been corrected at all.

'Were these dates all with the same fellow?'

'No. Different guys mostly. A few repeats.'

'So she liked to play the field, is that correct?'

'I guess so.'

'Is that a yes or no, Ms. Gilley?'

'It's a yes.'

'Thank you. In the ten weeks prior to her death, weeks in which you said she most often had at least two dates, how many different men did she see?'

Gilley shook her head in exasperation.

'I have no idea. I didn't count them. Besides, what does this have to do—'

'Thank you, Ms. Gilley. I would appreciate it if you would just answer the questions I pose to you.'

He waited. She said nothing.

'Now, did Jody ever encounter difficulties when she stopped dating a man? When she moved on to the next?'

'I don't know what you mean.'

'I mean were all the men happy not to have a return engagement?'

'Sometimes they'd get mad if she didn't want to go out again. Nothing serious.'

'No threats of violence? She wasn't afraid of anyone?'

'Not that she told me about.'

'Did she tell you about every man she dated?'

'No.'

'Now, on these dates, did she often bring the men back to the home you two shared?'

'Sometimes.'

'Did they stay over?'

'Sometimes, I don't know.'

'You often weren't there, is that correct?'

'Yes, I often stayed at my boyfriend's.'

'Why is that?'

She gave a short laugh.

'Because I love him.'

'Well, did you ever stay together overnight at your home?'

'I don't remember him ever staying over.'

'Why is that?'

'I guess because he lives alone. It was more private.'

'Isn't it true, Ms. Gilley, that you stayed overnight several times a week at your boyfriend's home?'

'Sometimes. So what?'

'And that this was because you were unhappy with your roommate's constant procession of overnight guests.'

Langwiser stood up.

'Your Honor, that's not even a question. I object to its form and content. Jody Krementz's lifestyle is not on trial here. David Storey is on trial for her murder and it's not fair for the defense to be allowed to go after someone who—'

'Okay, Ms. Langwiser, that's enough,' Judge Houghton said. He looked over at Fowkkes. 'Mr. Fowkkes, that's about all the string I'm going to allow you to run with in that direction. Ms. Langwiser makes her point. I want you to move on with this witness.'

Fowkkes nodded. Bosch studied him. He was a perfect actor. In his demeanor he was able to convey the frustration of a man being pulled back from a hidden truth. He wondered if the jury would see it as an act.

'Very well, Your Honor,' Fowkkes said, putting the frustration into the inflection of his voice. 'I have no further questions for this witness at this time.'

The judge adjourned for the afternoon break of fifteen minutes. Bosch ushered Gilley through the reporters, down the elevator and out to her car. He told her she had done very well and handled Fowkkes's cross-examination perfectly. He then joined Kretzler and Langwiser in the second-floor DA's office where the prosecution team had a temporary office during the trial. There was a small coffeemaker in the room and it was half-filled with coffee brewed during the morning break. There wasn't enough time for a fresh brew so they all drank the stale coffee while Kretzler and Langwiser considered the progress of the day.

'I think the she's-a-whore defense is going to backfire on them big time,' Langwiser said. 'They have to have more than that.'

'He's just trying to show there were a lot of men,' Kretzler said. 'And it could have been any of them. The shotgun defense. You shoot a lot of pellets and one's bound to hit the target.'

'It's still not going to work.'

'I'll tell you one thing, with John Reason reserving on all of these wits, we're moving really quickly. He keeps this up, we're going to finish our case Tuesday or Wednesday.'

'Good. I can't wait to see what they've got.'

'I can,' Bosch interjected.

Langwiser looked at him.

'Oh, Harry. You've weathered these storms before.'

'Yeah, but I've got a bad feeling about this one.'

'Don't worry about it,' Kretzler said. 'We're going to

kick their ass across the courtroom. We're in the tube, man, and we ain't coming out.'

They put their three Styrofoam cups together in a toast.

Bosch's current partner, Jerry Edgar, and former partner, Kizmin Rider, testified during the afternoon session. Both were asked by the prosecutors to recall the moments after the search of David Storey's home when Bosch got into the car and reported to them that Storey had just bragged of committing the crime. Their testimony was solidly in tandem with Bosch's own testimony and would act to buttress the case against defense assaults on Bosch's character. Bosch also knew that the prosecutors hoped to gain additional credence with the jury because both Edgar and Rider were black. Five members of the jury and the two alternates were black. In a time when the veracity of any white police officer in Los Angeles would fall under suspicion by black jurors, having Edgar and Rider join a line of solidarity with Bosch was a plus.

Rider testified first and Fowkkes passed on cross-examination. Edgar's testimony mirrored hers but he was asked additional questions because he had delivered the second search warrant issued in the case. This one was a court order seeking hair and blood samples from David Storey. It had been approved and signed by a judge while Bosch was in New York following the *Architectural Digest* lead and Rider was on a Hawaiian vacation planned before the murder. With a patrol officer in tow, Edgar had once again appeared at Storey's house at 6 A.M. with the warrant. He testified that Storey kept them waiting outside while he contacted his lawyer, who by now was the criminal defense attorney J. Reason Fowkkes.

Once Fowkkes was apprised of the situation he told Storey to cooperate and the suspect was taken to Parker Center in downtown where samples of his pubic hair, scalp hair and blood were collected by a lab nurse.

'Did you at any point during this traveling time and

collection process question the defendant about the crime?' Kretzler asked.

'No, I did not,' Edgar responded. 'Before we left his residence he gave me his phone and I spoke to Mr. Fowkkes. He told me his client did not wish to be questioned or harassed, as he put it, in any way. So we basically drove in silence – at least on my part. And we didn't talk at Parker Center either. When we were finished, Mr. Fowkkes was there and he drove Mr. Storey home.'

'Did Mr. Storey make any unsolicited comments to you during the time he was with you?'

'Just one.'

'And where was that?'

'In the car while we were driving to Parker Center.'

'And what did he say?'

'He was looking out the window and just said, "You people are fucked if you think I'm going down for this."'

'And was this piece of conversation tape-recorded?'

'Yes, it was.'

'Why is that?'

'Because of his earlier admission to Detective Bosch, we thought there was a chance he might go ahead and make another statement like that. On the day I served the hair and blood warrant, I used a car borrowed from the narcotics unit. It's a car they use for making street buys. It is wired for sound.'

'Did you bring the tape from that day with you, Detective?'

'Yes.'

Kretzler introduced the tape as evidence. Fowkkes objected, saying that Edgar had already testified as to what was said and the audio wasn't necessary. Again the judge overruled and the tape was played. Kretzler started the tape well before the statement made by Storey so that the jurors would hear the hum of the car engine and traffic noise and know that Edgar did not violate the defendant's rights by questioning him in order to elicit the statement.

When the tape came to Storey's comment, the tone of arrogance and even hate for his investigators came through loud and clear.

Wanting that tone to be what carried the jurors into the weekend, Kretzler ended his questioning of Edgar.

Fowkkes, perhaps understanding the ploy, said he would have a brief cross-examination. He proceeded to ask Edgar a series of innocuous questions that added little to the record in favor of the defense or disfavor of the prosecution. At precisely 4:30 P.M. he ended the cross-examination and Judge Houghton promptly recessed for the weekend.

As the courtroom emptied into the hallway, Bosch looked around for McEvoy but didn't see him. Edgar and Rider, who had hung around after her testimony, came up to him.

'Harry, how 'bout we go get a drink?' Rider said.

'How 'bout we go get drunk?' Bosch replied.

28

They waited until ten-thirty Saturday morning for their charter clients to arrive but no one showed. McCaleb was sitting silently on the gunwale in the stern doing a slow burn over everything. The missing charter, his dismissal from the case, the most recent phone call from Jaye Winston, everything. Before he left the house Winston had called to apologize for how things had gone the day before. He feigned indifference and told her to forget about it. And he still didn't tell her about Buddy Lockridge overhearing them on the boat two days earlier. When Jaye said Twilley and Friedman had decided it would be best if he returned the copies of all the documents relating to the case, he told her to tell them they could come get them if they wanted them. He said he had a charter and had to go. They abruptly said good-byes and hung up.

Raymond was bent over the stern, fishing with a little spinner reel McCaleb had gotten him after they moved to the island. He was looking through the clear water at the moving shapes of the orange garibaldi fish twenty feet below. Buddy Lockridge was sitting in the fighting chair reading the Metro section of the *Los Angeles Times.* He seemed as relaxed as a summer wave. McCaleb had not yet confronted him with his suspicions that he was the leak. He had been waiting for the right moment.

'Hey, Terror, you see this story?' Lockridge said. 'About Bosch giving his testimony yesterday in Van Nuys court?'

'Nope.'

'Man, what they're hinting at here is that this director's a serial killer. Sounds like one of your old cases. And here the guy on the witness stand putting the finger on him is a—'

'Buddy, I told you, don't talk about that. Or did you forget what I said?'

'Okay, sorry. I was just saying, if this ain't irony I don't know what is, that's all.'

'Fine. Leave it at that.'

McCaleb checked his watch again. The clients should have been there at ten. He straightened up and went to the salon door.

'I'll make some calls,' he said. 'I don't want to be waiting around all day for these people.'

At the little chart table in the boat's salon he opened a drawer and took out the clipboard where they attached the charter reservations. There were only two pages on it. The current day's charter and a reservation for the following Saturday. The winter months were slow. He looked at the information on the top sheet. He was unfamiliar with it because Buddy had taken the reservation. The charter was for four men from Long Beach. They were supposed to come over Friday night and stay at the Zane Grey. A four-hour charter – ten to two on Saturday – and then they'd take a late ferry back to overtown. Buddy had taken the organizer's home number and the name of the hotel as well as a deposit of half the charter fee.

He looked at the list of hotels and phone numbers taped to the chart table and called the Zane Grey first. He quickly learned that no one with the charter organizer's name – the only one of the four names McCaleb had – was staying at the hotel. He then called the man's home number and got his wife. She said her husband wasn't home.

'Well, we're kind of waiting for him on a boat over here

on Catalina. Do you know if he and his friends are on their way?'

There was a long silence.

'Ma'am, you there?'

'Uh, yes, yes. It's just that, they're not going fishing today. They told me they canceled that trip. They're out golfing right now. I can give you my husband's cell phone if you would like. You could talk—'

'That's not necessary, ma'am. Have a nice day.'

McCaleb closed his phone. He knew exactly what had happened. Neither he nor Buddy had checked the answering service that handled calls to the phone number they had placed on their charter ads in various phone books and fishing publications. He called the number now, punched in the code and, sure enough, there had been a message waiting since Wednesday. The party canceled the charter. They'd reschedule later.

'Yeah, sure,' McCaleb said.

He erased the message and closed the phone. He felt like throwing it through the glass slider at Buddy's head but he tried to calm himself. He walked into the little galley and got a quart carton of orange juice out of the cooler. He took it out with him to the stern.

'No charter today,' he said before taking a long drink from the carton.

'Why not?' Raymond asked, his disappointment obvious.

McCaleb wiped his mouth on the sleeve of his long-sleeve T-shirt.

'They canceled.'

Lockridge looked up from the newspaper and McCaleb hit him with a laser stare.

'Well, we keep the deposit, right?' Buddy asked. 'I took a two-hundred-dollar deposit on Visa.'

'No, we don't keep the deposit because they canceled on Wednesday. We've both been too *busy* I guess to check the charter line like we're supposed to.'

'Ah, fuck! That's my fault.'

'Buddy, not in front of the boy. How many times do I have to tell you that?'

'Sorry. Sorry.'

McCaleb continued to stare at him. He had not wanted to talk about the leak to McEvoy until after the charter because he needed Buddy's help running a four-man fishing party. Now it didn't matter. Now was the time.

'Raymond,' he said while still staring at Lockridge. 'Do you still want to earn your money?'

'Yeah.'

'You mean "yes," don't you?'

'Yeah. I mean, yes. Yes.'

'Okay, then reel in, hook your line and start taking these rods in and put them in the rack. Can you do that?'

'Sure.'

The boy quickly reeled in his line, took off his bait and threw it into the water. He attached the hook to one of the rod's eyelets and then leaned it in the corner of the stern so he could take it home with him. He liked to practice his casting technique on the rear deck of the house, dropping a rubber practice weight onto the roofs and backyards below.

Raymond started taking the deep-sea rods out of the holders where Buddy had placed them in preparation for the charter. Two by two he took them into the salon and put them in the overhead racks. He had to stand on the couch to do it but it was an old couch in dire need of a new slipcover and McCaleb didn't care about it.

'Something wrong, Terror?' Buddy tried. 'It's just a charter, man. We knew it was going to be slow this month.'

'It's not the charter, Bud.'

'Then what? The case?'

McCaleb took a smaller gulp of juice and put the carton down on the gunwale.

'You mean the case I'm not on anymore?'

'I guess. I don't know. You're not on it anymore? When did that—'

'No, Buddy, I'm not on it. And there's something I want to talk to you about.'

He waited for Raymond to move another set of rods into the salon.

'You ever read the *New Times*, Buddy?'

'You mean that free weekly?'

'Yeah, that free weekly. The *New Times*, Buddy. Comes out every Thursday. There's always a stack in the laundry building at the marina. In fact, why am I asking this? I know you read the *New Times*.'

Lockridge's eyes suddenly fell to the deck. He looked crestfallen with guilt. He brought one hand up and rubbed his face. He kept it over his eyes when he spoke.

'Terry, I'm sorry. I never thought it would get back to you. What happened?'

'What's the matter, Uncle Buddy?'

It was Raymond in the door of the salon.

'Raymond, would you go inside and close that door for a few minutes?' McCaleb said. 'You can put on the TV. I need to talk to Buddy by myself.'

The boy hesitated, staring the whole time at Buddy covering his face.

'Raymond, please. And take this back to the cooler.'

The boy finally stepped out and took the orange juice carton. He went back in and slid the door closed. McCaleb looked back at Lockridge.

'How could you not think it would get back to me?'

'I don't know. I just thought nobody would know.'

'Well, you were wrong. And it has caused me a lot of trouble. But most of all it's a fucking betrayal, Buddy. I just can't believe you would do something like this.'

McCaleb glanced at the glass door to make sure the boy wasn't in earshot. There was no sign of Raymond. He must've gone down to one of the staterooms. McCaleb realized his breathing was way up. He was so angry he was hyperventilating. He had to end this and calm down.

'Does Graciela have to know about it?' Buddy asked in a pleading voice.

'I don't know. It doesn't matter what she knows. What matters is that we had this relationship and then you do something like this behind my back.'

Lockridge still hid his eyes behind his hand.

'I just didn't think it would mean that much to you, even if you found out. It was no big deal. I'm—'

'Don't try to mitigate it or tell me what kind of deal it is, okay? Don't even talk to me in that pleading, whiny voice. Just shut up.'

McCaleb walked to the stern, pressing his thighs against the padded combing. His back to Lockridge, he looked up the hillside above the commercial part of the little town. He could see his house. Graciela was on the deck holding the baby. She waved and then held Cielo's hand up in a baby wave. McCaleb waved back.

'What do you want me to do?' Buddy said from behind him. His voice was more controlled now. 'What do you want me to say? I won't do it again? Fine, I won't do it again.'

McCaleb didn't turn around. He continued looking up at his wife and his daughter.

'It doesn't matter what you won't do again. The damage is done. I have to think about this. We're partners as well as friends. Or we were, at least. All I want now is for you to just go. I'm going inside with Raymond. Take the skiff and go back to the pier. Take a ferry back tonight. I just don't want you around here, Buddy. Not now.'

'How will you guys get back to the pier?'

It was a desperate question with an obvious answer.

'I'll call the water taxi.'

'We've got a charter next Saturday. It's five people and—'

'I'll worry about Saturday when I come to it. I can cancel it if I have to or turn it over to Jim Hall's charter.'

'Terry, are you sure about this? All I did was—'

'I'm sure. Go on, Buddy. I don't want to talk anymore.'

McCaleb turned from the view and walked past Lockridge and to the salon door. He opened it and stepped in, then slid the door closed behind him. He didn't look back at Buddy. He went to the chart table and got an envelope out of the drawer. He slipped a five-dollar bill from his pocket into it, sealed it and wrote Raymond's name on it.

'Hey, Raymond where are you?' he called out.

For dinner they had grilled cheese sandwiches and chili. The chili was from the Busy Bee. McCaleb had picked it up on his way up from the boat with Raymond.

McCaleb sat across the table from his wife with Raymond to his left and the baby to his right in a jumper seat perched on the table. They were eating inside as an evening fog had enshrouded the island in a chilly grip. McCaleb remained morosely quiet through the meal, as he had been through much of the day. When they had come back early, Graciela decided to keep her distance. She took Raymond for a hike in the Wrigley Botanical Garden in Avalon Canyon. McCaleb was left with the baby, who fussed most of the day. He didn't mind, though. It took his mind off things.

Finally, at dinner, there was no avoiding each other. McCaleb had made the sandwiches so he was the last to sit down. He had barely begun eating when Graciela asked him what his trouble was.

'Nothing,' he said. 'I'm fine.'

'Raymond said you and Buddy had an argument.'

'Maybe Raymond should mind his own business.'

He looked at the boy as he said this and Raymond looked down at his food.

'That's not fair, Terry,' Graciela said.

She was right. McCaleb knew it. He reached over and

tousled the boy's hair. It was so soft. He liked doing it. He hoped the gesture conveyed his apology.

'I'm off the case because Buddy leaked it to a reporter.'

'What?'

'We came up – I came up – with a suspect. A cop. Buddy overheard me telling Jaye Winston about my findings. He turned around and told a reporter. The reporter turned around and started making calls. Jaye and her captain think I was the leak.'

'That doesn't make sense. Why would Buddy do that?'

'I don't know. He didn't say. Actually, he did say. He said he didn't think I'd care or that it mattered. Words to that effect. That was today on the boat.'

He gestured toward Raymond, meaning this was the tense conversation he had caught part of and told Graciela about.

'Well, did you call Jaye and tell her it was him?'

'No, it doesn't matter. It came through me. I was dumb enough to let him on the boat. Can we talk about something else? I'm tired of thinking and talking about this.'

'Fine, Terry, what else do you want to talk about?'

He was silent. She was silent. After a long moment he started to laugh.

'I can't think of anything right now.'

Graciela finished eating a bite of her sandwich. McCaleb looked over at Cielo, who was looking at a blue-and-white ball that was suspended over her on a wire attached to the side of her bouncer seat. She was trying to reach for it with her tiny hands but couldn't quite make it. McCaleb could see her getting frustrated and he understood the feeling.

'Raymond, tell your father what you saw today in the gardens,' Graciela said.

She had recently begun referring to McCaleb as Raymond's father. They had adopted him but McCaleb didn't want to put any pressure on the boy to think of or refer to him as his father. Raymond usually called him Terry.

'We saw a Channel Islands fox,' he said now. 'It was hunting in the canyon.'

'I thought foxes hunted at night and slept during the day.'

'Well, somebody woke him up then because we saw him. He was big.'

Graciela nodded, confirming the sighting.

'Pretty cool,' McCaleb said. 'Too bad you didn't get a picture.'

They ate in silence for a few minutes. Graciela used her napkin to clean spittle off the baby's chin.

'Anyway,' McCaleb said, 'I'm sure you're happy that I'm off it and things will be normal around here again.'

Graciela looked at him.

'I want you to be safe. I want the whole family to be together and safe. That's what makes me happy, Terry.'

He nodded and finished his sandwich. She continued.

'I want you to be happy but if that means working these cases, then that is a conflict with your personal well-being as far as your health is concerned and the well-being of this family.'

'Well, you don't have to worry about it anymore. I don't think anybody will come calling on me again after this.'

He got up to clear the table. But before picking up plates he leaned over his daughter's chair and bent the wire so that the blue-and-white ball would be within her reach.

'It's not supposed to be like that,' Graciela said.

McCaleb looked at her.

'Yes, it is.'

29

McCaleb stayed up into the early morning hours with the baby. He and Graciela alternated nights on duty so that at least one of them got a decent night of sleep. Cielo seemed to have an almost hourly feed clock. Each time she awoke he would feed her and walk her through the dark house. He would gently pat her back until he heard her burp and then he would put her down again. In an hour the process would begin again.

After each cycle McCaleb would walk through the house and check the doors. It was a nervous habit, his routine. The house, by virtue of being up on the hillside, was fogged in tight. Looking through the rear windows, he couldn't even see the lights of the pier down below. He wondered if the fog stretched across the bay to the mainland. Harry Bosch's house was up high. He wondered if he was standing at his window looking into the misty nothingness as well.

In the morning Graciela took the baby and McCaleb, exhausted from the night and everything else, slept until eleven. When he came to he found the house to be quiet. In his T-shirt and boxer shorts he wandered down the hall and found the kitchen and family room empty. Graciela had left a note on the kitchen table saying she had taken the children to St. Catherine's for the ten o'clock service and then to the market afterward. The note said they'd be back by noon.

McCaleb went to the refrigerator and got out the gallon jug of orange juice. He poured a full glass and then took his keys off the counter and went back into the hallway to the locking cabinet. He opened it up and got out a plastic Ziploc bag containing a morning dose of the drug therapy that kept him alive. The first of every month he and Graciela carefully put together the doses and put them in plastic bags marked with dates and whether they were the A.M. or P.M. dosage. It made it easier than having to open dozens of pill bottles twice a day.

He took the bag back to the kitchen and began taking the pills two and three at a time with gulps of juice. As he followed this routine he looked through the kitchen window and down to the harbor below. The fog had moved out. It was still misty but clear enough for him to see *The Following Sea* and a skiff tied at its fantail.

He went to one of the kitchen drawers and pulled out the set of binoculars Graciela liked to use when she was watching him on the boat heading in or out of the harbor with a charter party. He went out onto the deck and to the railing. He focused the binoculars. There was no one in the cockpit or up on the bridge of the boat. His view could not penetrate the reflective film on the sliding door of the salon. He moved his focus to the skiff. It was weathered green with a one-and-a-half-horse outboard. He recognized it as being one of the rentals from the concession on the pier.

McCaleb went back inside and left the binoculars on the counter while he swiped the remaining pills into his hand. He took them and the orange juice back to the bedroom. He quickly ingested the pills while he got dressed. He knew Buddy Lockridge would not have rented a boat to get to *The Following Sea.* Buddy knew which Zodiac was McCaleb's and would simply have borrowed that.

Somebody else was on his boat.

It took him twenty minutes to walk down to the pier because Graciela had the golf cart. He went to the boat rental booth first to ask who had rented the boat but the window was closed and there was a sign with a clock face that said the operator would not be back until twelve-thirty. McCaleb checked his watch. It was ten after twelve. He couldn't wait. He went down the ramp to the skiff dock and stepped onto his Zodiac and started the engine.

As McCaleb moved down the fairway toward *The Following Sea* he studied the side windows of the salon but still could not see any movement or indication that someone was on the boat. He cut the engine on the Zodiac when he was twenty-five yards away and the inflatable skiff glided the rest of the way silently. He unzipped the pocket of his windbreaker and removed the Glock 17, his service weapon from his time with the bureau.

The Zodiac bumped lightly into the fantail next to the rental skiff. McCaleb first looked into the skiff but saw nothing other than a life vest and a flotation cushion, nothing that indicated who had rented the boat. He stepped onto the fantail and while crouched behind the stern wrapped the Zodiac's line around one of the rear cleats. He looked over the transom and saw only himself in the sliding door. He knew he would have to approach the door not knowing if there would be someone on the other side watching him come in.

He crouched down again and looked around. He wondered if he should retreat and come back with the harbor patrol boat. After a moment he decided against it. He glanced up the hill at his house and then raised himself and swung his body over the transom. With the gun carried low and hidden behind his hip he walked to the door and looked down at the lock. There was no damage or indication it had been tampered with. He pulled the handle and the door slid open. McCaleb was sure he had locked it the day before when leaving with Raymond.

He stepped inside. The salon was empty, no sign of intruder or burglary. He slid the door closed behind him and listened. The boat was silent. There was the sound of water lapping against the outside surfaces and that was it. His eyes moved toward the steps leading to the lower-deck staterooms and the head. He moved that way, raising the gun in front of him now.

On the second of the four steps down McCaleb hit a cracked board that sighed with his weight. He froze and listened for a response. There was only silence and the relentless sound of water against the sides of the boat. At the bottom of the stairs was a short hallway with three doors. Directly ahead was the forward stateroom, which had been converted into an office and file storage room. To the right was the master stateroom. To the left was the head.

The door to the master stateroom was closed and McCaleb could not remember if it had been that way when he had left the boat twenty-four hours earlier. The door to the head was wide open and hooked on the inside wall so it wouldn't swing and slam when the boat was moving. The office door was partially open and swaying slightly with the movement of the boat. There was a light on inside the room and McCaleb could tell it was the light over the desk, which was built into the lower berth of a set of bunk beds to the left of the door. McCaleb decided he would check the head first, followed by the office and then the master last. As he approached the head he realized that he smelled cigarette smoke.

The head was empty and too small to be used as a hiding place anyway. As he turned toward the office door and raised his weapon, a voice called out from within.

'Come on in, Terry.'

He recognized the voice. He cautiously stepped forward and used his free hand to push open the door. He kept the gun raised.

The door swung open and there was Harry Bosch sitting at the desk, his body in a relaxed posture, leaning back and looking toward the door. Both his hands were in sight. Both were empty except for the unlit cigarette between two fingers of his right hand. McCaleb slowly moved into the small room, still holding the gun up and aimed at Bosch.

'You going to shoot me? You want to be my accuser *and* my executioner?'

'This is breaking and entering.'

'Then I guess that makes us even.'

'What are you talking about?'

'That little dance at my place the other night, what do you call that? "Harry, I gotta couple more questions about the case." Only you never asked any real questions, did you? Instead, you take a look at my wife's picture and ask about that, and you ask about the picture in the hallway and you drink my beer and, oh, yeah, you tell me all about finding God in your baby daughter's blue eyes. So what do you call all of that, Terry?'

Bosch casually turned the chair and glanced over his shoulder at the desk. McCaleb looked past him and saw his own laptop computer was open and turned on. On the screen he could see that Bosch had called up the file containing the notes for the profile he was going to compose until everything changed the day before. He wished he had protected it with a password.

'It feels like breaking and entering to me,' Bosch said, his eyes on the screen. 'Maybe worse.'

In Bosch's new posture the leather bomber jacket he was wearing fell open and McCaleb could see the pistol holstered on his hip. He continued to hold his own weapon up and ready.

Bosch looked back at him.

'I didn't get a chance to look at all of this yet. Looks like a lot of notes and analysis. Probably all first-rate stuff, knowing you. But somehow, someway, you got it wrong, McCaleb. I'm not the guy.'

McCaleb slowly slid back into the lower berth of the opposite set of bunks. He held the gun with a little less precision now. He sensed there was no immediate danger from Bosch. If he had wanted to, he could have ambushed him as he'd come in.

'You shouldn't be here, Harry. You shouldn't be talking to me.'

'I know, anything I say can and will be used against me in a court of law. But who am I going to talk to? You put the bead on me. I want it off.'

'Well, you're too late. I'm off the case. And you don't want to know who's on it.'

Bosch just stared at him and waited.

'The bureau's civil rights division. You think Internal Affairs has been a pain in your ass? These people live and breathe for one thing, taking scalps. And an LAPD scalp is worth more than Boardwalk and Park Place put together.'

'How'd that happen, the reporter?'

McCaleb nodded.

'I guess that means he talked to you, too.'

Bosch nodded.

'Tried to. Yesterday.'

Bosch looked around himself, noticed the cigarette in his hand and put it in his mouth.

'You mind if I smoke?'

'You already have been.'

Bosch pulled a lighter out of his jacket pocket and lit the cigarette. He pulled the trash can out from beneath the desk and next to his seat to be used as an ashtray.

'Can't seem to quit these.'

'Addictive personality. A good and bad attribute in a detective.'

'Yeah, whatever.'

He took a hit off the cigarette.

'We've known each other for what is it, ten, twelve years?'

'More or less.'

'We worked cases and you don't work a case with somebody without taking some kind of measure. Know what I mean?'

McCaleb didn't answer. Bosch flicked the cigarette on the side of the trash can.

'And you know what bothers me, even more than the accusation itself? It's that it came from you. It's how and why you could think this. You know, what was the measure you took of me that allowed you to make this jump?'

McCaleb gestured with both hands as if to say the answer was obvious.

'People change. If there was anything I learned about people from my job, it's that any one of us is capable of anything, given the right circumstances, the right pressures, the right motives, the right moment.'

'That's all psycho-bullshit. It doesn't . . .'

Bosch's sentence trailed off and he didn't finish. He looked back at the computer and the papers spread across the desk. He pointed the cigarette at the laptop's screen.

'You talk about darkness . . . a darkness more than night.'

'What about it?'

'When I was overseas . . .' He dragged deeply on the cigarette and exhaled, tilting his head back and shooting the smoke toward the ceiling. '. . .I was put into the tunnels and let me tell you, you want darkness? That was darkness. Down in there. Sometimes you couldn't see your fucking hand three inches in front of your face. It was so dark it hurt your eyes from straining to see just anything. Anything at all.'

He took another long hit from the cigarette. McCaleb studied Bosch's eyes. They were staring blankly at the memory. Then suddenly he was back. He reached down and ground the half-finished cigarette into the inside edge of the can and dropped it in.

'This is my way of trying to quit. I smoke these shitty menthol things and never more than a half at a time. I'm down to about a pack a week.'

'It's not going to work.'

'I know.'

He looked up at McCaleb and smiled crookedly in a sort of apologetic way. Quickly his eyes changed and he moved back to his story.

'And then sometimes it wasn't that dark down there. In the tunnels. Somehow there was just enough light to make your way. And the thing is, I never knew where it came from. It was like it was trapped down there with the rest of us. My buddies and me, we called it lost light. It was lost but we found it.'

McCaleb waited but that was all Bosch said.

'What are you telling me, Harry?'

'That you missed something. I don't know what it is but you missed something.'

He held McCaleb with his dark eyes. He reached back to the desk and picked up the stack of copied documents from Jaye Winston. He tossed them across the small room onto McCaleb's lap. McCaleb made no move to catch them and they spilled to the floor in a jumble.

'Look again. You missed something and what you did see added up to me. Go back in and find the missing piece. It will change the addition.'

'I told you, man, I'm off it.'

'I'm putting you back on it.'

It was said with a tone of permanence, as if there was no choice for McCaleb.

'You've got till Wednesday. That writer's deadline. You have to stop his story with the truth. You don't, and you know what J. Reason Fowkkes will do with it.'

They sat in silence for a long moment looking at each other. McCaleb had met and talked with dozens of killers in his time as a profiler. Few of them readily admitted their crimes. So in that Bosch was no different. But the intensity with which he stared unblinkingly at him was something McCaleb had never seen before in any man, guilty or innocent.

'Storey's killed two women, and those are just the two

we know about. He's the monster you spent your life chasing, McCaleb. And now . . . and now you're giving him the key that unlocks the door to the cage. He gets out, he'll do it again. You know his kind. You know he will.'

McCaleb could not compete with Bosch's eyes. He looked down at the gun in his hands.

'What made you think I would listen, that I would do this?' he asked.

'Like I said, you take somebody's measure. I got yours, McCaleb. You'll do this. Or the monster you set free will haunt you the rest of your life. If God is really in your daughter's eyes, how will you be able to look at her again?'

McCaleb unconsciously nodded and immediately wondered what he was doing.

'I remember you once told me something,' Bosch said. 'You said if God is in the details, so is the Devil. Meaning, the person you are looking for is usually right there in front of us, hiding in the details all the time. I always remember that. It still helps me.'

McCaleb nodded again. He looked down at the documents on the floor.

'Listen, Harry, you should know. I was convinced about this when I took it to Jaye. I'm not sure I can be turned the other way. If you want help, I'm probably the wrong one to go to.'

Bosch shook his head and smiled.

'That's exactly why you're the right one. If you can be convinced, the world can be convinced.'

'Yeah, where were you on New Year's Eve? Why don't we start with that.'

Bosch shrugged his shoulders.

'Home.'

'Alone?'

Bosch shrugged his shoulders again and didn't answer. He stood up to go. He put his hands in the pockets of his jacket. He went through the narrow door first and up the steps to the salon. McCaleb followed, now holding the gun at his side.

Bosch slid the door open with his shoulder. As he stepped out onto the cockpit he looked up at the cathedral of the hillside, then he looked at McCaleb.

'So all that talk at my place about finding God's hand, was that bullshit? Interview technique or something? A statement designed to get a response that could fit into a profile?'

McCaleb shook his head.

'No, no bullshit.'

'Good. I was hoping it wasn't.'

Bosch climbed over the transom to the fantail. He untied his rental boat and got in and sat down on the rear bench. Before starting the engine he looked once more at McCaleb and pointed to the back of the boat.

'*The Following Sea.* What's that mean?'

'My father named the boat. It was his originally. The following sea is the wave that comes up behind you, that hits you before you see it coming. I guess he named the boat as sort of a warning. You know, always watch your back.'

Bosch nodded.

'Overseas we used to tell each other, "Watch six."'

Now McCaleb nodded.

'Same thing.'

They were silent a moment. Bosch put his hand on the boat motor's pull handle but didn't start the engine.

'You know the history of this place, Terry? I'm talking about back before the missionaries came.'

'No, do you?'

'A little. I used to read a lot of history books. When I was a kid. Whatever they had in the library. I liked local history. L.A. mostly, and California. I just liked reading it. We took a field trip here from the youth hall once. So I read up on it.'

McCaleb nodded.

'The Indians that lived out here – the Gabrielinos – were sun worshippers,' Bosch said. 'The missionaries came and changed all of that – in fact, they were the ones who called them Gabrielinos. They called themselves something else but I don't remember what it was. But before all that happened they'd been here and they worshipped the sun. It was so important to life on the island I guess they figured it had to be a god.'

McCaleb watched Bosch's dark eyes scan across the harbor.

'And the mainland Indians thought of the ones out here as these fierce wizards who could control weather and waves through worship and sacrifices to their god. I mean, they had to be fierce and strong to be able to cross the bay so they could trade their pottery and sealskins on the mainland.'

McCaleb studied Bosch, trying to get a bead on the message he was sure the detective was trying to convey.

'What are you saying, Harry?'

Bosch shrugged his shoulders.

'I don't know. I guess I'm saying that people find God where they need Him to be. In the sun, in a new baby's eyes . . . in a new heart.'

He looked at McCaleb, his eyes as dark and as unreadable as the painted owl's.

'And some people,' McCaleb began, 'find their salvation in truth, in justice, in that which is righteous.'

Now Bosch nodded and offered his crooked smile again.

'That sounds good.'

He turned and started the engine with one pull. He then mock saluted McCaleb and pulled away, angling the rental boat back toward the pier. Not knowing the etiquette of the harbor, he cut across the fairway and between unused mooring buoys. He didn't look back. McCaleb watched him all the way. A man all alone on the water in an old wooden boat. And in that thought came a question. Was he thinking about Bosch or himself?

30

On the ferry ride back Bosch bought a Coke at the concession stand and hoped it would settle his stomach and prevent seasickness. He asked one of the stewards where the steadiest ride on the boat was and he was directed to one of the middle seats on the inside. He sat down and drank some of the Coke, then pulled the folded pages he had printed in McCaleb's office out of his jacket pocket.

He had printed two files before he had seen McCaleb approaching in the Zodiac. One was titled SCENE PROFILE and the other was called SUBJECT PROFILE. He had folded them into his jacket and disconnected the portable printer from the laptop before McCaleb entered the boat. He'd only had time to glance at them on the computer and now began a thorough reading.

He took the scene profile first. It was only one page. It was incomplete and appeared to be simply a listing of McCaleb's rough notes and impressions from the crime scene video.

Still, it gave an insight into how McCaleb worked. It showed how his observations of a scene turned into observations about a suspect.

SCENE

1. Ligature
2. Nude
3. Head wound
4. Tape/gag – 'Cave'?

5. Bucket?
6. Owl – watching over?

highly organized
detail oriented
statement – the SCENE is his statement
he was there – he watched (the owl?)
exposure = victim humiliation
  = victim hatred, contempt
bucket – remorse?
killer – PRIOR KNOWLEDGE of victim
personal knowledge – previous interaction
personal hatred
KILLER INSIDE THE WIRE
what is the statement?

Bosch reread the page and then thought about it. Though he did not have full knowledge of the crime scene from which McCaleb's notes were drawn, he was impressed by the leaps in logic McCaleb had made. He had carefully gone down the ladder to the point where he concluded that Gunn's killer was someone he knew, that it was someone who would be found inside the perimeter wire that circled Gunn's existence. It was an important distinction to make in any case. Investigative priorities were usually set upon the determination of whether the suspect being sought had intersected with the victim only at the point of the killing or before. McCaleb's read on the nuances of the scene were that the killer was someone known to Gunn, that there was a prelude to this final and fatal crossing of killer and victim.

The second page continued the listing of shorthand notes that Bosch assumed McCaleb planned to turn into a fleshed-out profile. As he read he realized that some of the word groupings were phrases McCaleb had taken from him.

SUSPECT
Bosch:
institutional – youth hall, Vietnam, LAPD
outsider – alienation
obsessive-compulsive
eyes – lost, loss
mission man – avenging angel
the big wheel always turning –
  nobody walks away
what goes around comes around

alcohol
divorce – wife? why?
alienation/obsession
mother
cases
justice system – 'bullshit'
carriers of the plague
guilt?

Harry = Hieronymus
owl = evil
evil = Gunn
death of evil = release stressors

paintings – demons – devils – evil
darkness and light – the edge
punishment
mother – justice – Gunn
God's hand – police – Bosch
punishment = God's work

A darkness more than night – Bosch

Bosch wasn't sure how to interpret the notes. His eyes were drawn to the last line and he repeatedly read it, unsure what it was that McCaleb was saying about him.

After a while he carefully folded the page closed and sat

still for a long moment. It felt somehow surrealistic to be sitting there on the boat, having just tried to interpret someone else's notes and reasons as to why he should be considered a murder suspect. He felt himself getting queasy and realized he might be getting seasick. He gulped down the rest of the Coke and got up, putting the pages back into his jacket pocket.

Bosch headed toward the front of the boat and pushed through the heavy door to the bow. The cool air blasted him immediately. He could see the dim outline of the mainland in the distance. He kept his eyes on the horizon and breathed in deeply. In a few minutes he started feeling better.

31

McCaleb sat on the old couch in the salon thinking about his encounter with Bosch for a long time. It was the first time in all of his experiences as an investigator that a murder suspect had come to him to enlist his aid. He had to decide if it had been the act of a desperate or a sincere man. Or, possibly, something else. What if McCaleb had not noticed the rental skiff and come to the boat. Would Bosch have waited for him?

He went down to the front stateroom and looked at the documents spread on the floor. He wondered if Bosch had intentionally tossed them so that they would fall to the floor and become mixed up. Had he taken something?

He went to the desk and studied his laptop. It was not attached to the printer but he knew that didn't mean anything. He closed the file that was on the screen and opened the print manager window. He clicked the jobs file and saw that two files had been printed that day – the scene and suspect profiles. Bosch had taken them.

McCaleb imagined Bosch riding on the *Express* ferry back across, sitting by himself and reading what McCaleb had written about him. It made him feel uncomfortable. He didn't think any suspect he had ever profiled had read the report McCaleb had put together on him.

He shook it off and decided to occupy his mind with something else. He slid off the chair to his knees and began picking up the murder book reports, putting them into a neat pile first before worrying about putting them back in order.

Once he had the mess cleaned up he sat down at the desk, the reports in a squared-off pile in front of him. McCaleb took a blank page of typing paper out of a drawer and wrote on it with the thick black marker he used for labeling cardboard boxes containing his files.

YOU MISSED SOMETHING

He took a piece of tape off a dispenser on the desk and taped the page to the wall behind the desk. He looked at it for a long time. Everything Bosch had said to him came down to that one line. He now had to decide if it was true, if it was possible. Or if it was the last manipulation of a desperate man.

He heard his cell phone begin to chirp. It was in the pocket of his jacket, which he had left on the couch in the salon. He hustled up the stairs and grabbed the jacket. When he reached into the pocket his hand closed around his gun. He then tried the other pocket and got the phone. It was Graciela.

'We're home,' she said. 'I thought you'd be here. I thought maybe we could all go down to lunch at El Encanto.'

'Um . . .'

McCaleb didn't want to leave the office or his thoughts about Bosch. But the last week had strained things with Graciela. He needed to talk to her about that, about how he saw things changing.

'Tell you what,' he finally said. 'I'm just finishing some stuff here. Why don't you take the kids down and I'll meet you there.'

He looked at his watch. It was quarter of one.

'Is one-thirty too late?'

'Fine,' she said abruptly. 'What stuff?'

'Oh, just . . . I'm sort of wrapping up this thing for Jaye.'

'I thought you told me you were off it.'

'I am but I have all the reports and I wanted to write up my final . . . you know, just wrap it up.'

'Don't be late, Terry.'

She said it with a tone that implied that he would miss more than his lunch if he was.

'I won't. I'll see you there.'

He closed the phone and went back down to the office. He looked at his watch again. He had about a half hour before he'd have to get on the skiff and go back to the pier. The El Encanto was about a five-minute walk from there. It was one of the few restaurants that remained open on the island during the winter months.

He sat down and started putting the stack of investigative documents in order. It was not a difficult task. Each page had a date stamp on the upper right-hand corner. But McCaleb stopped almost as soon as he started. He looked up at the message he had taped on the wall. He decided that if he was going to look for something he had not noticed before, that he had missed, he should come at the information from another angle. He decided not to put the documents in their correct order. Instead, he would read them in the random order they were now in. Doing it this way he would avoid thinking about the flow of the investigation and how one step followed the other. He would simply have each report to consider as a single piece of the puzzle. It was a simple mind trick but he had used it before on cases with the bureau. Sometimes it shook something new out, something he had previously missed.

He checked his watch again and began with the first document on the pile. It was the autopsy protocol.

32

McCaleb walked briskly to the front steps of the El Encanto. He saw his golf cart parked at the curb. Mostly, the carts on the island looked the same, but he could identify his because of the baby seat with the pink-and-white cushioning. His family was still here.

He went up the steps and the hostess, recognizing him as a local, pointed to the table where his family was seated. He hurried over and pulled out a chair next to Graciela. They were close to being finished. He noticed that the waitress had already left the check on the table.

'Sorry I'm late.'

He took a chip out of the basket at the center of the table and dragged it through the salsa and guacamole bowls before shoving it into his mouth. Graciela looked at her watch and then pierced him with her deep brown eyes. He weathered it and got ready for the next one which he knew was surely coming.

'I can't stay.'

She loudly put her fork down on her plate. She was finished.

'Terry . . .'

'I know, I know. But something's come up. I have to go across tonight.'

'What could've possibly come up? You're off the case. It's Sunday. People are watching football, not running around trying to solve murders that they're not even asked to.'

She pointed to a television mounted in the upper corner

of the room. Three talking heads with thick necks sat at a counter with a football field behind them. McCaleb knew that the day's games would determine the Super Bowl contenders. He couldn't care less, though he did suddenly remember he had promised Raymond that they would watch at least one of the games together.

'I have been asked, Graciela.'

'What are you talking about? You said they asked you *off* the case.'

He told her about discovering Bosch on the boat that morning and what he had asked McCaleb to do.

'And this is the guy you told Jaye probably did it?'

McCaleb nodded.

'How'd he know where you lived?'

'He didn't. He knew about the boat, not where we live. You don't have to worry about that.'

'I think I do. Terry, you are going too far with this and you are going completely blind to the dangers to yourself and your family. I think—'

'Really? I think—'

He stopped and reached into his pocket and pulled out two quarters. He turned to Raymond.

'Raymond, are you finished eating?'

'Yeah.'

'You mean yes?'

'Yes.'

'Okay, take these. Go play the video machine over there by the bar.'

The boy took the quarters.

'You're excused.'

Raymond hesitantly hopped down and then trotted into the next room where there were tabletop video games that they had played before. He chose a game McCaleb knew was Pac-Man and sat down. He was not out of McCaleb's sight.

McCaleb looked back at Graciela, who had her purse up

on her lap and was taking money out and putting it down on the check.

'Graciela, forget about that. Look at me.'

She finished with the money and pushed her wallet back into the purse. She looked at him.

'We have to go. CiCi has to take her nap.'

The baby was in her bouncing chair on the table, one hand grasping the blue-and-white ball on the wire.

'She's fine. She can sleep right there. Just listen to me for a minute.'

He waited and she put a conceding look on her face.

'All right. Say what you have to say and then I have to leave.'

McCaleb turned and leaned close to Graciela so that his words would be heard only by her. He noticed the edge of one of her ears poking through her hair.

'We are heading toward a big problem here, aren't we?'

Graciela nodded and immediately the tears came down her cheeks. It was as if his saying the words out loud had knocked down the thin defensive mechanism she had constructed inside to protect herself and her marriage. McCaleb pulled the unused napkin out from beneath his silverware setting and handed it to her. He then put his hand on the back of her neck and pulled her toward him and kissed her on the cheek. Over the top of her head he saw Raymond watching them with a scared look on his face.

'We've talked about this, Graci,' he began. 'You have it in your head that we can't have our home and our family and everything else if this is what I do. The problem is in that word "if." That is the mistake here. Because there is no "if" here. It's not "if this is what I do." It *is* what I do. And I've gone too long thinking otherwise, trying to convince myself of something else.'

More tears came and she held the napkin to her face. She cried silently but McCaleb was sure people in the restaurant had noticed and were watching them instead of the television above them. He checked on Raymond and saw the boy was back to playing the video game.

'I know,' Graciela managed to say.

He was surprised by her acknowledgment. He took it as a good sign.

'So then what do we do? I'm not talking about just now and this case. I mean, for now and forever. What do we do? Graci, I am tired of trying to be what I'm not and of ignoring the thing inside that I know is what I am truly all about. It took this case to finally make me realize it and admit it to myself.'

She didn't say anything. He wasn't expecting her to.

'You know I love you and the kids. That's not the issue. I think I can have both and you think I can't. You've adopted this one-or-the-other attitude and I don't think it's right. Or fair.'

He knew his words were hurting her. He was drawing a line. One of them had to capitulate. He was saying it wasn't going to be him.

'Look, let's think about this. This isn't a good place to talk. What I am going to do is finish my work on this thing and then we'll sit down and talk about our future. Is that okay?'

She slowly nodded but didn't look at him.

'You do what you have to do,' she said in a tone McCaleb knew would make him feel guilty forever. 'I just hope you'll be careful.'

He pulled himself over and kissed her again.

'I've got too much here with you not to be.'

He got up and came around the table to the baby. He kissed her on top of the head and then unhitched the chair's safety belt and lifted her out.

'I'll take her down to the cart,' he said. 'Why don't you get Raymond?'

He carried the baby down to the cart and secured her in the safety seat. He put her bouncing chair in the rear storage compartment. Graciela came down with Raymond a few minutes later. Her eyes were swollen from the crying. McCaleb put his hand on Raymond's shoulder and walked him to the front passenger seat.

'Raymond, you're going to have to watch the second game without me. I have some work I have to do.'

'I can go with you. I can help you.'

'No, it's not a charter.'

'I know, but I can still help you.'

McCaleb knew Graciela was looking at him and he felt the guilt like the sun on his back.

'Thanks but maybe next time, Raymond. Put on your seat belt.'

Once the boy was safely in, McCaleb stepped back from the cart. He looked at Graciela, who was no longer looking at him.

'Okay,' he said. 'I'll be back as soon as I can. And I'll have the phone with me if you want to call.'

Graciela didn't acknowledge him. She pulled the cart away from the curb and headed up Marilla Avenue. He watched them until they were out of sight.

33

On the walk back to the pier his cell phone chirped. It was Jaye Winston returning his call. She was talking very quietly and said she was calling from her mother's house. McCaleb had difficulty hearing so he sat down on one of the benches along the casino walk. He leaned forward with his elbows on his knees, one hand holding the phone tightly to one ear, his other hand clasped over the other.

'We missed something,' he said. 'I missed something.'

'Terry, what are you talking about?'

'In the murder book. In Gunn's arrest record. He was—'

'Terry, what are you doing? You're off the case.'

'Says who, the FBI? I don't work for them anymore, Jaye.'

'Then says me. I don't want you getting any further—'

'I don't work for you, either, Jaye. Remember?'

There was a long silence on the phone.

'Terry, I don't know what you are doing but it's got to stop. You have no authority, no standing in this case anymore. If those guys Twilley and Friedman find out you're still snooping around on this, they can arrest you for interference. And you know they're just the type that will.'

'You want standing, I have standing.'

'What? I withdrew my authorization to you yesterday. You can't use me on this.'

McCaleb hesitated and then decided to tell her.

'I have standing. I guess you could say I'm working for the accused.'

Now Winston's silence was even longer. Finally she spoke, her words delivered very slowly.

'Are you telling me that you went to Bosch with this?'

'No. He came to me. He showed up on my boat this morning. I was right about the other night. The coincidence; me showing up at his place, then the call from his partner about you. He put it together. The reporter from the *New Times* called him, too. He knew what was going on without me having to tell him a thing. The point is, Jaye, none of that matters. What matters is that I think I jumped on Bosch too soon. I missed something and now I'm not so sure. There's a chance all of this could be a setup.'

'He's convinced you.'

'No, I convinced myself.'

There were voices in the background and Winston told McCaleb to hold on. He then heard voices muffled by a hand over the phone. It sounded like arguing. McCaleb stood up and continued walking toward the pier. Winston came back on in a few seconds.

'Sorry,' she said. 'This is not a good time. I'm in the middle of something right now.'

'Can we meet tomorrow morning?'

'What are you talking about?' Winston said, her voice almost shrill. 'You just told me you are working for the target of an investigation. I'm not going to meet with you. How the fuck would that look? Hold on—'

He heard her muffled voice apologizing for her language to someone. She then came back on the line.

'I really have to go.'

'Look, I don't care how it would look. I'm interested in the truth and I thought you would be, too. You don't want to meet me, fine, don't meet me. I've gotta go myself.'

'Terry, wait.'

He listened. She said nothing. He sensed that she was distracted by something there.

'What, Jaye?'

'What is this thing you said we missed?'

'It was in the arrest package from Gunn's last duice. I guess after Bosch told you he had spoken to him in lockup you pulled all the records. I just scanned through it the first time I looked at the book.'

'I pulled the records,' she said in a defensive tone. 'He spent the night of December thirtieth in the Hollywood tank. That's where Bosch saw him.'

'And he bonded out in the morning. Seven-thirty.'

'Yeah. Okay? I don't get it.'

'Look who bailed him out.'

'Terry, I'm at my parents'. I don't have—'

'Right, sorry. He was bailed out by Rudy Tafero.'

Silence. McCaleb was at the pier. He walked out toward the gangway that led down to the skiff dock and leaned on the railing. He cupped his free hand over his ear again.

'Okay, he was bailed out by Rudy Tafero,' Winston said. 'I assume he is a licensed bail bondsman. What does that mean?'

'You haven't been watching your TV. You're right, Tafero is a licensed bail bondsman – at least he put a license number on the bail sheet. But he's also a PI and security consultant. And – ready for this – he works for David Storey.'

Winston didn't say anything but McCaleb could hear her breathing into the phone.

'Terry, I think you better slow down. You are reading too much into this.'

'No coincidences, Jaye.'

'What coincidence? The man's a bail bondsman. It's what he does. He gets people out of jail. I'll bet you a box of doughnuts his office is right across the street from Hollywood station with all the others. He probably bails every third drunk and fourth prostitute out of the tank there.'

'You don't believe it's that simple and you know it.'

'Don't tell me what I believe.'

'This was when he was in the middle of preparing for Storey's trial. Why would Tafero come over and write a duice ticket himself?'

'Because maybe he's a one-man show and maybe, like I said, all he had to do was cross the street.'

'I don't buy it. And there's something else. On his booking slip it says Gunn got his one phone call at three A.M. December thirty-first. The number's on the slip – he called his sister in Long Beach.'

'Okay, what about it? We knew that.'

'I called her today and asked if she'd called a bondsman for him. She said no. She said she was tired of getting calls in the middle of the night and literally bailing him out all the time. She told him he was on his own this time.'

'So he went with Tafero. What about it?'

'How'd he get him? He already used his call.'

Winston had no answer for that. They were both silent for a while. McCaleb looked out across the harbor. The yellow taxi boat was moving slowly down one of the fairways, empty except for the man at the wheel. Men alone in their boats, McCaleb thought.

'What are you going to do?' Winston finally asked. 'Where are you going with this?'

'I'm coming back across tonight. Can you meet me in the morning?'

'Where? When?'

The tone of her voice revealed that she was put out by the prospect of a meeting.

'Seven-thirty, out front at the Hollywood station.'

There was a pause and then Winston said, 'Wait a minute, wait a minute. I can't do this. If Hitchens gets wind of it, that will be the end. He'll ship me out to

Palmdale. I'll spend the rest of my career pulling bones out of the desert sand.'

McCaleb was ready for that protest.

'You said the bureau guys want the murder book back, right? You meet me, I'll have it with me. What's Hitchens going to say about that?'

There was silence as Winston considered this.

'Okay, that'll work. I'll be there.'

34

When Bosch got home that evening he found the message light on his phone machine was blinking. He pushed the button and listened to two messages, one from each of the prosecutors on the Storey case. He decided to call Langwiser back first. As he punched her number into the phone, he wondered what urgency had caused both members of the prosecution team to call him. He thought maybe they had been contacted by the FBI agents McCaleb had mentioned. Or possibly by the reporter.

'What's up?' he asked when Langwiser answered. 'With both of you guys calling me I know it must be big and bad.'

'Harry? How are you?'

'Hanging in. What do you two have cooking?'

'It's funny you should mention that. Roger's on his way over and I'm going to cook tonight. We're going to go over Annabelle Crowe's grand jury testimony one more time. You want to come by?'

He knew she lived up in Agua Dulce, an hour's drive north.

'Uh, you know what, I've been driving all day. Down to Long Beach and back. You think you really need me there?'

'Totally optional. Just didn't want you to feel left out. But that's not why we were calling.'

'What was the reason?'

He was in the kitchen, sliding a six-pack of Anchor

Steam onto a shelf in the refrigerator. He pulled one bottle out of its sleeve and closed the door.

'Roger and I have been conferencing all weekend about this. We also talked to Alice Short about it.'

Alice Short was a chief deputy who was in charge of major trials. Their boss. It sounded as though they had been contacted about the Gunn case.

'What's the "it" you're talking about?' Bosch asked.

He slid the bottle into the opener and yanked down, popping the cap.

'Well, we think the case has really gone by the numbers. Really fallen together. In fact, it's bulletproof, Harry, and we think we should pull the trigger tomorrow.'

Bosch was quiet a moment while he tried to decipher all the weaponry coding.

'You're saying you're going to rest tomorrow?'

'We think so. We'll probably talk about it again tonight but we have Alice's blessing and Roger really thinks it's the right move. What we'd do is put on a bunch of cleanup wits in the morning and then bring Annabelle Crowe out after lunch. We'd end with her – a human story. She'll be our closer.'

Bosch was speechless. It might be the right move from a prosecutorial point of view. But that would put J. Reason Fowkkes in control of things as early as Tuesday.

'Harry, what do you think?'

He took a long pull on the bottle. The beer wasn't that cold. It had been in the car for a while.

'I think you only get one shot,' he said, continuing the weaponry imagery. 'You two better think long and hard about it tonight while you're making the pasta. You don't get a second chance to put on a case.'

'We know, Harry. And how'd you know I was making pasta?'

He could hear the smile in her voice.

'Lucky guess.'

'Well, don't worry, we'll think long and hard. We have been.'

She paused, allowing him a chance to respond but he was silent.

'In case we go this way, what's the status on Crowe?'

'She's waiting in the wings. Good to go.'

'Can you reach her tonight?'

'No problem. I'll tell her to be there by noon tomorrow.'

'Thanks, Harry. See you in the morning.'

They hung up. Bosch thought about things. He wondered if he should call McCaleb and tell him what was happening. He decided to wait. He walked out into the living room and turned on the stereo. The Art Pepper CD was still in the play slot. The music soon filled the room.

35

McCaleb was leaning against the Cherokee parked in front of the LAPD's Hollywood station when Winston pulled up in a BMW Z3 and parked. When she got out she saw McCaleb studying her car.

'I was running late. I didn't have time to pick up a company car.'

'I like your wheels. You know what they say about L.A., you are what you drive.'

'Don't start profiling me, Terry. It's too fucking early. Where's the book and the tape?'

He noted her profanity but kept his thoughts on that to himself. He pushed off the car and went around to the passenger side. He opened the door and took out the murder book and the crime scene tape. He handed them to her and she took them back to her car. McCaleb closed and locked the Cherokee, looking down through the window to the floor of the backseat where he had covered the Kinko's box with the morning newspaper. Before coming to the rendezvous he had gone to the twenty-four-hour shop on Sunset and photocopied the entire murder book. The tape was a problem; he didn't know where to get it dubbed on short notice. So he'd simply bought a videocassette at the Rite-Aid near the marina and slipped the blank tape into the case Winston had given him. It was his guess that she wouldn't check to make sure he had returned the correct tape.

When she came back from her car he pointed with his chin across the street.

'I guess I owe you a box of doughnuts.'

She looked. Across Wilcox from the station was a shabby two-story building with a handful of storefront bail bond operations with phone numbers advertised in each window in cheap neon, maybe to help prospective clients memorize them from the backseat of passing patrol cars. The middle business had a painted sign above the window: Valentino Bonds.

'Which one?' Winston asked.

'Valentino. As in Rudy Valentino Tafero. That's what they used to call him when he worked this side of the street.'

McCaleb appraised the small business again and shook his head.

'I still don't see how a neon bondsman and David Storey ever hooked up.'

'Hollywood is just street trash with money. So what are we doing here? I don't have a lot of time.'

'You bring your badge?'

She gave him a don't-fuck-with-me look and he explained what he wanted to do. They went up the steps and into the station. At the front desk Winston flashed her badge and asked for the A.M. watch sergeant. A man with Zucker on his name plate and sergeant's stripes on the sleeve of his uniform came out from the small office. Winston showed her badge again, introduced herself and then introduced McCaleb as her associate. Zucker knitted his healthy set of eyebrows together but didn't ask what associate meant.

'We're working a homicide case from New Year's Eve. The victim spent the night before in your tank. We—'

'Edward Gunn.'

'Right. You knew him?'

'He'd been in a few times. And of course I heard he won't be coming back.'

'We need to talk to whoever runs the tank on A.M. watch.'

'Well, that would be me, I guess. We don't have a specific duty. It's sort of catch as catch can around here. What do you want to know?'

McCaleb took a set of photocopies from the murder book out of his jacket pocket and spread them on the counter. He noticed Winston's look but ignored it.

'We're interested in how he made bail,' he said.

Zucker turned the pages around so he could read them. He put his finger on Rudy Tafero's signature.

'Says it right here. Rudy Tafero. He's got a place across the street. He came over and bailed him out.'

'Did someone call him?'

'Yeah, the guy did. Gunn.'

McCaleb tapped his finger on the copy of the booking slip.

'It says here that when he got his call he called this number. It's his sister.'

'Then she must've called Rudy for him.'

'So nobody gets two calls.'

'Nope, 'round here we're usually so busy they're lucky if they get the one.'

McCaleb nodded. He folded the photocopies and was about to put them back in his pocket when Winston took them from his hand.

'I'll hang on to those,' she said.

She slipped the folded copies into a back pocket of her black jeans.

'Sergeant Zucker,' she said. 'You wouldn't be the kind of nice guy who would call Tafero, being that he's former LAPD, and tip him that he had a potential fish over here in the tank, would you?'

Zucker stared at her for a moment, his face a stone.

'It's very important, Sergeant. If you don't tell us, it could come back on you.'

The stone cracked into a humorless smile.

'No, I'm not that kind of nice guy,' Zucker said. 'And I don't have any nice guys like that on A.M. watch. And speaking of which, I just got off shift which means I don't have to be talking to you anymore. Have a nice day.'

He started to step away from the counter.

'One last thing,' Winston said quickly.

Zucker turned back to her.

'Were you the one who called Harry Bosch and told him Gunn was in the tank?'

Zucker nodded.

'I had a standing request from him. Any and every time Gunn was brought in here, Bosch wanted to know about it. He'd come in and talk to the guy, try to get him to say something about that old case. Bosch wouldn't give up on it.'

'It says Gunn wasn't booked until two-thirty,' McCaleb said. 'You called Bosch in the middle of the night?'

'That was part of the deal. Bosch didn't care what time it was. And actually, the procedure was that I would page him and then he'd call in.'

'And that's what happened that last night?'

'Yeah, I paged and Bosch called in. I told him we had Gunn again and he came down to try to talk to him. I tried to tell him to wait until morning 'cause the guy was on his ass drunk – Gunn, I mean – but Harry came down anyway. Why are you asking so much about Harry Bosch?'

Winston didn't answer so McCaleb jumped in.

'We're not. We're asking about Gunn.'

'Well, that's all I know. Can I go home now? It's been a long one.'

'Aren't they all,' Winston said. 'Thank you, Sergeant.'

They stepped away from the counter and walked out to the front steps.

'What do you think?' Winston asked.

'He sounded legit to me. But you know what, let's watch the employee lot for a few minutes.'

'Why?'

'Humor me. Let's see what the sergeant drives home.'

'You're wasting my time, Terry.'

They got into McCaleb's Cherokee anyway and drove around the block until they came to the entrance–exit of the Hollywood station employee parking lot. McCaleb drove fifty yards past it and parked in front of a fire hydrant. He adjusted the side-view mirror so he could see any car that left the lot. They sat and waited in silence for a couple of minutes until Winston spoke.

'So if we are what we drive, what's this make you?'

McCaleb smiled.

'Never thought about it. A Cherokee . . . I guess that makes me the last of a breed or something.'

He glanced at her then looked back at the mirror.

'Yeah, and what about this coating of dust on everything, what does that—'

'Here we go. Think it's him.'

McCaleb watched a car leave the exit and turn left in their direction.

'Coming this way.'

Neither of them moved. The car drove up and stopped right next to them. McCaleb looked over casually and his eyes met Zucker's. The cop lowered his passenger-side window. McCaleb had no choice. He lowered his.

'You're parked in front of a plug there, Detective. Don't get a ticket.'

McCaleb nodded. Zucker saluted with two fingers and drove off. McCaleb noted that he was driving a Crown Victoria with commercial bumpers and wheels. It was a secondhand patrol car, the kind you pick up at auction for four hundred bucks and slap on an $89.95 paint job.

'Don't we look like a couple of assholes,' Winston said.

'Yeah.'

'So what's your theory about *that* car?'

'He's either an honest man or he drives the beater to work because he doesn't want people to see the Porsche.'

He paused.

'Or the Z3.'

He turned to her and smiled.

'Funny, Terry. Now what? Eventually, I have to get some real work done today. And I'm supposed to meet with your bureau buddies this morning as well.'

'Stick with me – and they aren't my buddies.'

He started the Cherokee and pulled away from the curb.

'You really think this car's dirty?' he asked.

36

The post office on Wilcox was a large World War II-era building with twenty-five-foot-high ceilings and murals depicting bucolic scenes of brotherhood and good deeds covering the upper walls. As they walked in, McCaleb's eyes scanned the murals but not for their artistic or philosophic merit. He counted three small cameras mounted above the public areas of the office. He pointed them out to Winston. They had a chance.

They waited in line and when it was their turn Winston flashed her badge and asked for the on-site security officer. They were directed to a door next to a row of vending machines and they waited nearly five minutes before it was opened and a small black man with gray hair looked out.

'Mr. Lucas?' Winston asked.

'That's right,' he said with a smile.

Winston showed the badge once more and introduced McCaleb simply by name. McCaleb had told her on the way over from Hollywood station that calling him an associate wasn't working.

'We're working a homicide investigation, Mr. Lucas, and an important piece of evidence is a money order that was purchased here and probably mailed here on December twenty-second.'

'The twenty-second? That's right in the Christmas rush.'

'That's right, sir.'

Winston looked at McCaleb.

'We noticed your cameras out there on the walls, Mr. Lucas,' she said. 'We'd be interested in knowing if you have a videotape from the twenty-second.'

'Videotape,' Lucas said, as if the word was foreign to him.

'You are the security officer here, right?' Winston said impatiently.

'Yes, I'm the security man. I run the cameras.'

'Can you take us back and show us your surveillance system, Mr. Lucas?' McCaleb said in a gentler tone.

'Yup, sure can. Just as soon as you get authorization I'll take you on back.'

'And how and where do we get authorization?' Winston asked.

'From L.A. Regional. Downtown.'

'Is there a specific person we talk to? We're on a homicide investigation, Mr. Lucas. Time is of the essence.'

'That would be Mr. Preechnar – he's a postal inspector – you would talk to. Yes.'

'Do you mind if we come back to your office and we call Mr. Preechnar together?' McCaleb asked. 'It would save us a lot of time and then Mr. Preechnar could just talk directly to you.'

Lucas thought about this for a moment and decided it was a good idea. He nodded.

'Let's see what we can do.'

Lucas opened the door and led them through a warren of huge mail baskets to a cubbyhole office with two desks squeezed together. On one of the desks was a video monitor with its screen cut into four camera views of the public area of the post office. McCaleb realized he had missed one of the cameras when he had searched the walls earlier.

Lucas ran his finger down a list of phone numbers taped to the top of the desk and made the call. Once he got ahold of his supervisor he explained the situation and then turned the phone over to Winston. She went through their explanation again and then turned the phone back over to Lucas. She nodded to McCaleb. They got the approval.

'Okay, then,' Lucas said after hanging up. 'Let's see what we've got here.'

He reached to his hip and pulled up a ring of keys on a retractable wire attached to his belt. He went to the other side of the office and unlocked a closet door which he opened to reveal a rack of video recorders and four upper shelves of videotapes marked with the numbers one through thirty-one on each shelf. On the floor were two cartons containing fresh videotapes.

McCaleb saw all of this and suddenly realized it was January 22, exactly one month from the day the money order was purchased.

'Mr. Lucas, stop the machines,' he said.

'Can't do that. The machines always gotta roll. If we're open for business, then the tapes are rolling.'

'You don't understand. December twenty-second is the day we want. We're taping over the day we want to look at.'

'Hold your horses, Detective McCallan. I have to explain the setup.'

McCaleb didn't bother correcting him on the name. There wasn't time.

'Then hurry, please.'

McCaleb looked at his watch. It was eight forty-eight. The post office had been open for forty-eight minutes. That was forty-eight minutes of the December 22 tape erased with forty-eight minutes of the current day's taping.

Lucas started explaining the taping procedure. One VCR for each of the four cameras. One tape in each machine at the start of each day. The cameras were set at thirty frames a minute, allowing one tape to cover the entire day. The tape for an individual day was held for a month and used again if not reserved because of an investigation by the postal inspectors service.

'We get a lot of scam artists and whatnot. You know how it is in Hollywood. We end up with a lot of tapes on reserve. The inspectors come in and get 'em. Or we send 'em on down in dispatch.'

'We understand, Mr. Lucas,' said Winston, an urgent tone in her voice as she apparently came to the same realization as McCaleb. 'Can you please turn off the machines or replace the tapes in them. We are taping over what could be valuable evidence.'

'Right away,' Lucas said.

But he proceeded to reach into the carton of new tapes and take out four cassettes. He then peeled labels off a dispenser roll and put them on the tapes. He took a pen from behind his ear and wrote the date and some sort of coding on the labels. Then, finally, he started popping tapes out of the VCRs and replacing them with the new cassettes.

'Now, how do you want to do this? These tapes are post office property. They are not leaving the premises. I can set you up over here at the desk. I've got a portable TV with built-in VCR if you want to use it.'

'Are you sure we just can't borrow them for the day?' Winston said. 'I could have them back by—'

'Not without a court order. That's what Mr. Preechnar told me. That's what I'm going to do.'

'Then I guess we don't have a choice,' Winston said, looking at McCaleb and shaking her head in frustration.

While Lucas went to get the TV, McCaleb and Winston decided that McCaleb would stay and watch the videotape while Winston went to her office for an 11 A.M. meeting with the bureau men, Twilley and Friedman. She said she would not be mentioning McCaleb's new investigation or the possibility that his earlier focus on Bosch might have been in error. She would return the copied murder book and crime scene tape.

'I know you don't believe in coincidences but that's all you have at the moment, Terry. You come up with something on the tape and I'll bring it to the captain and we'll blow Twilley and Friedman out of the water. But until you have it . . . I'm still in the doghouse and need something more than a coincidence to look anywhere other than at Bosch.'

'What about the call to Tafero?'

'What call?'

'Somehow he knew Gunn was in the tank and he came and bailed him out – so they could kill him that night and pin it on Bosch.'

'I don't know about the call – if it wasn't Zucker, it was probably somebody else in the station he's got a sweetheart deal with. And the rest of what you just said is pure speculation without a single fact backing it up.'

'I think it's—'

'Stop, Terry. I don't want to hear it until you have something backing it up. I'm going to work.'

As if on cue, Lucas came back pushing a cart with a small television on top of it.

'I'll set you up with this,' he said.

'Mr. Lucas, I need to go to an appointment,' Winston said. 'My colleague is going to look at the tapes. Thank you for your cooperation.'

'Happy to be of service, ma'am.'

Winston looked at McCaleb.

'Call me.'

'You want me to drive you back to your car?'

'It's just a few blocks. I'll walk it.'

He nodded.

'Happy hunting,' she said.

McCaleb nodded. She had said that to him once before on a case that had not turned out so happily for him.

37

Langwiser and Kretzler told Bosch they were going ahead with the plan to rest their case by the close of the day.

'We got him,' Kretzler said, smiling and enjoying the adrenaline ride that came with making the decision to pull the trigger. 'By the time we're done he'll be tied down nine ways till Sunday. We've got Hendricks and Crowe today. We've got everything we need.'

'Except motive,' Bosch said.

'Motive is not going to be important with a crime that is obviously the work of a psychopath,' Langwiser said. 'Those jurors aren't going to go back into their little room at the end of this and say, "Yeah, but what was his motive?" They're going to say this guy is a sick fuck and—'

Her voice dropped to a whisper when the judge entered the courtroom through the door behind the bench.

'– we're going to put him away.'

The judge called for the jury and after a few minutes the prosecutors were putting on their last witnesses of the trial.

The first three witnesses were film business people who had attended the premiere party on the night of Jody Krementz's death. Each testified to having seen David Storey at the film premiere and the following party with a woman they identified from exhibit photos as Jody Krementz. The fourth witness, a screenwriter named Brent Wiggan, testified that he left the premiere party a few minutes before midnight and that he waited at the valet stand for his car along with David Storey and a woman he also identified as Jody Krementz.

'Why are you so sure it was just a few minutes before midnight, Mr. Wiggan?' Kretzler asked. 'It was, after all, a party. Were you watching the clock?'

'One question at a time, Mr. Kretzler,' the judge barked.

'Sorry, Your Honor. Why are you so sure it was a few minutes before midnight, Mr. Wiggan?'

'Because I *was* watching the clock, actually,' Wiggan said. 'My watch, that is. I do my writing at night. I am most productive from midnight until six. So I was watching the clock, knowing I had to get back to my house at close to midnight or I would fall behind in my work.'

'Would that also mean you were not drinking alcoholic beverages at the premiere party?'

'That is correct. I wasn't drinking because I didn't want to become tired or have my creativity dampened. People don't usually drink before they go to work at a bank or as a plane pilot – well, I guess most of them don't.'

He paused until the titters of laughter subsided. The judge looked annoyed but didn't say anything. Wiggan looked like he was enjoying his moment of attention. Bosch started feeling uneasy.

'I don't drink before I go on the job,' Wiggan finally continued. 'Writing is a craft but it is also a job and I treat it as such.'

'So are you crystal clear in your memory and identification of who David Storey was with at a few minutes before midnight?'

'Absolutely.'

'And David Storey, you personally already knew him, correct?'

'Yes, that's true. For several years.'

'Have you ever worked for David Storey on a film project?'

'No, I haven't. But not for lack of trying.'

Wiggan smiled ruefully. This part of the testimony, right down to the self-deprecating comment, had been carefully planned by Kretzler earlier. He needed to limit the potential for damage to Wiggan's testimony by walking him through the weak spots on direct.

'What do you mean by that, Mr. Wiggan?'

'Oh, I would say that in the last five years or so I have pitched film projects to David directly or to people in his production company maybe six or seven times. He never bought any of them.'

He hiked his shoulders in a sheepish gesture.

'Would you say this created a sense of animosity between you two?'

'No, not at all – at least not on my part. That's the way the Hollywood game is played. You keep pitching and pitching and hopefully somebody eventually bites. It helps to have a thick skin, though.'

He smiled and nodded to the jury. He was giving Bosch a full set of the creeps. He wished Kretzler would end it before they lost the jury.

'Thank you, that's all, Mr. Wiggan,' Kretzler said, apparently getting the same vibes as Bosch.

Wiggan's face seemed to fall as he realized his moment was ending.

But then Fowkkes, who had passed on cross-examining the first three witnesses of the day, stood up and went to the lectern.

'Good morning, Mr. Wiggan.'

'Good morning.'

Wiggan raised his eyebrows in a what-do-we-have-here look.

'Just a few questions. Could you list for the jury the titles of films that you have written that have been produced?'

'Well . . . so far, nothing's been made. I've got some options and I think in a few—'

'I understand. Would you be surprised to know that in

the last four years you have pitched Mr. Storey or submitted film treatments to him on a total of twenty-nine occasions, all of which were rejected?'

Wiggan's face flushed with embarrassment.

'Well, I . . . I guess that could be true. I . . . don't really know. I don't keep a record of my rejections, as Mr. Storey apparently does.'

He delivered the last line in a snippish manner and Bosch almost winced. There was nothing worse than a witness on the stand who is caught in a lie and then gets defensive about it. Bosch glanced at the jury. Several of them were not looking at the witness, a sign that they were as uncomfortable as Bosch.

Fowkkes moved in for the kill.

'You were rejected by the defendant on twenty-nine occasions and yet you say to the jury that you bear him no malice, is that correct, sir?'

'That's just business as usual in Hollywood. Ask anyone.'

'Well, Mr. Wiggan, I am asking you. Are you telling this jury that you bear this man no ill will when he is the same man who has constantly and repeatedly said to you your work is not good enough?'

Wiggan almost mumbled his answer into the microphone.

'Yes, that is true.'

'Well, you're a better man than me, Mr. Wiggan,' Fowkkes said. 'Thank you, Your Honor. Nothing further at this time.'

Bosch could feel a good bit of the air go out of the prosecution's balloon. With four questions and less than two minutes Fowkkes had put Wiggan's entire credibility into question. And what was so absolutely perfect about the defense attorney's skillful surgery was that there was little Kretzler could do on redirect to resuscitate Wiggan. The prosecutor at least knew better than to try to perhaps dig the hole deeper. He dismissed the witness and the judge called for the mid-morning break of fifteen minutes.

After the jury was out and people started working their way out of the courtroom, Kretzler leaned across Langwiser to whisper to Bosch.

'We should've known that this guy was going to blow up,' he said angrily.

Bosch just looked around to make sure no reporters were within earshot. He leaned toward Kretzler.

'You're probably right,' he said. 'But six weeks ago you were the one who said he would do the vetting on Wiggan. He was your responsibility, not mine. I'm going to get coffee.'

Bosch got up and left the two prosecutors sitting there.

After the break the prosecutors decided they needed to come back strong immediately after the disastrous cross-examination of Wiggan. They dropped plans to have another witness testify about seeing Storey and the victim together at the premiere party and Langwiser called a home security technician named Jamal Hendricks to the stand.

Bosch walked Hendricks in from the hallway. He was a black man wearing blue pants and a light blue uniform top, his first name embroidered over one pocket and the Lighthouse Security emblem over the other. He was planning to go to work following his testimony.

As they went through the first set of doors to the courtroom Bosch asked Hendricks in a whisper if he was nervous.

'Nah, man, piece of cake,' Hendricks replied.

On the stand Langwiser took Hendricks through his pedigree as a service technician for the home security company. She then moved specifically to his work on the security system at David Storey's house. Hendricks said that eight months earlier he had installed a deluxe Millennium 21 system in the house on Mulholland.

'Can you tell us what some of the features are on the deluxe Millennium Twenty-one system?'

'Well, it's top of the line. It's got everything. Remote sensing and operation, voice recognition command software, automatic sensor polling, an innkeeper program . . . you name it and Mr. Storey got it.'

'What is an innkeeper program?'

'Essentially, it's operation recording software. It lets you know what doors or windows have been opened and when, when the system has been turned on and off, what personal codes were used and whatnot. It keeps track of the whole system. It's primarily used in commercial-industrial applications but Mr. Storey wanted a commercial system and it came included.'

'So he didn't specifically ask for the innkeeper program?'

'I don't know about that. I didn't sell him the system. I only installed it.'

'But he could have had this program and not known about it.'

'Anything's possible, I guess.'

'Now did there come a time when Detective Bosch called Lighthouse Security and asked for a technician to meet him at Mr. Storey's home?'

'Yeah, he made the call and it was given to me because I had installed the system. I met him there at the house. This was after Mr. Storey had been arrested and was in lockup. Mr. Storey's lawyer was there, too.'

'When was that exactly?'

'That was November eleventh.'

'What did Detective Bosch ask you to do?'

'Well, first he showed me a search warrant. It allowed him to collect information from the system's chip.'

'And did you help him with that?'

'Yeah. I downloaded the innkeeper data file and printed it out for him.'

Langwiser first introduced the search warrant – the

third executed during the investigation – as an exhibit, then she introduced the printout Hendricks had just testified about.

'Now Detective Bosch was interested in the innkeeper records for the evening of October twelfth going into the morning of October thirteenth, is that correct, Mr. Hendricks?'

'Right.'

'Can you look at the printout and read the entries for that time period?'

Hendricks studied the printout for several seconds before speaking.

'Well, it says the interior door leading to the garage was opened and the alarm system was engaged by Mr. Storey's voiceprint at seven-oh-nine the night of the twelfth. Then nothing happened until the next day, the thirteenth. At twelve-twelve A.M. the alarm system was disengaged by Mr. Storey's voiceprint and the interior garage door was opened again. He then put the alarm back on – once he was in the house.'

Hendricks studied the printout before continuing.

'The system remained at status until three-nineteen, when the alarm was shut off. The interior garage door was then opened and the alarm system was engaged once more by Mr. Storey's voiceprint. Then, forty-two minutes later, at four-oh-one A.M., the alarm was disengaged by Mr. Storey's voiceprint, the garage door was opened and the alarm system was engaged again. There was no other activity until eleven A.M., when the alarm was disengaged by the voice print of Betilda Lockett.'

'Do you know who Betilda Lockett is?'

'Yes, when I installed the system I set up her voice acceptance program. She's Mr. Storey's executive assistant.'

Langwiser asked permission to set up an easel with a board displaying the times and activities Hendricks had just testified to. It was approved over objection and Bosch helped Langwiser set up the display. The poster board had two columns on it showing the record of the house alarm's engagement and the usage of the door between the house and the garage.

		ALARM	INTERIOR GARAGE DOOR
10/12	7:09 P.M.	– engaged by D. Storey	opened/closed
10/13	12:12 A.M.	– disengaged by D. Storey	opened/closed
10/13	12:12 A.M.	– engaged by D. Storey	
10/13	3:19 A.M.	– disengaged by D. Storey	opened/closed
10/13	3:19 A.M.	– engaged by D. Storey	
10/13	4:01 A.M.	– disengaged by D. Storey	opened/closed
10/13	4:01 P.M.	– engaged by D. Storey	

Langwiser continued her questioning of Hendricks.

'Does this illustration accurately reflect your testimony about the alarm system in David Storey's home on the evening of October twelfth going into October thirteenth?'

The technician looked at the poster carefully and then nodded.

'Is that a yes?'

'It's a yes.'

'Thank you. Now, because these activities were instigated with the system's recognition and approval of David Storey's voiceprint, are you telling the jury that this is the record of David Storey's comings and goings during the time period in question?'

Fowkkes objected, saying the question assumed facts not in evidence. Houghton agreed and told Langwiser to rephrase or ask another question. Her point made with the jury, she moved on.

'Mr. Hendricks, if I had a tape-recording of David Storey's voice, could I play it into the Millennium Twenty-one's station microphone and receive clearance to engage or disengage the alarm?'

'No. There are two fail-safe mechanisms. You must use a password recognized by the computer and you must say the date. So you need voice, password, correct date or the system won't accept the command.'

'What was David Storey's password?'

'I don't know. It's private. The system is set so that he can change his password as often as he likes.'

Langwiser looked at the poster on the easel. She went up and took a pointer off the easel's ledge and used it to underline the entries for 3:19 and 4:01 in the morning.

'Can you tell from these entries whether someone with Mr. Storey's voice left the house at three-nineteen and returned at four-oh-one, or if it was the other way around; someone came in at three-nineteen and then left at four-oh-one?'

'Yes, I can.'

'How is that?'

'The system also records which transmitter stations are used to engage and disengage the system. In this house the stations are set on either side of three doors – you know, outside and inside the door. The three are the front door, the door to the garage and one of the doors to the rear deck. The transmitters are on the outside and the inside of each door. Whatever one is used gets recorded in the innkeeper program.'

'Can you look at the printout from Mr. Storey's system that you looked at earlier and tell us what transmitters were used during the three-nineteen and four-oh-one entries?'

Hendricks studied his paperwork before answering.

'Uh, yes. At three-nineteen the exterior transmitter was used. That means somebody was in the garage when they turned the alarm on in the house. Then at four-oh-one the same exterior transmitter was used to turn the alarm off. The door was then opened and closed, then the alarm was turned back on from the inside.'

'So someone came home at four-oh-one, is that what you are saying?'

'Yes. Right.'

'And the system computer registered this someone as David Storey, correct?'

'It identified his voice, yes.'

'And this person would have to have used Mr. Storey's password and given the correct date as well?'

'Yes, that's right.'

Langwiser said she had no further questions. Fowkkes told the judge he had a quick cross-examination. He bounded to the lectern and looked at Hendricks.

'Mr. Hendricks, how long have you worked for Lighthouse?'

'Three years next month.'

'So you were employed by Lighthouse on January first a year ago, the so-called Y-two-K changeover?'

'Yes,' Hendricks said hesitantly.

'Can you tell us what happened to many of Lighthouse's clients on that day?'

'Uh, we had a few problems.'

'A *few* problems, Mr. Hendricks?'

'We had system failures.'

'What system in particular?'

'The Millennium Twos had a program malfunction. But it was minor. We were able to—'

'How many clients with Millennium Twos were affected in the Los Angeles area?'

'All of them. But we found the bug and—'

'That's all, sir. Thank you.'

'We got it fixed.'

'Mr. Hendricks,' the judge barked. 'That's enough. The jury will disregard the last statement.'

He looked at Langwiser.

'Redirect, Ms. Langwiser?'

Langwiser said she had a few quick questions. Bosch had known about the Y2K problems and reported them to the prosecutors. Their hope had been that the defense would not learn of them or raise them.

'Mr. Hendricks, did Lighthouse fix the bug that infected the systems after Y-two-K?'

'Yes, we did. It was fixed right away.'

'Would it in any way have affected data gathered from the defendant's system a full ten months after Y-two-K?'

'Not at all. The problem was resolved. The system was repaired.'

Langwiser said that was all she had for the witness and sat down. Fowkkes then rose for re-cross.

'The bug that was fixed, Mr. Hendricks, that was the bug they knew about, correct?'

Hendricks gave a confused look.

'Yeah, that was the one that caused the problem.'

'So what you're saying is that you only know about these "bugs" when they cause a problem.'

'Uh, usually.'

'So there could be a program bug in Mr. Storey's security system and you wouldn't know about it until it creates a problem, correct?'

Hendricks shrugged his shoulders.

'Anything's possible.'

Fowkkes sat down and the judge asked Langwiser if she had anything else. The prosecutor hesitated a moment but then said she had nothing further. Hendricks was dismissed by Houghton, who then suggested an early break for lunch.

'Our next witness will be very brief, Your Honor. I'd like to get him in before the break. We plan to concentrate on one witness during the afternoon session.'

'Very well, go on.'

'We recall Detective Bosch.'

Bosch got up and went to the witness stand, carrying the murder book. This time he did not touch the microphone. He settled in and was reminded by the judge that he was still under oath.

'Detective Bosch,' Langwiser began. 'At some point

during your investigation of the murder of Jody Krementz were you directed to drive from the defendant's home to the victim's home and then back again?'

'Yes, I was. By you.'

'And did you follow that direction?'

'Yes.'

'When?'

'On November sixteenth at three-nineteen A.M.'

'Did you time your drive?'

'Yes, I did. Both ways.'

'And can you tell us those times? You can refer to your notes, if you wish.'

Bosch opened the binder to a previously marked page. He took a moment to study the notations even though he knew them by heart.

'From Mr. Storey's house to Jody Krementz's house it took eleven minutes and twenty-two seconds, driving within posted speed limits. Coming back it took eleven minutes and forty-eight seconds. The round trip was twenty-three minutes, ten seconds.'

'Thank you, Detective.'

That was it. Fowkkes passed again on cross-examination, reserving the right to call Bosch back to the stand during the defense phase. Judge Houghton recessed the trial for lunch and the crowded courtroom slowly drained into the outside hallway.

Bosch was pushing and moving through the crowd of lawyers, spectators and reporters in the hallway and looking for Annabelle Crowe when a hand strongly grabbed his upper arm from behind. He swung around and looked into the face of a black man he didn't recognize. Another man, this one white, came up to them. The two men had on almost identical gray suits. Bosch knew they were bureau men before the first man said his first word.

'Detective Bosch, I'm Special Agent Twilley with the FBI. This is Special Agent Friedman. Can we talk to you somewhere privately?'

38

It took three hours to go carefully through the videotape. At the end of it McCaleb had nothing to show for his time except a parking ticket. Tafero had appeared nowhere in the video of the post office on the day the money order was purchased. Neither had Harry Bosch, for that matter. The missing forty-eight minutes of video, which had been taped over before McCaleb and Winston got there, now haunted him. If they had gone to the post office first and Hollywood station second, they might have had the killer on tape. Those forty-eight minutes might be the difference in the case, the difference in being able to clear Bosch or convict him.

McCaleb was thinking about what-if scenarios when he got to the Cherokee and found the parking ticket under the wiper. He cursed and pulled it off and looked at it. He had been so absorbed in watching the tape he had forgotten he had parked in a fifteen-minute zone in front of the post office. The ticket would cost him forty dollars and that stung. With few fishing charters in the winter months, his family had been living mostly off Graciela's small paycheck and his monthly pension from the bureau. There wasn't a lot of leeway with expenses for the two kids. This, coupled with Saturday's canceled charter, would hurt.

He slipped the ticket back into place on the windshield and started walking down the sidewalk. He decided he wanted to go into Valentino Bonds, even if he knew Rudy Tafero would likely be up in Van Nuys in court. It was in keeping with his practice of viewing the target subject in comfortable surroundings. The target might not be there this time, but the surroundings where he felt safe would.

As he walked he took out his cell phone and called Jaye Winston but got her machine. He hung up without leaving a message and paged her. Four blocks later, when he was almost to Valentino Bonds, she called back.

'I got nothing,' he reported.

'Nothing?'

'No Tafero and no Bosch.'

'Damn.'

'It had to have been on that missing forty-eight minutes.'

'We should have—'

'Gone to the post office first. I know. My fault. The one thing I did get was a parking ticket.'

'Sorry, Terry.'

'Which at least gives me an idea. It was right before Christmas and crowded. If he was in a fifteen-minute zone he might have gone over while waiting in line. The parking enforcement goons in this city are like Nazis. They wait in the shadows. There's always a chance there was a ticket. It should be checked.'

'Son of Sam?'

'Right.'

She was referring to the New York City serial killer who was tripped up in the 1970s by a parking ticket.

'I'll take a shot at it. See what I can do. What are you going to do?'

'I'm about to check out Valentino Bonds.'

'Is he there?'

'He's probably up in court. I'm going to go up there next, see if I can talk to Bosch about all of this.'

'Better be careful. Your colleagues from the bureau said they were going up to see him at lunch. They might still be around when you get there.'

'What, they're expecting Bosch to be so impressed by their suits that he confesses or something?'

'I don't know. Something like that. They were going to brace him. Get some stuff on the record and then go find the contradictions. You know, routine word trap.'

'Harry Bosch is not routine. They're wasting their time.'

'I know. I told 'em. But you can't tell an FBI agent anything, you know that.'

He smiled.

'Hey, if this goes the other way and we take down Tafero, I want the sheriff to pay for this ticket.'

'Hey, you're not working for me. You're working for Bosch, remember? He pays parking tickets. The sheriff only pays for pancakes.'

'All right. I'm gonna go.'

'Call me.'

He slid the phone into the pocket of his windbreaker and opened the glass door of Valentino Bonds.

It was a small white room with a waiting couch and a counter. It reminded McCaleb of a motel office. There was a calendar on the wall depicting a beach scene from Puerta Vallarta. Behind the counter a man sat with his head down, filling in a crossword puzzle. Behind him was a closed door to what was probably a rear office. McCaleb put a smile on his face and started walking with purpose around the counter before the man there even looked up.

'Rudy? Hey, Rudy, come on outta there!'

The man looked up as McCaleb passed him and opened the door. He stepped into an office that was more than twice the size of the front room.

'Rudy?'

The man from the counter came in right behind him.

'Hey, man, what are you doing?'

McCaleb turned, scanning the room.

'Looking for Rudy. Where is he?'

'He's not here. Now, if you would step—'

'He told me he'd be here, that he didn't have to be in court until later.'

Scanning the office, he saw the rear wall was covered

with framed photos. He took a step closer. Most of them were shots of Tafero with celebrities he had either bailed out or worked with as a security consultant. Some of the photos were clearly from his days working across the street at the cop shop.

'Excuse me, just who are you?'

McCaleb looked at the man as if insulted. He looked like he might be Tafero's younger brother. The same dark hair and eyes with rough good looks.

'I'm a friend. Terry. We used to work together when he was across the street.'

McCaleb pointed to a group photo that was on the wall. It showed several men in suits and a few women standing in front of the brick facade of the Hollywood Division station. The detective squad. McCaleb saw both Harry Bosch and Rudy Tafero in the back row. Bosch's face was turned slightly away from the camera. There was a cigarette in his mouth and smoke rising from it partially obscured his face.

The man turned and started looking at the photo.

McCaleb's eyes took another swing around the office. The room was nicely appointed with a desk to the left and a sitting area to the right with two short couches and an oriental rug. He stepped closer to the desk to look at a file sitting at center on the blotter but the file, though an inch thick with documents, had nothing written on the tab.

'What the fuck, you're not on here.'

'Yes, I am,' McCaleb said without turning from the desk. 'I was smoking. You can't see my face.'

There was a file tray to the right of the blotter that was stacked with folders. McCaleb leaned his head at an angle to check the tabs. He saw an assortment of names, some of them recognizable as entertainers or actors but none of them correlating to his investigation.

'Bullshit, man, that ain't you. That's Harry Bosch.'

'Really? You know Harry?'

The man didn't answer. McCaleb turned around. The man was looking at him with angry, suspicious eyes. For the first time McCaleb saw that he held an old billyclub down at his side.

'Let me see.'

He walked over and looked at the framed photo.

'You know, you're right, that's Harry. I must've been in the one they took the year before. I was working undercover when they took this one and couldn't be in the picture.'

McCaleb nonchalantly took a step toward the door. Inside he was bracing to get hit with the bat.

'Just tell him I was here, okay? Tell him Terry stopped by.'

He made it to the door but one last framed photo caught his eye. It showed Tafero and another man side by side, jointly holding a polished wood plaque in their hands. The picture was old, Tafero looked almost ten years younger. His eyes were brighter and his smile seemed genuine. The plaque itself was hanging on the wall next to the photo. McCaleb leaned closer and read the brass plate attached at the bottom.

RUDY TAFERO

HOLLYWOOD BOOSTERS DETECTIVE OF THE MONTH

FEBRUARY 1995

He glanced back at the photo again and then moved through the door to the front room.

'Terry what?' the man said as he passed.

McCaleb walked to the front door before turning back to him.

'Just tell him it was Terry, the undercover guy.'

He left the office and walked back up the street without looking back.

McCaleb sat in his car in front of the post office. He felt uneasy, the way he always did when he knew the answer was within reach but he just couldn't quite see it. His gut told him he was on the right track. Tafero, the PI who hid his upscale Hollywood practice behind a bail bonds shack, was the key. McCaleb just couldn't find the door.

He realized he was very hungry. He started the car and thought about a place to eat. He was a few blocks from Musso's but had eaten there too recently. He wondered if they served food at Nat's but figured if they did that it would be dangerous to the stomach. Instead, he drove over to the In 'n Out on Sunset and ordered at the drive-through.

While he was eating his hamburger over the to-go box in the Cherokee, his phone chirped. He put the burger down in the box, wiped his hands on a napkin and opened the phone.

'You're a genius.'

It was Jaye Winston.

'What?'

'Tafero got a ticket on his Mercedes. A black four-thirty CLK. He was in the fifteen-minute zone right in front of the post office. The ticket was written at eight-nineteen A.M. on the twenty-second. He hasn't paid it yet. He has till five today and then it's overdue.'

McCaleb was silent as he considered this. He felt nerve synapses firing like dominoes running up his backbone. The ticket was a hell of a break. It proved absolutely nothing but it told him that he was following the correct path. And sometimes knowing you were on the right path was better than having the proof.

His thoughts jumped to his visit to Tafero's office and the photographs he had seen.

'Hey, Jaye, did you get a chance to look up anything on the case with Bosch's old lieutenant?'

'I didn't have to go looking. Twilley and Friedman already had a file on it with them today. Lieutenant Harvey Pounds. Somebody beat him to death about four weeks after he had that altercation with Bosch over Gunn. Because of the bad blood Bosch was a likely suspect. But he apparently was cleared – by the LAPD at least. The case is open but inactive. The bureau kind of watched from afar and has kept an open file, too. Twilley told me today that there are some people in the LAPD who think Bosch was cleared on it a little too quickly.'

'Oh, and I bet Twilley loves that.'

'He does. He already has Bosch down for it. He thinks Gunn is only the tip of the iceberg with Harry.'

McCaleb shook his head but immediately moved on. He couldn't dwell on other peoples' foibles and motivations. There was a lot to think about and plan for with the investigation at hand.

'By the way, do you have a copy of the parking ticket?' he asked.

'Not yet. It was all phone work. But it's being faxed. The thing is, you and I know what it means but it's a long way off from being proof of anything.'

'I know. But it will make a good prop when the time comes.'

'When the time comes for what?'

'To make our play. We'll use Tafero to get to Storey. You know that's where this is heading.'

'We? You've got it all planned out, don't you, Terry?'

'Not quite but I'm working on it.'

He didn't want to have an argument with her about his role in the investigation.

'Listen, my lunch is getting cold here,' he said.

'Well, excuse me. Go ahead and eat.'

'Call me later. I'm going up to see Bosch later on. Anything from Twilley and Friedman on that?'

'I think they're still up there with him.'

'All right. Check you later.'

He closed the phone, got out of the car and carried the food box to a trash can. He then jumped back in and started the engine. On the way back to the post office on Wilcox he opened all the windows to air the smell of greasy food out of the car.

39

Annabelle Crowe walked to the witness stand, drawing all eyes in the courtroom. She was stunningly attractive but there was an almost awkward quality about her movements. This mixture made her seem old and young at the same time and even more attractive. Langwiser would do the questioning. She waited until Crowe was seated before disturbing the room's vibe and getting up to go to the lectern.

Bosch had barely noticed the entrance of the final witness for the prosecution. He sat at the prosecution table with his eyes down, deep in thought about his visit from the two FBI agents. He had sized them up quickly. They smelled blood in the water and knew if they bagged Bosch on the Gunn case that there would be no end to the media ride they would get from it. He expected them to make their move at any moment.

Langwiser quickly moved through a series of general questions with Crowe, establishing that she was a neophyte actress with a few plays and commercials on her resume as well as one line in a feature film that had yet to be released. Her story seemed to confirm the difficulties of making it in Hollywood – a knock-down beauty who was only one in a town full of them. She still lived on stipends sent from her parents in Albuquerque.

Langwiser moved on to more salient testimony, keying in on the night of April 14 of the previous year when Annabelle Crowe went out on a date with David Storey. After quickly drawing brief descriptions of the dinner and drinks the couple enjoyed at Dan Tana's in West Hollywood, Langwiser moved to the latter half of the evening, when Annabelle accompanied Storey to his home on Mulholland Drive.

Crow testified that she and Storey shared a whole pitcher of margaritas on the back deck of his house before they went to his bedroom.

'And did you go willingly, Ms. Crowe?'

'Yes, I did.'

'You engaged in sexual relations with the defendant?'

'Yes, I did.'

'And this was consensual sexual intercourse?'

'Yes, it was.'

'Did anything happen that was unusual once you began having sexual relations with the defendant?'

'Yes, he started to choke me.'

'He started to choke you. How did that occur?'

'Well, I guess I closed my eyes at one point and it felt like he was changing positions or moving. He was on top of me and I felt his hand slide behind my neck and he sort of lifted my head off the pillow. Then I felt him slide something down . . .'

She stopped and put her hand to her mouth as she appeared to fight to maintain her composure.

'Take your time, Ms. Crowe.'

The witness looked as though she was genuinely trying to hold back tears. She finally dropped her hand and picked up her cup of water. She sipped from it and then looked up at Langwiser, a new resolve in her eyes.

'I felt him slide something down over my head and around my neck. I opened my eyes and he was tightening a necktie around my neck.'

She stopped and took another sip of water.

'Can you describe this necktie?'

'It had a pattern. It was blue diamonds on a field of purple. I remember it exactly.'

'What happened when the defendant pulled the tie tightly around your neck?'

'It was choking me!' Crowe replied shrilly, as if the question was stupid and the answer was obvious. 'He was choking me. And he kept . . . moving in me . . . and I tried to fight him but he was too strong for me.'

'Did he say anything at this time?'

'He just kept saying, "I have to do this, I have to do this," and he was breathing really hard and he kept on having sex with me. His teeth were clenched tight when he said it. I . . .'

She stopped again and this time single tears slid down both her cheeks, one slightly behind the other. Langwiser went to the prosecution table and took a box of tissues from her spot. She held them up and said, 'Your Honor, may I?'

The judge allowed her to approach the witness with the tissues. Langwiser made the delivery and then went back to the lectern. The courtroom was silent save for the crying sounds of the witness. Langwiser broke the moment.

'Ms. Crowe, do you need a minute?'

'No, I'm fine. Thank you.'

'Did you pass out when the defendant choked you?'

'Yes.'

'What do you remember next?'

'I woke up in his bed.'

'Was he there?'

'No, but I could hear the shower running. In the bathroom next to the bedroom.'

'What did you do?'

'I got up to get dressed. I wanted to leave before he came out of the shower.'

'Were your clothes where you had left them?'

'No. I found them in a bag – like a grocery bag – by the bedroom door. I put on my underwear.'

'Did you have a purse with you that night?'

'Yes. That was in the bag, too. But it was opened. I looked inside and he had taken the keys out. I—'

Fowkkes objected, saying the answer assumed facts not in evidence and the judge sustained it.

'Did you see the defendant take your keys out of your purse?' Langwiser asked.

'Well, no. But they had been inside my purse. I didn't take them out.'

'Okay, then someone – someone you didn't see because you were unconscious on the bed – took your keys out, is that correct?'

'Yes.'

'Okay, where did you find your keys after you realized they were not in your purse?'

'They were on his bureau next to his own keys.'

'Did you finish getting dressed and leave?'

'Actually, I was so scared I just grabbed my clothes and my keys and my purse and I ran out of there. I finished getting dressed when I got outside. I then ran down the street.'

'How did you get home?'

'I got tired of running and so I walked on Mulholland for a long time until I came to a fire station with a pay phone out front. I used it to call a cab, then I went home.'

'Did you call the police when you got home?'

'Um, I didn't.'

'Why not, Ms. Crowe?'

'Well, two things. When I got home David was leaving a message on my machine and I picked up. He apologized and said he got carried away. He told me he thought that the choking was going to increase my satisfaction while we had sex.'

'Did you believe him?'

'I don't know. I was confused.'

'Did you ask him why he had put your clothes in a bag?'

'Yes. He said he thought he was going to have to take

me to the hospital if I didn't wake up by the time he was out of the shower.'

'Did you ask him why he thought he should take a shower before taking an unconscious woman in his bed to the hospital?'

'I didn't ask that.'

'Did you ask him why he didn't call for paramedics?'

'No, I didn't think of that.'

'What was the other reason you did not call the police?'

The witness looked down at her hands, which were grasping each other in her lap.

'Well, I was embarrassed. After he called I wasn't sure anymore what had happened. You know, whether he had tried to kill me or was . . . trying to satisfy me more. I don't know. You always hear about Hollywood people and weird sex. I thought maybe I was . . . I don't know, just being uncool and square about it.'

She kept her eyes down and two more tears went down the slopes of her cheeks. Bosch saw a drop hit the collar of her chiffon blouse and leave a wet mark. Langwiser continued in a very soft tone.

'When did you contact the police about what happened that night with you and the defendant?'

Annabelle Crowe responded in a softer tone.

'When I read about him being arrested for killing Jody Krementz the same way.'

'You talked to Detective Bosch then?'

She nodded.

'Yes. And I knew that if I'd . . . I'd called the police that night that maybe she'd still . . .'

She didn't finish. She grabbed tissues out of the box and started a full force cry. Langwiser told the judge she was finished with her examination. Fowkkes said there would be a cross-examination but suggested that it should follow a break during which time the defendant could compose herself. Judge Houghton said that was a good idea and called a fifteen-minute break.

Bosch stayed in the courtroom watching over Annabelle Crowe as she went through the box of tissues. When she was done her face was no longer as beautiful. It was distorted and red, her eye sockets swollen. Bosch thought she had been convincing but he knew she hadn't faced Fowkkes yet. How she fared during the cross would determine whether the jury believed anything she had said on direct.

When Langwiser came back in she told Bosch there was someone at the outer door of the courtroom who wanted to speak to him.

'Who is it?'

'I didn't ask. I just overheard him talking to the deputies as I went in. They wouldn't let him in.'

'Was he in a suit? A black guy?'

'No, street clothes. A windbreaker.'

'Keep an eye on Annabelle. And you better find another box of tissues.'

He got up and went to the courtroom doors, working his way past all of the people coming back in at the end of the break. At one point he came face-to-face with Rudy Tafero. Bosch moved to his right to go around him but Tafero moved to his left. They danced back and forth a couple of times and Tafero smiled broadly. Bosch finally stopped and didn't move until Tafero pushed by him.

In the hall he looked around but didn't see anyone he recognized. Then Terry McCaleb walked out of the men's room and they nodded to each other. Bosch walked over to the railing in front of one of the floor-to-ceiling windows that looked out on the plaza below. McCaleb walked up.

'I've got about two minutes, then I've got to get back in there.'

'I just want to know if we can talk after court today. Things are happening and I need some time with you.'

'I know things are happening. Two agents showed up here today.'

'What did you tell them?'

'To fuck off. It made them mad.'

'Federal agents don't take that sort of language that well, you should know that, Bosch.'

'Yeah, well, I'm a slow learner.'

'What about after?'

'I'll be around. Unless Fowkkes creams this wit. Then I don't know, my team might have to retreat somewhere to lick our wounds.'

'All right, then I'll hang out, watch it on TV.'

'Later.'

Bosch went back into the courtroom, wondering what McCaleb had come up with so quickly. The jury was back and the judge was giving Fowkkes the go-ahead. The defense attorney waited politely as Bosch moved by him to get to the prosecution table. Then he began.

'Now Ms. Crowe, is acting your full-time occupation?'

'Yes.'

'Have you been acting here today?'

Langwiser immediately objected, angrily accusing Fowkkes of harassing the witness. Bosch thought her reaction was a bit extreme but knew she was sending a message to Fowkkes that she was going to defend her witness tooth and nail. The judge overruled the objection, saying Fowkkes was within bounds in cross-examining a witness hostile to his client.

'No, I am not acting,' Crowe answered forcefully.

Fowkkes nodded.

'You testified that you have been in Hollywood three years.'

'Yes.'

'I counted five paying jobs you spoke of. Anything else?'

'Not yet.'

Fowkkes nodded.

'Good to be hopeful. It's very difficult to break in, isn't it?'

'Yes, very difficult, very discouraging.'

'But you are on TV right now, aren't you?'

She hesitated a moment, the realization that she had walked into a trap showing on her face.

'And so are you,' she said.

Bosch almost smiled. It was the best answer she could have given.

'Let's talk about this . . . event that allegedly took place between you and Mr. Storey,' Fowkkes said. 'This event is, in fact, something you concocted from newspaper stories following David Storey's arrest, correct?'

'No, not correct. He tried to kill me.'

'So you say.'

Langwiser stood up to object but before she did the judge admonished Fowkkes to keep such editorial comments to himself. The defense lawyer moved on.

'Now, after Mr. Storey supposedly choked you to the point of unconsciousness, did you develop bruises on your neck?'

'Yes, I had a bruise for almost a week. I had to stay inside. I couldn't go to auditions or anything.'

'And you took photographs of the bruise to document its existence, correct?'

'No, I didn't.'

'But you showed the bruise to your agent and friends, did you not?'

'No.'

'And why is that?'

'Because I didn't think it would ever come to this, where I would have to try to prove what he did. I just wanted it to go away and I didn't want anyone to know.'

'So we only have your word for the bruise, is that correct?'

'Yes.'

'Just as we only have your word for the entire alleged incident, correct?'

'He tried to kill me.'

'And you testified that when you got home that evening

David Storey happened at that very moment to be leaving a message on your phone machine, correct?'

'Absolutely.'

'And you picked that call up – a call from the man you say tried to kill you. Do I have that right?'

Fowkkes gestured as if grabbing a telephone. He held his hand up until she answered.

'Yes.'

'And you saved that message on that tape to document his words and what had happened to you, correct?'

'No, I taped over it. By mistake.'

'By mistake. You mean you left it in the machine and eventually taped over it?'

'Yes. I didn't want to but I forgot and it got taped over.'

'You mean you forgot that someone tried to kill you and taped over it?'

'No, I didn't forget that he tried to kill me. I'll never forget that.'

'So as far as this tape goes, we only have your word for it, correct?'

'That's right.'

There was a measure of defiance in her voice. But in a way it seemed pitiful to Bosch. It was like yelling, 'Fuck you' into a jet engine. He sensed that she was about to be thrown into that jet engine and torn apart.

'Now, you testified that you are supported in part by your parents and that you have earned some monies as an actress. Is there any other source of income you haven't told us about?'

'Well . . . not really. My grandmother sends me money. But not too often.'

'Anything else?'

'Not that I can think of.'

'Do you take money from men on occasion, Ms. Crowe?'

There was an objection from Langwiser and the judge called the lawyers to a sidebar. Bosch watched Annabelle

Crowe the whole time the lawyers whispered. He studied her face. There was still a brushstroke of defiance but it was being crowded by fear. She knew something was coming. Bosch decided that Fowkkes had something legitimate that he was going after. It was something that was going to hurt her and thereby hurt the case.

When the sidebar broke up Kretzler and Langwiser returned to their seats at the prosecution table. Kretzler leaned over to Bosch.

'We're fucked,' he whispered. 'He's got four men that will testify they paid her for sex. Why didn't we know about this?'

Bosch didn't answer. She had been assigned to him for vetting. He had questioned her at length about her personal life and had run her prints for an arrest record. Her answers and the computer run were clean. If she'd never been popped for prostitution and she denied any criminal activities to Bosch, there wasn't much else he could have done.

Back at the lectern, Fowkkes rephrased the question.

'Ms. Crowe, have you ever taken money from men in exchange for sex?'

'No, absolutely not. That is a lie.'

'Do you know a man named Andre Snow?'

'Yes, I do.'

'If he were to testify under oath that he paid you for sexual relations, would he be lying?'

'Yes, he would.'

Fowkkes named three other men and they went through the same loop of Crowe acknowledging that she knew them but denying she had ever sold them sex.

'Then have you ever taken money from these men, but not for sex?' Fowkkes asked in a false tone of exasperation.

'Yes, on occasion. But it had nothing to do with whether we had sex or not.'

'Then what did it have to do with?'

'Them wanting to help me. I considered them friends.'

'Did you ever have sex with them?'

Annabelle Crowe looked down at her hands and shook her head.

'Are you saying no, Ms. Crowe?'

'I am saying that I didn't have sex with them every time they gave me money. They didn't give me money every time we had sex. One thing had nothing to do with the other. You are trying to make it look like something it's not.'

'I'm just asking questions, Ms. Crowe. As it is my job to do. As it is your job to tell this jury the truth.'

After a long pause Fowkkes said he had no further questions.

Bosch realized that he had been gripping the arms of his chair so tightly that his knuckles were white and had gone numb. He rubbed his hands together and tried to relax but he couldn't. He knew that Fowkkes was a master, a cut-and-run artist. He was brief and to the point and as devastating as a stiletto. Bosch realized that his discomfort was not only for Annabelle Crowe's helpless position and public humiliation, but for his own position. He knew the stiletto would be pointed at him next.

40

They settled into a booth at Nat's after getting bottles of Rolling Rock from the bartender with the tattoo of the barbed-wire-wrapped heart. While she pulled the bottles from the cold case and opened them, the woman hadn't said anything about McCaleb having come in the other night asking questions about the man he had now returned with. It was early and the place was empty except for groups of hard-cores at the bar and crowded into the booth all the way to the rear. Bruce Springsteen was on the jukebox singing, 'There's a darkness on the edge of town.'

McCaleb studied Bosch. He thought he looked preoccupied by something, probably the trial. The last witness had been a wash at best. Good on direct, bad on cross. The kind of witness you don't use – if you have the choice.

'Looked like you guys got sandbagged there with your wit.'

Bosch nodded.

'My fault. I should've seen it coming. I looked at her and thought she was so beautiful she couldn't possibly . . . I just believed her.'

'I know what you mean.'

'Last time I trust a face.'

'You guys still look like you're in good shape. What else you got coming?'

Bosch smirked.

'That's it. They were going to rest today but decided to

wait until the morning so Fowkkes wouldn't have the night to get ready. But we've fired all the bullets in the gun. Starting tomorrow we see what they've got.'

McCaleb watched Bosch take down almost half the bottle in one long pull. He decided he'd better get to the real questions while Bosch was still sharp.

'So tell me about Rudy Tafero.'

Bosch shrugged his shoulders in a gesture of ambivalence.

'What about him?'

'I don't know. How well do you know him? How well *did* you know him?'

'Well, I knew him when he was on *our* team. He worked Hollywood detectives about five years while I was there. Then he pulled the pin, got his twenty-year pension and moved across the street. Started working on getting people we put in the bucket out of the bucket.'

'When you were both on the same team, both in Hollywood, were you close?'

'I don't know what close means. We weren't friends, we weren't drinking buddies, he worked burglaries and I worked homicides. What are you asking so much about him for? What's he got to do with—'

He stopped and looked at McCaleb, the wheels obviously turning inside. Rod Stewart was now singing 'Twisting the Night Away.'

'Are you fucking kidding me?' Bosch finally asked. 'You're looking at—'

'Let me just ask some questions,' McCaleb interjected. 'Then you can ask yours.'

Bosch drained his bottle and held it up until the bartender noticed.

'No table service, guys,' she called over. 'Sorry.'

'Fuck that,' Bosch said.

He slid out of the booth and went to the bar. He came back with four more Rocks, though McCaleb had barely begun to drink his first one.

'Ask away,' Bosch said.

'Why weren't you two close?'

Bosch put both elbows on the table and held a fresh bottle with both hands. He looked out of the booth and then at McCaleb.

'Five, ten years ago there were two groups in the bureau. And to a large extent it was this way in the department, too. It was like the saints and the sinners – two distinct groups.'

'The born agains and the born againsts?'

'Something like that.'

McCaleb remembered. It had become well known in local law enforcement circles a decade earlier that a group within the LAPD known as the 'born agains' had members in key positions and was holding sway over promotions and choice assignments. The group's numbers – several hundred officers of all ranks – were members of a church in the San Fernando Valley where the department's deputy chief in charge of operations was a lay preacher. Ambitious officers joined the church in droves, in hopes of impressing the deputy chief and enhancing their career prospects. How much spirituality was involved was in question. But when the deputy chief delivered his sermon every Sunday at the eleven o'clock service, the church would be packed to standing room only with off-duty cops casting their eyes fervently on the pulpit. McCaleb had once heard a story about a car alarm going off in the parking lot during an eleven o'clock service. The hapless hype rummaging through the vehicle's glove compartment soon found himself surrounded by a hundred guns pointed by off-duty cops.

'I take it you were on the sinners' team, Harry.'

Bosch smiled and nodded.

'Of course.'

'And Tafero was on the saints'.'

'Yeah. And so was our lieutenant at the time. A paper pusher named Harvey Pounds. He and Tafero had their little church thing going and so they were tight. I think anybody who was tight with Pounds, whether because of church or not, wasn't somebody I was going to gravitate toward, if you know what I mean. And they weren't going to gravitate toward me.'

McCaleb nodded. He knew more than he was letting on.

'Pounds was the guy who messed up the Gunn case,' he said. 'The one you pushed through the window.'

'He's the one.'

Bosch dropped his head and shook it in self-disgust.

'Was Tafero there that day?'

'Tafero? I don't know, probably.'

'Well, wasn't there an IAD investigation with witness reports?'

'Yeah, but I didn't look at it. I mean, I pushed the guy through a window in front of the squad. I wasn't going to deny it.'

'And later – what, a month or so? – Pounds ends up dead in the tunnel up in the hills.'

'Griffith Park, yeah.'

'And it's still open . . .'

Bosch nodded.

'Technically.'

'You said that before. What does that mean?'

'It means it's open but nobody's working it. The LAPD has a special classification for cases like it, cases they don't want to touch. It's what is called closed by circumstances other than arrest.'

'And you know those circumstances?'

Bosch finished his second bottle, slid it to the side and pulled a fresh bottle in front of him.

'You're not drinking,' he said.

'You're doing enough for both of us. Do you know those circumstances?'

Bosch leaned forward.

'Listen, I'm going to tell you something very few people know about, okay?'

McCaleb nodded. He knew better than to ask a question now. He would just let Bosch tell it.

'Because of that window thing I went on suspension. When I got tired of walking around my house staring at the walls, I started investigating an old case. A cold case. A murder case. I went freelancing on it and I ended up following a blind trail to some very powerful people. But at the time I had no badge, no real standing. So a few times, when I made some calls, I used Pounds's name. You know, I was trying to hide what I was doing.'

'If the department found out you were working a case while on suspension things would've gotten worse for you.'

'Exactly. So I used his name when I made what I thought were some routine, innocuous calls. But then one night somebody called Pounds up and told him that they had something for him, some urgent information. He went to the meet. By himself. Then they found him later in that tunnel. He'd been beaten pretty bad. Like they had tortured him. Only he couldn't answer their questions because he was the wrong guy. I was the one who had used his name. I was the one they wanted.'

Bosch dropped his chin to his chest and was silent for a long moment.

'I got him killed,' he said without looking up. 'The guy was a pure-bred asshole but my actions got him killed.'

Bosch suddenly jerked his head up and drank from his bottle. McCaleb saw his eyes were dark and shiny. They looked weary.

'Is that what you wanted to know, Terry? Does that help you?'

McCaleb nodded.

'How much of this would Tafero have known?'

'Nothing.'

'Could he have thought you were the one who called Pounds out that night?'

'Maybe. There were people who did and probably still do. But what does it mean? What's it got to do with Gunn?'

McCaleb took his first long drink of beer. It was cold and he felt the chill in his chest. He put the bottle down and decided it was time to give something back to Bosch.

'I need to know about Tafero because I need to know about reasons, motives. I have no proof of anything – yet – but I think Tafero killed Gunn. He did it for Storey. He set you in the frame.'

'Jesus . . .'

'Nice perfect frame. The crime scene is connected to the painter Hieronymus Bosch, the painter is connected to you as his namesake and then you are connected to Gunn. And you know when Storey probably got the idea for it?'

Bosch shook his head. He looked too stunned to talk.

'The day you tried to interview him in his office. You played the tape in court last week. You identified yourself on it by your full first name.'

'I always do. I . . .'

'He then connects with Tafero and Tafero has the perfect victim to put in the frame. Gunn – a man he knew walked away from you and a murder charge six years ago.'

Bosch lifted his bottle a couple of inches off the table and brought it back down hard.

'I think the plan was twofold. If they got lucky the connection would be made quickly and you'd be fighting a murder charge before Storey's trial even started. If that didn't happen, then Plan B. They would still have it to crush you with at trial. Destroy you, they destroy the case. Fowkkes already took out that woman today and potshotted a few of the other wits. What does the case rest on? You, Harry. They knew it would come down to you.'

Bosch turned his head slightly and his eyes seemed to

go blank as he stared at the scarred table top while considering what McCaleb had said.

'I needed to know your background with Tafero. Because that's a question; why would *he* do this? Yes, there probably is money in it and a hook into Storey if he walks. But there had to be something more. And I think you just told me what it was. He's probably hated you for a long time.'

Bosch looked up from the table and directly at McCaleb.

'It's a payback.'

McCaleb nodded.

'For Pounds. And unless we get the proof of it, it might just work.'

Bosch was silent. He stared down at the table. He looked tired and washed out to McCaleb.

'Still want to shake his hand?' McCaleb asked.

Bosch raised his eyes.

'Sorry, Harry, that was a cheap shot.'

Bosch shook his head, shrugging it off.

'I deserve it. So tell me, what *do* you have?'

'Not a lot. But you were right. I missed something. Tafero bailed Gunn out on New Year's Eve. I think the plan was to kill him that night, set the scene and let things take their course. The Hieronymus Bosch connection would come to light – either through Jaye Winston or a bureau VICAP inquiry – and you'd become a natural target. But then Gunn went and got himself drunk in here.'

He raised his bottle and gestured to the bar.

'And then he got himself duiced while driving home. Tafero had to get him out so they could stay with the plan. So he could kill him. That bail slip is the one direct link we have.'

Bosch nodded. McCaleb could tell he was seeing the scheme.

'They leaked it to that reporter,' Bosch said. 'Once it hit

the media they could jump on it and use it and act like it was news to them, like they were behind the curve when all along they were bending the goddamn curve.'

McCaleb nodded hesitantly. He didn't bring up Buddy Lockridge's admission because it threw a jam into the working theory.

'What?' Bosch asked.

'Nothing. I'm just thinking.'

'You've got nothing other than Tafero posting the bail?'

'A traffic ticket and that's it for now.'

In detail McCaleb described his morning's visits to Valentino Bonds and the post office and how his being forty-eight minutes late at the post office might be the difference in being able to clear Bosch and take down Tafero.

Bosch winced and picked up his bottle, but then put it down without drinking from it.

'The parking ticket puts him at the post office,' McCaleb offered.

'It's nothing. He's got an office five blocks away. He could claim it was the only parking place he could find. He could say he lent his car to somebody. It's nothing.'

McCaleb didn't want to concentrate on what they didn't have. He wanted to fill in pieces.

'Listen, the morning watch sergeant told us you had a standing request to be notified every time Gunn was brought in. Would Tafero have known about it? Either from before when he was still in the squad or some other way?'

'He could have. It wasn't a secret. I was working on Gunn. Someday I was going to break him.'

'By the way, what did Pounds look like?'

Bosch gave him a confused look.

'Short, wide and balding with a mustache?'

Bosch nodded and was about to ask a question when McCaleb answered it.

'His picture is on the wall in Tafero's office. Pounds

giving him the detective-of-the-month plaque. I bet you never got one of those, Harry.'

'Not with Pounds making the pick.'

McCaleb looked up and saw that Jaye Winston had entered the bar. She was carrying a briefcase. He nodded to her and she started toward the booth, walking with her shoulders up as though she were carefully stepping through a landfill.

McCaleb moved over and she slid into the booth next to him.

'Nice place.'

'Harry,' McCaleb said, 'I believe you know Jaye Winston.'

Bosch and Winston looked at each other.

'First thing,' Winston said, 'I'm sorry about the thing with Kiz. I hope—'

'We do what we have to do,' Bosch said. 'You want a drink? They don't come to the table here.'

'I'd be shocked if they did. Maker's Mark, rocks, if they have it.'

'Terry, you cool?'

'Cool.'

Bosch slid out to get the drink. Winston turned to look at McCaleb.

'How is it going?'

'Little pieces, here and there.'

'How's he taking it?'

'Not bad, I guess, for a guy who's been put into a pretty big box. How'd you do?'

She smiled in a way that McCaleb could tell meant she had come up with something.

'I got you the photo and a couple other . . . interesting . . . pieces.'

Bosch put Winston's drink down in front of her and slid back into the booth.

'She laughed when I said Maker's Mark,' he said. 'That's the house swill there.'

'Wonderful. Thank you.'

Winston moved her glass to the side and brought her briefcase up onto the table. She opened it, removed a file and then closed the briefcase and put it back on the floor next to the booth. McCaleb watched Bosch watching her. There was an expectant look on his face.

Winston opened the file and slid a five-by-eight photo of Rudy Tafero over to McCaleb.

'That's from his bonding license. It's eleven months old.'

She then referred to a page of typed notes.

'I went to county lockup and pulled everything on Storey. He was held there until they transferred him to Van Nuys jail for the trial. During his stay in county he had nineteen visits from Tafero. The first twelve visits coming during the first three weeks he was in there. During that same period, Fowkkes only visited him four times. A lawyer in Fowkkes's office visited an additional four times and Storey's executive assistant, a woman named Betilda Lockett, visited six times. That's it. He was meeting with his investigator more often than his lawyers.'

'That's when they planned it,' McCaleb said.

She nodded and then smiled in that same way again.

'What?' McCaleb asked.

'Just saving the best for last.'

She brought her briefcase back up and opened it.

'The jail keeps records of all property and possessions of inmates – things that were brought in with them, things approved and passed to them by visitors. There is a notation in Storey's records that his assistant, Betilda Lockett, was allowed to give him a book during the second of her six visits. According to the property report, it was called *The Art of Darkness*. I went to the downtown library and checked it out.'

From her briefcase she took a large, heavy book with a blue cloth cover. She started opening it on the table. There was a yellow Post-it sticking out as a marker.

'It's a study of artists who used darkness as a vital part of the visual medium, according to the introduction.'

She looked up and smiled as she got to the Post-it.

'It has a rather long chapter on Hieronymus Bosch. Complete with illustrations.'

McCaleb lifted his empty bottle and clicked against her glass, which she still hadn't touched. He then leaned in, along with Bosch, to look at the pages.

'Beautiful,' he said.

Winston turned the pages. The book's illustrations of Bosch's work included all of the paintings from which pieces of the crime scene could be traced: *The Stone Operation*, *The Seven Deadly Sins* with the eye of God, *The Last Judgment* and *The Garden of Earthly Delights*.

'He planned the thing right there from his cell,' McCaleb marveled.

'Looks like it,' Winston said.

They both looked at Bosch, who was nodding his head almost imperceptibly.

'Now your turn, Harry,' McCaleb said.

Bosch looked perplexed.

'My turn at what?'

'At making good luck.'

McCaleb slid the picture of Tafero across the table and nodded toward the bartender. Bosch slid out and took the photo to the bar.

'We're still just dancing around the edges,' Winston said as they both watched Bosch question the bartender about the photo. 'We've got little pieces but that's it.'

'I know,' McCaleb said. He couldn't hear what was being said at the bar. The music was too loud, Van Morrison singing, 'The wild night is coming.'

Bosch nodded to the bartender and came back to the booth.

'She recognizes him – drinks Kahlúa and cream of all things. She can't put him here with Gunn, though.'

McCaleb shrugged his shoulders in a no-big-deal gesture.

'It was worth the shot.'

'You know where this is going, don't you?' Bosch said, his eyes shifting from McCaleb's to Winston's and then back. 'You're going to have to make a play. It's going to be the only way. And it's gotta be a damn good play because my ass is on the line.'

McCaleb nodded.

'We know,' he said.

'When? I'm running out of time.'

McCaleb looked at Winston. It was her call.

'Soon,' she said. 'Maybe tomorrow. I haven't gone into the office with this yet. I have to finesse my captain on it because last he knew, Terry here was banished and I was working with the bureau on you. I also have to get a DA involved because when we make the move we'll have to move fast. If it all works out I say we take Tafero in tomorrow night and make the play to him.'

Bosch looked down at the table with a rueful smile. He slid an empty bottle back and forth between his hands.

'I met those guys today. The agents.'

'I heard. You didn't exactly assure them of your innocence. They came back all hot and bothered.'

Bosch looked up.

'So what do you need from me on this?'

'We need you to sit tight,' Winston said. 'We'll let you know about tomorrow night.'

Bosch nodded.

'There is one thing,' McCaleb said. 'The exhibits from the trial, do you have access to them?'

'During court, yeah. Otherwise they stay with the clerk. Why?'

'Because Storey obviously had existing knowledge of the painter Hieronymus Bosch. He had to have recognized your name during that interview and known what he could do with it. So I'm thinking that book his assistant brought him in jail had to be his own. He told her to bring it to him.'

Bosch nodded.

'The picture of the bookcase.'

McCaleb nodded.

'You got it.'

'I'll let you know.' Bosch looked around the place. 'Are we done here?'

'We're done,' Winston said. 'We'll be in touch.'

She slid out of the booth, followed by Bosch and McCaleb. They left two beers and a whiskey rocks untouched on the table. At the door, McCaleb glanced back and saw a couple of the hard-cores moving in on the treasure. From the jukebox John Fogerty was singing, 'There's a bad moon on the rise . . .'

41

The chill off the water worked its way into McCaleb's bones. He shoved his hands deep into the pockets of his windbreaker and turtled his neck as far down into the collar as he could as he carefully made his way down the ramp to the Cabrillo Marina docks.

Though his chin was down his eyes were alert and scanning the docks for unusual movement. Nothing caught his attention. He glanced at Buddy Lockridge's sailboat as he passed. Despite all the junk – surfboards, bikes, gas grill, an ocean kayak and other assorted equipment and debris – crowding the deck, he could see the cabin lights were on. He walked quietly on the wood planking. He decided that whether Buddy was awake or not it was too late and McCaleb was too tired and cold to deal with his supposed partner. Still, as he approached *The Following Sea*, he couldn't help but move his mind over the sharp-edged anomaly in his working theory on the case. Back at the bar Bosch had been correct when he deduced that someone from the Storey camp had to have leaked the story of the Gunn investigation to the *New Times*. McCaleb knew that the only way the current case theory hung together was if Tafero, or maybe Fowkkes or even Storey from jail, had been Jack McEvoy's source. The problem was that Buddy Lockridge had told McCaleb that he had leaked the investigation to the weekly tabloid.

Now the only way, at least as it appeared to McCaleb, that this could work would be if both Buddy and someone in Storey's defense group leaked the same information to the same media source. And this, of course, was a coincidence that even a believer in coincidence would have a difficult time accepting.

McCaleb tried to put it out of his mind for the moment. He got to the boat, looked around again, and stepped down into the cockpit. He unlocked the slider and went in, turning on the lights. He decided that in the morning he would go over and question Buddy more carefully about what he had done and who he had talked to.

He locked the door and put his keys and the videotape he'd been carrying down on the chart table. He immediately went to the galley and poured a large glass of orange juice. He then turned the upper deck lights off and took the juice with him down to the lower deck where he went into the head and quickly began his evening pill ritual. As he swallowed the pills and orange juice he looked at himself in the small mirror over the sink. He thought about what Bosch had looked like. The weariness clearly set deep in his eyes. McCaleb wondered if he would get the same look in a few years, after a few more cases.

When he was finished with his medicine routine he stripped off his clothes and took a quick shower, the water feeling ice cold because the water heater hadn't been on since he had crossed in the boat the day before.

Shivering, he went into the master cabin and put on a pair of boxer shorts and a sweatshirt. He was dead tired but once he got into the bed he decided he should write a few notes about his thoughts on how Jaye Winston should run the play with Tafero. He reached down to the nightstand's drawer, where he kept pens and scratch pads. When he opened it he found a folded newspaper crammed into the small drawer space. He pulled it out, unfolded it and found it was the previous week's issue of *New Times*. The pages had been folded backward so that the rear advertising section was at the front. McCaleb was looking at a page full of matchbook-sized ads under a heading that said OUTCALL MASSAGE.

McCaleb got up quickly and went to his windbreaker, which he had tossed onto a chair. He pulled the cell phone out of the pocket and went back to the bed with it. Though McCaleb had been carrying the phone with him in recent days, it usually stayed in its charger on the boat. It was paid for out of charter funds and was carried as a business expense. It was used by clients during charter trips and by Buddy Lockridge while confirming reservations and running credit card authorizations.

The phone had a small digital screen with a menu he scrolled through. He opened the call log program and began scrolling through the last hundred numbers the phone had been used to call. Most of the numbers he quickly identified and eliminated. But every time he did not recognize a number he compared it to the phone numbers at the bottom of the ads on the massage page. The fourth unrecognized number he compared to the ads was a match. The number was for a woman who advertised herself as an 'Exotic Japanese-Hawaiian Beauty' named Leilani. Her ad said she specialized in 'full-service relaxation' and was not associated with any massage agency.

McCaleb closed the phone and got off the bed again. He started pulling on a pair of sweatpants as he tried to recall exactly what had been said when he had accused Buddy Lockridge of leaking the case information to the *New Times*.

By the time he was dressed, McCaleb realized he had never specifically accused Buddy of leaking information to the newspaper. He had only mentioned the *New Times* and Buddy had immediately begun to apologize. McCaleb now understood that Buddy's apology and embarrassment could have been over his using *The Following Sea* the week before when it was in the marina as a rendezvous point with the full-service masseuse. It explained why he had asked if McCaleb was going to tell Graciela what he had done.

McCaleb looked at his watch. It was ten after eleven. He grabbed the newspaper and went topside. He didn't want to wait until the morning to confirm this. He guessed that Buddy had used *The Following Sea* to meet the woman because his own boat was so small and cramped and looked like a forbidding floating rat trap. There was no master cabin – just one open space that was as crowded with junk as the deck above. If Buddy had *The Following Sea* available to him, he would have used it.

In the salon he didn't bother turning on the lights. He leaned over the couch and looked out the window to the boat's left. Buddy's boat, the *Double Down*, was four slips away and he could see the cabin lights were still on. Buddy was still awake, unless he had passed out with the lights on.

McCaleb went to the slider and was about to unlock it when he realized it was already open a half inch. He realized someone was on the boat, probably having entered while he had been in the shower and unable to hear the lock pop or feel the added weight on the boat. He quickly slid the door all the way open in an effort to escape. He was just stepping through when he was grabbed from behind. An arm came over his right shoulder and across the front of his neck. It bent at the elbow and his neck was shoved into the V it formed. His attacker's other forearm closed the triangle behind his neck. The hold closed like a vise on both sides of his neck, compressing the carotid arteries that carried oxygenated blood to his brain. McCaleb had an almost clinical understanding of what was happening. He was caught in a textbook choke hold. He began to struggle. He brought his arms up and tried to dig his fingers under the forearm and biceps on either side of his neck but it was no use. He was already weakening.

He was dragged back away from the door and into the darkness of the salon. He reached his left hand back to the point where his attacker's right hand gripped his left forearm – the weak point of the triangle. But he had no leverage and was losing power quickly. He tried to yell. Maybe Buddy would hear. But his voice was gone and nothing came out.

He remembered another defensive measure. He raised his right foot up and drove it down, heel first, toward his attacker's foot, with the last strength he could muster. But he missed. His heel hit the floor ineffectively and his attacker took another step backward, violently pulling McCaleb off balance and unable to attempt the kick release again.

McCaleb was quickly losing consciousness. His vision of the marina lights through the salon door was being crowded by a closing blackness with a reddish outline. His last thoughts were that he was in the grip of a classic choke hold, the kind taught at police departments across the country until too many deaths resulted from its use.

Soon even that thought drifted away and he saw no lights. The darkness moved in and took him.

42

McCaleb came awake to tremendous muscular pain in his shoulders and upper legs. When he opened his eyes he realized he was lying chest down across the master cabin's bed. His head was lying flat on the mattress, his left cheek down, and he was staring at the headboard. It took him a moment before he remembered that he had been on his way to visit Buddy Lockridge when he was attacked from behind.

He became completely conscious and tried to relax his aching muscles but realized he could not move. His wrists were bound behind his back and his legs were bent backward at the knees and were being held in that position by someone's hand.

He lifted his head off the mattress and tried to turn. He couldn't get the angle. He dropped back to the mattress and turned his head to the left. He lifted up once again and turned to see Rudy Tafero, standing next to the bed, smiling at him. With one gloved hand he was holding McCaleb's feet, which were bound at the ankles and folded back toward his thighs.

Comprehension rushed over him. McCaleb realized he was naked and that he was bound and held in the same posture as he had seen the body of Edward Gunn. The reverse fetal pose from the painting by Hieronymus Bosch. The cold chill of terror exploded in his chest. He instinctively flexed his leg muscles. Tafero was ready for it. His feet barely moved. But he heard three clicks behind his head and became aware of the ligature around his neck.

'Easy,' Tafero said. 'Easy now. Not yet.'

McCaleb stopped his movement. Tafero continued to press his ankles down toward the back of his thighs.

'You've seen the setup before,' Tafero said matter of factly. 'This one's a little different. I strung together a bunch of snap-cuffs, like every L.A. cop carries around in the trunk of his car.'

McCaleb understood the message. The plastic strips first invented to bundle cables together but found to be useful by police agencies faced with occasional social unrest and the need to make mass arrests. A cop can carry one set of handcuffs but hundreds of snap cuffs. String them around the wrists, slide the end through the lock. Tiny grooves in the plastic strip click and lock as the tie gets tighter. The only way to remove it is to cut it off. McCaleb realized that the clicking sound he had just heard had been a snap cuff tightening around his neck.

'So you be careful now,' Tafero said. 'Hold real steady.'

McCaleb put his face down into the mattress. His mind was racing, looking for the way out. He thought if he could engage Tafero he might buy some time. But time for what?

'How'd you find me?' he spoke into the mattress.

'Easy enough. My little brother followed you from my shop and got your plate. You should look around more often, make sure you aren't being followed.'

'I'll remember that.'

He understood the plan. It would look as if Gunn's killer had gotten McCaleb when he had come too close. He turned his head again so he could see Tafero.

'It's not going to work, Tafero,' he said. 'People know. They're not going to buy that it was Bosch.'

Tafero smiled down at him.

'You mean Jaye Winston? Don't worry about her. I'm going to go pay her a visit when I'm done here with you. Eighty-eight-oh-one Willoughby, apartment six, West Hollywood. She was easy to find, too.'

He raised his free hand and waved the fingers as though he were playing the piano or typing.

'Let your fingers do the walking through the voters registration – I've got it on CD-ROM. She's a registered Democrat, if you can believe it. A homicide cop who votes Democrat. Wonders never cease.'

'There are others. The FBI's on this. You—'

'They're on Bosch. Not me. I saw them today at the courthouse.'

He reached down and ticked one of the snap cuffs strung from McCaleb's legs to his neck.

'And these, I'm sure, will help bring them directly to Detective Bosch.'

He smiled at the genius of his own plan. And McCaleb knew his thinking was sound. Twilley and Friedman would go after Bosch like a pair of dogs chasing either side of a car.

'Hold steady now.'

Tafero let go of his feet and moved out of his sight. McCaleb strained to keep his legs from unfolding. Almost immediately he felt the muscles in his legs start to burn. He knew he didn't have the strength to hold them for long.

'Please . . .'

Tafero returned to view. He was holding a plastic owl in both hands, a delighted smile on his face.

'Took this off one of the boats down the dock. A little weathered but it'll work out nice. Gonna get another one for Winston.'

He looked around the room as if looking for a place for the owl. He settled on a shelf above the built-in bureau. He placed the owl there, looked back at McCaleb once and then adjusted it so the plastic bird's gaze was upon him.

'Perfect,' he said.

McCaleb closed his eyes. He could feel his muscles vibrating with the strain. An image of his daughter appeared in his mind. She was in his arms, her eyes were watching him over the bottle and telling him not to worry or be afraid. It soothed him. He concentrated on her face and somehow thought he could even smell her hair. He felt tears going down his face and his legs started to give way. He heard the clicking of the cuffs and –

Tafero grabbed his legs and held them.

'Not yet.'

Something hard banged off McCaleb's head and thudded on the mattress next to him. He turned his face and opened his eyes and saw it was the videotape he had gone back to borrow from Lucas, the post office security officer. He looked at the post office emblem of the flying eagle on the sticker Lucas had put on the tape for him.

'I hope you don't mind but while you were sleeping off the choke hold I took a look at the tape on your VCR. I couldn't find anything on it. It's blank. Why is that?'

McCaleb felt a pang of hope. He realized that the only reason he wasn't already dead was because of the tape. Tafero had found it and it raised too many questions. It was a break. McCaleb tried to think of a way to turn it further to his advantage. The tape was supposed to be blank. They had planned to use it as a prop when they brought Tafero in and tried to play him. It would have been part of a bluff. They would hold it up and tell him they had him on tape sending the money order. But they wouldn't actually play it. Now McCaleb thought he might be able to still use it – but in reverse.

Tafero shoved down hard on his ankles, so hard they came close to touching McCaleb's buttocks. McCaleb groaned from the stress on his muscles. Tafero eased back.

'I asked you a question, motherfucker. Now you fucking answer it.'

'It's nothing. It's supposed to be blank.'

'Bullshit. The label says "December twenty-second." It says "Wilcox surveillance." Why is it blank?'

He increased the pressure on McCaleb's legs but not to the point of a few moments before.

'Okay, I'll tell you the truth. I'll tell you.'

McCaleb took a deep breath and tried to relax. In the moment his body was still, when the air was held in his lungs, he thought he detected a movement of the boat that was out of rhythm with the gentle rise-and-fall cycle of the marina's wake. Somebody had stepped onto the boat. He could only think of Buddy Lockridge. And if it was him then he was most likely walking into his own doom. McCaleb started to speak quickly and loudly, hoping his voice would warn Lockridge off.

'It's just a prop, that's all. We were going to bluff you, tell you we had you on tape buying the money order that bought the owl. The plan, the plan was to get you to turn on Storey. We know it was his plan from the jail. You just followed orders. They want Storey more than they want you. I was going to—'

'All right, shut up!'

McCaleb was quiet. He wondered if Tafero had felt the boat move unusually or if he had heard something. But then McCaleb watched as the tape was lifted off the bed. He realized he had Tafero thinking. After a long moment of silence Tafero finally spoke.

'I think you are full of shit, McCaleb. I think this tape is out of one of those multiplex surveillance systems they use. It won't read on a regular VCR.'

If it didn't seem that every muscle in his body was screaming in pain, McCaleb might have smiled. He had Tafero. He was helplessly hogtied on the bed but he was playing his captor. Tafero was second-guessing his own plan.

'Who else has copies?' Tafero asked.

McCaleb didn't answer. He started thinking that he had been wrong about the boat's movement. Too much time had gone by. There was no one else onboard.

Tafero rapped the tape hard on the back of McCaleb's head.

'I said who else has copies?'

There was a new note in the tone of his voice. One part confidence had been removed and replaced with one equal part fear that there was a flaw in his perfect plan.

'Fuck you,' McCaleb said. 'You do what you have to do with me. Either way, you'll be finding out who's got copies soon enough.'

Tafero pushed down on his legs and leaned over him. McCaleb could feel his breath close to his ear.

'Listen to me, you fucking—'

There was a sudden loud crash from behind McCaleb.

'Don't fucking move!' a voice called.

In the same instant Tafero stood up and let go of McCaleb's legs. The sudden release of pressure coupled with the jarring noise made McCaleb startle and involuntarily flex his muscles at once. He heard the zipping sound of snap cuffs clicking in several places of his bindings. In chain reaction, the cuff around his neck pulled tight and locked. He tried to raise his legs but it was too late, the cuff was set. It was biting into his neck. He had no air. He opened his mouth but not a sound came out.

43

Harry Bosch stood in the doorway of the boat's downstairs cabin and pointed his gun at Rudy Tafero. His eyes widened as he took in the whole room. Terry McCaleb was naked on the bed, his arms and legs bound behind him. Bosch saw that several snap cuffs had been linked together and used to bind his wrists and ankles while a leader ran from his ankles and under his wrists to a loop around his neck. He couldn't see McCaleb's face but saw the plastic was digging tightly into his neck and the skin was a dark rouge. He was strangling.

'Turn around,' he yelled at Tafero. 'Get back against the wall.'

'He needs help, Bosch. You—'

'I said get back against the fucking wall! Now!'

He raised the gun to Tafero's chest level to drive home the order. Tafero raised his hands and started turning to the wall.

'Okay, okay, I'm turning around.'

As soon as Tafero had turned Bosch moved quickly into the room and shoved the big man up against the wall. He glanced at McCaleb. He could see his face now. It was getting redder. His eyes were opened and bugged. His mouth was opened in a desperate but fruitless bid for air.

Bosch pushed the barrel of his gun into Tafero's back and reached his other hand around him to check for a weapon. He pulled a handgun out of Tafero's belt and then stepped back. He looked at McCaleb again and knew he didn't have any time. The problem was controlling

Tafero and getting to McCaleb to cut him free. He suddenly knew what needed to be done. He stepped back and brought his hands together so that the guns were side by side. He raised them over his head and brought the butts of both guns down violently into the back of Tafero's head. The big man pitched forward, going face-first into the wood-paneled wall and then dropping to the floor motionless.

Bosch turned and dropped both guns onto the bed and quickly pulled out his keys.

'Hold on, hold on, hold on.'

His fingers scrabbling, he pulled the blade out of the penknife attached to the key chain. He reached to the plastic cuff embedded around McCaleb's neck but couldn't get his fingers underneath it. He shoved McCaleb onto his side and quickly worked his fingers under the cuff at the front of his neck. He slipped the blade in and sliced through the cuff, the point of the knife just nicking the skin beneath it.

A horrible sound came from McCaleb's throat as he gulped air into his lungs and tried to speak at the same time. The words were unintelligible, lost in the instinctive urgency for oxygen intake.

'Shut up and breathe!' Bosch yelled. 'Just breathe!'

There came an interior rattling sound with each breath McCaleb took. Bosch saw a vibrant red line running the circumference of his neck. He gently touched McCaleb's neck, wanting to feel for possible damage to the trachea or larynx or the arteries. McCaleb roughly turned his head on the mattress and tried to move away.

'Just . . . cut me loose.'

The words made him cough violently into the mattress, his whole body shaking from the trauma.

Bosch used the knife to cut his hands free and then his ankles. He saw red ligature marks on both sets of limbs. He pulled all the snap cuffs away and threw them on the floor. He looked around and saw the sweatpants and shirt on the floor. He picked them up and threw them onto the bed. McCaleb was slowly turning back to face him, his face still red.

'You . . . you . . . saved . . .'

'Don't talk.'

There was a groan from the floor and Bosch saw Tafero start moving as he began to regain consciousness. Bosch stepped over and stood straddling him. He took his handcuffs off his belt, bent down and then violently pulled Tafero's arms behind his back to cuff him. While he worked he talked to McCaleb.

'Hey, you want to take this guy out, tie him to the anchor and drop him over the side, it'd be fine by me. I wouldn't even blink about it.'

McCaleb didn't respond. He was pulling himself into a sitting position. Finished with the cuffing process, Bosch straightened up and looked down at Tafero, who had now opened his eyes.

'Stay still, shithead. And get used to those cuffs. You are under arrest for murder, attempted murder and general conspiracy to be an asshole. I think you know your rights but do yourself a favor and don't say a word until I get the card out and read it to you.'

The moment he was done speaking Bosch became aware of a creaking sound coming from the hallway. In that second he realized someone had used his words as cover to get close to the doorway.

Things seemed to drop into a slow-motion sense of clarity. Bosch instinctively brought his left hand up to his hip but realized his gun was not there. He had left it on the bed. He started to turn to the bed but saw McCaleb sitting up, still naked, and already pointing one of the guns at the doorway.

Bosch's eyes followed the aim of the gun to the door. A man was swinging into the opening in a crouched position, two hands on a pistol. He was taking aim at Bosch. There was a shot and wood splintered from the doorjamb. The gunman flinched and squinted his eyes. He recovered and started to level the aim of his gun. There was another shot and another and then another. The noise was deafening in the confines of the wood-paneled room. Bosch watched one bullet hit the wall and two hit the gunman in the chest, throwing him backward into the hallway wall. He sank to the floor but was still visible from the bedroom.

'No!' Tafero shouted from the floor. 'Jesse, no!'

The wounded gunman was still moving but having difficulty with motor controls. With one hand he awkwardly raised the gun again and made a pathetic attempt to aim it once more at Bosch.

There was another shot and Bosch saw the gunman's cheek explode with blood. His head snapped back against the wall behind him and he became still.

'No!' Tafero cried out again.

And then there was silence.

Bosch looked at the bed. McCaleb still held the gun aimed at the door. A cloud of blue gunpowder smoke was rising into the center of the room. The air smelled acrid and burned.

Bosch picked his gun up off the bed and went out to the hallway. He squatted down next to the gunman but didn't need to touch him to know he was dead. During the shooting he had thought he recognized him as Tafero's younger brother who worked in the bail bonds office. Now most of his face was gone.

Bosch got up and went into the head to grab a tissue, which he then used to take the gun out of the dead man's grip. He carried it back into the master cabin and put it down on the nightstand. The gun McCaleb had used was now lying on the bed. McCaleb stood on the other side of the bed. He had the sweatpants on and was pulling the shirt over his head. Once his head came through he looked at Bosch.

Their eyes held for a long moment. They had saved each other. Bosch finally nodded.

Tafero worked his way up into a sitting position against the wall. Blood had run out of his nose and down around both sides of his mouth. It looked like a grotesque Fu Manchu mustache. Bosch guessed that his nose had been broken when he'd gone face-first into the wall. He sat slumped against the wall, his eyes staring in horror through the doorway to the body in the hallway.

Bosch used the tissue to pick the gun up off the bed and put it next to the other one on the nightstand. He then took a cell phone out of his pocket and punched in a number. While he waited for the call to connect he looked at Tafero.

'You got your little brother killed, Rudy,' he said. 'That's too bad.'

Tafero lowered his eyes and started crying.

Bosch's call was answered at central dispatch. He gave the address of the marina and said he was going to need a homicide team from the officer involved–shooting unit. He would need a coroner's crew and techs from Scientific Investigation Division to respond as well. He told the dispatcher to make all notifications by landline. He didn't want the media to get wind of the incident from a police scanner until the time was right.

He closed the phone and held it up for McCaleb to see.

'You want an ambulance? You should get checked out.'

'I'm fine.'

'Your neck looks like it could—'

'I said I'm fine.'

Bosch nodded.

'Suit yourself.'

He came around the bed and stood in front of Tafero.

'I'm going to get him out of here, put him in the car.'

He dragged Tafero to his feet and pushed him to the door. As he passed his brother's body in the hallway Tafero let out a loud animal-like wail, a kind of sound Bosch was surprised to hear coming from such a big man.

'Yeah, it's too bad,' Bosch said without a note of

sympathy in his voice. 'The kid had a bright future helping you kill people and getting people out of jail.'

He shoved Tafero toward the steps up to the salon.

On the way up the gangway to the parking lot Bosch saw a man standing on the deck of a sailboat cluttered with rafts and surfboards and other junk. The man looked at Bosch and then Tafero and then back to Bosch. His eyes were wide and it was clear he recognized them, probably from the trial coverage on TV.

'Hey, I heard shots. Is Terry okay?'

'He's going to be fine.'

'Can I go talk to him?'

'Better not. The cops are coming. Let them handle it.'

'Hey, you're Bosch, aren't you? From the trial?'

'Yeah. I'm Bosch.'

The man said nothing else. Bosch kept moving with Tafero.

When Bosch came back onto the boat a few minutes later McCaleb was in the galley drinking a glass of orange juice. Behind him and down the steps the splayed legs of the dead man were visible.

'A neighbor of yours out there asked about you.'

McCaleb nodded.

'Buddy.'

That's all he said.

Bosch looked out the window and back up at the parking lot. He thought he could hear sirens in the distance but thought it might just be the wind playing sound games.

'They're going to be here any minute,' he said. 'How's the throat? I hope you can talk, 'cause we're going to have a lot of explaining to do.'

'It's fine. Why were you here, Harry?'

Bosch put his car keys down on the countertop. He didn't answer for a long moment.

'I just sort of guessed you might be drawing a bead, that's all.'

'How so?'

'You busting in on his brother at the office this morning. I figured that if he followed you, he might've gotten a plate or something they could trace to you here.'

McCaleb looked pointedly at him.

'And what, you were hanging out in the marina and saw Rudy but not the little brother?'

'No, I just drove down and cruised around a little. I saw Rudy's old Lincoln parked up there in the lot and figured something was going on. I never saw the little brother – he must've been hiding somewhere and watching.'

'I'm thinking he was on the docks looking for an owl he could take off a boat to use at Winston's. They were improvising tonight.'

Bosch nodded.

'Anyway, I was looking around and saw the door open on your boat and decided to check it out. I thought it was too cold a night and you were too careful a guy to sleep with the door open like that.'

McCaleb nodded.

Bosch now heard the unmistakable sound of approaching sirens and looked out the window and across the docks to the parking lot. He saw two patrol cars glide in and stop near his slickback where Tafero was locked in the back. They killed the sirens but left the blue lights flashing.

'I better go meet the boys in blue,' he said.

44

For most of the night they were separated and questioned and then questioned again. Then the interrogators switched rooms and they heard the same questions once more from different mouths. Five hours after the shooting on *The Following Sea* the doors were opened and McCaleb and Bosch stepped out into a hallway at Parker Center. Bosch came up to McCaleb then.

'You okay?'

'Tired.'

'Yeah.'

McCaleb watched him put a cigarette in his mouth but not light it.

'I'm heading out to the sheriff's,' Bosch said. 'I want to be there.'

McCaleb nodded.

'I'll see you there.'

They stood side by side behind the one-way glass, squeezed in next to the videographer. McCaleb was close enough to smell Bosch's menthol cigarette breath and the glove-box cologne he had seen him put on in his car while driving behind him out to Whittier. He could see the faint reflection of Bosch's face in the glass and he realized he was looking through it into what was happening in the next room.

On the other side of the glass was a conference table with Rudy Tafero seated next to a public defender named

Arnold Prince. Tafero had white tape spread across his nose and cotton in both nostrils. He had six stitches in the crown of his head which could not be seen because of his full head of hair. Paramedics had treated him for a broken nose and the head laceration at Cabrillo Marina.

Across from Tafero sat Jaye Winston. To her right was Alice Short, from the DA's office. To her left were Deputy Chief Irvin Irving of the LAPD and Donald Twilley of the FBI. The early morning hours had been spent with all law enforcement agencies remotely involved in the investigation jockeying for the best position to take advantage of what all players knew to be a major case. It was now six-thirty in the morning and time to question the suspect.

It had been decided that Winston would handle the questioning – it being her case from the beginning – while the other three looked on and were available to her for advice. She began the interview by stating the date, time and identities of those in the room. She then read Tafero his constitutional rights and had him sign an acknowledgment form. His attorney said that Tafero would not be making a statement at the present time.

'That's fine,' Winston said, her eyes on Tafero. 'I don't need him to talk to me. I want to talk to him. I want to give him an idea of what he is facing here. I don't want there to be any regrets down the line over miscommunications or his passing up the one opportunity to cooperate that he'll be given.'

She looked down at the file in front of her and opened it. McCaleb recognized the top sheet as a DA's office complaint form.

'Mr. Tafero,' Winston began, 'I want you to know that this morning we are charging you with the first-degree murder of Edward Gunn on January first of this year, the attempted murder of Terrell McCaleb on this date, and the murder of Jesse Tafero, also on this date. I know you know the law but I am compelled to explain the last charge. Your brother's death occurred during the commission of a felony. Therefore, under California law you, as his co-conspirator, are held responsible for his death.'

She waited a beat, staring into Tafero's seemingly dead eyes. She went back to reading the complaint.

'Further, you should know that the district attorney's office has agreed to file a count of special circumstances in regard to the murder of Edward Gunn. To wit, murder for hire. The addition of special circumstances will make it a death penalty case. Alice?'

Short leaned forward. She was an attractive, petite woman in her late thirties with big, engaging eyes. She was the deputy chief in charge of major trials. It was a lot of power in such a small body – especially when contrasted with the size of the man across the table from her.

'Mr. Tafero, you were a policeman for twenty years,' she said. 'You more than most know the gravity of your actions. There is not a case I can think of that cries out more for the death penalty. We will ask a jury for it. And I have no doubt we will get it.'

Her rehearsed part of the play finished, Short leaned back in her chair and deferred to Winston. There was a long silence while Winston stared at Tafero and waited for him to look back at her. Eventually, his eyes came up and held on hers.

'Mr. Tafero, you've been around and you've even been in the opposite position in rooms just like this before. I don't think we could play a game on you if we had a year to work it out. So no game. Just the offer. A one-time offer that will be rescinded, permanently, when we walk out of this room. It comes down to this.'

The focus of Tafero's eyes had dropped to the table again. Winston leaned forward and looked up into them.

'Do you want to live or do you want to take your chances with the jury? It's as simple as that. And before you answer, there are a few things to consider. Number one, the jurors are going to see photographic evidence of what you did to Edward Gunn. Two, they are going to hear Terry McCaleb describe what it was like to be so helpless and to feel his own life being choked away by your design. You know, I don't usually bet on such things but I'd give it less than an hour. My bet is that it will be one of the quickest death verdicts ever returned in the state of California.'

Winston pulled back and closed the file in front of her. McCaleb found himself nodding. She was doing very well.

'We want your employer,' Winston said. 'We want physical evidence that will link him to the Gunn case. I have a feeling that someone like you would take precautions before carrying out such a scheme. Whatever it is, we want what you have.'

She looked at Short and the prosecutor nodded, her way of saying well done.

Almost half a minute went by. Finally, Tafero turned to his attorney and was about to whisper a question. Then he turned back to Winston.

'Fuck it, I'll ask myself. Without acknowledging a fucking thing here, what if you drop the special circumstances? What am I facing?'

Winston immediately burst out laughing and shook her head. McCaleb smiled.

'Are you kidding?' Winston asked. '"What am I facing?" Man, you are going to be buried in concrete and steel. That's what you are facing. You are never, *ever* going to see the light of day again. Deal, no deal, that is a given and non-negotiable.'

Tafero's attorney cleared his throat.

'Ms. Winston, this is hardly a professional manner in which—'

'I don't give a shit about my manner. This man is a killer. He's no different from a hit man except, no, he's worse. He used to carry a badge and that makes it all the more despicable. So this is what we'll do for your client, Mr. Prince. We'll take guilty pleas to the murder of

Edward Gunn and the attempted on Terry McCaleb. Life without on both counts. Non-negotiable. We'll no-bill the charge on his brother. Maybe it will help him live with it better if he doesn't carry the charge. I don't really care. What I care about is that he understands that his life as he knows it is over. He's gone. And he can either go to death row or super max, but he's going to one of them and not coming back.'

She looked at her watch.

'You've got about five minutes and then we're out of here. You don't want the deal, fine, we'll take both of them to trial. Storey might be a long shot but there's no question about Mr. Tafero here. Alice is going to have prosecutors knocking down her door, sending her flowers and chocolates. Every day's going to be Valentine's Day – or Valentino's day, as the case may be. This one's a ticket to prosecutor of the year.'

Prince brought a slim briefcase up onto the table and slid his legal pad into it. He hadn't written a word on it.

'Thank you for your time,' he said. 'I think what we'll do is proceed to a bail hearing and go from there with discovery and other matters.'

He pushed his chair back and stood up.

Tafero slowly raised his head and looked at Winston, his eyes badly bloodshot from the hemorrhaging of his nose.

'It was his idea to make it look like a painting,' he said. 'David Storey's idea.'

There was a moment of stunned silence and then the defense attorney sat down heavily and closed his eyes in pain.

'Mr. Tafero,' Prince said. 'I am strongly advising—'

'Shut up,' Tafero barked. 'You little pissant. You're not the one facing the needle.'

He looked back at Winston.

'I'll take the deal. As long as I don't get charged with my brother.'

Winston nodded.

Tafero turned to Short and pointed his finger and waited. She nodded.

'Deal,' she said.

'One thing,' Winston said quickly. 'We're not going into this with your word against his. What else have you got?'

Tafero looked at her and a thin, dead smile cracked across his face.

In the viewing room, Bosch stepped closer to the glass. McCaleb saw his reflection more clearly on the glass. His eyes stared unblinking.

'I've got pictures,' Tafero said.

Winston hooked her hair behind her ear and narrowed her eyes. She leaned across the table.

'Pictures? What do you mean, photographs? Photographs of what?'

Tafero shook his head.

'No. Pictures. He drew pictures for me while we were in the attorney visiting room in the jail. Drawings of what he wanted the scene to look like. So it would look like the painting.'

McCaleb gripped his hands into fists at his sides.

'Where are the drawings?' Winston said.

Tafero smiled again.

'Safe-deposit box. City National Bank, Sunset and Doheny. The key's on the ring that was in my pocket.'

Bosch brought his hands up and slapped them together.

'Bang!' he exclaimed, loud enough that Tafero turned and looked toward the glass.

'Please!' the videographer whispered. 'We're taping.'

Bosch went to the door of the little room and stepped out. McCaleb followed. Bosch turned and looked at him. He nodded.

'Storey goes down,' he said. 'The monster goes back into the darkness from which it came.'

They looked at each other silently for a moment and then Bosch broke it away.

'I gotta go,' he said.

'Where?'

'Get ready for court.'

He turned and started walking through the deserted bullpen of the sheriff's department homicide squad. McCaleb saw him bang a fist on a desk and then punch it into the air above him.

McCaleb went back into the viewing room and watched the interview continue. Tafero was telling the assemblage in the interview room that David Storey had demanded that the killing of Edward Gunn take place on the first morning of the new year.

McCaleb listened for a while and then thought of something. He stepped out of the observation room and into the bullpen. Detectives were now filtering in to start the day of work. He went to an empty desk and tore a page off a notepad on its top. He wrote, 'Ask about the Lincoln' on it. He folded it and took it to the door of the interview room.

He knocked and after a moment Alice Short opened the door. He handed her the folded note.

'Give this to Jaye before the interview is over,' he whispered.

She nodded and closed the door. McCaleb went back into the observation room to watch.

45

Freshly showered and shaved, Bosch stepped off the elevator and headed toward the doors to the Division N courtroom. He walked with purpose. He felt like a true prince of the city. He had taken only a few strides when he was accosted by McEvoy, who stepped out of an alcove like a coyote that had been waiting in a cave for his unsuspecting prey. But nothing could dent Bosch's demeanor. He smiled as the reporter fell into stride with him.

'Detective Bosch, have you thought any more about what we talked about? I've got to start writing my story today.'

Bosch didn't slow his pace. He knew that once he got into the courtroom he wouldn't have a lot of time.

'Rudy Tafero,' he said.

'Excuse me?'

'He was your source. Rudy Tafero. I figured it out this morning.'

'Detective, I told you that I can't reveal—'

'Yeah, I know. But, see, I'm the one who's revealing it. Anyway, it doesn't matter.'

'Why not?'

Bosch suddenly stopped. McEvoy walked a few steps past and then came back.

'Why not?' he asked again.

'Today's your lucky day, Jack. I've got two good tips for you.'

'Okay. What?'

McEvoy started pulling a notebook from his back pocket. Bosch put his hand on his arm to stop him.

'Don't take that out. The other reporters see that, they'll think I'm telling you something.'

He gestured up the hall to the open door of the media room where a handful of reporters were loitering and waiting for the day's court session to begin.

'Then they'll come over and I'll have to tell them.'

McEvoy left the notebook in place.

'Okay. What are the tips?'

'First of all, you're full of shit on that story. In fact, your source was arrested this morning for the murder of Edward Gunn as well as the attempted murder of Terry McCaleb.'

'What? He got—'

'Wait. Let me talk. I don't have a lot of time.'

He waited and McEvoy nodded.

'Yeah, Rudy got popped. He killed Gunn. The plan was to put it on me and spring it on the world during the defense case.'

'Are you saying that Storey was a part of—'

'Exactly. Which brings me to tip number two. And that is, if I were you, I would be in that courtroom today long before the judge comes in and starts things. You see those guys standing down there? They're going to miss it, Jack. You don't want to be like them.'

Bosch left him there. He nodded to the deputy on the courtroom door and was allowed in.

Two deputies were walking David Storey to his place at the defense table as Bosch came into the courtroom. Fowkkes was already there and Langwiser and Kretzler were seated at the prosecution table. Bosch looked at his watch as he came through the gate. He had about fifteen minutes before the judge would take the bench and call for the jury.

He went to the prosecution table but remained standing. He leaned down and put both palms on the table and looked at the two prosecutors.

'Harry, you ready?' Langwiser began. 'Today's the day.'

'Today's the day but not because of what you think. You two would take a plea on this wouldn't you? If he copped to Jody Krementz *and* Alicia Lopez, you wouldn't go for the needle, right?'

They both looked at him with blank stares of confusion.

'Come on, we don't have a lot of time before the judge comes out. What if I could go over there and in five minutes get you two murder ones? Alicia Lopez's family would love you for it. You told them you didn't have a case.'

'Harry, what are you talking about?' Langwiser said. 'We floated a plea. Twice. Fowkkes shot it down both times.'

'And we don't have the evidence on Lopez,' Kretzler added. 'You know that – the grand jury passed. Nobody, no—'

'Listen, you want the plea or not? I think I can go over there and get it. I arrested Rudy Tafero for murder this morning. It was a setup orchestrated by Storey to get to me. It backfired and Tafero is taking a deal. He's talking.'

'Jesus Christ!' Kretzler said.

He said it too loudly. Bosch turned and looked over at the defense table. Both Fowkkes and Storey were looking at them. Just past the defense table he saw McEvoy take a seat in the media gallery that was closest to the defense table. No other reporters had come in and sat down yet.

'Harry, what are you talking about?' Langwiser said. 'What murder?'

Bosch ignored the questions.

'Let me go over there,' Bosch said. 'I want to look in Storey's eyes when I tell him.'

Kretzler and Langwiser looked at each other. Langwiser

shrugged her shoulders and waved her hands in exasperation.

'Worth a try. We were only holding death as an ace in the hole.'

'Okay then,' Bosch said. 'See if you can get the clerk to buy me some time with the judge.'

Bosch stepped around the defense table and stood in front of it so he could look equally at Fowkkes and Storey. Fowkkes was writing something on a legal pad. Bosch cleared his throat and after a few moments the defense attorney slowly looked up.

'Yes, Detective? Shouldn't you be at your table preparing for—'

'Where's Rudy Tafero?'

Bosch looked at Storey as he asked it.

Fowkkes looked behind him to the seat against the rail where Tafero normally sat during court sessions.

'I'm sure he's on his way,' he said. 'We have a few minutes.'

Bosch smiled.

'On his way? Yeah, he's on his way. Up to super max at Corcoran, maybe Pelican Cove if he's lucky. I really wouldn't want to be a former cop doing my time in Corcoran.'

Fowkkes seemed unimpressed.

'Detective, I don't know what you are talking about. I am trying to prepare a defense strategy here because I think the prosecution is going to fold its tent today. So, if you don't mind.'

Bosch looked at Storey when he responded.

'There is no strategy. There is no defense. Rudy Tafero was arrested this morning. He's been charged with murder and attempted murder. I'm sure your client can tell you all about it, Counselor. That is, if you didn't know already.'

Fowkkes stood up abruptly as though he were making an objection.

'Sir, it is highly irregular for you to come to the defense table and—'

'He cut a deal about two hours ago. He's laying it all out.'

Again Bosch ignored Fowkkes and looked at Storey.

'So here's the deal. You've got about five minutes to go over there to Langwiser and Kretzler and agree to plead to murder one on Krementz *and* Lopez.'

'This is preposterous. I am going to complain to the judge about this.'

Bosch now looked at Fowkkes.

'You do that. But it doesn't change things. Five minutes.'

Bosch stepped away but went to the clerk's desk in front of the judge's bench. The exhibits were lying stacked on a side table. Bosch looked through them until he found the poster he wanted. He slid it out and carried it with him back to the defense table. Fowkkes was still standing but bending down so Storey could whisper in his ear. Bosch dropped the poster, containing the blowup photo of the bookcase in Storey's house, on the table. He tapped his finger on two of the books on an upper shelf. The titles on the spines were clearly readable. One title was *The Art of Darkness* and the other book was merely titled *Bosch*.

'There's your prior knowledge right there.'

He left the exhibit on the defense table and started to walk back to the prosecution table. But after two steps he came back and put his palms down flat on the defense table. He looked directly at Storey. He spoke in a voice that he knew would be loud enough for McEvoy to hear in the media gallery.

'You know what your big mistake was, David?'

'No,' Storey said, a sneer in his voice. 'Why don't you tell me?'

Fowkkes immediately grabbed his client's arm in a silencing gesture.

'Drawing out the scene for Tafero,' Bosch said. 'What

he did was, he went and put those pretty pictures you made right into his safe-deposit box at City National. He knew they might come in handy and they sure did. He used them this morning to buy *his* way out of a death sentence. What are you going to use?'

Bosch saw the falter in Storey's eyes, the tell. For just a moment his eyes blinked without really blinking. But in that moment Bosch knew it was over because Storey knew it was over.

Bosch straightened up and casually looked at his watch, then at Fowkkes.

'About three minutes now, Mr. Fowkkes. Your client's life is on the line.'

He returned to the defense table and sat down. Kretzler and Langwiser leaned toward him and urgently whispered questions but Bosch ignored them.

'Let's just see what happens.'

Over the next five minutes he never once looked over at the defense table. He could hear muffled words and whispers but couldn't make out any of it. The courtroom filled with spectators and members of the media.

Nothing came from the defense table.

At precisely 9 A.M. the door behind the bench opened and Judge Houghton bounded up the steps to his spot. He took his seat and glanced at both the prosecution and defense tables.

'Ladies and gentlemen, are we ready for the jury?'

'Yes, Your Honor,' Kretzler said.

Nothing came from the defense table. Houghton looked over, a curious smile on his face.

'Mr. Fowkkes? Can I bring in our jury?'

Now Bosch leaned back so he could look past Langwiser and Kretzler at the defense table. Fowkkes sat slouched in his chair, a posture he had never exhibited in the courtroom before. He had an elbow on the arm of the chair and his hand up. He was wagging a pen in his fingers and seemed to be lost in deep, depressing thought. His client sat rigid next to him, face forward.

'Mr. Fowkkes? I'm waiting for an answer.'

Fowkkes finally looked up at the judge. Very slowly he rose from the seat and went to the lectern.

'Your Honor, may we approach at sidebar for a moment?'

The judge looked both curious and annoyed. It had been the routine of the trial to submit all non-public conference requests by 8:30 A.M. so that they could be considered and argued in chambers without cutting into court time.

'This can't be handled in open court, Mr. Fowkkes?'

'No, Your Honor. Not at this time.'

'Very well. Come on up.'

Houghton signaled the lawyers forward with both hands as though he were giving signals to a truck backing up.

The attorneys approached the side of the bench and huddled with the judge. From his angle Bosch could see all of their faces and he didn't need to hear what was being whispered. Fowkkes looked ashen and after a few words Kretzler and Langwiser seemed to grow in stature. Langwiser even glanced over at Bosch and he could read the victory message in her eyes.

He turned and looked over at the defendant. He waited and David Storey slowly turned and their eyes locked one final time. Bosch didn't smile. He didn't blink. He didn't do anything but hold the stare. Eventually, it was Storey who looked away and down at his hands lying in his lap. Bosch felt a trilling sensation move over his scalp. He'd felt it before, times when he had glimpsed the normally hidden face of the monster.

The sidebar conference broke up and the two prosecutors came back quickly to the table, excitement clearly showing in their strides and on their faces. By contrast J. Reason Fowkkes moved slowly to the defense table.

'That's all, Fowkkes,' Bosch said under his breath.

Langwiser grabbed Bosch by the shoulder as she sat down.

'He's going to plead,' she whispered excitedly. 'Krementz *and* Lopez. When you went over there, did you say consecutive or concurrent sentencing?'

'I didn't say either.'

'Okay. We just agreed on concurrent but we're going into chambers to work it out. We need to formally charge Storey with Lopez first. You want to come in and make the arrest?'

'Whatever. If you want me to.'

Bosch knew it was just a legal formality. Storey was already in custody.

'You deserve it, Harry. We want you to be there.'

'Fine.'

The judge tapped his gavel once and drew the courtroom's attention. The reporters in the media gallery were all leaning forward in their seats. They knew something big was going on.

'We'll stand in recess until ten o'clock,' the judge announced. 'I'll see all parties in chambers now.'

He stood up and quickly went down the three stairs to the rear door before the deputy had time to call, 'All rise.'

46

McCaleb stayed away from *The Following Sea*, even after the last detective and forensic technician had finished with it. From early afternoon until dark the boat was staked out by reporters and television news crews. The coupling of the shooting aboard the boat plus the arrest of Tafero and abrupt guilty pleas from David Storey had turned the boat into the central image of a story that had developed quickly through the day. Every local channel plus the networks shot their stand-up reports from the marina, *The Following Sea* serving as the backdrop with its yellow police tape strung across the salon door.

McCaleb hid out for most of the afternoon in Buddy Lockridge's boat, staying below decks and donning one of Buddy's floppy fishing hats if he poked his head up through a hatch to see what was going on outside. The two were talking again. Soon after leaving the sheriff's department and getting to the marina ahead of the media, McCaleb had sought out Buddy and apologized for assuming that his charter partner had leaked the story. Buddy in turn apologized for using *The Following Sea* – and McCaleb's cabin – as a rendezvous point for encounters with erotic masseuses. McCaleb agreed to tell Graciela he had been wrong about Buddy being the leak. He also agreed not to tell her about the masseuses. Buddy had explained that he didn't want Graciela thinking less of him than she probably already did.

While they hid out in the boat, they watched Buddy's little twelve-inch TV and remained up-to-the-minute with the day's developments. Channel 9, which had been carrying the Storey trial live, remained most current, staying on live and continuously reporting from the Van Nuys courthouse and the sheriff's Star Center.

McCaleb was left stunned and in awe by the day's events. David Storey abruptly filed guilty pleas in Van Nuys to two murders as he was simultaneously charged in the downtown Los Angeles courthouse with being a conspirator in the Gunn case. The movie director had avoided the death penalty in the first cases but still would face it in the Gunn case if he did not make another plea arrangement with prosecutors.

A televised news conference at the Star Center had featured Jaye Winston prominently. She answered questions from reporters after the sheriff, flanked by LAPD and FBI brass, read a statement announcing the day's events from an investigative standpoint. McCaleb's name was mentioned numerous times in the discussion of the investigation and subsequent shooting aboard *The Following Sea*. Winston also mentioned it at the end of the news conference when she expressed her thanks to him, saying it was his volunteer work on the case that broke it open.

Bosch was also prominently mentioned but took no part in any press conferences. After Storey's guilty verdicts were entered in the Van Nuys court, Bosch and the lawyers involved in the case were mobbed outside the doors to the courtroom. But McCaleb had seen video on one channel of Bosch pushing his way through the reporters and cameras and refusing to comment as he moved to a fire escape and disappeared down the stairs.

The only reporter who got to McCaleb was Jack McEvoy, who still had his cell phone number. McCaleb talked to him briefly but declined to comment on what had happened in the master cabin of *The Following Sea* and how close he had come to death. His thoughts about that were too personal and he would never share them with any reporter.

McCaleb had also talked to Graciela, calling her and filling her in on the events before she saw them on the news. He told her he probably wouldn't get home until the next day because he was sure the media pack would be watching the boat until well after dark. She said she was glad it was over and that he'd be coming home. He sensed there was still a high level of stress in her voice and knew it was something he would have to address when he got back to the island.

Late in the day McCaleb was able to slip out of Buddy's boat unnoticed when the media pack was distracted by activity in the marina parking lot. The LAPD was towing off the old Lincoln Continental that the Tafero brothers had been using the night before when they had come to the marina to kill McCaleb. While the news crews filmed and watched the mundane task of a car being hooked up and towed away, McCaleb was able to get to his Cherokee without being spotted. He started the car and drove out of the lot ahead of the tow truck. Not a single reporter followed.

It was fully dark by the time he got to Bosch's house. The front door was open as it had been the time before, the screen door in place. McCaleb rapped on the wooden frame and peered through the mesh into the darkness of the house. There was a single light – a reading light – on in the living room. He could hear music and thought it was the same Art Pepper CD that had been playing during his last visit. But he didn't see Bosch.

McCaleb looked away from the door to check the street and when he looked back Bosch was standing at the screen and it startled him. Bosch unhooked a latch and opened the screen. He was wearing the same suit McCaleb had seen him in on the news. He was holding a bottle of Anchor Steam down at his side.

'Terry. Come on in. I thought maybe you were a

reporter. Bugs the hell out of me when they come to your house. Seems like there should be one place they can't go.'

'Yeah, I know what you mean. They're all over the boat. I had to get away.'

McCaleb passed by Bosch in the entrance hallway and stepped into the living room.

'So reporters aside, how's it going, Harry?'

'Never better. A good day for our side. How's your neck doing?'

'Sore as hell. But I'm alive.'

'Yeah, that's what's important. Want a beer?'

'Uh, that would be good.'

While Bosch got the beer McCaleb went out to the rear deck.

Bosch had the deck lights off, making the lights of the city more brilliant in the distance. McCaleb could hear the ever-present sound of the freeway at the bottom of the pass. Searchlights cut across the sky from three different locations on the valley floor. Bosch came out and handed him a beer.

'No glass, right?'

'No glass.'

They looked out into the night and drank their beers silently for a little while. McCaleb thought about how he should say what he wanted to say. He was still working on it.

'The last thing they were doing before I left was hooking up Tafero's car,' he said after some time.

Bosch nodded.

'What about the boat? They finished with it?'

'Yeah, they're done.'

'Is it a mess? They always leave things a mess.'

'Probably. I haven't been inside. I'll worry about it tomorrow.'

Bosch nodded. McCaleb took a long draw on his beer and put the bottle down on the railing. He had taken too much. It backed up in his throat and burned his sinuses.

'Okay?' Bosch asked.

'Yeah, fine.' He wiped his mouth with the back of his hand. 'Harry, I came up to tell you I'm not going to be your friend anymore.'

Bosch started to laugh but then stopped.

'What?'

McCaleb looked at him. Bosch's eyes were still piercing in the darkness. They had caught a speck of reflected light from somewhere and McCaleb could see the two pinpoints holding on him.

'You should've hung around a little longer this morning while Jaye interviewed Tafero.'

'I didn't have the time.'

'She asked him about the Lincoln and he said it was his undercover car. He said he used it on jobs when he didn't want there to be any chance of a trace. It has stolen plates on it. And the registration is phony.'

'Makes sense, a guy like that, having a car for the wet work.'

'You don't get it, do you?'

Bosch had finished his beer. He was leaning with his elbows on the railing. He was peeling the label off the bottle and dropping the little pieces into the darkness below.

'No, I don't get it, Terry. Why don't you tell me what you're talking about?'

McCaleb picked up his beer but then put it back down without drinking any more.

'His real car, the one he used every day, is a Mercedes 430 CLK. That was the one he caught the ticket with. For parking at the post office when he sent the money order.'

'Okay, the guy had two cars. His secret car and his show car. What does it mean?'

'It means you knew something you shouldn't have known.'

'What are you talking about? Knew what?'

'Last night I asked you why you came onto my boat.

You said you saw Tafero's Lincoln and knew there was something wrong. How did you know that Lincoln was his?'

Bosch was silent for a long moment. He looked out into the night and nodded.

'I saved your life,' he said.

'I saved yours.'

'So we're even. Leave it at that, Terry.'

McCaleb shook his head. It felt like there was a fist in his stomach pushing up into his chest, trying to get to his new heart.

'I think you knew that Lincoln and knew it meant trouble for me because you had watched Tafero before. Maybe on a night he was using the Lincoln. Maybe on a night he was watching Gunn and setting up the hit. Maybe on the night he made the hit. You saved my life because you knew something, Harry.'

McCaleb was quiet for a moment, giving Bosch an opportunity to say something in his defense.

'That's a lot of maybes, Terry.'

'Yeah. A lot of maybes and one guess. My guess is that somehow you knew or you figured out back when Tafero hooked up with Storey that they would have to come after you in court. So you watched Tafero and you saw him draw the bead on Gunn. You knew what was going to happen and you let it happen.'

McCaleb took another long drink of beer and put the bottle back down on the railing.

'A dangerous game, Harry. They almost pulled it off. But I guess if I hadn't come along you would've figured out some way of pointing it back at them.'

Bosch continued to stare out into the darkness and say nothing.

'The one thing I hope is that you weren't the one who tipped Tafero that Gunn was in the tank that night. Tell me you didn't make that call, Harry. Tell me you didn't help get him out so they could kill him like that.'

Again Bosch said nothing. McCaleb nodded.

'You want to shake somebody's hand, Harry, shake your own.'

Bosch dropped his gaze and looked down into the darkness below the deck. McCaleb watched him closely and saw him slowly shake his head.

'We do what we have to do,' Bosch said quietly. 'Sometimes you have choices. Sometimes there is no choice, only necessity. You see things happening and you know they're wrong but somehow they're also right.'

He was silent for a long moment and McCaleb waited.

'I didn't make that call,' Bosch said.

He turned and looked at McCaleb. Again McCaleb could see the shining points of light in the blackness of his eyes.

'Three people – three monsters – are gone.'

'But not that way. We don't do it that way.'

Bosch nodded.

'What about your play, Terry? Pushing past the little brother into the office. Like you didn't think that would start some shit. You pushed the action with that little move and you know it.'

McCaleb felt his face growing hot under Bosch's stare. He didn't answer. He didn't know what to say.

'You had your own plan, Terry. So what's the difference?'

'The difference? If you don't see it, then you have completely fallen. You are lost.'

'Yeah, well, maybe I'm lost and maybe I've been found. I'll have to think about it. Meantime, why don't you just go home now. Go back to your little island and your little girl. Hide behind what you think you see in her eyes. Pretend the world is not what you know it to be.'

McCaleb nodded. He'd said what he wanted to say. He stepped away from the railing, leaving his beer, and walked toward the door to the house. But Bosch hit him with more words as he entered the house.

'You think naming her after a girl nobody cared about or loved can make up for that lost girl? Well, you're wrong, man. Just go home and keep dreaming.'

McCaleb hesitated in the doorway and looked back.

'Good-bye, Harry.'

'Yeah, good-bye.'

McCaleb walked through the house. When he passed the reading chair where the light was on he saw the printout of his profile of Bosch sitting on the arm of the chair. He kept going. When he got to the front door he pulled it closed behind him.

47

Bosch stood with his arms folded on the deck railing and his head down. He thought about McCaleb's words, both spoken and printed. They were pieces of hot shrapnel ripping through him. He felt a deep tearing of his interior lining. It felt as though something within had seized him and was pulling him into a black hole, that he was imploding into nothingness.

'What did I do?' he whispered. 'What did I do?'

He straightened up and saw the bottle on the railing, its label gone. He grabbed it and threw it as far as he could out into the darkness. He watched its trajectory, able to follow its flight because of moonlight reflecting off the brown glass. The bottle exploded in the brush on the rocky hillside below.

He saw McCaleb's half-finished beer and grabbed it. He pulled his arm back, wanting to throw this one all the way to the freeway. Then he stopped. He put the bottle back on the railing and went inside.

He grabbed the printed profile off the arm of the chair and started ripping the two pages apart. He went to the kitchen, turned the water on and put the pieces into the sink. He flicked on the garbage disposal and pushed the pieces of paper into the drain. He waited until he could tell by the sound that the paper had been chewed into nothing and was gone. He turned off the disposal and just watched the water running into the drain.

Slowly, his eyes came up and he looked through the kitchen window and out through the Cahuenga Pass. The lights of Hollywood glimmered in the cut, a mirror reflection of the stars of all galaxies everywhere. He thought about all that was bad out there. A city with more things wrong than right. A place where the earth could open up beneath you and suck you into the blackness. A city of lost light. His city. It was all of that and, still, always still, a place to begin again. His city. The city of the second chance.

Bosch nodded and bent down. He closed his eyes, put his hands under the water and brought them up to his face. The water was cold and bracing, as he thought any baptism, the start of any second chance, should be.

48

He could still smell burned gunpowder. McCaleb stood in the master cabin and looked around. There were rubber gloves and other debris scattered on the floor. Black fingerprint dust was everywhere, on everything. The door to the room was gone and so was the doorjamb, cut right out of the wall. In the hallway an entire wall panel had been removed as well. McCaleb walked over and looked down at the floor where the little brother had died from the bullets he had fired. The blood had dried brown and would permanently stain the alternating light and dark wood strips in the floor. It would always be there to remind him.

Staring at the blood, he replayed the shots he had fired at the man, the images in his mind moving much slower than real time. He thought about what Bosch had said to him, out on the deck. About letting the little brother follow him. He considered his own culpability. Could his guilt be any less than Bosch's? They had both set things in motion. For every action there is an equal and opposite reaction. You don't go into the darkness without the darkness going into you.

'We do what we have to do,' he said out loud.

He went up into the salon and looked out the door at the parking lot. The reporters were still up there with their vans. He had sneaked in. Parked at the far end of the marina and then borrowed a skiff from somebody's boat to get to *The Following Sea*. He had climbed aboard and slipped in without anyone seeing him.

He noticed that the vans had their microwave towers cranked up and each crew was getting ready for the eleven o'clock report, the camera angles set so that *The Following Sea* would once more be in all the shots. McCaleb smiled and opened his phone. He hit a number on speed dial and Buddy Lockridge answered.

'Buddy, it's me. Listen, I'm on the boat and I gotta go home. I want you to do me a favor.'

'You gotta go tonight? Are you sure?'

'Yeah, this is what I want you to do. When you hear me turn the Pentas over, you come over and untie me. Do it fast. I'll do the rest.'

'You want me to go with you?'

'No, I'll be fine. Catch an *Express* over on Friday. We've got the charter on Saturday morning.'

'All right, Terror. I heard on the radio it's pretty flat out there tonight and no fog, but be careful.'

McCaleb closed the phone and went to the salon door. Most of the reporters and their crews were preoccupied and not looking at the boat because they had already assured themselves it was empty. He slid open the door and stepped out, shut the door and then quickly climbed the ladder to the bridge. He unzipped the plastic curtain that enclosed the bridge and slipped in. Making sure both throttles were in neutral, he engaged the choke and slid his key into the ignition.

He turned the key and the starters began to whine loudly. Looking back through the plastic curtain he saw the reporters had all turned to the boat. The engines finally turned over and he worked the throttles, revving the engines into a quick-start warm-up. He glanced back again and saw Buddy coming down the dock to the boat's stern. A couple of the reporters were hurrying down the gangway to the dock behind him.

Buddy quickly uncleated the two stern lines and threw them into the cockpit. He then moved down the side pier to get the bow line. McCaleb lost sight of him but then heard his call.

'Clear!'

McCaleb took the throttles out of neutral and moved the boat out of the slip. As he made the turn into the fairway he looked back and saw Buddy standing on the side pier and the reporters behind him on the dock.

Once he was away from the cameras he unzipped the curtains and took them down. The cool air swept into the bridge and braced him. He sighted the flashing red lights of the channel markers and put the boat on course. He looked ahead, past the markers, into the darkness but saw nothing. He turned on the Raytheon and saw that which he could not see ahead. The island was there on the radar screen.

Ten minutes later, after he had cleared the harbor break line, McCaleb pulled the phone out of his jacket and speed-dialed home. He knew it was too late to call and that he was risking waking the children. Graciela answered in a whispered urgency.

'Sorry, it's just me.'

'Terry, are you all right?'

'I am now. I'm coming home.'

'You're crossing in the dark?'

McCaleb thought a moment about the question.

'I'll be all right. I can see in the dark.'

Graciela didn't say anything. She had an ability to know when he was saying one thing and talking about something else.

'Put the deck light on,' he said. 'I'll look for it when I get close.'

He closed the phone and pushed the throttles up. The bow started to rise and then leveled off. He passed the last channel marker twenty yards to his left. He was right on course. A three-quarter moon was high in the sky ahead and laying down a shimmering path of liquid silver for him to follow home. He held on tightly to the wheel and thought about the moment when he had truly thought he was going to die. He remembered the image of his daughter that had come to him and had comforted him. Tears started to roll down his cheeks. Soon the wind off the water dried them on his face.

Acknowledgments

The author gratefully acknowledges the help of many people during the writing of this book. They include John Houghton, Jerry Hooten, Cameron Riddell, Dawson Carr, Terrill Lankford, Linda Connelly, Mary Lavelle and Susan Connelly.

For words of support of inspiration just when they were needed, thanks go to Sarah Crichton, Philip Spitzer, Scott Eyman, Ed Thomas, Steve Stilwell, Josh Meyer, John Sacret Young and Kathy Lingg.

The author is indebted to Jane Davis for her excellent management of *www.michaelconnelly.com.* Gerald Petievich and Robert Crais are owed many thanks for excellent career advice foolishly ignored – to this point, at least – by the author.

This book, like those before it, would not exist in publishable form without the excellent efforts of its editor, Michael Pietsch, and copy editor, Betty Power, and the entire team at Little, Brown and Company.

And all this work would be for nought if not for the efforts of the many booksellers who put the stories into readers' hands. Thank you.

Lastly, special thanks to Raymond Chandler for inspiring the title of the book. Describing in 1950 the time and place from which he drew his early crime stories, Chandler wrote, 'The streets were dark with something more than night.'

Sometimes they still are.

Michael Connelly
Los Angeles

Bosch returns in the next gripping thriller in this bestselling series

CITY OF BONES

A dog unearths a human bone in the Hollywood hills. It's evidence from a cold case more than 20 years old. But Bosch just can't let this one go.

'A stunningly good novel . . .
Perhaps, indeed, the best of the series'
EVENING STANDARD

Read on for an extract now.

Available in paperback, ebook and audio.

I

The old lady had changed her mind about dying but by then it was too late. She had dug her fingers into the paint and plaster of the nearby wall until most of her fingernails had broken off. Then she had gone for the neck, scrabbling to push the bloodied fingertips up and under the cord. She broke four toes kicking at the walls. She had tried so hard, shown such a desperate will to live, that it made Harry Bosch wonder what had happened before. Where was that determination and will and why had it deserted her until after she had put the extension cord noose around her neck and kicked over the chair? Why had it hidden from her?

These were not official questions that would be raised in his death report. But they were the things Bosch couldn't avoid thinking about as he sat in his car outside the Splendid Age Retirement Home on Sunset Boulevard east of the Hollywood Freeway. It was 4:20 P.M. on the first day of the year. Bosch had drawn holiday call-out duty.

The day more than half over and that duty consisted of two suicide runs — one a gunshot, the other the hanging. Both victims were women. In both cases there was evidence of depression and desperation. Isolation. New Year's Day was always a big day for suicides. While most people greeted the day with a sense of hope and renewal, there were those who saw it as a good day to die, some — like the old lady — not realizing their mistake until it was too late.

Bosch looked up through the windshield and watched as the latest victim's body, on a wheeled stretcher and covered in a green blanket, was loaded into the coroner's blue van. He saw there was one other occupied stretcher in the van and knew it was from the first suicide — a thirty-four-year-old actress who had shot herself while parked at a Hollywood overlook on Mulholland Drive. Bosch and the body crew had followed one case to the other.

Bosch's cell phone chirped and he welcomed the intrusion into his thoughts on small deaths. It was Mankiewicz, the watch sergeant at the Hollywood Division of the Los Angeles Police Department.

"You finished with that yet?"

"I'm about to clear."

"Anything?"

"A changed-my-mind suicide. You got something else?"

"Yeah. And I didn't think I should go out on the radio with it. Must be a slow day for the media — getting more what's-happening calls from reporters than I am getting service calls from citizens. They all want to do something on the first one, the actress on Mulholland. You know, a death-of-a-Hollywood-dream story. And they'd probably jump all over this latest call, too."

"Yeah, what is it?"

"A citizen up in Laurel Canyon. On Wonderland. He just called up and said his dog came back from a run in the woods with a bone in its mouth. The guy says it's human — an arm bone from a kid."

Bosch almost groaned. There were four or five call outs like this a year. Hysteria always followed by simple explanation: animal bones. Through the windshield he saluted the two body movers from the coroner's office as they headed to the front doors of the van.

"I know what you're thinking, Harry. Not another bone run. You've done it a hundred times and it's always the same thing. Coyote, deer, whatever. But listen, this guy with the dog, he's an MD. And he says there's no doubt. It's a humerus. That's the upper arm bone. He says it's a child, Harry. And then, get this. He said . . ."

There was silence while Mankiewicz apparently looked for his notes. Bosch watched the coroner's blue van pull off into traffic. When Mankiewicz came back he was obviously reading.

"The bone's got a fracture clearly visible just above the medial epicondyle, whatever that is."

Bosch's jaw tightened. He felt a slight tickle of electric current go down the back of his neck.

"That's off my notes, I don't know if I am saying it right. The point is, this doctor says it was just a kid, Harry. So could you humor us and go check out this humerus?"

Bosch didn't respond.

"Sorry, had to get that in."

"Yeah, that was funny, Mank. What's the address?"

Mankiewicz gave it to him and told him he had already dispatched a patrol team.

"You were right to keep it off the air. Let's try to keep it that way."

Mankiewicz said he would. Bosch closed his phone and started the car. He glanced over at the entrance to the retirement home before pulling away from the curb. There was nothing about it that looked splendid to him. The woman who had hung herself in the closet of her tiny bedroom had no next of kin, according to the operators of the home. In death, she would be treated the way she had been in life, left alone and forgotten.

Bosch pulled away from the curb and headed toward Laurel Canyon.

2

Bosch listened to the Lakers game on the car radio while he made his way into the canyon and then up Lookout Mountain to Wonderland Avenue. He wasn't a religious follower of professional basketball but wanted to get a sense of the situation in case he needed his partner, Jerry Edgar. Bosch was working alone because Edgar had lucked into a pair of choice seats to the game. Bosch had agreed to handle the call outs and to not bother Edgar unless a homicide or something Bosch couldn't handle alone came up. Bosch was alone also because the third member of his team, Kizmin Rider, had been promoted nearly a year earlier to Robbery-Homicide Division and still had not been replaced.

It was early third quarter, and the game with the Trail Blazers was tied. While Bosch wasn't a hardcore fan he knew enough from Edgar's constant talking about the game and begging to be left free of call-out duty that it was an important matchup with one of the Los Angeles team's top rivals. He decided not to page Edgar until he had gotten to the scene and assessed the situation. He turned the radio off when he started losing the AM station in the canyon.

The drive up was steep. Laurel Canyon was a cut in the Santa Monica Mountains. The tributary roads ranged up toward the crest of the mountains. Wonderland Avenue dead-ended in a remote spot where the half-million-dollar homes were surrounded by heavily wooded and steep terrain. Bosch instinctively knew that searching for bones in the area would be a logistical nightmare. He pulled to a stop behind a patrol car already at the address Mankiewicz had provided and checked his watch. It was 4:38, and he wrote it down on a fresh page of his legal pad. He figured he had less than an hour of daylight left.

A patrol officer he didn't recognize answered his knock. Her nameplate said Brasher. She led him back through the house to a home office where her partner, a cop whom Bosch recognized and knew was named Edgewood, was talking to a white-haired man who sat behind a cluttered desk. There was a shoe box with the top off on the desk.

Bosch stepped forward and introduced himself. The white-haired man said he was Dr. Paul Guyot, a general practitioner. Leaning forward Bosch could see that the shoe box contained the bone that had drawn them all together. It was dark brown and looked like a gnarled piece of driftwood.

He could also see a dog lying on the floor next to the doctor's desk chair. It was a large dog with a yellow coat.

"So this is it," Bosch said, looking back down into the box.

"Yes, Detective, that's your bone," Guyot said. "And as you can see . . ."

He reached to a shelf behind the desk and pulled down a heavy copy of *Gray's Anatomy.* He opened it to a previously marked spot. Bosch noticed he was wearing latex gloves.

The page showed an illustration of a bone, anterior and posterior views. In the corner of the page was a small sketch of a skeleton with the humerus bone of both arms highlighted.

"The humerus," Guyot said, tapping the page. "And then we have the recovered specimen."

He reached into the shoe box and gently lifted the bone. Holding it above the book's illustration he went through a point-by-point comparison.

"Medial epicondyle, trochlea, greater and lesser tubercle," he said. "It's all there. And I was just telling these two officers, I know my bones even without the book. This bone is human, Detective. There's no doubt."

Bosch looked at Guyot's face. There was a slight quiver, perhaps the first showing of the tremors of Parkinson's.

"Are you retired, Doctor?"

"Yes, but it doesn't mean I don't know a bone when I see —"

"I'm not challenging you, Dr. Guyot." Bosch tried to smile. "You say it is human, I believe it. Okay? I'm just trying to get the lay of the land here. You can put that back into the box now if you want."

Guyot replaced the bone in the shoe box.

"What's your dog's name?"

"Calamity."

Bosch looked down at the dog. It appeared to be sleeping.

"When she was a pup she was a lot of trouble."

Bosch nodded.

"So, if you don't mind telling it again, tell me what happened today."

Guyot reached down and ruffled the dog's collar. The dog looked up at him for a moment and then put its head back down and closed its eyes.

"I took Calamity out for her afternoon walk. Usually when I get up to the circle I take her off the leash and let her run up into the woods. She likes it."

"What kind of dog is she?" Bosch asked.

"Yellow Lab," Brasher answered quickly from behind him.

Bosch turned and looked at her. She realized she had made a mistake by intruding and nodded and stepped back toward the door of the room where her partner was.

"You guys can clear if you have other calls," Bosch said. "I can take it from here."

Edgewood nodded and signaled his partner out.

"Thank you, Doctor," he said as he went.

"Don't mention it."

Bosch thought of something.

"Hey, guys?"

Edgewood and Brasher turned back.

"Let's keep this off the air, okay?"

"You got it," said Brasher, her eyes holding on Bosch's until he looked away.

After the officers left, Bosch looked back at the doctor and noticed that the facial tremor was slightly more pronounced now.

"They didn't believe me at first either," he said.

"It's just that we get a lot of calls like this. But I believe you, Doctor, so why don't you continue with the story?"

Guyot nodded.

"Well, I was up on the circle and I took off the leash. She went up into the woods like she likes to do. She's well trained. When I whistle she comes back. Trouble is, I can't whistle very loud anymore. So if she goes where she can't hear me, then I have to wait, you see."

"What happened today when she found the bone?"

"I whistled and she didn't come back."

"So she was pretty far up there."

"Yes, exactly. I waited. I whistled a few more times, and

then finally she came down out of the woods next to Mr. Ulrich's house. She had the bone. In her mouth. At first I thought it was a stick, you see, and that she wanted to play fetch with it. But as she came to me I recognized the shape. I took it from her — had a fight over that — and then I called you people after I examined it here and was sure."

You people, Bosch thought. It was always said like that, as if the police were another species. The blue species which carried armor that the horrors of the world could not pierce.

"When you called you told the sergeant that the bone had a fracture."

"Absolutely."

Guyot picked up the bone again, handling it gently. He turned it and ran his finger along a vertical striation along the bone's surface.

"That's a break line, Detective. It's a healed fracture."

"Okay."

Bosch pointed to the box, and the doctor returned the bone.

"Doctor, do you mind putting your dog on a leash and taking a walk up to the circle with me?"

"Not at all. I just need to change my shoes."

"I need to change, too. How about if I meet you out front?"

"Right away."

"I'm going to take this now."

Bosch put the top back on the shoe box and then carried it with two hands, making sure not to turn the box or jostle its contents in any way.

Outside, Bosch noticed the patrol car was still in front of the house. The two officers sat inside it, apparently writing out reports. He went to his car and placed the shoe box on the front passenger seat.

Since he had been on call out he had not dressed in a suit. He had on a sport coat with blue jeans and a white oxford shirt. He stripped off his coat, folded it inside out and put it on the backseat. He noticed that the trigger from the weapon he kept holstered on his hip had worn a hole in the lining and the jacket wasn't even a year old. Soon it would work its way into the pocket and then all the way through. More often than not he wore out his coats from the inside.

He took his shirt off next, revealing a white T-shirt beneath. He then opened the trunk to get out the pair of work boots from his crime scene equipment box. As he leaned against the rear bumper and changed his shoes he saw Brasher get out of the patrol car and come back toward him.

"So it looks legit, huh?"

"Think so. Somebody at the ME's office will have to confirm, though."

"You going to go up and look?"

"I'm going to try to. Not much light left, though. Probably be back out here tomorrow."

"By the way, I'm Julia Brasher. I'm new in the division."

"Harry Bosch."

"I know. I've heard of you."

"I deny everything."

She smiled at the line and put her hand out but Bosch was right in the middle of tying one of the boots. He stopped and shook her hand.

"Sorry," she said. "My timing is off today."

"Don't worry about it."

He finished tying the boot and stood up off the bumper.

"When I blurted out the answer in there, about the dog,

I immediately realized you were trying to establish a rapport with the doctor. That was wrong. I'm sorry."

Bosch studied her for a moment. She was mid-thirties with dark hair in a tight braid that left a short tail going over the back of her collar. Her eyes were dark brown. He guessed she liked the outdoors. Her skin had an even tan.

"Like I said, don't worry about it."

"You're alone?"

Bosch hesitated.

"My partner's working on something else while I check this out."

He saw the doctor coming out the front door of the house with the dog on a leash. He decided not to get out his crime scene jumpsuit and put it on. He glanced over at Julia Brasher, who was now watching the approaching dog.

"You guys don't have calls?"

"No, it's slow."

Bosch looked down at the MagLite in his equipment box. He looked at her and then reached into the trunk and grabbed an oil rag, which he threw over the flashlight. He took out a roll of yellow crime scene tape and the Polaroid camera, then closed the trunk and turned to Brasher.

"Then do you mind if I borrow your Mag? I, uh, forgot mine."

"No problem."

She slid the flashlight out of the ring on her equipment belt and handed it to him.

The doctor and his dog came up then.

"Ready."

"Okay, Doctor, I want you to take us up to the spot where you let the dog go and we'll see where she goes."

"I'm not sure you'll be able to stay with her."

"I'll worry about that, Doctor."

"This way then."

They walked up the incline toward the small turn-around circle where Wonderland reached a dead end. Brasher made a hand signal to her partner in the car and walked along with them.

"You know, we had a little excitement up this way a few years ago," Guyot said. "A man was followed home from the Hollywood Bowl and then killed in a robbery."

"I remember," Bosch said.

He knew the investigation was still open but didn't mention it. It wasn't his case.

Dr. Guyot walked with a strong step that belied his age and apparent condition. He let the dog set the pace and soon moved several paces ahead of Bosch and Brasher.

"So where were you before?" Bosch asked Brasher.

"What do you mean?"

"You said you were new in Hollywood Division. What about before?"

"Oh. The academy."

He was surprised. He looked over at her, thinking he might need to reassess his age estimate.

She nodded and said, "I know, I'm old."

Bosch got embarrassed.

"No, I wasn't saying that. I just thought that you had been somewhere else. You don't seem like a rookie."

"I didn't go in until I was thirty-four."

"Really? Wow."

"Yeah. Got the bug a little late."

"What were you doing before?"

"Oh, a bunch of different things. Travel mostly. Took me a while to figure out what I wanted to do. And you want to know what I want to do the most?"

Bosch looked at her.

"What?"

"What you do. Homicide."

He didn't know what to say, whether to encourage her or dissuade her.

"Well, good luck," he said.

"I mean, don't you just find it to be the most fulfilling job ever? Look at what you do, you take the most evil people out of the mix."

"The mix?"

"Society."

"Yeah, I guess so. When we get lucky."

They caught up to Dr. Guyot, who had stopped with the dog at the turnaround circle.

"This thc place?"

"Yes. I let her go here. She went up through there."

He pointed to an empty and overgrown lot that started level with the street but then quickly rose into a steep incline toward the crest of the hills. There was a large concrete drainage culvert, which explained why the lot had never been built on. It was city property, used to funnel storm water runoff away from the homes on the street. Many of the streets in the canyon were former creek and river beds. When it rained they would return to their original purpose if not for the drainage system.

"Are you going up there?" the doctor asked.

"I'm going to try."

"I'll go with you," Brasher said.

Bosch looked at her and then turned at the sound of a car. It was the patrol car. It pulled up and Edgewood put down the window.

"We got a hot shot, partner. Double D."

He nodded toward the empty passenger seat. Brasher frowned and looked at Bosch.

"I hate domestic disputes."

Bosch smiled. He hated them too, especially when they turned into homicides.

"Sorry about that."

"Well, maybe next time."

She started around the front of the car.

"Here," Bosch said, holding out the MagLite.

"I've got an extra in the car," she said. "You can just get that back to me."

"You sure?"

He was tempted to ask for a phone number but didn't.

"I'm sure. Good luck."

"You too. Be careful."

She smiled at him and then hurried around the front of the car. She got in and the car pulled away. Bosch turned his attention back to Guyot and the dog.

"An attractive woman," Guyot said.

Bosch ignored it, wondering if the doctor had made the comment based on seeing Bosch's reaction to Brasher. He hoped he hadn't been that obvious.

"Okay, Doctor," he said, "let the dog go and I'll try to keep up."

Guyot unhooked the leash while patting the dog's chest.

"Go get the bone, girl. Get a bone! Go!"

The dog took off into the lot and was gone from sight before Bosch had taken a step. He almost laughed.

"Well, I guess you were right about that, Doc."

He turned to make sure the patrol car was gone and Brasher hadn't seen the dog take off.

"You want me to whistle?"

"Nah. I'll just go in and take a look around, see if I can catch up to her."

He turned the flashlight on.